William M Nesbitt Brian Beard

THE JORVIK CHRONICLE

AUSTIN MACAULEY PUBLISHERS™
LONDON • CAMBRIDGE • NEW YORK • SHARJAH

A CIP catalogue record for this title is available from the British Library.

ISBN 9781788780247 (Paperback)
ISBN 9781398427709 (Hardback)
ISBN 9781398416970 (ePub e-book)

www.austinmacauley.com

10 9 8 7 6 5 4 3 2 1

First Published (2020)
Austin Macauley Publishers Ltd
25 Canada Square
Canary Wharf
London
E14 5LQ

FOR

THE AUTHOR
WHO, HAVING BEEN BORN IN **STREONSHALH**,
AND SPENDING MUCH OF HIS YOUTH IN **JORVIK**,
HAS BEEN PROMISING HIMSELF TO WRITE THIS
BOOK FROM THE AGE OF THIRTEEN.

AT LAST, HE CAN NOW ENTER VALHOLL
WITH A CLEAR CONSCIENCE

MA GUDERNE FREMSKYNDE DIG

* * *

To Jenny

Books by William M Nesbitt

As Bill Nesbitt:

Travails Abroad

As Sean Collins:

Last of the Cold War Warriors

Last of the Cold War Warriors II

When Twilight Ends

The Kyushu Contract

The Jorvik Chronicle

Books by Brian Beard

The Breedon Book of Premiership Records

Three Lions

Collins Gems Disaster Survival

A Game of Three Halves
(Autobiography of Kenny Swain)

Lincoln Born, Football Bred: John Ward

The Jorvik Chronicle

Memo to Bill

More people than will ever be known owe a debt of gratitude to you. I count myself privileged to have known you. I am more than grateful to have had the opportunity to complete your lifetime work with the blessing of Jenny.

What began as a massive task, the magnitude of which I could not fathom, became an all-encompassing obsession that would not let go. It took on a life of its own, growing organically, and I constantly felt as if two huge hands were reaching out from the story, grabbing me warmly by the throat and pulling me in until I was there, at the heart of the Saga, in 9th-century England.

Once in a lifetime one might get the chance to be part of something special. *The Jorvik Chronicle* was that for me.

Thanks Bill. Enjoy Valhalla.

Brian

Where is the horse gone? Where is the rider?

Where the giver of treasure?
Where are the seals at the feast?
Where are the revels in the hall?
Alas for the bright cup!
Alas for the mailed warrior!
Alas for the splendour of the prince!
How that time has passed away,
Dark under the cover of night.
As if it had never been.

The Wanderer

SIMON GARTH, professor of pre-medieval languages at Cambridge University, found himself in North Yorkshire at the behest of the York Archaeological Trust, who had been aware of his reputation and expertise, not least from his several highly respected books on the translation of Old East Norse and 9th-century Latin, in particular the similarity of what were often called the Anglo-Saxon and Viking languages, both based in Old Germanic; this had enabled them to understand each other to a large extent. As he specialised in Old Danish, it seemed particularly apt that he now found himself in the city of York, given that, as Jorvik, it had been the capital of the Danelaw—Viking England.

Simon's invitation from the YAT was about to present him with a unique opportunity: a two-volume journal, discovered on an archaeological dig north of the city. This in itself was a rare occurrence. The history and stories of the Danes were usually in aural form, with no written records or accounts. Evidently, the Chronicle had a cover of leather on wood with inlaid silver decoration and had suffered minimal damage.

The pages were of treated calfskin vellum; the wet, un-haired and limed skins would have been dried under tension in wooden stretching frames. The text had been written in late 9th-century Latin with iron gall ink, in a practised and educated hand—almost certainly a Christian monk or scribe.

This did not surprise Simon. Following the onslaught of what had become known as the Great Heathen Army in AD 866, Paganism and Christianity had been practised side by side, albeit uneasily.

The Chronicle had been deliberately and carefully interred in a solid stone chest, some 40cm x 25 cm, intended, as Simon could only imagine, as a 'time capsule' of the 9th century. It would not have survived so well—if at all—had it not been found located some nine feet under the surface, in moist, peaty earth, which was organic-rich and oxygen-free—ideal conditions for preserving wood and leather.

The chest had been removed with great care by the YAT and taken back to their laboratories for analysis. A non-invasive Raman spectroscopy analysed the molecular vibrations of the pigments and inks used, without the necessity of taking a sample. Any pressure on the parchment had to be avoided. Iron gall ink could corrode the vellum in humid conditions so the journal had to be kept in 30 degrees relative humidity.

Simon's train of thought was interrupted by two members of the YAT carrying in an acid- and lignin-free archival box. He sat with anticipation as they opened the box and placed the Chronicle in front of him, beneath the spectral lamp, on a prepared cushion of foam. With its silver ornamentation, the cover was a work of art in itself. Simon donned a pair of white cotton gloves and prepared to enter the past.

The first thing he noticed was a Runor—an inscription in the Runic alphabet—carved into the cover with extreme care. On closer examination, Simon recognised the alphabet as the Younger Futark, an alphabet that contained 16 characters in the long-branch of the Danes. The word 'Futark' came from the names of the first five of the Runes. This system of runic writing became known in Europe as the 'alphabet of the Norsemen'. Simon studied the runic inscription and began making notes on the laptop to his left. Although he knew the Runes could have several meanings, the nearest translation he could determine suggested the life story of its owner.

'Travel across the sea. A new beginning with a change in world rhythms. A life of challenge and sacrifice. Achieving success, wealth and honour. Happiness and a time of peace and prosperity, when all problems are resolved and all loose ends are tied.'

Simon paused as the moment took hold. Carefully, he opened the cover by the top right-hand corner, ensuring he caused no damage. There was a further runic inscription on the first page:

Osgar of the Angelfolc, also known as Sigrvard, Jarl of the Deniscan, caused me to be made.

Simon leaned back in his chair. He rubbed his eyes with the palms of his hands. This could possibly be the most important chronicle of 9th-century life found to date. If the content proved the inscription, it would shed light on the life of an Angle, who became a Danish Jarl, and the circumstances under which he achieved this.

A Danish Jarl was similar to an Anglo-Saxon Earl in rank, with acquired estates and wealth—wealth that was counted in land, horses and slaves; honour-bound to provide men and to command part or all of an army on behalf of his king. The majority of his time would have been spent in administration, the law, politics and hunting and—as a *drengr**—expeditions, both raiding and trading, across the seas.

As the timeline was stated in years after the birth of Christ, it would enable events in the Chronicle to be checked against existing historical facts—perhaps with unexpected revelations.

As Simon turned the first page, hesitantly, his hand trembled slightly as he realised he would be the first person to read the journal for over 1,100 years, a window into the past.

He began to read.

* *Warrior.*

CHAPTER ONE

AD 857

IT was forenoon.

The sunlight's reflection, shimmering on the sea, appeared as a golden pathway, a glistening bridge, beckoning Osgar from the earth to the kingdom of Sigel, goddess of the sun.

He walked slowly along the eastern bank of the River Esk, barefoot and wearing only his rough woven undershirt and baggy trousers secured by a belt, in which was his small knife for everyday chores. The day was too hot for his wool tunic.

Over his right shoulder were slung the four trout he had caught upriver with his hook and line, on which his prizes hung. The family would all dine well that evening along with the fresh mussels he had collected earlier beneath the western headland. He continued on home, following the river towards the mouth of the estuary where it joined the sea between the headland cliffs.

Atop the eastern headland lay his village, Streonshalh*—the strong bend of the river—the settlement clustered around the monastery built by Hild in 657. In 658, the Great Synod had been held there to establish the form of Christianity which would be followed, Roman rather than Celtic, and to set the date for the celebration of Easter throughout the Christian world.

Streonshalh, in the kingdom of Deira,** was isolated by the sea, moorland and forests. All trade was waterborne. Cut off from the nearest villages in winter, the Streonshalh folk cared little for what

* *Whitby.*

** *Deira, an Anglo-Saxon kingdom in northern England, stretched from the Humber estuary in the south to the River Tees in the north.*

happened outside their own village; a village made up of ten wooden, mud and wattle, thatched houses with wickerwork cattle enclosures and their chief's hall, a place for his family, council meetings and feasting. All were overshadowed by the monastery of Hild that sat atop the hill like a shepherd watching his flock. All, save the fishermen's houses and curing shed down by the beach and small harbour area for landing their catch and for trade.

The villagers, numbering less than forty, were farmers and, with their families, cultivated crops of einkorn, barley, rye and vegetables. They also husbanded a motley assembly of cattle, sheep, goats and swine: livestock that occasionally gave meat, mainly for feast days and celebrations, and cured ham and mutton. However, the main diet remained the cauldron of stew over the central fire-hearth. As with all farming families, Osgar's parents gave a share of all they produced to the monastery on whose lands they farmed. Osgar now being of nine winters, his was a working day, helping his father in the fields and tending the livestock. His sister and younger brother would collect firewood and help their mother grind flour, churn butter and collect the sheep and goats' wool for spinning into yarn for weaving.

Osgar had also grown, over his nine winters, being frightened on occasion by the elder's night-time stories from the past—including those of the feared *Vikingr*—the pirates. In the year of seventy winters ago, the longships of the Northmen had raided the holy island of Lindisfarne, off the coast of the kingdom of Bernicia to the north. They had fallen upon the monastery and small settlement with ferocity, slaughtering the monks at their altars, throwing some of them into the sea to drown, stripping survivors naked, driving them from the monastery. The Vikings pillaged gold crucifixes, ivory relics, silver pyres, tapestries, illuminated scrolls and books with precious stones inset. That for which they had no purpose, they sold back to the Christian Church.

They also loaded their ships with cattle and sheep from the pastures and captives to be sold as slaves; nothing of worth was ignored and slaves were prized above all. The Vikings then compounded their infamy by raiding the monastery of Jarrow and the holy island of Iona.

Osgar pinched the bridge of his nose with thumb and index finger, a family habit when deep in thought, and forced those images from his mind—he was no longer a bairn to be frightened by stories. Soon would be the feast in the hall to celebrate *Eostre*, the goddess of birth, which the Christians had stolen into their religion, renaming it the Celebration of Easter.

There would be much feasting and drinking of barley ale and mead, music from lyres and horn flutes and circle dancing.

Osgar's mother Aebbe, his sister Godkifu and Godwine, his younger brother of seven winters, had all been baptised as Christians at the monastery, as had he, but his father, Deorwine, and himself had continued to practice the old religion of Woden and Tiw. And while fishing, Osgar always prayed to Wade, the god of the sea, for a good catch.

His parents had always told him that he was to be betrothed but that would not be until he reached twelve winters. He was not surprised, for he knew his family could not feed him forever.

He was more than aware that a man was considered old at forty winters and a woman at thirty, many of them dying in childbirth. It was important to safeguard the future of his bloodline. His only hope as he grew older was that he would not be paired with someone ugly or a shrew.

But those thoughts disappeared as he neared the mouth of the river estuary. His blood ran cold as he saw black smoke spiralling into the clear blue sky.

In the small harbour, the village's three small fishing boats and the curing shed had almost been reduced to ashes; the fisher-folk's homes were in flames, their bodies strewn around them. On the sandy beach, three longships were beached, prow in, their square sails down, oars stowed. The sides of the boats were bereft of shields—a raiding party of at least ninety fully-armed warriors had struck. Osgar dropped his catch in the dust and ran as he had never run before. His name meant 'Spear of God'. He wished out loud to Tiw that he had one now. His only weapon was the knife now grasped in his hand. He was halfway to the village when he saw smoke from the monastery and settlement. He could hear the crackling of the timbers and the crash of collapsing roofs in the still summer air. He cursed the Christian God for the monastery that had led the Northmen to them and prayed to Woden to protect his family.

He reached the boundary of the village and looked upon the body of Ealdred, chief of their village, his axe by his side.

Next to him lay Osgar's father, his sword still in hand, his skull cleaved in twain; around them lay the corpses of five more pairs of sightless eyes, men who had tried to defend their village and their families. The Vikings were still screaming their bloodlust as they burned every house after ransacking it for spoils. Others were rounding up cattle and sheep from the pastures to drive them down to their ships. The monks and nuns who had not yet been raped and slaughtered had been barricaded in the church before it was torched. Osgar covered his ears as he heard their prayers turn to screams.

The only survivors, two young female novices, dressed in only their undershifts, were being dragged along by their hair, screaming for mercy and appealing to their God. It was He who would decide their fate: rape, mutilation or death or, if He were magnanimous, a lifetime of slavery.

The high wooden fence, surrounding the village for protection from wolves, foxes and boars more than enemies, had collapsed in flames, the Northmen's fire-arrows making short work of their only defence. Osgar moved forward in a crouch, using the burning houses and thick, acrid smoke as cover, running from one house to the next until he reached the back wall of his family home. He began to kick a hole in the mud and wattle wall, praying he would not be heard amongst the cacophony of the looting.

Finally, he crawled through the opening and stood erect, frozen, gripping his knife even tighter as he surveyed the carnage that lay before his young eyes.

From the way they lay, their belts having been sliced through and their brooch-fastened wool tunics and long-sleeved shifts having been torn from their bodies by brute force, his mother and sister had been raped, probably several times, before their throats were slit and their bodies mutilated. His younger brother of just seven winters, Godwine, lay on the floor. His genitals had been cut off. His head lay nearby. The knife in his hand showed he had tried to protect his mother and sister.

Osgar could hear the Northmen setting torch to the rear of the house. He must escape, whatever the odds. He ran for the doorway. The daylight was blocked by a giant in a helmet with his eyes hovering behind gaping black holes that almost floated above an elaborate nasal-guard. Wearing a full suit of chain mail, as for battle, he was the tallest warrior Osgar had ever seen, although the youngster's attention was more focussed on the swinging double-hand axe that menaced him.

The full suit of chain mail denoted wealth and identified its wearer as the *Vikingr* leader. He stood over Osgar, scratching his long but neatly trimmed beard.

"*Nakkvar ungra drenga, ha!*" said the deep voice that boomed from beyond its metal cave.

Osgar could understand the words 'young' and 'warrior', though nothing more. He lunged forward with his knife. The Vikingr laughed as he parried the blow with his shield, knocking Osgar breathless to the ground, though he still managed to swipe his pitiful blade across the invader's unprotected ankle.

Further enraged, the Northman raised his axe above his head.

Osgar prayed to Tiw, the god of war, to intervene.

"*Letta! Neinn!*"

It wasn't the intervention Osgar prayed for but it had the desired effect for, at the cry of 'Stop', the *Vikingr* leader froze and his axe stayed at mid-swing. The life-saving command had come from a tall, grey-haired, white-bearded man in a long, light-brown robe, now striding purposefully towards them, throwing-spear in hand, which he used as a walking-pole.

"I want this boy for my *thrall*."

Osgar recognised the word 'thrall'—it meant slave in his own language. He could understand most of their words so he had an idea that his life was hanging in the balance.

"*Nakkar Litt harfagri? Hri?*"

"I need him as a *seidmadhr*—a Seer—to train for when I am no more. It is written in the Runes: I saw an eagle hovering over the boy. But I also saw he himself was the eagle."

The Northman looked down at a quivering Osgar thoughtfully. Then slowly lowered his axe and spoke, "Very well, Seer. I will not anger Odinn—I will abide by his will. He tried to stick me with a woman's blade, Seer." He laughed, pointing down at Osgar. "Me! He has courage. You say he is an eagle—very well." He ceased laughing. "You may have him—but as he grows taller, he will also be trained as a warrior, agreed?"

"*Ja*—as you say, my Jarl!" The Seer bent his head.

"Then take him to the ship—we are done here. He is now your responsibility."

"As you say."

The Seer led Osgar away. As they left, Osgar glanced back at the

Northman who was shouting at his warriors, axe held high, "*Skynda—ver segl—we sail.*"

Osgar was dragged aboard the ship with the other captives but he noticed he was the only one not bound.

The Seer led him to the high stern and sat him under the *styrimadr*, the helmsman, on his raised board, the large steering blade—the *stjornbord** to the right of the stern.

"I am Froda, Seer to the Jarl."

Osgar knew Froda meant 'enlightened and wise'. He realised a Jarl must hold the same status as an Angle Eorl or Thane. He now had the opportunity to observe the Seer more closely. He appeared to be taller than the average *Vikingr*, with the exception of the Jarl, with piercing blue eyes that seemed to read Osgar's heart and thoughts.

They were now well out to sea. Osgar looked over the stern as the longship began to pitch through the waves. The cliffs of Deira were quickly fading into the horizon as was the dark cloud of smoke that hung where Streonshalh had once stood. His home no more. He wiped an involuntary tear. He knew he must not show grief or fear in front of his captors. Froda had noticed the tear and placed his hand on Osgar's shoulder. "Only warriors can cry. Cowards or fools cannot."

Osgar stared into the rolling waters.

"*Ja!* You could jump, boy, but your young life would be ended by an arrow before you could drown dead. Your name, my little firebrand, if you please to give it?"

"Osgar!" he declared defiantly.

"Not for too much longer. You will be given a new name more befitting a Seer—and a warrior." Froda searched Osgar's face for a reaction. He saw none. "You are fair-haired and blue-eyed, which is highly prized and will bode well for your future."

The longship, which Osgar would come to know as the 'Raven of Odinn', was being rowed apace through the open sea eastwards. He would learn that only warriors were allowed to crew a longship of war. Nevertheless, Osgar noted that the places of three dead warriors had been taken by captives. Against his will, he found the longship impressive. The 'Raven', which was taking him to slavery, was sixty-six feet long and built to carry twenty warriors with their own weapons and shields—which were hung from the sides of the ship.

* *Origin of the term 'starboard'.*

Lightweight and clinker-built, the longships were designed to sail at speed but also to flex and to withstand rough seas. Their shallow draught was purposely designed to enable navigation of inland rivers and beaching on land more easily. The fearsome carving on the prow of each ship announced the *Vikingr* intent. Every inch of space on board was used wisely. The warriors sat on a chest of personal possessions to row, helmets stowed nearby.

Suddenly, a wind sprang up and the Jarl gave the order to raise sail. On its single mast, the longship's large square sail was made of treated wool and decorated with checked red and white squares. The sails, depending on size, could take two and a half years to weave.

Once raised on the 'Raven', the sail billowed in the wind, increasing the speed greatly and as the bow sliced through the black water, the crew took advantage of stowed oars to eat and drink. Osgar was given a wooden bowl of sun-dried cod and bread with a wooden goblet of water to wash it down.

As Froda ate, he told Osgar it would take just 30 hours to reach his 'new home', though the youngster wondered if he would ever get used to 'new home'. "If the weather holds fair," added the Seer. "Sleep now, my young friend."

As the night smothered the 'Raven' with a blanket of darkness, the heavens revealed myriad stars sparkling overhead, offering some light as the crew sailed under and by those very same heavenly bodies. The Seer-to-be had no knowledge of how those stars would affect the life that lay ahead for him.

The crew took it in turns to sleep, each of them welcoming their turn to crawl inside their sealskin sleeping bags, a warm and welcome shield against the cold sea air. They were soon asleep, as was the helmsman who had stood down to be replaced by another for the rather uncomfortable night's work ahead. Ignar, before he took up his position, still had time and thought to smile at Osgar as he ruffled the youngster's hair before settling down to steer the ship home.

Osgar too was soon deep in slumber. Froda looked down on his new charge, wondering what thoughts must have been swirling around that young mind from the 24 hours just passed.

There was light on the eastern horizon as Osgar awoke but his eyes could not see as he was leaning over portside, vomiting up his earlier meal. The ship, its sail now down, was pitching and rolling in the heavy swell and high winds that lashed the 'Raven' with the freezing torrential rain of a lightning storm. The flashes of dazzling light lit up the faces of the fearful crew, followed by rolls of thunder as Thor in Asgard gave voice to his mighty hammer. Osgar turned his head back from his projectile vomiting towards the helmsman who was lashed to his post, literally. The crew fought to manhandle the heavy sail, sodden by the storm, over the ship, providing a cover under which to ride out the storm.

"Do not worry, little one," comforted Froda. "It will not last. This is but a squall compared to some of the storms we have weathered." Once more in his young life, Osgar was afraid.

The storm finally abated and once more the sail was raised.

Osgar heard the helmsman inform the Jarl that the storm had blown them off course. That meant they would have to wait for the other two ships to find them; therefore, the voyage would take longer.

"If they are not already at the bottom of the sea!"

The Jarl was not best pleased as he cast an accusatory glance towards the heavens.

"How do we know where we are?" Osgar asked with genuine concern.

"By day, we travel by the sun," explained Froda, "and by night, the stars."

"But how do you navigate with neither sun nor stars?" said the youngster with what he thought a reasonable question.

Froda smiled as he answered, for he too had once asked a similar question, many winters since.

"Then they ask the Seer."

"And are you always right?" Osgar inquired.

"If I was, we would not sail close to the coast," Froda laughed. "Do not be in such haste, you will learn all, in good time."

After what seemed to be a never-ending voyage of saga-like proportions to the edge of the world, they sighted land.

The other two ships of the raiding party had re-joined the 'Raven' in the forenoon, with no losses, and together the trio sailed parallel to the coastline. Just two hours later, the lookout cried out from atop 'Raven's' mast and the Jarl ordered the sail be lowered and the crew to their oars as they turned for shore.

The Jarl's longship led into the inlet and, within minutes, Osgar could see a village getting closer and closer. It wasn't a huge settlement and what few buildings there were seemed to be clinging to the steep hillside for dear life. Osgar later learnt that was by design.

Osgar's new place of residence, for it was too soon after the massacre of his family and the destruction of Streonshalh to call it home, lay before him as the longships approached their destination.

The entrance to the inlet was virtually invisible from the sea as two rocky promontories overlapped like lovers' arms about to interlock, leaving the narrowest of entry points. Osgar was to later learn that was but a small part of the Denisc obsession with subterfuge and deception. Had he but looked skywards, he would have spied more of the defences that made the settlement of Eirikr impregnable.

The thick forest surrounding Eirikrsby's north and western flank had been carefully coppiced, man giving nature a hand. At one time, it had been impenetrable until Eirikr's father's father's father had ordered a snaking line be cut as a swathe through the trees. The path was seven leagues long but a mere quarter part of that as the crow flies. But, as Osgar later learned, the protective pines were huddled so close together that even birds could not fly in a straight line. The pathway through the silent sentries protecting the settlement had been cut in such an ingenious way that each section of the route was a precise seven strides long and, for added security, anyone moving through the pathway could not see the next section until reaching the end of the one before it.

So, a straight-line traverse of the forest was impossible, unless you knew where you were going, as all youngsters did, generation after generation. Potential invaders attempting to breach Eirikrsby's outer perimeter on that particular flank faced an even more impenetrable barrier, again testimony to Eirikr's great-grandfather, Boldon the Clever and his far-sightedness. To supplement the felling of the trees to create a pathway, Boldon employed a programme of planting of pine saplings, each no more than three strides from the next, some nine feet. The man-traps, located in any gaps that were not planted, with their sharpened stakes were an added deterrent to a barrier that was never breached. Neither had there ever been a need to use the pathway as an escape route.

But Boldon saved the best until last with a line of hollowed tree trunks, containing thick, black pitch, that weaved in and out of the man-traps. "Just to be sure," as Boldon told his son, who told his, who

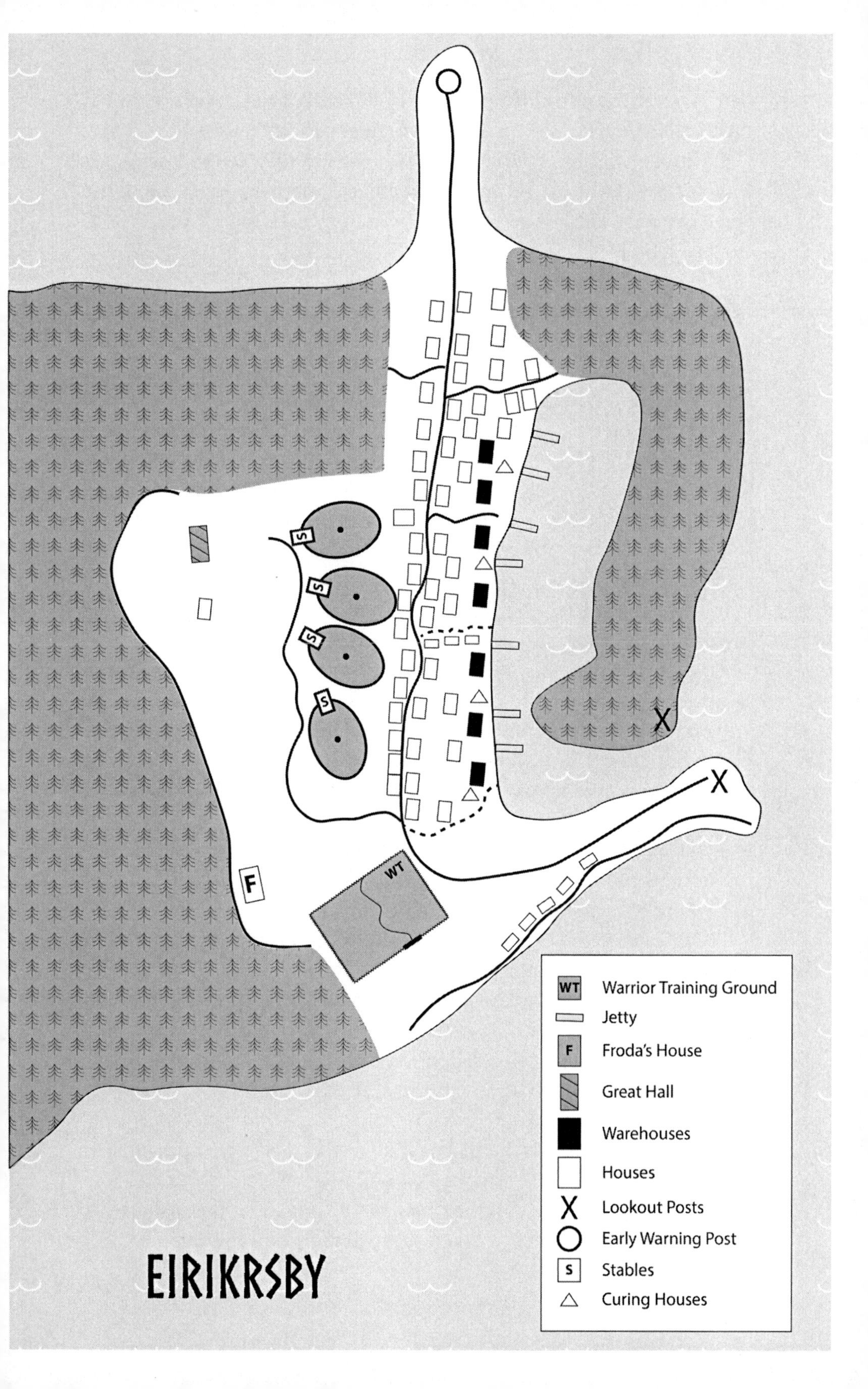
WT
S
F
Warrior Training Ground
Jetty
Froda's House
Great Hall
Warehouses
Houses
Lookout Posts
Early Warning Post
Stables
Curing Houses
EIRIKRSBY

told Eirikr. 'The Ring of Fire' had never been used. Osgar hoped it stayed that way. He had endured enough fire for a lifetime.

It wasn't long after he arrived at Eirikrsby that Osgar discovered why knowledge of the settlement's defences, particularly through the Silent Sentries, became second nature to the young folk. It was Jultide and party time.

The order 'up oars' boomed out from the Jarl as the 'Raven' glided with precision to nestle softly against the wharf with barely enough impact to disturb the goblet of beer that Froda always imbibed on his safe return from a raid; "Purely for medicinal purposes, you understand" was how he put it to his newly acquired apprentice.

Once the other two ships glided into place with similar precision, Osgar noticed the large number of ships already moored at Eirikrsby—longships for raiding as well as knarrs designed for carrying cargo and trading goods—adjacent to warehouses and curing sheds.

As the villagers cheered a safe return of their loved ones, the Jarl leapt from his longship and strode up the jetty to where a *thrall* stood with a white stallion, the finest horse Osgar had ever seen. The Jarl leapt onto his ornate saddle and rode off through the village.

Osgar could see many houses, some of similar construction to those in his own village, and many that were much larger, built completely of wood with thatched or turf roofs. Even though he couldn't see the entire settlement, he still counted at least thirty houses he could see and knew there were many more he could not. The buildings appeared to be lining wide streets, something he had not seen before.

Compared to his own village, this must be a city, he thought.

He knew of only one other, the capital Eoforwic in Deira.

"Where are we?" Osgar turned towards Froda.

"Your new home, my village. Welcome to the Denisc kingdom of Jylland."

Once ashore, past the laughing and screaming boys diving from the jetty and weaving their way through the two score or more men unloading the three heavily-laden longships, Froda led Osgar, whose land-legs were none too steady, through the village.

He noted the great respect with which Froda was greeted as they made their way through the throng and he was met with looks of curiosity as he stared at the people and buildings of his new home. The village was even bigger than he had first thought. In the distance, a forest of pines looked over Eirikrsby, the Settlement of Eirikr.

There was more to the location than first met the eye, as Osgar was to soon discover.

It wasn't difficult for Osgar to work out that Eirikr was the Jarl who now ruled him. But his thoughts were rudely interrupted by a cacophony of sounds that assailed his ears, the most he had ever heard: dogs barking and whelping, men shouting and women talking and laughing almost as loudly as they called to their children to behave; timber was being chopped and sawn, hammers struck anvils as cleavers prepared meat for salting as well as for the feasting that lay ahead. Osgar heard the neighing of horses and the clash of steel on steel as warriors practised their skills.

Then there were the smells and odours, some of which he recognised, some he did not. Smells that assaulted his senses like an unstoppable wave as it swamped him. The smells of animals and humans, sometimes indistinguishable from each other.

Villagers passed by steaming cauldrons of boiling meat and ovens of roasting beef and boar as well as clay ovens that could not keep cloaked the aeons-old aroma of fresh bread. The smoke from the houses mixed with that of the forges: cakes and pancakes on skillets mixed with the smell of freshly-mown corn and barley. Osgar was grateful for those welcoming aromas, for lying heavily alongside such favourable essences were the less pleasant odours of animal detritus and urine from open latrines and the sour smell of rotting vegetables—and worse—from the middens. There were simply too many for him to assimilate.

He looked at the villagers as they walked. Their garments appeared to be of coarse wool, coloured with dyes. The men wore outer kyrtills, long-sleeved, knee-length shirts over linen undervests with tight-fitting long cloth trousers. Their leather shoes were secured with criss-crossed leather thongs up their calves, tied just below the knee. They also wore a leather belt to secure their clothing—some with ornate buckles—from which hung a leather purse and a *seax*, or small knife. Some wore a fur-trimmed cap, others a long cloak secured by a ringed pin, placed so as not to encumber the sword arm. Osgar noticed the majority of men wore a sword; he was later to learn that all freemen were entitled, and obliged, to carry weapons at all times.

If Osgar had known what a learning curve was, he would have understood that he was on one that was very steep; but under the tutelage of Froda, he was best equipped to negotiate the process.

Froda educated Osgar as to the importance of hair, especially for men where the length of beard and hair on the head were visible signs of power, wealth and virility.

Short hair was for slaves. *Not for me, then,* thought the apprentice Seer. Beard lengths varied: some were shaped to a point, some sported as the *tjuguskegg* or forkbeard. Shorter hair and a neatly-trimmed beard were a sign of rank, two more things the boy of nine winters would not need worry about for a while.

The attire of Denisc women, noted Osgar, was less like the Angle. They seemed to favour a long shift, also with a cloak, but the over-dress was embroidered and decorated and held up by two shoulder straps fastened with oval brooches. From the brooch's attached chain hung combs, scissors and other feminine necessities. The women also wore more jewellery than the men, who restricted their ornamentation to amulets and pins in the main. The women adhered to no such limitation and Osgar noticed that many seemed burdened down by varying quantities of rings, ornate brooches and necklaces as well as amulets.

Whether silver or gold, amber or precious stones or even simple pieces of pewter, bronze or animal bone, the quality of the jewellery was determined by rank and social standing.

Among the women, blonde hair was the most highly prized so brunettes would dye their hair red or red-gold, using lye. Their hair was worn long and loose, in two braids or in a *kransen*—a circlet—for formal occasions. If the woman was married, Osgar would find, to his expense, that the hair was gathered up and worn under a *hustrilinet*—a headscarf.

Osgar's sartorial meandering ended as they arrived at Froda's house on the outskirts of the village. Froda bade him enter.

CHAPTER TWO

IT was a little different to the houses of his home village, in construction, except larger, with walls of pine. Froda strode across the rush floor, leaning his spear-cum-walking pole against the door. He lit four carved soapstone oil lamps, dispelling the room's darkness and throwing threatening shadows across its walls. The house appeared to be about twenty-five feet in length and fifteen feet deep, as a single room. In the centre of the room was a large rectangular fire-hearth, edged with stone. It was already lit with a cauldron suspended above it; Osgar also noted a spit and skillet with knives and spoons in a pot beaker nearby. As he had expected, there was a large hole in the centre of the roof above. Upright poles were set at intervals along the walls, a heavy timber lintel over the doorway and small windows closed by shutters at night.

By the wall near the fire was a chest bed with a down mattress and pillow, woollen blankets and furs. Osgar had heard of such things, but only in the homes of the wealthy. One wall was lined with benches for guests, he presumed, with sheepskins and furs bundled beneath. For the first time, Osgar saw what he later learned were tapestries, hung from the walls, depicting mythical scenes from Norse legends with runic inscriptions. Two chests, a table and four stools completed the sparse furnishings in the room. Almost incongruously, held by two large metal brackets, hung a lightweight sword; the sword had a three-foot iron and steel double-edged blade—intended for cutting and slashing—with runic letters and a hilt decorated with silver.

"Froda?" Osgar pointed to the sword. "May I ask a question? The sword?"

"Ah, *ja*. The sword. Its name is 'Bone Eater', it is a warrior's sword."

He held Osgar's gaze with piercing eyes. "I have slain men in battle but only of necessity."

"But you did not carry it in battle or wear armour?"

"I have no need of them." Froda smiled.

"But why?"

"Fate," Froda answered simply.

"Fate?" Now Osgar was totally perplexed.

"It is our belief. If it be my time to die, then so be it, there is little I can do to avoid it. We Denisc believe in the Nornar—the three women of destiny. At the birth of a child, they choose when it will die. No man can live beyond his time so we have nothing to lose in battle, but should we die, we gain the most important thing to a Denisc warrior—honour. *Nothing* comes before honour."

"Nothing?"

"Nothing! I shall try to enlighten you as to our beliefs as you grow. We also have the maidens of Odinn—the Valkyries. They cannot be seen by man but appear the night before a battle and touch the men who are to die. That is why all the Denisc warriors are fierce in battle, they expect to be killed."

Osgar could now understand why the *Vikingr* were feared.

"We are not barbarians. We have many laws to ensure men are brave, honest and fair. We detest cowards and thieves. If someone commits a crime, they must stand trial."

"And if found guilty?"

"A man must carry a piece of red-hot iron—a woman hot stones from boiling water—for a required distance. If they drop them, they are guilty. If not dropped, then their hands are cleansed and dressed. After seven days, if their hands are healed, they are innocent."

Osgar knew he had to ask. "And if not—if they are guilty?" he repeated his question.

"Then their fate would be decided by the *thing*.* The guilty must pay a fine levied by the court, be sentenced to become a *thrall*—a slave—or be banished from our lands, which means anyone can kill them without fear of punishment. Do you understand?"

"These are the rules by which you live?" muttered a rapidly maturing captive.

"Precisely—you have understood well, boy."

* *A meeting where judgements and punishments are given.*

Osgar immediately decided to be incredibly law-abiding.

"But now we need to eat, it was a long voyage. This was prepared for our return," said Froda, pointing towards the basket by the door. "Bring it here, this will be our main meal of the day."

He did as Froda bade. Beneath the wickerwork basket's square of linen lay butter, eggs, bread, cheese, honey and fresh fruit.

"Once we were seen on the horizon, the villagers put together this basket of food for our arrival."

"Do they do this for everyone?"

Froda smiled, tapping the side of his nose. "They do if they may need the knowledge of a Seer in their future."

Osgar laughed and placed the basket away from the heat.

Froda sampled the cauldron's contents and declared them ready.

Sat on two stools at the table, they dined on bowls of the stew of mutton, carrots, wild celery and cabbage, flavoured with juniper berries, wild garlic and thyme from Froda's garden, with crusty bread and honey and beakers of barley ale. It tasted delicious as Osgar realised it was more than he was given at home, his former home.

Osgar washed down a piece of bread with a gulp of ale then took the chance of asking Froda why he lived apart from the main village.

"That," Froda rose, collecting their empty bowls and spoons, "I will tell you when your lessons begin. But for now, boy, may Odinn protect you. *Goda nott.*"

And with that, Froda retired to his bed.

Osgar sat, staring into the embers of the fire and feeding it to ensure it would be ready for the morning, as he had at home, his former home, until he too was forced to take his sleeping place on the bench, to dream of Streonshalh and his family and his former home. He would never know that Streonshalh, following the *Vikingr* raid, would lay abandoned for the next two centuries.

Osgar had already learned that the Denisc usually ate only twice a day—the breakfast offered to him now and *nattverthr*, the evening meal—rather like their two seasons of the year, summer and winter.

He rose and walked to the table.

"You eat when you have washed." Froda pointed to the doorway.

"Wash? But I—" was as far as he got.

"We wash daily and bathe and sauna on Saturday. You wish breakfast?"

Osgar found a pail of water by the door. He looked around but there was no one in sight; he stripped and washed in the ice-cold spring water.

"Good, now I will not have your stink in my house."

Osgar, meanwhile, wondered how Froda could possibly tell amongst the other smells in the house.

"Here," Froda continued, "put these on," handing him a set of new clothing. He stooped to pick up Osgar's discarded tunic.

"This, I will burn." Froda wrinkled his nose as he stepped outside with the offending tunic.

Taking his new clothes, Osgar dressed in the undershift, baggy woollen trousers and the long-sleeved tunic, securing it with a leather belt and fur-trimmed cap.

Froda examined him. "Much better. Now you look Denisc." Osgar had no intention of becoming one. "Now, try those on and let me know which fit best." Froda pointed towards two pairs of leather shoes with leather thongs, by the fire-hearth.

After trying both pairs, Osgar informed Froda that one pair was too small, the other too large.

"*Gott*—now put on the bigger pair."

Osgar did as he was bid.

"Now," Froda ordered, "pack them with straw until they feel comfortable. Breakfast?"

He sat at the table as Froda filled their wooden bowls with yesterday's stew—now more like soup—and brought them over, giving Osgar a spoon. After the soup, they breakfasted on buttermilk with crusty bread and honey with beakers of ale—safer than water was one of the earliest lessons Osgar learned the other side of the North Sea.

"Shall I wash our bowls?"

"No, leave them. I have something for you." And with that, Froda produced a wrapped package and unfolded the linen in which it had been rolled. He placed it in front of Osgar on the table. Osgar beheld the most beautiful knife he had seen in his nine winters.

The iron, steel-edged, pointed blade with runic inscriptions was six inches long with an intricately carved ivory handle decorated with silver. The *seax* was an all-purpose knife but this one could be used as a weapon. He balanced it in his hand, turning to Froda.

"Is this from—" Yet again, Froda cut him off mid-sentence.

"No, it is not from me. It is a gift from Eirikr, our Jarl, and with it a message: do your best to stay alive until it is time to learn to be a warrior."

Osgar stuck the *seax* into his belt.

"Now boy, can we begin your lessons to become a Seer?"

It was a rhetorical question.

"You asked two questions over last night's dinner: why do I live on the edge of the village and how can I navigate without sun and stars? Let us begin your education by dispelling the myths surrounding my gifts.

"*Sva vel.* Very well. Legends and myths tell us Odinn has two ravens: memory and thought. At dawn, he has them fly around the world. In the evening, they return to impart to him everything they have seen and heard—so Odinn knows exactly what is happening in the world of man. A Seer is the only channel with access to Odinn in Asgard from our world, Midgard."

Osgar sat, his mouth open in awe. "So, you can talk to Odinn?" he asked incredulously.

"We Seers interpret what we hear, or what the magic of the Runestones tell us."

Froda produced the Runestones and cast them on the floor. "The stones will tell us Odinn's will."

"What do they say?" asked the excited Osgar.

"They say you are ignorant, superstitious and gullible if you believe in magic."

"This is what Odinn is telling me?" Osgar asked, his voice trembling with fear and uncertainty.

"No! That is what *I* am telling you! Now, be quiet and listen to me, boy. A Seer is one of the most important members of Denisc society. They believe, blindly, in fate and we provide counsel from the god, the ultimate warrior, to our king, his Jarls and to anyone who seeks us out and is honest and lives an honourable life."

"But—"

"Be quiet if you wish to become a Seer. Our advice is based upon the exercise of logic, personal experience and a lifetime of knowledge, and then, our reading of the Runes. Do you understand?"

"*Ja,*" came the subdued reply.

"*Gott.* Every night for the next three summers, you will learn the meanings and mysteries of the Runes, the Younger Futark's sixteen stones carved by the Runemaster. Far more importantly, I will teach you how to interpret them without the use of magic. But Osgar, with that knowledge comes power—power that should never be misused."

Osgar nodded, trying hard to understand that which he was being told.

"The Denisc believe that fate dictates their lives—and their afterlife."

Froda realised he now had the young Englar's complete attention.

"They believe that if they have led their life with honour as a warrior and died in battle, sword in hand, then they will go to *Valholl*—the Hall of the Slain—and feast with the gods for eternity.

"An alternative destination for a warrior is *Folkvangar*—a field ruled over by the goddess Freya, who can choose half of the warriors who died in battle to live their afterlife there in contentment."

"But what happens to those who are not warriors—and the women and children?"

"A very intelligent question, my would-be Seer. *Helgafjell*, the holy mountain, is held to be a wonderful place to spend your afterlife for those who have not died in battle—but you must have led an honest and blameless life.

"The one you may wish to avoid, Osgar, is *Helheim*—a dark and sinister realm ruled by the goddess Hel. Places are reserved there for those who have died in a dishonourable way. Unfortunately, this includes dying in bed."

Osgar made an immediate decision to die standing.

"As a Seer," Froda continued, "bear in mind that no funeral celebrations can be held until seven days after the death. Then, they can mark the passing with the drinking of ale, which confirms the disposition of property.

"Now, beardless one, you asked why I live on the outskirts of the village. I practise magic, I talk to Odinn, I am a mystery to the villagers—an enigma. They bring me provisions and gifts, knowing they may need my services themselves sometime in the future. I would hardly retain my mystery should I live in the centre of the village."

Osgar could see the logic in that. He was learning already.

"Now, as a Seer, are you expected to live on charity? Far from it. As the Jarl's Seer, my recompense is substantial and paid in silver. The villagers who seek out my talents seldom pay a fee but in eggs and cheese, poultry, meat, ale and mead, or even a whole sow. I assure you I am no danger of starvation."

Osgar chuckled as Froda pointed out, "In reality, I have considerable means—as will you once you are a Seer."

He took off his gold arm amulet and handed it to Osgar.

"Remember, with we Denisc, if it does not move, we shall decorate it," he chuckled.

Osgar scrutinised the symbols engraved on the amulet as Froda explained their meaning, "They are the symbols of the Helm of Awe and the Hammer of Thor. The *aegish jalmr*—the helm of awe or terror—is 'magic' and can induce memory loss or delusions, designed to hide someone from their pursuers."

Osgar's attention then switched to the very recognisable Hammer of Thor.

"And the hammer?"

"Ah, the *Mjolnir*—the lightning. Again, 'magic'. The hammer returns to Thor's hand when thrown. The symbol indicates the god's power of thunder and lightning. This is the symbol you will see everywhere, worn as protection as an amulet or pendant."

"Our gods are almost the same," Osgar observed.

"*Gott*—then you should have no problem understanding ours. Now, I need to explain to you about respect. As a Seer, you will not gain respect as a right: respect must be earned, which is a matter of time and the accuracy of your prophecies. I shall give you the opportunity to earn it."

Osgar moved forward and proffered the amulet back towards its owner. Its owner, gesturing with his right hand inclined, palm forward, declined. The silent gesture spoke volumes.

Osgar was now its owner.

He slipped the amulet onto his left arm and smiled as it slipped from wrist to elbow.

"Something else that will take time," whispered Froda.

As he twisted the amulet around and around his skinny arm, Osgar, realising the lesson was not yet over, continued, "You said you would explain how you can find your way across the sea without the sun or stars."

"I forgot not, so pay close attention to me. Many of our voyages follow a coastline until reaching a river, but we also have the skills to sail in open seas, away from land.

"We have a long history of seafaring and have built up a knowledge of coasts and currents, navigation marks and the birds which signify land is near—all are part of a chart in our memories."

"Navigation marks?" Osgar was thirsting for knowledge.

"Mountains, hills, signs of habitation, strangely-shaped rocks, avoiding the *brim-sker*, the rocks on which waves break. The seafarers also use a weight on the end of a line to measure the depth of the water in relation to the longship's draft. The shadow of the *gnomen* on a marked circle of wood, from the sun's rays, helps them determine their latitude."

"But the Seer's 'magic'—navigating without sun or stars. In thick fog, perhaps?" Osgar interrupted.

"Patience, child." Froda frowned. "The magic you refer to is the sun stone—a Norse spar. It will show the position of the sun through fog or cloud."

Froda reached down under the neck of his gown and produced a pendant chain from which hung a crystal.

"Lo, the sun stone. And this," producing a piece of magnetised iron oxide, "is the lodestone.* It will always show you the direction of the *Nordn Stiarna* or Pole Star, which will ensure you will always find your destination." Froda next produced an ellipsoid lens of rock crystal. "This is a spy-glass, with which you can scan the horizon for land or ships. This will bring them closer to you and you will see them before they can see you. But do not hasten, young one. You will gain first-hand experience of sea voyages soon enough, I predict."

By then, it was late forenoon.

"For the remainder of the day," Froda instructed, "I wish you to explore your new home, and the people within it.

"But do not be over-familiar. You must create a distance—a barrier—between the Seer and the villagers."

"But how will they know I am to become a Seer dressed like this?" Osgar spread his arms to indicate the way he was attired. "Do I not need a robe?"

Froda laughed heartily, hands on hips and back arched.

"*Du skal kravle, for du can ga*—you must learn to crawl before you can walk. By now most of the villagers will know you are my pupil—but take this."

* *An early form of compass.*

He handed Osgar a four-foot staff, decorated with Runes and topped with a silver representation of a serpent's head.

"This will signify that you will become my successor and that you are a freeman, not a *thrall*. Now, I suggest you begin to appreciate your fellow-villagers. They will, no doubt, also be appraising you.

"When you return, we shall have *nattverthr*, after which you can tell me of your day and continue your lessons in reading the Runes."

CHAPTER THREE

OSGAR walked the length and breadth of the village, pausing to introduce himself to those outside their houses or tending their livestock or poultry in their wickerwork enclosures. Froda had been right: most of them knew of him, if only by name.

"*Hvat segir thu?*" and its response of "*Alt gott. Thakka!*" were becoming a part of his vocabulary by mid-afternoon.

He made a point of stopping at each artisan's workshop or stall. Their services he may well need to call upon in the future.

He introduced himself to the fletcher, producing goose-feather flighted arrows for the ash and *ybogi*—yew bows; the butchers in the Shambles, cleaving the bodies of pigs, sheep, goats, hunted wild boar and, for feasts, horses. He talked with the farmers selling their produce in the market—a living he knew well—and with the carpenter, busy fulfilling orders for furniture, plates and beakers.

At the jewellers, goldsmiths and silversmiths, he was amazed by the range of their expertise—brooches, rings, pendants, amulets and talismans and more, some intricately decorated with precious metals; they were also ornamenting weapons for the warriors, and even spoons and drinking horns of ivory and bone. At the kilns, he examined the potter's wares, and bread at the bakery with its communal clay ovens. The leather craftsmen were busy producing helmets, belts, sheaves, shoes and boots and tack for the horses.

Reaching the *smidja*, he approached the smithy, who was busy producing farm implements, tools, blades, horseshoes and a range of ironwork. The heat in the smithy was almost unbearable.

"*Sael!*" Osgar held out his arm. It was not taken.

"*Velkomminn, utlender.*"

Osgar was not sure if it had been meant as a friendly greeting or an insult. The smithy introduced himself, putting aside his tools by the red-hot, glowing forge fire.

"I see you make horseshoes," said Osgar, trying hard to make conversation. "For war-horses?" he asked.

"We value our horses highly, Angle."

Osgar could sense the smithy's scorn at the lack of his knowledge.

"They are too valuable to use in battle. The warriors use them to seek out the enemy and to take them to the scene of the battle where they dismount and fight on foot."

"*Far vel, thakka.*" Osgar made good his escape, wending his way to the weapon-maker.

"*Hei Seer*! I am called Magnus." He held out his arm and Osgar clasped it, although he had difficulty wrapping his hand around a considerably bulky forearm.

"Not Seer yet, my friend."

"Then Seer-to-be." Magnus smiled.

Osgar looked around the walls of the workshop. There were many stands of weapons: double-edged swords, short axes and long axes, capable of slicing through helmets and shields as a knife through butter.

There were *seaxan* (small knives), metal helmets, long- and short-shafted spears for throwing and close-quarter fighting.

Some of the weapons were awaiting the engraving of the Runes or decoration with gold and silver. Hanging on one wall was a *brynja*, the only coat of chain mail, with its flexible links, in the workshop. Only the very rich would be able to afford the price.

Magnus followed his gaze. "That is for the Jarl," he stated.

Osgar should have guessed.

"Your work is truly impressive, Magnus."

"*Thakka fyrir*, Seer-to-be." He smiled in gratitude. "If what I have heard is true then I shall be making a *brynja* and a *hervapna*—a full set of weapons—for you in the future."

"I also have that hope, my friend."

"You are being treated well?" Magnus asked, passing him a *bjor-ker* of barley ale, and one for himself.

"Yes, but I think your smithy has taken a dislike to me," Osgar confessed.

"Balder the smithy? He is a *bacraut*, but unfortunately, an asshole who is an excellent smith. I assure you it is nothing personal. Many summers ago, his mother was dying and he did not like, or believe, it when Froda told him this truth. So he went to a *volva*—a sorceress—in Ribe.

"She took his silver and told him to return here and sacrifice his horse to the gods, then his mother would recover. She died just seven nights later. Balder has hated Seers ever since. If he gives you any trouble, let me know. Now, have you time, I suggest you visit my friend, Loki, the shield-maker. Tell him I sent you."

At the shield-maker's, Loki let Osgar try several of the three-foot diameter, lightweight, wooden shields, held by putting his hand through a leather-covered iron handgrip at its centre. Although defensive, the iron rim of the shield and the domed iron boss in its centre could be useful in an offensive situation.

"When it is time, you may choose your own colours and decoration." Osgar could not wait.

At the far end of the village, Osgar found his path halted, his way blocked by a six-foot-high, semi-circular wooden rampart with a guard tower over its gate, a stockade and a deep defensive ditch. The ramparts were well guarded.

On reflection, Osgar realised it was logical to protect the western, inland approach to the village; the harbour to the east was equally well protected with its lookouts scanning the horizon above a series of sharpened wooden stakes submerged below the surface, onto which an enemy ship could impale itself, not knowing the only safe course into the inlet.

Osgar retreated, passing through the market and stopping to chat at the stalls before he reached the harbour. Hearing giggling laughter, he turned to see a group of children, younger than himself, playing kingy bats, hitting a ball of tied fabric from bat to bat trying to keep it from falling to the ground.

Like their warrior fathers, two older boys were fighting with wooden swords and small shields. The children, he knew, would also play *Hnefatafl*—a board game played between red and white armies of intricately carved pieces.

Osgar thought of his home and childhood in Streonshalh, but only for a moment. His brief nostalgia was interrupted by the sudden need for a latrine. Apart from Magnus' ale, during his talk with the owner of the weaving workshop, his wife had brought Osgar some cottage cheese wrapped in soggy linen and some stale bread. Unfortunately, that intake was now fighting a successful battle to escape his bowels. He spied a wickerwork-screened latrine at the rear of the house opposite and seized his chance.

Pulling up his tunic and dropping his baggy trousers, he squatted over the hole in the ground and relieved himself of lunch with a loud trumpet of wind. The smell of the latrine was indescribable and he pitied the poor *thrall* whose job it would be to empty it.

Walking between the houses to an open field, he found the *skeps*—the beehives made of straw. The keeper of the honey explained the bees would be killed by filling the *skeps* with smoke from a sulphur fire, then six to eight honeycombs could be collected from each hive. Osgar chatted for a while and accepted some fresh honey as a gift for Froda.

On his return, he passed the women in the brew-house. It was a woman's job to make the ale and beer and the men's to drink it—as it should be. One of the younger women, aged around 13 winters, shouted out what she would like to give him.

"*Nae, thakka,*" he shouted back through cupped hands. "*Alt er gott!*"

"*Heimskr skitkarl?*" came her reply.

He walked on and soon reached the harbour. He had noticed on his walk through the village that half of the villagers were under 16 summers. This did not surprise him, given that the life expectancy was twenty to thirty summers, or less.

On the quayside, *thralls* were unloading the *knarrs*, cargo ships, and transferring their load to the warehouses, overseen by Denisc dockers. Osgar could easily identify the owner of the ships, the *kaupmadr*, by the merchant's richly and expensively embroidered clothing, soft leather boots, fur-trimmed cap and gold hanging around his neck and on his forearms. He announced his wealth to the world. Osgar sauntered over to him and introduced himself.

"So, Froda's apprentice, *Ja?* My name is Vidar. I am a merchant trader." *Stating the obvious,* thought Osgar. "Have you come to tell me you can predict the storms for the next year?"

"*Ja*, there will be many of them," Osgar replied with a perfectly serious face.

Vidar exploded with a great guffaw of laughter, shaking his two chins, and slapped Osgar on the back, almost knocking him into the harbour. No one could accuse Vidar of being slight in build. He obviously lived well.

"May I ask what cargo you carry?"

"Certainly. Over here," pointing to two upturned wooden crates. "Now, imports. I bring in spices, oils and perfumes, also glassware and silk from the east and ivory as well as Rhineland wines for the Jarls."

"And then you set sail in search of another cargo?" quipped Osgar.

"*Ymir's eistna, nei!*"

Osgar wondered how Ymir's balls had become part of the conversation.

"Are you trying to bankrupt me, boy? I am a merchant, I cannot afford to sail empty ships. Once unladen, the ships will take on a cargo for export."

"Which will be?"

Osgar was genuinely interested—trading seemed to generate great wealth.

"On their next voyage," he pointed towards his ships, "they will carry jet and amber beads and ornaments; pine marten, fox, otter, beaver and bear furs; the highest quality cloth and wool; and *thralls* for sale to our Arab friends for large amounts of silver." He smiled. "Should you ever decide to involve yourself with trading, seek me out: Vidar the merchant, everyone knows me. But now, I must go and check my manifests."

With that, he turned and strode up the *bruggja* to his warehouse.

"*Thakka! Far vel!*" Osgar shouted after the disappearing merchant, whom he felt sure he would meet again.

Being by the harbour, Osgar decided to seek out the boatyard of the shipwright. He was pointed in the direction of the shipbuilder's yard, who noticed his silver-topped rod as he approached.

"*Hversu ferr*, Seer-to-be?"

"*Allt vel, thakka.* May we speak?"

"*Allt er gott*—what do you wish to know?"

"Everything about shipbuilding," Osgar explained.

Arne the shipwright laughed as if Osgar had said something to amuse him.

"You have twenty summers to spare?" he asked, raising an eyebrow.

"Your point is well taken, master shipbuilder," Osgar returned his smile. "Perhaps only the basics?"

"*Ja*, that is possible. We are all hard at work, building a ship for the Jarl."

"A longship?"

"Of course; only, this one will be the best to ever sail the seas."

"The longship is very big," Osgar suggested thoughtfully.

"We have built bigger," Arne stated proudly, "for King Horvik, son of Guthred; it held over a hundred warriors." He beamed with pride.

Osgar had trouble imaging such a vast craft.

"Tomorrow, we are laying the frame into the hull. As you may find yourself aboard her in the future time, I suggest you return in the fore-noon and I will explain it to you."

"*Thakka*, that would please me greatly. Does she have a name?"

"That will be up to the Jarl, when she is completed. Whatever name he chooses, we will carve a prow to suit the name."

"I shall look forward to tomorrow, master shipbuilder."

"As you say, Seer."

Osgar left the scent of freshly-cut oak, pine glue and the sound of the axes of the builders behind him as he made his way back through the village. He passed the Jarl's *langhus* on the way, wondering when he would be summoned there.

Froda had told his young charge that the Jarl was following his progress with a personal interest and had explained the function of the longhouse.

Unlike many longhouses that provided a home for many families, having one large room, this longhouse housed only the Jarl and his extended family, with additional rooms separated by partitions for his *huskarls*—his personal bodyguards—and their families. Osgar stood, trying to imagine its interior used for council meetings, as a court for trials and punishments and for feasting.

The Jarl's visiting guests would also be allocated rooms. Externally, the longhouse was some two hundred feet long and twenty feet in width, reflecting the Jarl's status. Built on stone footings with a wooden frame, it had walls of wooden planking, no windows and was roofed with turf. Froda had told Osgar that, for a feast, trestle tables were set, normally stored on the crossbeams of the roof.

Arriving back at Froda's house as twilight fell, they dined on venison, fresh from the hunt and cooked on the skillet, and fresh vege-tables. As they sipped *bjorr* from beakers, Froda questioned him as to how he had spent the day and what he had learned. The Seer seemed pleased with the answers.

"Good, you have begun your journey. The word I have is that you are wise beyond your years. That is good, they will accept you. Next, you must earn their respect as a Seer. In the near time, I shall allow you to cast the Runes for the villagers and I shall hear your predictions with great interest."

Osgar felt elated to think of the opportunity of casting the Runes.

"As to the forenoon," Froda continued, "your day with my friend Arne will be a long one and, I hope, will give you an understanding of our most important weapon—the longship. Now, I think it is time for sleep."

Osgar needed no second bidding. He slept as a log.

Early the next morning, Osgar took fresh fruit and bread in a knotted linen cloth and made his way to the boatyard.

"*Godan dag, Seer. Velkommin.*"

"*Godan morgin,* master stemsmith," Osgar returned his greeting. Froda had explained to him that stemsmith was Arne's title, as well as shipwright. For part of his craft in assembling longships was, when the basic shape of keel and frame was assembled, to stretch a line from stem to stern to measure the proportions of each plank and rib, using radii marked on a knotted line.

"Come," said Arne as he led Osgar to where his craftsmen and *thralls* were gathered around the wooden hull of the ship-to-be, some fifty feet in length.

"This is a *skeid,*" as he smacked the hull with his calloused palm, "which means 'that which cuts through water'.

"When she is launched," Arne continued, "she will ride over the tops of the waves for greater speed. Her shallow draft of only three feet not only makes her swifter but allows her to navigate an *oss*, shallow river, and beach prow into land."

Arne continued with Osgar's education and the hours slipped away from him. He next learned that only the finest oak was used. *Strakes*, the planks, were cut with the grain of the wood to give them added strength. Arne pointed to one of his workmen using an axe to make a split in a tree trunk, then driving wooden wedges in along that cut until it separated the tree.

"From that two-hundred-year-old oak tree, he will go on splitting it until it yields us sixty-four planks. I choose only the best craftsmen." He smiled in satisfaction.

Osgar learned the tools used to build the ships had never changed: the axe, adze, plane, drawknife. Augers would be used to begin the holes needed for the rivets and treenails.

Channels would be cut for caulking, made from sheep's wool dipped in tree resin to ensure watertight seals. All Arne's boats were clinker-built, with overlapping planks riveted together.

They sat with *bjor-kers*—beakers—as Arne talked Osgar through the various stages of building a longship, "or as you Englars call them—dragonships," he laughed.

The ship began with the laying of the keel, its shape determined by two curved stem and stern posts. It was not flat wood but was a V-shape to take the first planks. The first *strake* in the building of the hull was the *Garboard,* the next plank being riveted to it. Once the hull was completed, the planks were caulked.

"And now, Seer," he stood, "we are ready to put the frame into the shell. This ship does not need a heavy frame; again, it is built for speed."

Osgar watched as the futtocks—the interior frames—and cross beams were put in place, joined to the timbers running across the hull to form the deck. The important part, Arne stressed, was the *keelson,* a long timber to sit inside the boat on its ribs above the keel, with the hole made in it to take the mast for the sail. Osgar marvelled as he watched the longship take shape before his eyes. He realised the longship that had brought him here as a captive had probably been built on that same spot by Arne and his craftsmen.

Arne called for a break and invited Osgar to take some salted herring and bread.

"I use a spacing of thirty-three inches between rowing stations. This leaves them the space to use their chests as *thwarts,* their seats."

"And you work from your plans to build the ship, *ja?*"

"*Neinn,* it is all in here," said Arne, tapping the side of his head.

Osgar recalled the *Denisc* communicated literally everything orally, with nothing written or recorded. Arne had learned his skills over many years of amassed experience. As with all master shipwrights, he built them the way he knew best.

"Do you only build longships?"

"*Nei,* Seer. This is a *skeid,* but we also build *snekkjas,* a smaller ship with twenty crew, also *drekkars*, more ornately carved but still built for raiding and war. And, of course, we build the *knarrs*—cargo ships for trading in many lands."

"Arne, as a Seer-to-be, I am interested as to the reason for the carved prow figures."

"There is more than one," Arne explained. "It is said they protect the ship and crew; others believe they ward off the real sea monsters we all fear. They are also useful for terrifying our enemies," he laughed.

"And the stem and the stern both being the same shape?"

"It enables us to back-row so the ship does not have to turn about; useful if you are heading for treacherous currents or rocks, *nei?*"

"I shall avoid the currents and rocks," Osgar decided.

The day had passed quickly—too quickly—and the light was already fading into a darkened sky. Osgar thanked Arne profusely, gripping both arms to express his deep gratitude for his time.

"You are welcome, Seer. It was a pleasure. You have shown a genuine interest in my craft and you have a quick mind."

"I hope I get the chance to sail in her someday," Osgar wished aloud.

Arne smiled and placed his hand on Osgar's shoulder, leaning forward as if to say something no one else should hear.

"Knowing our Jarl and Froda well, Seer, I have no doubt you shall."

Osgar made his way through the now lamp-lit village with a strange sense of elation. Today, not only had he learned that which had fired his imagination from Arne the master stemwright, but, also, Froda had told him that tonight he was to be given his first opportunity to give an actual reading of the Runes to Sweyn, leader of the fisher folk.

He quickened his pace.

CHAPTER FOUR

AD 860

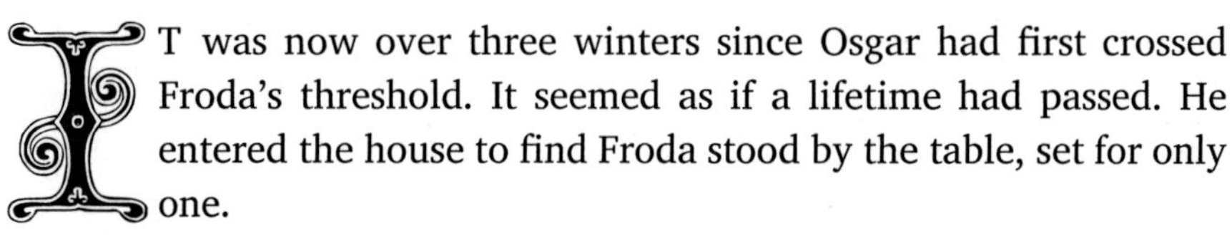

IT was now over three winters since Osgar had first crossed Froda's threshold. It seemed as if a lifetime had passed. He entered the house to find Froda stood by the table, set for only one.

"The time has come, as we knew it would. Eirikr has summoned you to the *langhus*. Now you are *tolf* and grown, it is time for you to begin your training as a *drengr—a rekkr*—and the next chapter of your *aevi*—your life story. I have taught you almost all I know. I can only pray to Odinn that one of them is wisdom—use it wisely, Osgar the Angle. Visit me if you are passing; my house will always be your home."

"Seer—Froda—I need no summons; of course, I shall return many times."

"The Runes tell me you are destined to become the first Seer of the Denisc to also become a Jarl, and that you will live a long and successful life."

"A Jarl?" Osgar reacted in surprise, laughing. "Me? A Jarl? I am as like to fly as an eagle."

"Then you will fly high," Froda responded. "Do you remember what I told the Jarl I saw, when we first met?"

"Of course, I was—" He stopped; Froda's vision that day, as he had stood under Eirikr's axe, came back to him.

"Remember it well. And now, as I detest long farewells, you must not keep the Jarl waiting, beardless one," Froda smiled.

Osgar crossed the distance between them and Froda hugged him to his chest. "*Far vel*, Osgar, the warrior-to-be. May Odinn keep you and protect you."

"*Far vel*, my teacher, mentor and friend."

Osgar turned and left the room quickly. As he strode away, knowing Froda would be watching him from the doorway, he dared not turn lest Froda see the tears on his face. Emotions, he learned that moment, were for only close friends and family and shared with no other.

As he walked, he remembered these past three winters of learning and laughter, interspersed with admonishments. He remembered his first reading of the Runes for Sweyn, the leader of the fishermen. He had rightly predicted a mighty storm as a sign of Thor's anger and advised Sweyn to beach his boats and not put to sea.

"How, in Odinn's name," Froda had questioned the next day, "did you know that there was going to be a storm? Did the Runes tell you?"

"In a way. They predicted the anger of Thor and I coupled this with my own understanding of the *himinn* and the cloud formations over the horizon I saw on my way here. Knowledge and observation."

"Ha! You are learning quickly, boy—make sure not too quickly," Froda laughed, slapping him on the shoulder. "Sweyn has been grateful ever since. Look at his latest offering." He pointed to the fish and food from the sea by the hearth. "There is enough there to feed us for a month," he laughed.

Over the next two winters, Osgar was called upon to give many readings, to the poor and the far from poor. The latter rewarded him well, in silver. He well remembered Froda teaching him how to use his own intelligence and experience as well as the stones and by now he was well versed in the art of ambiguous predictions. When a trader asked whether he should expand his stall, Osgar suggested he let his competitor know his plans. His competitor's reaction would be the gods' answer to his problem. The competitor's immediate reaction had been to buy the trader's stall for more than three times its worth. The stallholder was ecstatic and, having bought a shop twice the size of his stall, he had still made a sizeable profit, a proportion of which Osgar had put into his rapidly accumulating 'trading' purse.

He had sought out Vidar the merchant trader, with whom he had talked over two winters past and who had offered his help. After a friendly and constructive meeting, Osgar left the warehouse having invested his savings in half of an export cargo of jet jewellery, gold and silver rings, as well as arm rings, leather clothes, shoes, helmets and body armour with an assortment of swords, axes and knives.

Vidar assured him it was a lucrative manifest.

"There is, of course, another high-yield commodity bought for silver—*thralls*."

"I will not invest in the misery of the sale of slaves," Osgar replied. "I was taken captive as one, remember?"

Vidar also predicted that the return trip imports of silk, spices and oils, glass and wine would gain them a very high return on their investment. Osgar prayed to Odinn it would return safely with his recent profits, which he had agreed with Vidar would be reinvested by the merchant. Froda was right, he would be a seer-warrior, but as a Seer foremost. He could see no profit in being a warrior unless there was pillage from raiding, and such opportunity would probably not be offered for several years. He would continue his trading, guided by Vidar, with whom he was establishing a close relationship. Learning the art of the Runes was ongoing but Froda also taught him about the Deniscan. He was in the kingdom of Jylland* on *Den Kimbriske Halvo*—the Cimbrian Peninsula in the land of Ribe, a trading city, the land of which Eirikr was Jarl.

The most important trading town was Hedeby to the south on the border.

"We are protected by the *Danevirke* on our southern border. This defensive wall, running for fifty miles from the Schflei fjord to the river Treene," Froda explained to him, "means that all trading coming from north to south must use the Ox Road, which runs through the *Danevirke* at Hedeby—hence its importance."

"Our economy is based on farming, trade and fishing, not on raiding as you might think—but Eirikr will explain the reasons better than I."

At a later stage in his education, Froda explained to Osgar the social structure of the *Denisc* hierarchy.

"Think of it as a pyramid," Froda advised. "At the point is the king—the most important. Our present ruler of all the Danes is Horik II to whom all must answer. He has the ultimate decision over the people.

"Below the king come the Jarls. They are the warrior leaders, wealthy landowners with many horses and slaves. All people in their

* *Jutland.*

'kingdom' are under their rule. They are fiercely independent and guard their positions and possessions by whatever means necessary. Personal honour they value above all things. If not called to the king's court, they spend the greater amount of their time in the administration of his kingdom, politics, hunting and expeditions across the seas.

"They are honour-bound to provide men and arms for war if the king calls upon them.

"Next come the Karls—the freemen. They are our warriors, artisans in many trades, merchant traders and farmers of cattle and crops, who own their own farms.

"At the base of the pyramid are the *thralls*—the slaves."

"As I am," Osgar stated.

"As you are not!" Froda replied angrily. "You are a freeman and have been since I took you to be a Seer. I am not your owner. I hoped I was your friend."

"I am sorry—I did not mean that. Of course, I look upon you as my friend," Osgar said reassuringly, as much for Froda as for himself.

"You must learn to control your emotions before giving them tongue, my Englar friend." It was a lecture and a lesson, which Froda continued the next day.

"We were discussing the *thralls, ja?*"

"*Ja*, Seer."

"They are the lowest order in our society and are treated as such. Some we train as servants and housemaids; others we use as labourers to build our fortifications, ditches, mounds, roads and as farm labourers. Their lives are dependent upon their masters and mistresses. Every freeman has the right to punish them or to sell them in the slave markets. Some are brought back from our raids specifically to be sold, a very lucrative export, to many lands far afield."

"And the Denisc women?" Osgar inquired.

"Do not worry, my young stallion, you will learn about them soon enough," said a laughing Seer. "For now, all you need to know is that they are free women.

"If there is no son, then as head of the family, the daughter inherits from the father until she marries, then the estate and rights are passed to the husband. Marriages are arranged by the family clan; as no doubt yours will be by the Jarl." He smiled again.

"As a widow, she regains all her estates and rights as well as her husband's, if there is no son, and carries the same independent social status as any unmarried woman."

Osgar's thoughts came back to the present as he approached the longhouse and his much willed-for audience with the Jarl. He realised he knew not what to expect. He knew only that Eirikr was a terrifying presence.

He reached the doorway, guarded by a fully-armed *huskarl*, one of the Jarl's personal bodyguards, who opened the heavy wooden door, gesturing him to enter. The interior of the longhouse was very much as Osgar had imagined it, except that it was neither lacking light nor filled with smoke.

Beams of light shone down from the smoke holes in the roof and from the dished lamps, placed at intervals around the longhouse. The lamps were carved from soapstone, burning fish-liver oil with a wick of cotton-grass. The floor on which he stood was made of packed earth, made absorbent by the scattering of ashes from the fires.

A large rectangular fire-pit ran down the centre of the hall; by the evidence of the other smoke holes, each of the other rooms had its own circular fire. There was only one bed closet, probably containing the longhouse's only box bed, no doubt with linen sheets, a silken quilt and down-filled pillows, as the largest room, presumably for the Jarl and his family. There were other smaller rooms for the Jarl's most important retainers and guests. Much later, Osgar learned that the Jarl had no family, having lost his wife and son in childbirth.

On either side of the *langhus* were raised wooden benches, topped with planks, running the length of its walls. They provided the only option for sitting, eating, working and sleeping, with the use of sheepskins and furs. The only other furniture Osgar could discern were the several wooden chests around the hall.

Around one wall, throwing and close-quarter spears were stacked, with collections of short and long axes, swords and helmets: an armoury in case of attack.

Men, women and children were milling around the longhouse, some doing chores or cooking. The children were playing and the men discussing war and battles from sagas or sharpening their weapons.

Another *huskarl* approached him and gestured to Osgar to follow him. As they walked the length of the hall, he could see the Jarl sat in a huge, ornate, carved wooden chair—more a throne—with a boy stood in front of him. The Jarl ceased whatever he had been saying to the fair-haired youngster and lifted his head as he saw Osgar approach. The Jarl stood as Osgar took his place beside the boy. Eirikr nodded at the *huskarl*, who turned and left them.

Osgar studied the Jarl, who had the power of life or death over his people. *He's tall, very tall*, thought Osgar. *Perhaps six foot, a giant among the Denisc.* Eirikr's blonde hair and beard were carefully trimmed, as befitted his rank.

Osgar looked upon Eirikr's deep blue eyes. He appeared, to Osgar anyway, to be over forty winters in age—*langlifr* in Denisc terms, old age. Though, looking into those penetrating eyes, Osgar could see no signs of dotage.

The lord was dressed in black leather, a long tunic covered in pointed silver studs over unusually tight trousers of finest red-dyed wool with embroidered hems. Around his neck, on a gold chain, hung a gold Hammer of Thor—as a talisman, Osgar presumed. On his arms were finely engraved gold amulets, one with his dragon house and battle-flag symbol; the other, smaller amulet on his right arm, his sword arm, was dedicated to Odinn. Eirikr was not taking any chances on his entrance to Valhalla, mused Osgar. On his right index finger, the Jarl also wore his clan-ring, a serpent of gold.

From his broad leather belt hung his sword of fame—*Farbjodr*—The Destroyer.

Suddenly, Osgar realised the Jarl was addressing him in a voice of gravel.

"So, Osgar the Angle, you come to us to train as a *drengr?*"

"Yes, my Jarl."

"So has your friend next to you. I suggest you get to know each other as you will be living and training together for the next three winters."

As Osgar turned to his left and lowered his gaze, he caught his first glimpse of Einar. And from that point onwards, their destiny was cast.

"I am Osgar the Seer," he said proudly as he grasped his new friend's outstretched arm.

"Einar," was the single-word reply as he took Osgar's arm.

Einar means 'He who fights alone'.

Osgar studied his new friend. His hair was, unusually, almost brown, as were his eyes. He was dressed in the mandatory plain tunic and baggy trousers.

Osgar estimated him to be at least four inches shorter than himself, although Osgar knew he was taller than the average.

He also noted that Einar was scrutinising his silver-topped rod.

"Now!" the Jarl continued. "Osgar, you will continue to be a Seer, where those who need your services can find you here, but remember, first and foremost, you are my personal Seer and I shall call you whenever necessary. Understood?"

"Absolutely, my lord," Osgar replied, while thinking, *I have a choice?*

"*Gutt*! Your weapons training will be under Svein Ragnarsson, the head of my *heimthegar*, my housekarls, the bravest of my warriors, my personal bodyguards."

Osgar knew from Froda's teachings that the *huskarls'* primary role was the defence of the Jarl. In battle, if the Jarl was in immediate danger, the housekarls would form a *skjald-borg*—a shield wall—around the Jarl and fight fiercely to the last man to protect him. They lived in the longhouses with their families, in a state of instant readiness, hence the presence of one on each side of the Jarl's chair, fully armed.

"If you fail me," the Jarl continued, "I shall sell you as *thralls*."

Osgar looked deep into his eyes. He believed him.

"You will train in the use of all weapons. Svein will decide with which weapon you show the most skill and courage in fighting.

"I personally will train you in the art of war. You will learn battle tactics, offensive and defensive manoeuvres, the structure of my army and how to be a leader in battle, and peace. My hope is that you will excel in all things, but especially leadership, eh Svein?"

Eirikr stopped the conversation as a tall, fair-bearded man in leather defensive armour approached. He wore his sword and a long *seax*, with a blade long enough to be used as a weapon, in his belt. His face was weathered, a scar running the entire length of his right cheek, testimony to a life as a warrior who had seen many battles. Beneath his penetrating blue eyes was a nose of a hawk.

Osgar and Einar exchanged glances. From that time on, they would refer to him as *hauknefr*—hawknose, but only out of his hearing.

"Svein, you are timely, I was just telling our two warriors-to-be here that you will be responsible for their training."

"As you say, my lord."

He looked at the two boys and smiled. The smile did not reach his eyes, only making him appear even more as a hawk.

"So, tomorrow you begin your training, *litt Englar*," he spoke directly to Osgar. "At twelve summers, you are no longer children who play with wooden swords. You will train with the same weapons you will use in battle," he smiled, or rather curled his lips.

"Remember, Svein, I do not want them sending each other to the afterlife—at least not yet. I need them here in Midgard. I have an investment in their future."

"As you say, my lord."

"And now, I think you should show them to their living space, where they can eat and drink."

He made a sign of dismissal and they followed Svein to the space that was to be their home for the next three winters—if they survived.

Their living space was basically a rectangular box with two sleeping shelves built into one wall, covered with sheepskins, a small upturned wooden case as a table, two stools and two oil lamps. In the centre of the room was a small, circular firepit directly under the smoke-hole in the ceiling. By the pit was a small stewpot and a skillet with two spoons.

"All the comforts of home," Osgar joked.

"But not a comfortable home," replied Einar, not amused.

"It could be worse," Osgar spread his arms to take in the room. "It could have been the latrine—and we may not have liked our trainer-to-be."

This time Einar did laugh.

Osgar, seizing his opportunity, inquired

"Einar, you know of my history but I know nothing of you."

"There is little to tell," Einar replied. "I too am an orphan. My mother died giving me life. My father was the Jarl's best warrior, head of the *huskarls*. He was slain in battle and now drinks with the gods in Valhalla."

"*Fyrirgef mik*."

"You do not need to be sorry for me, Osgar. I was eight winters old when Svein was promoted to my father's position and the Jarl took me under his wing. Now, it seems we are destined to become *drengr*. There is no more to tell."

They were interrupted by a serving maid, a *grodkona*, with their meal: a bowl of hot lamb stew and vegetables, crusty bread and beakers of beer.

"Tell me," Osgar inquired of her, "why are we banished from the hall to our room to eat. Do you know?"

"*Ja*. I heard the Jarl and the *huskarl* talking." She dropped her voice to a whisper. "Svein does not consider you have yet earned the right to sit at the Jarl's table with the warriors."

Osgar and Einar exchanged glances yet again.

"What is your name?" Osgar asked.

"Cynfrith, my lord."

"I am not a lord, Cynfrith." He laughed. "I am not even a warrior."

"You are, compared to me, my lord," she smiled.

It was then Osgar realised.

"You are an Angle," he said.

"Yes, my lord. I was taken at twelve winters from my village on the estuary of the Humber."

"I am an Angle also. I was taken from my village of *Streonshalh* in *Deira* when I was nine winters," Osgar exclaimed with a burst of emotion he managed to keep in check. He hugged her to him as she sobbed for all that had ended.

"Cynfrith," with a change of tack, Osgar continued, "I need you to do something for me I can ask of no other."

"Anything, my lord," she answered, failing to keep emotion from her voice. "What is it you wish?"

"*Fregn*—information. Am I right in thinking you serve at the Jarl's table?"

"Yes, my lord."

"Then, could I ask you tell me any information you hear that may be of interest to me?"

"But what, my lord?"

"Anything and everything, no matter how small. Any scrap of information could be important."

"I shall try my best, my lord."

"And one more thing, Cynfrith."

"Yes, my lord?"

"Stop calling me lord."

"Yes, my lord…" she paused then giggled. "Yes." Osgar smiled.

He stooped and kissed her on the forehead.

"*Thakka*, Cynfrith, a thousand times."

She blushed, turned and left quickly.

"Well done, Osgar," Einar commented with his usual sub-tone of sarcasm, "you have made a conquest. Now she is in love with you. What possible purpose could she serve?"

"I may be a Seer, Einar, but I would like a little more information, particularly as to what the Jarl has planned for my future. That, I cannot see, yet. And does not a man's tongue run wild when released by horn after horn of beer?"

That was true, Einar thought to himself. He also remembered they had a big day ahead of them on the morrow.

"Come," he said, "we need to sleep before we face Svein and our first lesson in warrior craft." This time, it was Osgar who had to agree. They made their way to their bench and despite the cacophony of shouting and laughter from the hall, they fell into a deep sleep.

CHAPTER FIVE

ARLY in the forenoon, Osgar and Einar rose, washed and dressed. They breakfasted on porridge from their cauldron while awaiting the arrival of Svein and their first step on the long path to becoming a warrior.

"*Morgin*! With me."

It was not a request. Blocking the light from the doorway, Svein strode into the hall. They had no opportunity to return his greeting. He strode up the *langhus* to where the weapons were stored. He pointed to the stack of swords in their leather-covered scabbards.

"To begin, you will choose your best friend—your *sverd*."

They did as they were bid. Einar casually picked up the nearest sword and attached it to his belt. Osgar looked at three. He examined each for straightness of blade, balance and weight before making his choice. This did not go unnoticed by Svein, who rubbed his beard thoughtfully.

"Come," he sat down on a wall seat, gesturing for them to join him, "and pay attention.

"Swords are the costliest of weapons and are also a sign of rank—break your blade and you pay for it, in many ways. If you survive the training, you will be expected to provide your own weapons."

This would not be a problem to Osgar. He was continuing his role as Seer, which provided some income, but even more was provided from his investments in trading with Vidar.

"Forget what you may have heard of the two-handed sword; you will be trained to fight with one hand for the sword and one for your shield. You will be given a whetstone—it is up to each warrior to maintain his weapons.

"Your sword is made up of the blade, the cross-guard, above it the grip and on top the pommel, to counter-balance the weight of the blade."

Osgar looked down and saw his pommel was in the shape of an oyster shell; *ironic*, he mused. Svein continued.

"Your sword should be hung from your belt. You will see a leather strap on the hilt—the *hjalt*—this you hang from your hand, while using an axe, for example, to disarm your opponent, then run him through with the sword.

"As to the hand grip, bone or ivory is best—even when your hand is wet with blood or sweat. The blade is of iron but made double-edged with steel. Most *drengr* name their swords.

"When you begin your weapons training, you will use a thirty-five-inch blade sword, weighing a little over two pounds. When considered ready, you will be given a forty-inch blade with a weight of over three pounds. Any questions?"

Osgar resisted the temptation to ask, *Don't you ever stop talking, when do we fight*? Instead, he asked, "*Ja*, do we not get a shield?"

"First you learn the blows of the sword, then you will be trained to fight with sword and shield. Don't worry, you will be practising from *dagan* to *solarsetr*. Now, hang your weapons in your room within easy reach, then re-join me here."

In their quarters, Einar turned to Osgar with a look of puzzlement; although, to him, Einar always looked puzzled.

"I don't understand, why do we not need our swords with us to begin our training?"

"I fear Svein has another test for us before we pick up a sword."

"What?"

Osgar admitted he had no idea. They re-joined Svein in the hall.

"Before you pick up your weapons to fight an enemy, you must first decide upon your tactics. That is why, for the next four weeks, you will pit your skills not only against each other but also my warriors—at *Hnefatafl!*"

"At what?" questioned Einar.

"*Hnefatafl*," Svein smiled back at him.

"A board game for children?" responded Einar angrily.

The smile faded from Svein's face.

"As the board is a battlefield and the better strategy will win, I would say it is far from a child's game. Prowess at *Hnefatafl* is much admired by our Jarl and his counsellors, and by the king.

"Unless you know better?" as he turned towards Einar. Osgar said nothing. After being taught by Froda and playing the game for the last three winters, Froda had sworn Osgar had an innate talent for the tactics of the board that made him virtually unbeatable and usually unplayable. He still practised now, on every visit to Froda.

The board being divided into squares, the game was played with twelve red and an equal number of white pieces and a king, all intricately carved from ivory or bone. The basic strategy of the game was that one side must try and form a blockade around the king and his *huskarls*, closing the ring until the king's defenders are captured or killed, then kill the king or make him a prisoner.

The king's defenders must stop this outcome by breaking through the gaps in the blockade, attacking the enemy from behind and widening the gap to enable the king to break free. Froda had taught him that it was purely a game of logic, coupled with the ability to think deviously. Osgar had learnt from him its many variants and levels of sophistication. In games where the king must reach a corner in order to escape, Osgar blocked all the corners with his men.

Playing Froda, Osgar had learned to his cost that, unless the corners were blocked early in the game, the defenders need only hold one gate for the king to escape. Osgar had become adept in forcing his opponent's move, leading him into the trap of leaving him only one specific move possible.

The three winters of the game's tactics served him well, not only against Einar—who in one game had upturned the board in anger—but also against his *huskarl* and *drengr* opponents, some of whom insisted on playing for silver, even though it was illegal to do so, adding to Osgar's growing purse.

Finally, the weeks of *Hnefatafl* came to an end. As well as deciding he needed a bigger purse in which to hold his winnings, Osgar became undisputed champion of the board when he narrowly beat Svein in the best of three games, much to his annoyance.

"Enough! I admire your skill if not your arrogance, Angle, but remember, these games are taken seriously and often end in the death of one opponent."

Osgar could not determine whether this was a statement or a veiled threat.

"Now, it is time to move forward with your training."

At last, the sword.

"You will begin," Svein continued, "your training in *fang*—the sport of wrestling, which may save your life one day."

"For how long?" a disappointed Osgar asked. So much for the sword.

"Until I consider you proficient."

Osgar knew full well he was not as muscular as he would wish, despite much of his free time having been spent lifting stones. One advantage he did have was his height; some four inches taller than his peer group, he had a longer reach than opponents his own age, who would not be a problem.

Warriors and housekarls, on average five feet six inches tall, would be.

Wrestling was really a contest of strength where to win, your opponent must be thrown off his feet, or lifted and dropped, and any part of his body touch the ground, except the feet.

Denisc boys grew up with wrestling but Osgar had been somewhat distracted, busy training to be a Seer. Warriors saw wrestling competitions as a way to keep their fighting skills honed for unarmed combat.

Osgar was proven right. The first weeks of his training were extremely painful. Had he not worn a *fangastakkur*—the wrestling jacket—he would have had several broken bones, if not worse.

Serious long-term injuries and even deaths were not uncommon. He persuaded Einar to train with him to hasten muscle development. As Einar was also suffering, he readily agreed.

Toga honk literally meant 'tugging on a loop'. Osgar and Einar sat on the ground facing each other, their knees bent and the soles of their feet on the other. They held a loop of string rope, its middle marked by a tag. At an agreed signal, they pulled the rope with all their strength, while straightening their legs and pushing against each other's soles, until one of them was pulled over. As this used the same muscular movements as rowing, winners were often selected as crew for a longship.

This, and the stone-lifting, began to have an effect. As the weeks passed, both Einar and Osgar began to win some of their bouts. Osgar realised they had the advantage of age, agility and speed and he worked out tactical moves with Einar.

They then began to win the majority of their matches, including those against the *huskarls,* which did not go unnoticed by Svein. Finally, Svein told them they had the *megin*—power—to begin the *hervapn*—weapons training. They took down their swords from the wall of their room and followed Svein to the weapons field, where some twenty men were already engaged in training with various weapons.

The one *akra*—field—was set with straw targets for bowmen, wooden for the *fleinn*—the throwing spear—and straw figures dressed in sacking with leather *kyrtill* and helmets for practice with the *atgeirr*—the thrusting spear—the axe and the sword.

In one area of the field, warriors were fighting in *einvigi*—single combat—with shield, sword and axe. At the far side of the field, Osgar could see those yet to reach manhood being trained on horseback to become a *riddari.*

As the two fledgling warriors crossed the field, a tall, red-bearded warrior in full armour, a very expensive *brynja*—a full coat of mail—and a helmet decorated with silver, strode towards them.

"*Heill—velkommin, Svein. Hversu ferr?*"

"*Alt gutt, thakka.*"

Svein turned to Osgar and Einar.

"These are the two would-be-warriors you have been expecting, Ulfr."

"My name—" Osgar began to say, when cut off by the red-bearded warrior. "You will speak only when you are spoken to, you understand, Englar?"

His voice was growl-like, well-suited to a warrior named Wolf.

Osgar was about to apologise but thought better of it.

"Ulfr here," Svein smiled, "will be your trainer and, while in his charge, your god. He is our best warrior and standard bearer to the Jarl. He is expert in all weapons but can kill with or without them. He has great slaughter to his name and therefore great honour."

Svein pointed to Osgar. "This is the Seer you were told about."

Ulfr curled his bottom lip. "I have little time for superstition and magic." He patted the hilt of his sword in its Rune-covered scabbard. "I rely on Bone-Eater here."

Svein addressed Ulfr: "My orders from the Jarl, and now yours, are that the Seer is under your command in the afternoons but will be closeted with the Jarl in the mornings, when it suits his lordship. Understood?"

"And me?" Einar queried.

"I have no orders regarding you," Svein barked.

"Understood, I am at my Jarl's command."

Ulfr turned to Osgar.

"Well, Seer. It seems you will have to work twice as hard to make up for the mornings you miss."

"Now, I have my own commands to carry out, so must leave you." Svein turned to Ulfr, "*Vit sjaumst*, my friend."

He turned to leave, then stopped and spoke, as if in afterthought, "Oh, *ja*, my two warriors," he declared as if it amused him, "the Jarl has ordered that from tonight you eat in his hall."

It begins, thought Osgar to himself.

Not bright but by every means early, the following day began with the sword, under the personal tuition of Ulfr. The early lessons were learnt by rote, using the straw-stuffed warriors as opponents.

After hour upon hour of slash, parry, slash and thrust, with very little thrust, Osgar became convinced he could deliver repetitive sword blows in his sleep, which he realised was exactly the intention of their teacher.

All the drills began the same way, with Ulfr's growled, "*Buinn?*" Their reply to the question of 'Ready?' was to give the *herop*, the war cry, of *'Ja!'*

The drill itself was designed to ensure their blows were made by reflex, becoming second nature. Ulfr had pointed out that if you took seconds to decide your choice of blow, you were dead.

"*Hofud!*"

They responded with a strong, downward strike to the head.

"*Oxl!*"

Shoulder! The horizontal cutting stroke to the upper arm and shoulder.

"*Laer*!"

"Thigh!" The diagonal downward stroke to the upper leg to cripple an opponent and cause him to fall.

"*Til baka*!"

"Back!" Step back to deliver the killing blow.

"*Magi! Veg!*"

"Belly! Kill!" The killing thrust through the opponent's stomach.

"*Vend ther!*" The order to turn 180 degrees and begin the drill again, but in the opposite direction.

Once Ulfr was satisfied, they began to train with sword and *skjoldr*—the shield. By Ulfr's feet lay two shields, two helmets and a long sword, with a two-handed grip.

"Pick up your shields!"

Osgar and Einar picked up the three-foot diameter, round shields, both carrying the mark of the Jarl, so easily and instantly recognisable in battle.

"Your shields are made of linden wood, preference of the *huskarl;* it is lightweight and not easily cleaved. It is rimmed with leather edging, which shrinks after fitting and protects the shield from splitting, as do the three iron bands binding the wood. Oil prevents it from becoming waterlogged.

"The handle inside is secured with iron nails with a domed iron boss in the centre of the face of the shield to protect your hand. The sling of leather is to enable you to carry it over your shoulder. In all, the weaponry you carry will be fifteen pounds in weight.

"Obviously, in battle, your enemy will target your head and legs as the only parts of your body exposed. And although your shield is defensive, the rim can be used to 'punch' your opponent, giving you the element of surprise." As Osgar and Einar nodded approvingly at each other, Ulfr added, "You can also use the shield to carry the wounded from the field. Should one of you be on it, do not bother returning."

As he would have trained them, Osgar could see why Ulfr considered the threat justified.

"The shield can be slung along the sides of our longships, not only to save space but to help shield the crew from wind and rain. The shields you see on the walls of the feasting hall are those of the *drengr* who fell in battle, but could not be buried with them.

"Perhaps, my would-be warriors, you are thinking that with the shield you can become invisible. Seer, hold up your shield in defensive position."

Osgar did as he was bid, just as he saw Ulfr pick up the two-handed sword. Suddenly, Ulfr's blade arced down, biting into Osgar's shield—and through it, cleaving it in two. On its way, the blade missed Osgar's hand on the shield grip by inches.

"I will presume you now know that you are not immortal."

He placed his hand on his hips and roared with laughter. His lesson had achieved its desired effect.

"You will now begin practising with sword and shield until, once more, they become reflex, after which you will fight against each other as if you were in battle—no set moves. The best warrior will win. Then you will fight me."

Osgar and Einar exchanged glances. Personally, Osgar would prefer twenty-five years of practice before fighting Ulfr.

"Firstly, you will need these." He handed them each a helmet of metal. Osgar knew these were expensive pieces of equipment—*spangenhelm.*

Many of the *volk* wore helmets of leather or none at all. The helmet took the form of a metal bowl, the front shaped to surround the eyes and with a long nasal bar—nose-guard. An iron band ran around its brow, with two more meeting on its top. The helmet was lined with sheepskin to absorb sweat. At the back hung a curtain of chain mail to protect the back of the head and neck. Ulfr seemed to take satisfaction in telling them to remember a powerful sword blow could cleave both helmet and skull.

"And now you may begin, leading to single combat. I pray to Odinn, when it is time to move your training forward, I still have two warriors-to-be."

So too did Einar and Osgar, sincerely.

The afternoon seemed endless and a little monotonous as Osgar and Einar did battle with their straw-filled opponents, winning every time. And, whereas Einar saw little merit in countless hack and slash movements with his sword, Osgar, on the other hand, convinced himself that every single additional blow was one blow closer to the reflex memory that may well one day save his life.

They went to dinner in the *langhus*, totally exhausted. They had fought each other, and others, in weapons training for what seemed an eternity. Their young bodies were black and blue and every muscle ached; Einar, particularly, wondered if they would ever recover. But it wasn't just the physical exertions that exhausted them, it was the other aspects of warrior training, all important in their own way, that needed to train the mind.

It was in that respect that Osgar was far more proficient, and receptive, than his friend.

They also learnt that day how to insult their opponent when fighting and even before battle was joined. Insults from '*gleidr vitskertr*'—bowlegged shortwit—to the common or garden '*daufi bacraut*'—daft asshole—and much worse. It was very much part of the art of warfare. The premise being that if you shouted loud enough and long enough at your enemy, he may just run away; unlikely, but it had been known to happen.

"I think I'm too tired to eat," moaned Einar—he was good at that—as they took their seats at the lowest table, far from the Jarl at his raised top table, looking down the hall.

"I could eat a horse," Osgar admitted.

"A shame then it is not a feast," laughed Einar.

At important feasts, such as *Jol*, the mid-winter feast or mid-summer or to the gods, a horse would be sacrificed and its blood sprinkled, as a part of the ritual to the gods, and the meat eaten.

As the *Denisc* valued their horses highly, making such a sacrifice proved their allegiance to the gods. But not that night, they made do with spitted lamb, roast pork and vegetables with hot, fresh, crusty bread and cheeses, all washed down with copious amounts of *bjor* and *medu*.

Too copious. They later agreed that beer and mead did not mix, which was how they found themselves in a barn with Elli, sixteen winters of age and known in the village by her nickname—well-ridden.

She stripped with practised ease and lay back on the straw. It was agreed silently between the pair that Osgar would ride first. As a sensation of an eruption of pleasure filled his body and mind, Osgar swore no one would ever know this was his first time.

He lay down and fell asleep, vaguely aware of Einar atop Elli.

When he awoke, Elli was long gone. Einar wasn't. His naked body lay on the straw, as Osgar checked for signs of life. At least he was breathing. He was also *ofrolvi*—excessively drunk.

Finding a sheepskin, Osgar threw it over Einar's naked body and weaved his way back to the *langhus*, rolling gently from side to side as a longship in a heavy sea.

CHAPTER SIX

"MORGIN, Einar."

Einar rubbed the sleep from his eyes, in the vain hope that he could also remove his hangover by the same process.

"Why do you rise so early, Osgar?" he mumbled. "We are not expected by Ulfr for another hour."

"I shall not be at weapons training with you this morning. I have been summoned by the Jarl. I am to be trained in tactics and warfare, remember?"

"Do you know why it is only you?" Einar questioned him, sounding disgruntled, still half-asleep.

"I don't. I promise you I shall ask the Jarl."

"*Thakka.*"

"*Ekki at thakka.* I'll see you later at the field, *ja?*"

With that, Osgar took his leave and found the Jarl in his ornate chair, having set a stool for him.

"Good morning, my lord."

"*Velkominn,* Seer. Be seated," the Jarl smiled. "Svein and Ulfr tell me you have taken well to your weapons, Osgar."

"Thank you, my lord. I have good teachers."

He noticed Eirikr glancing down at his sword in its scabbard and his *seax* in his belt.

"Seer, remember to wear your weapons at all times in public, the *Den Lagu*—our law—demands it."

"*Ja,* my lord. May I ask a question?"

"That depends upon the question."

"I was wondering why Einar is not with me for your tuition?"

Loyalty to Osgar was as important as truth. The Jarl stroked his beard as he pondered the merits of the question before answering.

"This is not a decision I have faced in the past. A Seer you are but also to become a warrior and leader of men. I know not which I shall need the most but no doubt I will have need of them both.

"Einar is destined to become one of my *heimthegar*—one of my personal bodyguard. A singular honour."

"Thank you, my lord."

"And now, we begin your education in warfare."

AD 863

The weeks that followed quickly turned to months as Osgar's training, both in tactical warfare and weapons, continued apace. So intense was his focus on becoming the best he could, Osgar forgot that the prize at completion—though he wondered if anyone else would think if 'prize' was the correct word—was single-combat against Ulfr. That omission from his thinking ensured he was crowned the best.

Fellow warriors formed a huge circle, some twenty yards across, with a narrow gap at extreme ends of the diameter.

Osgar entered from the east, Ulfr from the west. As they entered the arena, the sound of swords beating against a hundred shields resonated throughout the village and swept down the narrow streets to the sea.

Ulfr, the seasoned veteran, towered above Osgar, despite him being taller than the average Denisc. There were no insults; indeed, no words at all. It was a simple test of how much of what had been taught had been learned.

They circled each other a couple of times. Osgar's eyes fixed upwards on Ulfr's, Ulfr's peripheral vision scanning everything around and in front of, him.

The veteran swung his sword in a wide arc to Osgar's left shoulder, which the youngster immediately parried away with his shield before impudently tapping the flat of his sword on Ulfr's right hip. The warrior circle roared in approval, and this was only the first move.

Osgar lunged forward but his inexperienced thrust had been seen a thousand times by Ulfr and a thousand times had been swept aside. Then began a period of hack and repulse, sword slash followed by shield parry on both sides, for what seemed like many minutes to the younger warrior.

Osgar tried thrusting again but soon realised that restricted reach and opponent's guard, not to mention his coat of mail, meant a foolish expending of energy. But the Seer-to-be learnt with every blow defended as much as every blow given and as the bigger man appeared to tire, Osgar changed tactics.

As Ulfr brought his sword down from a great height with the sole purpose of cleaving Osgar's leather helmet, Osgar dropped down on one knee and with perfect timing, rolled to one side as Ulfr's sword was buried in the churned-up mud they had created, halfway along the blade.

Seizing his momentary advantage, Osgar rolled once again, this time behind Ulfr, and tapped him on his arse with the flat of his blade. Once again, the warrior circle laughed. Osgar felt a smile but Ulfr did not see the funny side.

Face to face once more, the hacking and slashing continued. Ulfr slashed high, Osgar ducked. Ulfr slashed low, aiming to cut Osgar down to size at the knees, literally; Osgar jumped.

As each slash missed, Ulfr got angrier and more careless. But so did Osgar. He let his guard slip because he went against all his opponent had taught him in the preceding weeks of training and THOUGHT about his next move, instead of reflex. As he waited to parry Ulfr's slash to his sword arm, he failed to spot the sweep of Ulfr's shield arm and if Osgar had ever wondered what it would feel like to be hit by a falling tree, he found out at that moment and was bowled off his feet. He rolled several times before coming to a halt a full six yards from where he had been hit. Again the warrior ring roared with approving laughter, this time for Ulfr.

Another tactical change, thought Osgar. He raised his sword and made a frontal assault, not a usual Denisc ploy, but an instant before his sword hit its intended target, Ulfr's head, Osgar dropped his left shoulder, pushed off his left leg and darted to Ulfr's left and behind him; but this time, he continued his run and, full circle, came back from whence he had come.

Ulfr's response was an attempted shield blow followed immediately by a sweep of his sword; again Osgar dropped his shoulder, pushed off from his left leg and once more darted behind his older opponent before resuming his former position in front of his teacher who by this time was puffing with near exhaustion. He stood in front of Osgar, arms extended, so there was a huge gap between the point of his sword and the furthest edge of his huge shield, a good eleven-feet span. But Ulfr was clever enough to ensure Osgar was too far away to take advantage of an apparent surrender.

Instead, the old war-dog roared, "Stand still and fight like a man, don't run around like a boy!"

"But I am a boy," replied Osgar, who was as quick with his tongue as he was with his feet. "I am still a boy and I am still alive." He raced forward towards Ulfr but his sword and shield were not at battle-stance and as Ulfr, slowly but surely, readied his weapons to repel Osgar's attack, he feinted a strike with his sword that seemed to distract the fledgling warrior.

Osgar slipped and slid forward, coming to a halt with his head buried in mud between Ulfr's feet. This brought the loudest roar of the day from the ring of warriors, a day that was fast disappearing into dusk. No one had seen Osgar tap his left ankle with his right foot as he raced towards Ulfr, who leaned down to pick up his prize pupil; no one except Svein, who was a latecomer to the bout, which was the ceremonial ending of yet another season's warrior training.

Ulfr whispered to Osgar, "I think we will call that a draw." Osgar looked up to see Ulfr, minus his helmet, smiling. He smiled back. They both knew the true victor.

As Osgar walked through the now dispersed ring of warriors, it seemed each and every one wanted to slap him on the back for a sterling show against their best warrior.

Einar approached with an enhanced admiration for his friend.

"The Jarl wishes to see you, Osgar," pointing to the edge of the training field where Eirikr sat on his prize steed.

As Osgar approached his Jarl, Eirikr dismounted and placed his hands on Osgar's shoulders.

"I was about to admonish you for making a fool of a proud warrior who has served me and mine so loyally over the years. But then I saw what you did." Eirikr coughed and winked in the same movement. A very diplomatic way of ensuring that Ulfr saved face. Osgar looked at his Jarl with a look of innocence they both knew was contrived. Eirikr continued, "I knew you would become a warrior. I knew of your Seer gifts but now I know you possess the diplomacy of a born leader, which will serve you well politically, sooner than you may think."

"Of course, my lord," and he winked back at his Jarl for the first and, most assuredly, last time. Of that, Osgar was certain.

Unlike many of their enemies, the Denisc had a well-organised *volk*—army—based on the *leidang*—a levy. Under the levy, contribution was compulsory and provided ships, men, provisions and some arms upon the order of the king or his appointed Jarl. Raids were usually organised by the Jarls themselves. An infantryman in the *volk*, as a freeman, must own a sword, helmet, shield and spear. Given the expense of a sword and helmet especially, weapons were provided by their military leader.

The most common weapon was a spear because most economic use could be made of material as many more spearheads could be made from the same amount of iron as was required for a sword. It was also less labour-intensive.

Eirikr also provided horses and chain mail-curtained helmets for his *huskarl*.

The Jarl, it seemed, had his own preference as to tactics, some of which Osgar regarded as devious though he had to concede they won battles, excelling in sudden attacks. Those devious ploys included ambushes, particularly in forested areas, which was especially favoured by Eirikr. There were also feigned retreats, encirclement and making the enemy believe the army opposing them was larger than it actually was; it was amazing how convincing it was to build a fire at night for every other man instead of every four or five, equally misleading to tie twigs to a rope and drag it behind a horse so that from distance, a patrol looked like an army. Denisc *volk* also excelled in the rapid building of field defences of wood and earth, forcing enemy horsemen to dismount and fight on foot.

The Jarl had stressed upon Osgar that the most effective tactic for devastating an enemy force was the *svinfylking*—boar formation. This employed a wedge-shaped battle formation of thirty warriors, the point towards the enemy line and a rapid attack, breaking through by sheer weight of numbers.

Wherever a battle was fought, Eirikr stressed the golden rule was to fight with the sun behind you. Equally important was to divide the men into three groups: the centre and two wings. The king or Jarl used his *huskarl* bodyguard as exactly that, as they would surround him and form a defensive shield barrier. Failure to protect their leader was the greatest dishonour. Standing closest to the Jarl was his standard bearer, honoured for his prowess and courage. He would be the target for the enemy's attack. Now Osgar understood Ulfr's position as the Jarl's standard bearer.

A battle was usually preceded with two sides shouting and hurling insults at each other. Although rare, it sometimes happened that one side would be so frightened they would turn tail and run, far more preferable to risking death.

However, if shouting didn't win the day, the next step was a *skot-hrid*—a shower of arrows and spears. Denisc warriors were renowned for their proficiency with spears and many were so skilled that they could hurl a shaft with each hand, doubling the effectiveness of such prowess. The most skilled of all were also able to catch an enemy spear in full-flight and return it from whence it came.

If the arrow and spear storm failed to secure victory, then the two sides would clash in a melee of individual and bloody combat until the death of a leader or a forced retreat.

Eager to learn more, Osgar asked about the tactics of a battle at sea. After all, was not the longship the Viking's greatest weapon?

"Avoid them," replied Eirikr. Osgar was soon to learn that in their persona of *Vikingr*, they detested sieges and fighting at sea. They looked upon their longships as transports for warriors, horses and provisions. Where they were forced into a sea battle, they preferred to fight as close to the shore as possible. Here, the tactics were to tie the ships together and face the enemy, loosing showers of arrows and spears.

This then turned into hand-to-hand combat as the *Vikingr* boarded the enemy's ships. The aim, Eirikr explained, was not to destroy but to capture them. They could be used by the *Vikingr* and also represented an investment.

Sometime later, Osgar raised the question of the use of horses.

"Horses are purely for locating the enemy and to enable our warriors, as reinforcements, to reach the battlefield as quickly as possible, dismount and join the fight. Our horses are far too valuable to risk in battle—never!"

The Jarl noticed a glimpse of disappointment in Osgar's face.

He leaned forward in his chair, elbows on knees, his beard cupped in his hands as he studied the Seer carefully.

"You disagree? You have some different tactic in mind? Would you care to share it with me?"

Osgar answered the Jarl softly, with uncertainty in his voice, "*Nei.* I have none, only an unshaped thought," he admitted.

Eirikr did not respond immediately but leaned back in his ornate chair. Finally, he spoke, "Then I shall look forward to hearing it when it has a shape." The Jarl smiled.

* * *

"Well, my friend," Vidar laughed, "whichever way you look at it, the gods have smiled on you. You are a wealthy young man."

Osgar smiled as he pored over the manifest ledger. He was indeed a wealthy young man. Over the past year, he had invested all his income as a Seer into Vidar's ventures.

"It has been a good year," he agreed.

"And a better one to come," said Vidar, slapping him on the back. "You are effectively my equal partner in trading."

His voice then took on a more serious tone as he added, "And I have formalised exactly that partnership under law.

"*Nei,*" said Vidar as he put up his hand to curtail Osgar's protestation. "You know as much about my business as me—perhaps more. I have no family. What happens to my trading empire if aught should happen to me? It is logical you should be my heir—you are now a man of fifteen summers."

They sealed the agreement with a glass of imported wine. No wooden tankards any more for the partners, rich partners.

On his way back to the longhouse, Osgar called upon Froda, as he did twice or more each seven days. They sat and talked.

"Your reputation as a Seer outgrows my own," Froda smiled. "You have yet to make a false prediction, the Jarl tells me."

Osgar had been aware for some time that the Jarl, devious as ever, had been taking 'divine guidance' from both of them, then comparing their readings, one against the other.

"If so, it is due to your teaching," Osgar replied.

"*Nei,* it is down to your own intelligence, experience and logic."

Osgar protested to no avail, and stood to leave. Froda tried, but could not.

"I am afraid my years have grown beyond my body's feeble attempt to hold them back," he coughed.

Osgar knew not the age of his mentor but he was more than long-lived, that much was plain. He now appeared *forn*—ancient. He had lost weight and was like a framework of bones covered by thin parchment. Osgar was worried. His mind of a man held sway over his thoughts as a Seer. *Don't go there,* he told himself.

"*Far vel,* Froda. I shall call again soon," he clasped the Seer to him.

"I shall look forward to it, my young friend, though now not so young," he corrected himself, "but a man. Farewell."

* * *

On the field of weapons, Ulfr called Osgar and Einar to him.

"Bring your shields and *hjalmr.*"

They put on their helmets and carried their shields over to Ulfr at the trestle table.

"This is your war axe," he pointed to the weapons on the table. "As a *drengr,* your main weapon will be your sword but you must also become an expert with the axe. Heft it and feel its balance."

Osgar swung the axe, finding it light, quick and well-balanced.

"This axe," Ulfr continued, "has a single iron blade, welded with hardened steel and is made to be used one-handed, with a six-inch cutting edge. The haft of wood is sized to balance the axe-head. You will go into battle with the short haft of thirty-two inches, short enough to be hidden behind your shield, as an additional weapon, giving you the element of surprise—which could save your life."

He paused for effect.

"Farmers in the *volk* bring their own axes to war. An axe is *not* to be thrown, except as a last resort, is that understood?"

"Yes sir," they answered in unison.

"Then take up your weapons and begin. And try not to cleave your shields—if that happens, you will pay for them."

As time passed, Einar found his forte as an expert with the axe. Finally, the time had come to practice the art of the spear, the most common of all weapons in battle.

Arrayed before them was a row of ten-foot ash spears, stuck upright into the earth. Osgar pulled one from the ground. He found the centrepoint of balance, compensating for its eight-inch long, pointed spearhead.

"These are your *atgeirr* and *fleinn*—the throwing spear," came a voice behind them. Ulfr.

"What," queried Einar, "is the point of throwing your weapon away?"

"Why?" Ulfr asked sarcastically. "Are you planning to go into battle with only one weapon?" It was a rhetorical question. "That is why you have the *atgeirr*—the thrusting spear.

"A shield wall second rank can reach over the interlocking shields of the first rank and thrust it into the enemy. Or it can be used in single combat but remember, its shaft can be sliced through with a sword or axe. You will practice both until you are proficient. The thrusting spear you will practice using your shield for defence, the throwing spear you will use on the straw figures," he pointed across the field.

"At least there will be one opponent you can best," said Osgar with a friendly shove that Einar did not appreciate.

"That's a long way away," said Einar.

"Why?" responded Ulfr with his customary growl. "Would you like to ask your enemy to come closer?"

"This really is not Einar's best day," decided Osgar.

"I have warriors who could throw two spears at the same time, one in each hand!" *That,* thought Osgar, *is never going to happen.* He was wrong.

Several days later, their weapons training began drawing to a close; appropriate, considering their final weapon was *ybogi*—the yew bow—six feet eight inches long with a draw weight of ninety pounds, firing thirty-two-inch arrows.

"You will be practising with the five foot ten inch bow. It is not a weapon for a *drengr*, who would only use it for hunting; but nevertheless, it is an important weapon in our arsenal. In battle, our archers can open the fighting with showers of arrows onto the enemy, giving us the chance to advance and fight at close quarters; or on a longship, to clear the decks of the enemy to enable us to board. A variation is the *hornbogi*—the hornbow—better for a horseman, as it is easier to draw when on horseback."

This was of particular interest to Osgar.

"Now, my almost-warriors,"—*from Ulfr, that was almost a compliment,* Osgar thought—"you will shoot at your usual men of straw and leather, only this time from six hundred feet. The longer bow that you will soon be using has a range of six hundred and fifty feet. When you can place six arrows, one after another, into the head and chest, I shall consider you ready to move on."

* * *

Ulfr led them to the stockade at the far end of the field.

"Do you both ride?"

"*Ja,*" Osgar answered. He had been taught to ride as a farmer's son, in what now seemed another world, a lifetime ago.

"*Gott.* Einar?"

Eyes lowered, Einar conceded he could not.

"Then the next two weeks could be painful for you. After all my hard work, try your best not to break your neck." He pointed to the horses inside the stockade, next to the training field.

"You have already been told we do not use a *hestre* in battle, only as a means for our *drengr* to reach the battleground with haste. We breed them primarily as packhorses and pairs to pull wagons, carts and, in winter, cargo sleighs. Although only five foot in height, they are sturdy and fast at full gallop, for short periods."

Given that he was much taller than the five-foot horse, Osgar could see no problem, even leaping into the saddle to gain time.

"Now, choose your horse."

Osgar picked out the tallest horse, a grey, which he considered would have the stamina to match its size. Einar selected the smallest, for which Osgar did not blame him. It was to prove a good choice—Einar would have the least distance to fall when he parted company with the horse, which was frequent. They were then given the tack they would need: a wood and leather saddle with a pannier on each side and a pommel at the front complementing the cantle at the back of the seat; next, a snaffle bit, decorated bridle and tall stirrups.

Over the coming weeks, they would practise at walking pace, the canter, the trot and at full gallop.

At the end of their training period, Osgar arose before *dagan* and stopped only to pick up a *hornbogi* and arrows and four *fleinr*—throwing spears. Having saddled his horse, which he had named *grar draur*—Grey Wolf—Osgar practised controlling him with his knees, leaving his hands free.

For two hours, Osgar rode repeatedly towards the straw man at full gallop; each ride his loosed spear found its target. Drawing the bow, leaning forward in the saddle, Osgar found he could loose three arrows as he bore down on his target—all with deadly accuracy.

He had proven to himself that what he held as theory was now fact. He intended to also prove the tactical effectiveness of what he had learned, in battle.

He was back in their *svefnhus* before Einar awoke.

On the weapons field, Ulfr was waiting.

"And now for the completion of your training as a *drengr.*"

Einar whispered to Osgar from the side of his mouth, "There's nothing left to train in!" he hissed. "Unless it's to learn to fly and shit on the enemy!"

Osgar strained hard not to laugh as Ulfr removed a blanket from a trestle table, revealing two *brynja*—full chain mail shirts, signifying a leader and his wealth. Few people could afford them.

"Put them on," Ulfr commanded.

Osgar's shirt reached down to his thighs, with three-quarter length sleeves. The belt ensured the mail coat did not push down and burden its wearer. The interlocking iron rings making up the shirt took days to be made and many more days for its skilled craftsman to assemble. And the cost, in silver alone, put it out of the financial reach of the ordinary warrior.

"The mail is a second line of defence. Remember, it can still be penetrated by a powerful blow. These are for you to use only while training, at the end of which you will return them to me. Only two warriors own mail—the Jarl and Svein, chief of his bodyguard. You are expected to have your own made.

"You will practise wearing the mail, with all weapons, and as a *riddari.*"

Osgar could see Einar was not looking forward to being a rider once again.

"Your training as warriors is almost at an end. You are now men. I can see our seer-warrior is already growing his *skegg*. Take care, Osgar, lest I blow your beard from your chin," he laughed.

"To be serious," Ulfr's smile disappeared, "on *Tiwsdaeg* next, there will be a melee held, involving all those who wish to be warriors. You have practised with some of them, I think."

Tiwsdaeg, the day of the god of war—*very apt*, thought Osgar.

Although he knew there were another seventeen trainees apart from themselves; Ulfr had been overseeing Einar and his own training personally, and they had had little contact with the others so it would be yet another fresh aspect of their training for battle.

"In the melee, you will be split into opposing sides. The choice of weapons is yours. Once you have dealt a *banahogg*—death blow—or one to disable, your opponent must withdraw from the field. However, in the heat of the melee, this sometimes does not happen. I advise you to treat the melee with the utmost seriousness—your life could depend on it."

Tuesday came. Osgar chose the sword, Einar the axe.

The war cry came. The two sides attacked. Osgar found himself facing a thrusting spear and shield. The bearer thrust the spear point at his chest. He deflected it to the side with his shield and cut off the point, a foot up the shaft, swinging his sword to the assailant's chest.

"You are dead?" shouted Osgar triumphantly.

His opponent conceded. Not all did.

Osgar only had seconds to turn as his next opponent brought down the blade of his axe, biting into the rim of Osgar's shield. As taught by Ulfr, he twisted his shield sharply to the left, leaving his assailant's front open to attack. Osgar held the point of his sword to his throat and he signalled defeat.

Osgar turned to scan the melee for Einar.

He need not have worried; Einar was creating havoc with his war axe. Some sixth sense made Osgar spin around to face his last opponent.

The 'dead man' had drawn his *seax*, the knife descending into what would have been Osgar's back.

"*Dey saxar!*"

"*Danish skitkarl!*"

Osgar parried the knife with his shield and drove his sword blade through the attacker's shoulder, ensuring his withdrawal from the field. As he turned to face the centre, he realised the fight was over. He also realised something else was over. The vitriolic slur in that final attacker's assault on him was the last act of his life as Osgar. He was Osgar no more.

It was then he saw Svein stood with the Jarl, who had been watching the melee. Svein signalled Einar and himself over to them. As they approached, Ulfr reported to them on the outcome of the melee.

"Well, my wolf, how went it?" the Jarl asked. "Have I my new warriors?"

"*Ja*, my lord. We have four wounded and one dead."

He looked directly at Osgar and Einar. "These two *drengr* acquitted themselves well."

"I expected no less," Eirikr commented. "Who was responsible for the one sent to *Valholl* before his time?"

"Einar, my lord."

It was then that Osgar realised Einar was bleeding profusely from a sword wound to his right side.

"How did it happen?" Svein demanded.

"He intended to kill me," Einar grimaced in pain. "I had no choice."

"We all have a choice," the Jarl interrupted, "but you made the right one. I cannot afford to have my best warriors killed in a melee. Ulfr, take him to have his wound bound."

Ulfr and Einar left the field, but not before Einar had looked over his shoulder at Osgar with a wide grin.

"So," the Jarl turned to Osgar, "I understand you are the best of my warriors. It does not surprise me. Ulfr tells me you are almost as good as your Jarl." He turned to Svein. "You had better guard your position, my friend." He laughed.

"I shall, my lord," Svein smiled. The smile did not reach his eyes.

* * *

Froda was dying. He sent for Osgar.

Osgar took a deep breath before he entered the room. A woman neighbour was mopping his fevered brow. He saw Osgar enter and smiled.

"*Sva vel*, leave us."

The woman withdrew, giving a small bow to Osgar as she passed him.

"Osgar, come closer, the light dies." He smiled.

The sunlight shone brightly through the open windows.

"I am ready to go to my rest, to feast and drink in Valhalla with Odinn—or to Volkvangr and Freya, or to Helgafjell—I care not which." He attempted another smile.

"Osgar, you are my heir. Seer to the Jarl and the people.

"Remember my teachings well, my little one, now a man. In knowledge lies power, for good or evil. The Runes tell me you will become a great leader and lead your people to a new and better life. It will not be easy. There will be a great sorrow and hardship along the path the gods have chosen for you. Two in one."

Osgar failed to grasp the last three words as Froda attempted to raise himself onto his elbows.

"*Nei*, Seer! Rest."

"My pendant, take it from round my neck."

Osgar did as he was bid.

"And this," Froda then removed the gold amulet from his forearm, handing it to him. "The last gifts I can give you," he coughed. "They have served me well. Now, please bring me my *spjot* from the corner."

Osgar did as directed and brought the spear to the bed.

"Now, help me stand. I cannot die in bed."

Osgar knew there was no point in gainsaying him. Grasping the spear shaft, Froda pulled himself with great pain to his feet, pointing to his sword hanging on its brackets.

"*Minn sverd*—quickly, Osgar."

Froda took it from him and grasped it by the hilt.

"This I cannot give you," he smiled. "It travels with me."

His smile turned into a cough of bright, red blood.

Osgar could barely hear his whisper, "Beware, Osgar. You have a serpent in your midst. The Runes do not lie."

He raised his sword above him, pointing to the heavens.

"*Far vell*, Osgar the Angle, remember me."

Osgar caught him in his arms as he fell. He closed his eyes and kissed him gently on his forehead. He heard Froda's voice, echoing across the years, tapering away before him: "Only warriors cry..."

"Oh, Odinn, take Froda the Seer, your servant, into your care and set a place for him in Valhalla."

Osgar bent his head and wept silently, as the embers in Froda's fire-hearth died, for the first and the last time.

CHAPTER SEVEN

AD 864

NOW a muscular five feet ten inches, Osgar was a good four inches taller than the average *Dene*. His blonde hair was neatly trimmed and the growth of his matching beard was now noticeable. He had elected to move into Froda's *hus* as Seer to his Jarl and people. It also afforded him privacy. The prescribed time having passed, tonight was *erfi*—the funeral feast—to which Eirikr had invited fellow Jarls, his *huskarls*, selected *drengr* and many important guests with their families where custom demanded. He had also arranged for the presence of a *Skald*, a Denisc storyteller and poet, an important and respected member of society.

As he walked toward the *langhus*, his thoughts returned to the day of Froda's funeral. No matter the *Kristinn* way was to bury their dead, as a *Dene*, Froda had been entitled to be cremated, as the smoke would carry him on his journey to the afterlife.

His ashes would then be interred. It had taken several hours to build the wooden pyre to ensure the intense heat needed to burn all of the body. Osgar had stood directly in front of the blazing pyre as Froda's heir, flanked by Eirikr and Svein, as he intoned the words known only to a Seer.

Once the ashes had been put in the shallow grave, Froda's sword and rod of office had been buried with him, with the grave facing north-south, covered with a mound of stones.

Osgar had stepped forward to place the last stone with a last sign of *vindatta*.

"Odinn grant you a seat at his table. Farewell, old friend."

The day following the funeral, Osgar was summoned by the Jarl.

The purpose of the meeting was not one he could have envisaged. After the pleasantries, Eirikr came to the point.

"I wish to appoint you as *logsogu-madr* of the *Thing*."

"My lord, I cannot accept the position of law-speaker of the assembly. I have—"

"Seer, this is not a request!" Eirikr's voice took on a hard edge. "You are a *sextan*—a man, but more, you are a Seer and the foremost among my warriors. I have seen your intelligence and logic at work, both as a Seer and under my tutelage—where the student has overtaken the master," he smiled.

"The law-speaker of the governing assembly—freemen all—must have their respect. That you have earned over these years past. The law-speaker must have the ability to dispense *jafnadr*—justice. I can think of no one better suited to the role.

"It will give you power over the people, second only to myself."

"But, my lord, do you honestly believe the freemen council will accept a law-speaker who is not a Dene, but an Angle?"

"That," Eirikr smiled as a fox, "I shall ensure at the *erfi*."

And now, Froda's funeral feast was here.

Osgar entered the crowded longhouse to the cacophony of the shouts and babble of the assembled guests. It was evident the ale, beer and mead had been flowing freely. Osgar made his way to the top table and his seat at Eirikr's right hand. On the Jarl's left, Svein, and next to him sat the most beautiful girl he had ever seen. Osgar put her age at fourteen years. The majority of her peer group would be married.

Her long, blonde hair fell to her shoulders, framing her perfect features. The deep blue eyes over a petite nose sparkled brighter than the stars; her small mouth had lips with the promise of hidden sensuality.

Osgar was aware of the Jarl's voice over the noise of the hall.

Eirikr must have been watching, evidently with some amusement.

"This, Seer," he indicated with his arm, "is Svein's *dottir*, Assi."

Assi—beautiful as a god. *A more than fitting name,* Osgar decided. She leaned forward over the table and her smile lit up the hall.

"*Saell*, Seer."

Her voice told Osgar she was aware of her beauty. She was dressed in a long, richly and expensively embroidered *kyrtill* of blue, matching her eyes.

"*Gott kveld, hvat segir thu?*"

"*Allt vel, thakka*," she replied with a smile of amusement.

Osgar complimented her by telling her he could not understand why she was not married, unless she only knew warriors who had lost their eyes in battle.

"*Kvanlauss? Ja*, you know my *fadir*, I think?" she laughed.

Her laugh was as the gentle rippling of a shallow stream over pebbles. Osgar looked over at her father, at Svein, and understood why she was unmarried.

He held Osgar's look with eyes harder than stone as he, almost imperceptibly, shook his head.

He was, Osgar read, warning him that the attention he was paying his daughter was not welcome. Svein reinforced that hidden message by placing his hand on the hilt of his sword, in case the message was unclear. It was not.

A feast was usually an opportunity for guests to parade their unmarried daughters, of twelve and over, to potential suitors.

This was obviously not Svein's intention. As marriages were arranged between families, he would be the one to choose a husband for his daughter, and Osgar was certain it would not be him.

There was ample food prepared for the feast, as some could last several days. Horses had been sacrificed to the gods and their meat served to the tables, with roasted pig and beef, boiled hams, spitted chicken and game. There were also vast quantities of several varieties of fish, served with platters of boiled and roasted vegetables, fresh-baked bread, with butter, cheeses, sweet desserts and nuts.

And to wash it all down, ale and mead refilled the *hvitingr*—the drinking horns—of the guests with great regularity.

Meanwhile, at the top table, the Jarl had provided expensive glass beakers and imported wines.

As what little food left was cleared away, the guests settled down to some serious drinking and games. Important guests were paired with women, drawn by lot, to be their drinking partners, while lesser-rank guests chose their own.

The game, said to have been played by the gods, entailed matching each other drink for drink while composing and reciting a verse of poetry and insulting their opponents. As the game progressed, the insults became stronger. The winners were those who lasted the longest without showing signs of being totally drunk.

At a lower table, its occupants were playing *hnutukast*, using bones left over from the feasting. The intention was to hurl a bone at your opponent and cause as serious an injury as possible. Fatalities were not unknown. In other parts of the hall, knife and axe-throwing contests were also taking place.

Picking up a heavy wooden hammer set in front of him, the Jarl stood up at the table, striking it with the hammer until he had achieved complete silence, with a little assistance from his none too gentle *huskarls*. There was little likelihood of anyone in the hall missing what was said.

"I ask you now to be silent as the slain. We are honoured by the visit of Valrmar the Skald to the *konungs-gardr*—the court of the king."

The Skald was an imposing figure in a long, white, embroidered tunic, with white hair and beard, piercing eyes and a deeply furrowed brow—as if all knowledge of this world, and the next, was stored within. The Skald's role was, through Edda poetry and prose and the telling of sagas, to be a teacher of Norse culture, history and of the gods, honour and courage.

As the Denisc had no written language to record events, poetry, mythology or their history, the Skald's role was pivotal to the people and rulers alike. They were revered and gained high rewards in silver for their knowledge. No doubt tonight's recitations would prove expensive to the Jarl, who bore in mind that poetry was the gift of Odinn, the greatest of all the gods.

Silence blanketed the hall as the Skald began to relate the story of 'The Sword of Sigmund'.

Osgar listened quietly, as did the entire assembly.

"Siggeir was a mighty king who ruled over Gothland. He arranged to meet with King Volsung and asked him for the hand of Signy, his daughter, in marriage. The king and his sons looked upon this favourably. For the wedding feast, King Siggeir went to the court of King Volsung. Great fires were built the length of the hall, in the midst of which stood the great tree of Branstock.

"That night, a stranger did come into the hall, barefoot, in linen trousers and a cloak, wearing a slouched hat over an ancient face with only one eye. He drew his sword and sank it up to the hilt in the tree Branstock. He spoke, 'Whosoever can draw the sword from the tree shall have it as a gift from me. There exists no better sword.' With that he turned, left the hall and disappeared.

"None thought that Odinn had given one eye in exchange for a drink from the fountain of Mimir, the source of all wisdom.

"All present in the hall tried to pull the sword from the tree. None succeeded. Up stepped Sigmund, son of King Volsung, and drew it forth. Siggeir asked Sigmund to sell it to him for three times its weight in gold. Sigmund refused. 'You had an equal opportunity to pull the sword from the tree but could not. Now I have it and would not sell it for all the gold you have.'

"King Siggeir was as angry as could be, but hid it well, as if it was of no consequence. That evening, he planned to take his vengeance."

The Skald paused and took a glass of wine.

"And of the king's vengeance, I shall relate to you tomorrow evening."

Osgar recognised that the Skald certainly knew how to hold the hall's attention. No doubt through decades of practice. He had to admit, he also wanted to know how the saga ended; he commented so to the Jarl.

"I trust so," Eirikr pulled a face, "it is costing me the weight of my right leg in silver!"

The Skald continued in prose form, with a bone flute and harp accompanying him, which music was seldom heard in any *langhus*.

The Skald recounted the wisdom of Brynhild, supposedly the wisest woman in the world. The lesson was obviously for the benefit of the children, allowed to remain to hear the teaching.

"Be kind to friends and kin and forgive them their trespasses against you to the long-enduring praise of men.

"If you hear the words of a drunken fool, do not join him in drink. Many a grief, even death, can grow from this.

"Never trust in him whose father, brother or kinsman you have slain. Young he may be, but from him a wolf can awaken.

"Never swear you a false oath. Great is the punishment for the breaking of your given word."

As the rules for a *Dene* went on, there arose in Osgar a memory long passed, but it was a memory of Osgar the Angle. The familiar ring of Denisc rules were almost word for word that which he had learnt at his mother's side in his childhood. The rules for life set down by the *Kristinn Kirkja*. He began to think the Angle and the *Dene* had more in common than they realised. Seven winters since, he had considered them pagan pirates but now thought of them as seafarers and explorers, skilled artisans and farmers. He had grown to understand and respect them, as they had him. Buried deep in his mind, he felt a sense of betrayal. But betrayal for whom?

His Angle family, slaughtered in *Streonshalh*, or his 'family' with whom he had been embraced, seven winters past, and the knowledge and skills he had taken unto him? Try as he might, his slain family's faces had become less easy to recall, fading into memory as was any future he may have harboured as a farmer. No! He was proud of his role as a seer-warrior. His future, or not?

The decision was about to be taken out of his hands.

* * *

"Fill your drinks," Eirikr bellowed over the noise. Once this had been done, all at the tables and on the *sets*, stood, raising their drinking horns and beakers.

"I give you the *minni*—the toast to the dead: Froda, the Seer and friend to all here!"

"FRODA!" rang around the hall.

"Tonight, we are here to honour Froda, our Seer, and to confirm our new Seer and law-speaker of the *Thing*. He has proved himself as Seer and also as my finest warrior."

No one saw the scowl on Einar's face.

There was silence in the hall. Osgar glanced at Svein, who wore a far from friendly look.

The Jarl turned to Osgar and signalled for him to rise.

"Seer, could you slaughter your own people?" he asked.

"*Neinn*, my lord," Osgar answered.

The rumble of growing disapproval grew into a rage of anger and hostility that spread throughout the hall.

"How could I, my lord? My people are *Denisc*. I am a *Dene*—your enemies are mine," Osgar declared.

The rumble of dissent in the hall turned once more. This time there was loud approval and much banging of fists on tables and shouts of "Osgar! Osgar!"

The Jarl held up his hands to order silence.

"You honour the wrong name."

The silence of a windless night fell over those assembled.

"By my order, Osgar the Angle is dead. In his place stands Sigrvard

Eirikrsson—a *Dene*—my adopted son and your next Jarl, as approved by the king." Again, no one saw Einar scowl.

Osgar knew his newly given name meant 'Guardian of Victory'.

A reverberating cry of assent filled the hall.

Eirikr called Ulfr to him. In his arms he carried the necessities of war. Once more, the Jarl called for silence.

He took the coat of chain mail from Ulfr and presented it to the now Sigrvard the *Dene*—his son.

"A *brynja* befitting my heir and," he took the sword from Ulfr, "a sword for a Jarl."

Sigrvard drew the weapon from its rune and silver-engraved scabbard to find the finest blade he, or any present, had ever seen. It was also engraved with a runic invocation to Thor.

Eirikr once more raised his hands for silence, turning again to Sigrvard.

"Now that you have the *hervapn* of a *drengr*, what name will you give your sword?" His new *fadir* smiled.

Sigrvard, sword in hand, turned to face the assembled guests and raised his voice.

"My sword I call '*Fyrst Blood*' because it will draw the 'first blood' of our enemies!" he shouted.

The hall shook with the pounding of fists on tables and the shouting of his new name: "Sigrvard! Sigrvard!"

"I have arranged that, in the morning, your steel helmet and war shield, both bearing my crest, shall be brought to you by Ulfr. Then, I would be pleased if you would choose a horse to carry you to war. I recommend *Sigr*—Victory—to match your new name, a white stallion sired by my own."

"My lord," Sigrvard protested, "this is too much honour for—"

"*Neinn!*" Eirikr cut him off mid-protestation. "Remember, now you are my son and heir and must be seen to be so."

"Then I pray to Odinn I shall be white-bearded before I become Jarl," Sigrvard responded.

"Do not worry, my son," Eirikr laughed. "I have no intention of feasting in *Valholl* until *Ragnatokkr*!"

Ragnatokkr—the Twilight of the Gods. His people, as he now looked upon them, believed there would come a great battle resulting in the death of Odinn, Thor, Freya, Heimdallr and Loki, followed by a series of natural disasters, leaving the world submerged.

Then would come a fertile rebirth and the return of the surviving gods and the world would be repopulated by two mortal survivors, Lif and Lifthrasir.

The Jarl stood and clapped his hands, calling for a *danzleikr*. Those not too drunk took to the floor and began to dance. Sigrvard saw his chance and turned in the direction of Assi. She was no longer in the hall.

Her father had not left, he had made his way to behind where Sigrvard was seated. Svein leaned over, placing his mouth near Sigrvard's ear.

"The Jarl has made his wishes clear and informed me of what he has planned for you. I have agreed to a betrothal, if she will have you." Sigrvard gasped in surprise. His heart leapt too, in unison.

"Whatever plans my new father has for me, I shall fulfil them."

"See that you do, Jarl-to-be. *Goda nott, sof thu vel.*"

The hall was now quieter, most of those remaining snoring loudly under their sheepskins on the *flets*. Sigrvard took leave of his new father and made his way back to his *hus*.

As he opened the door, he was aware of someone else in the room. He drew his *seax* slowly and lit an oil lamp. By its light he could see, perched on his bed, peeking above the sheepskin blanket, Cynfrith, the Angle *grodkona* to the Jarl.

Sigrvard walked over to the bed. As she smiled at him nervously, he lifted the sheepskin. She was naked. Sigrvard undressed slowly and lay down beside her, as her arms reached out for him.

* * *

At the weapons field, Sigrvard was given his new *hkjold*—the helm decorated with a golden dragon on each side; his war shield was painted with a red dragon, the sign of Eirikr's clan.

He next chose the white stallion, 'Victory', his father had advised and after riding him around the field several times, he knew he had made the right choice.

He spent the rest of the morning in practice and training incomers at Ulfr's request, as he did three mornings in seven.

"You are ensured of the respect of the men," Ulfr stated. "They are convinced you are invincible," he smiled. "I did not foresee the day when I would be defeated in combat," he admitted. "You do know, do you not, they are also saying your sword has magical powers?"

"I defeated you only because the gods decreed it. Luck was smiling upon me that day. But wait, I recall it was a draw."

"It matters not why you defeated me, *Sigrvard*," Ulfr explained. "I have told my ego it was simply down to old age, my friend."

They laughed as friends.

"And now, I must see my father. I shall see you tomorrow, my friend."

On arrival at Eirikr's *langhus*, Sigrvard found his father in a pensive mood.

"My father, I need an answer to a question that has puzzled me."

"Which is?"

"Why would Svein change his mind so suddenly on my suitability to marry his daughter?"

"I simply told him you were to be my legal son, therefore my heir, and the next Jarl," he chuckled. "I also pointed out to him your wealth approaches mine, adding that mine came from plunder and fealty; yours as a Seer and trader, which will no doubt continue to swell. Where would he find a better match?"

It was Sigrvard's turn to laugh. "You are as devious as a fox."

"More so—that is why I live longer than a fox." Eirikr frowned. "Sit, my son, we have much to discuss." He took a deep breath. "*Hwaet drincst du*?"

"*Win, thakka.*"

Eirikr nodded to one of his *huskarl*, who left then returned with a *grodkona* bearing two drinking horns.

"I expected to see Cynfrith as your serving girl," noted Sigrvard.

"Leave us!" bellowed Eirikr to his two guards. "My son, you must remember the girl served me but belonged to Svein, who originally bought her as his *thrall* and as such, was perfectly within the law to sell her on the slave market."

"Why?" Sigrvard's voice dropped, as did his guard, to a low, threatening measure, despite who sat before him. He gripped his sword hilt.

More wisely than his new son, Eirikr continued, "I am sorry but you brought this on her."

"What! How?"

"Your *inn mtki munr*—your night of passion. Somehow Svein learnt of it. You are about to marry his daughter, did you intend to keep the girl as a mistress and shame your new wife? He had no choice. I am truly sorry for you."

"I do not seek sympathy, Father, only vengeance," said Osgar, putting aside that Svein could have exacted an even greater consequence upon his *thrall.*

"And vengeance I expressly forbid, do you understand me?" He raised his voice. "Do you understand?"

"Yes, my Jarl, I pledge my troth I shall not send my *swaer*—father-in-law—to the *hellgrind*—gates of hell."

"But now to more important matters. You have my people's respect as a Seer and a warrior, but you must also prove yourself as a *hilmir*—their leader in war."

"How?"

"In three weeks, you will lead a *skiphere* of the warriors of *Jylland* to raid and pillage the *Tyrrhenian Haf*, home of the Carolingians."

CHAPTER EIGHT

SIGRVARD felt his heart quicken at the thought.

"I am told by Arne, my shipwright, that you know as much about my new longship as he. Good. You will be in command on her first voyage. She is now completed. I have named her '*Raudr Dreki*'. She will carry my flag and my red dragon on her sail and at her prow. This emblem of my ancestors is now yours, my son."

Sigrvard had watched the construction of the ship at every stage; the best, Arne told him, he had ever built. It would be crewed by eighty warriors and be the largest in the war fleet.

"How many ships will I have in the fleet, Father?" Sigrvard asked.

"Apart from my new Red Dragon, you will also have my sixty-warrior and three thirty-warrior ships.

"Esbjerg are contributing four ships—one sixty-warrior and three thirty-warrior vessels with two ships each from Hanstholm and Skagen in the north."

Eirikr saved Sigrvard the mental calculation. "This gives you a war fleet of thirteen longships carrying an army of five hundred warriors. The choice of your second-in-command, your personal *huskarls*, standard bearer and crew, I leave to you. It would be advisable to ensure amicable relations with our allies in this, so include them on your war council and in your decisions—once you have made them.

"I shall arrange for you to meet Tryggr. He has forgotten more of *Vikingr* sea routes than you will ever learn. His name means 'trustworthy'—he is. I suggest you keep him near you.

"We shall talk more of this," Eirikr rose from his chair, "over the time remaining to us before you sail. For now, think carefully on the choice of your councillors and crews."

* * *

Sigrvard found Einar on the weapons field, sparring with a member of the recent recruits. After greeting them both, he drew Einar aside.

"How goes your life as a *huskarl*, my friend?"

"They have nicknamed me 'the axe-warrior'," he grimaced. "I must admit I prefer it to the sword—the axe feels like an extension of my arm."

"Perhaps," Sigrvard smiled, "I can find a use for an axe-warrior."

"As what?"

He had Einar's full attention.

"I am about to lead a war fleet against the Carolingians. I will need thirty *huskarls* as my personal bodyguards in battle who will join my flagship."

"And I am one of them?" Einar asked expectantly.

"I am afraid not." Sigrvard watched his friend's face fall. "But I am in need of a standard bearer; if you know anyone who might be interested...the rewards are high."

Sigrvard, practised as he was in leading his friend on a winding path, could keep up the pretence no longer. He extended his arm to his friend. Einar grasped it, then pulled Sigrvard into his arms in joy.

"Einar," Sigrvard extricated himself, "tomorrow forenoon, you have a coat of chain mail to pick up, as my standard bearer."

Einar's eyes widened as he shook his head in disbelief. "But the work time on a chain—"

Sigrvard raised his hand to silence him.

"It was ordered after the time of our melee, hence it is completed."

"But, I can never repay this *skuld*," he said despondently.

"What debt? You owe me nothing, you are my friend."

"But—"

"Einar, as I rise, so too do you, my friend. I am appointing you my second-in-command of my *huskarls*. If our planning is successful, we should both return with more than our own weight in gold and silver."

"Then there is only one thing I can offer you in return, my friend."

After hearing Einar out, Sigrvard agreed. Taking a spear from the weapons field, they made their way to an *akr gras* on the edge of the village. They selected a spot and Sigrvard drew his sword, scoring out a long rectangle of turf. Einar stepped forward with the spear, impaling the underside of the turf in its centre with the spear point. Both grasping the haft of the spear, they raised the turf to form an arch, the ends of the strip remaining in the earth, and took their places beneath it.

The Brotherhood of Blood was the closest bond that could be formed in life—and death—between two warriors. Einar and Sigrvard drew their knives and made a cut on their forearms.

As they clasped each other's arms in friendship, their blood mingled, dripping freely to form a red pool on the ground.

Einar crouched down and stirred their blood together—two into one.

Now bound for *ae*—in this life and the next—they solemnly swore their oath of blood to Odinn, that should harm befall the one, he would be avenged by the other. They would guard each other's lives and all contained therein as their own, as true brothers.

"Now," Einar ventured with a smile, "I suggest we replace spilt blood with good Denisc *bjorr!*"

About this, Sigrvard did not argue.

* * *

The next several days were to pass quickly; there were not enough hours in a day, nor days in a week. To Einar, Sigrvard delegated the selection of crews from the best and bravest warriors, the choosing of his personal *huskarls* and to provide a list of additional weapons he considered may be needed, and to liaise with the weapons and shield-makers, who had been forewarned of the upcoming voyage and had already begun their work.

In addition, he asked Einar to plan the provisioning of the ships with beer, ale, wine, mead and water; dried fish, salted meat, vegetables, bread, poultry and sheep—the sheep to be sacrificed to the gods before becoming food for the men.

Anything else needed would be foraged. In all things, Einar was to report to Sigrvard directly, and only to him.

"Einar, do you think you can achieve all of this in the time you have?"

"If I could not, I would not be worthy of being your second-in-command. Besides," he smiled, "for the amount of silver you are paying me, I would happily do twice as much and forgo sleep—but not women," qualifying his statement.

"Whom do you think I am ordering the sheep for?" Sigrvard asked.

Einar's hand dropped quickly to his *seax* in mock anger. They laughed together.

Sigrvard's next meeting was with Tryggr, whom, on his father's advice, he had appointed steersman of his flagship, The Red Dragon. Tryggr, with a red beard but a pate devoid of hair and shining as an ivory helmet, had the deeply lined, weathered face of a *forn flotnar*, who had spent his life at sea. Sigrvard knew he must discount his many years, which he would put at being at least fifty, as his father had advised him:

"His knowledge both proves his sharp memory and disclaims his years. His mind is as sharp as an axe-blade."

"*Hyversu ferr*, Tryggr?" Sigrvard extended his arm in friendship.

"*Allt vel, thakka*, my lord," as he took the offered arm.

Sigrvard had given up on correcting everyone who called him 'my lord'. He had brought it to his father's attention.

"But it is an insult to your name and rank, my Jarl and my father," Sigrvard protested.

"I do not take it so," he replied. "It is no bad thing that they begin to think of you as the next Jarl. You cannot rule without the respect and will of the people. My advice to you as your father and your Jarl is to accept it in the spirit in which it is given."

"Tryggr, tomorrow I go to Arne's, the shipwright, to trial my new flagship, the Red Dragon, at sea. Like my father, I value your opinion and advice, and would ask you to accompany me."

"Of course, my Jarl. As you command, my lord."

"I would rather you look upon this as an invitation from a would-be friend, rather than a command from a Jarl-to-be."

Tryggr answered with a wide grin, "You have your father's silver tongue, my lord. He was not nicknamed 'The Fox' for nought. He and I fought many battles in many lands. I understand your raid is to be against the land of the Carolingians. I know well the sea route we need to sail; this voyage, for me, would not be my first to that land."

"This is indeed pleasing to my ears. A better man for this voyage I could not wish for, and I give thanks to Odinn for it."

"*Thakka*, my lord."

"So, Tryggr, please join me at Arne's shipyard tomorrow forenoon, and we shall test this dragon at sea."

"And I, my lord, shall explain the route we need to take for a successful outcome to this voyage."

Sigrvard had given Einar his orders for the morrow. Now he needed to speak with Arne. As he approached the boatyard, he saw his new flagship moored next to the 'Raven of Odinn'.

He froze. He had never seen such an impressive, ornately carved and decorated ship. It took his breath away.

Arne approached him, accompanied by Einar, and he greeted them.

"What do you think?" Arne stretched out his arm to the new flagship, which dwarfed the other longships at anchor. "Is she not the most beautiful ship ever built? She is a *Busse*—a warship. A *Drakkar*—a dragon by name and nature."

"Arne, Odinn himself would be pleased to have this ship to sail from Asgard. You have excelled yourself, my friend."

Arne beamed broadly at the praise as Einar strode towards them.

"As ordered, my lord, I have assembled the crew and they are boarded: thirty *huskarls* and fifty of our best warriors. If I am permitted, I have a question."

"Of course. What worries you, Einar?"

"I am not worried, my lord, only curious as to why you ordered the crew to bring with them their personal chests, the seats for their voyage?"

"Weight," Sigrvard answered simply. "I cannot load her with the exact weight she will be carrying, but I am trying to get her as close as possible. I ordered Arne to load her cargo space with iron, as much as he thought might equal the weight of our provisions. On this trial today, she will tell us her greatest speed when fully laden. From that, Tryggr will be able to calculate the length of time for our voyage."

"Soon you will be known as 'Fox the Fair'," he smiled.

"Of course," Sigrvard pointed out, "our return voyage will be slower, due to the excessive weight of our riches."

Arne and Einar laughed aloud at the prospect.

"Also," Sigrvard's tone grew serious once more, "I have decided that unusual as it may be, Arne will have a share of our wealth, even though not with us. Without his great skill, we would not have this longship to sail in." His point was well taken.

"There will no dissent on this matter, and I can vouch for our crew," Einar pledged.

"Good. Do we know what delays Tryggr?" Sigrvard asked, looking around him.

"Nothing, my lord," Arne answered. "He was here even before myself and waits for us on board the ship."

"Then I suggest we do not keep him waiting," Sigrvard turned, noticing Arne's look of an expectant father having just been delivered of a new-born son, and led the way to the flagship. As she was anchored prow in, the first thing Sigrvard noticed was the carved red dragon on the bows. It was not possible to miss it. Arne's woodcarver had excelled himself: Sigrvard realised the dragon's eyes seemed to be watching him approach. 'Welcome' was the look the seer-warrior noted.

Standing at the prow of the ship, Sigrvard felt as if he were the *drakkar* itself, flying over the waves of the open sea. Once out of the inlet, the crew had the order 'oars in', as they picked up the wind and lowered the sail with its imposing red dragon at its centre.

As the waves became higher, she seemed to fly over their crests, pitching as she did so but with minimum roll. Sigrvard called for Tryggr, who had positioned himself at the helm to gain a 'feel' for the ship, to hand over the helm and join him in the bows.

"Please, sit. So, what think you?"

"I think, on this voyage, my lord, we must be careful not to leave the rest of the fleet in our wake," he grinned.

Sigrvard smiled. "So, you are pleased with her performance?"

"More than so," Tryggr replied. "Arne has made several innovations with the Red Dragon—one I have not seen before is the twin anchors."

"The anchors?"

"*Ja!* These are not the normal yoke of wood but of iron, and there are two—one fore and one aft—so the ship cannot be swept in any direction and is kept in the position in which she was anchored. Arne says it is to ensure his share of the riches stays where they are put."

They were still laughing when Arne and Einar joined them. Sigrvard turned to Einar, "How goes it with the crew?"

"More than pleased to have been chosen. They feel, in this ship, they can sweep all before them and return rich men. Rich enough to enhance their social standing and marriage prospects also."

"That is good. Tryggr," he turned, "where are your calculations?"

"Either with sail or the thirty-five oars each side, I have never sailed in a faster ship. The helm answers as a child obeying its father's every command. She sails at her ease at twelve miles in one hour but I honestly believe she could make seventeen sea miles at her fastest with a fair wind behind her. I shall base my calculations on the lower figure."

"Is it within your first estimates to tell me how long before we return from this voyage? Remember, I am a man who has to set a date for his wedding."

"To be safe, I would tell your father-in-law, shortly to be, that he should expect to see us enter the inlet in eight weeks and, we trust, fully laden," he grinned.

"Then I have yet eight weeks as unmarried," Sigrvard smiled in return. "If you are all satisfied with the Red Dragon, I suggest we return to the jetty for a toast of mead to Aegir, the god of the sea—we may need his blessing."

Assi and Sigrvard were summoned by the Jarl to the *langhus*.

Svein was stood by the Jarl's side. Also present were the six witnesses to the commitment, as required under Denisc law.

"The details of your betrothal and marriage contract have been agreed between our two families," Eirikr declared. "The *mundr* has been negotiated as has the dowry and it has been accepted."

Svein nodded in agreement.

Sigrvard wondered how much bride price—*mundr*—Svein had achieved and how much *heimangerd*—dowry—he had been willing to pay to reach agreement.

"Svein and I are of one mind, that both payments will take place on your wedding day. All we need now is a date. We have also agreed your marriage will take place after your return from your voyage," Eirikr confirmed with a smile of satisfaction.

Sigrvard took Assi's hand in his and kissed her gently on the lips. Svein coughed his disapproval, loudly. Eirikr said nothing. Svein's disapproval was understandable: a marriage contract was a matter of business, not emotion. Very seldom did 'love' between the couple enter into the arrangement.

The entire population of Eirikrsby stood on the quayside as the longships took on the last of their provisions. Assi and Sigrvard stood hand in hand. He turned to her and whispered, for there were too many close by, "Assi, did you know your father demanded the *mundr* be paid before we set sail?"

"*Nei*, but why?"

"I presume in case I do not return," he smiled.

"He shames me," Assi said with embarrassment.

"No. Who knows? I may have made the same request if in his place. No matter to us. We marry for love."

"*Sva vel*," Assi's voice took on a more serious tone, "promise me you will return alive and with your body as complete as when you leave." Her intonation was clear.

"Do not worry, my love. I have no intention of suffering a wound that could affect our wedding night."

Assi's cheeks coloured at the vision his words brought to her mind. She leaned over and whispered, "Oh, my love, it would be wonderful for us to see our children married."

Sigrvard nodded but knew only too well over half the children born did not live past their seventh winter.

"Our fate is in the hands of the gods but it would do us no ill to pray to Freya, wife of Odinn and the goddess of fertility, love and beauty. I shall pray to her as the goddess of war. As all do, we shall wed on a *Frjadagr*—her day—and make sacrifice to her to bless our marriage with children."

"*Ost min, kyss mik.*"

He did as she wished, taking her face in his hands. He held her with a slow, long kiss. As he released her, she took his hand in hers and looked deep into his eyes. She held back a tear.

"*Sigi, ek elska thik.*"

"And I you, my love," he responded. "I pledge you my troth, I will return for our wedding," he smiled.

"*Sva vel, Odinn*," she whispered softly, praying for his safe return.

The war fleet was an impressive sight, all thirteen vessels now gathered in the inlet, the crews ready to sail at high water. Earlier, Sigrvard had summoned a meeting of the leaders of their allies on this raid, from Esbjerg, Skagen and Hanstholm. They were all experienced warriors; he was not. The other reason Sigrvard had, for calling the meeting, was to establish his position as their warlord and leader.

"Any warrior disobeying my orders, no matter his allegiance, will be punished—severely. Understood?"

It was understood.

"My flagship, the Red Dragon, will be the lead ship, followed by the Raven of Odinn.

"Any ship falling behind, we shall heave to and wait for as long as possible. We are leaving as a fleet and I expect to return as one. We are not a hundred ships so I have planned for only that which I consider achievable. We are not equipped to lay siege to cities, neither have we the numbers. With a force of five hundred warriors, our biggest advantage is the element of surprise—and our enemies will not know if we are raiders or the advance party of a larger force."

All present nodded their heads in agreement. Sigrvard had successfully cemented his position as their leader.

"There remains only that we pray the gods are with us."

He raised his drinking horn, as did all assembled.

"To Odinn!"

"ODINN!"

Their roar echoed across the inlet.

"My friends, we sail on the tide."

* * *

As Eirikrsby disappeared from view over his right shoulder, Sigrvard smiled to himself as he stood on the prow of the Red Dragon. He mused over the additional name change 'requested' of him. Assi had told him, in no uncertain terms, she was unwilling to spend her entire life calling him Sigrvard. Reason, unknown. He had acceded to her demand and was now 'Siggi', but only to her. He made it clear that if he heard it from anyone else's lips but hers, he would divorce her.

"No one could say this raid was not well-planned," Einar congratulated him. "You make it sound as child's play."

"Bear in your mind, Einar," Sigrvard responded, "these children will send you to Valhalla at first chance."

"Einar the axe-warrior will ensure they do not gain that chance—and there will be great slaughter," he laughed. "The skalds will tell the saga of 'Sigrvard and Einar' for hundreds of years yet to come."

"Enough false praise, my brother," Sigrvard smiled, clapping him on the back. "Now, let each man to his task."

CHAPTER NINE

AS the ships reached one mile from shore, Sigrvard ordered Tryggr to take up position at the head of the fleet. The longships hoisted up their sails to catch the favourable wind on a southerly heading, following the Red Dragon sail that already seemed some way distant.

Sigrvard strode back to the stern to have words with the helmsman.

"Tryggr."

"My Lord?"

"You estimate a seven-day voyage to our first landfall?"

"Given good weather and favourable winds," Tryggr answered. "With respect, I know the longships prefer to hug the coast but until we are past the kingdom of the Frisians and well into the German Ocean, I would prefer to be on the three-mile horizon."

"So be it," Sigrvard agreed. "I defer to your knowledge."

"*Thakka*, my lord."

They continued sailing southward on the German Ocean, the crews working, eating in groups and sleeping at their posts. Every day, Sigrvard checked their position with the instruments of navigation he had inherited from Froda.

As they sailed south-west through the *Engelskanal*, between the coasts of the English kingdom of Wessex and the Carolingian Empire, the land of the Franks, the gods deserted them.

The fog appeared as a solid wall of still, dense smoke. As they entered the fogbank, Sigrvard could no longer see the prow of his ship. It seemed solid enough to cut a path through with a sword. He shouted his commands to the crew.

"Sail down! Oars out. Ahead slowly."

"Should we heave-to until the *thoka* clears?" Tryggr asked.

"No, we could be here for eternity. I can take us through the fog; you forget, I am the Seer."

He ordered lookouts to the prow and the masthead, and flaming torches to be set on the stern and the top of the mast, in the hope the other ships would follow them—that is, if they could see them. He also ordered the prow lookout to take regular soundings. In theory, they were sailing in deep water but he was not prepared to rely solely on fate. Sigrvard used Froda's sunstone to keep the ship on course, shouting up the corrections in heading to Tryggr.

After several nerve-wracking hours, they finally emerged from the fogbank. Tryggr asked for Sigrvard's orders.

"Oars in! Anchors out," he commanded. "We wait here, clear of the fog, for the rest of the ships—hopefully all of them—to join us."

Over the next two hours, ship by ship, all the fleet emerged from the fog and hove-to. Sigrvard shouted to the ships alongside for a report. They had been lucky.

Two had collided in the fog but the only damage had been several broken oars and three crew members injured, but not fatally. He ordered the fleet to resume formation and then issued his most popular order of the voyage: a beer for every man before they resumed their journey. He could hear his name being shouted as the toast from the other longships, and smiled.

* * *

On the eighth forenoon, having travelled southward down the Western Ocean and into the Cantabric Sea, they made landfall on the coast of Asturias,* north of the Emirate of Cordoba. Anchoring the fleet to the east of their destination, Sigrvard called a meeting of the war-leaders on his flagship. As they gathered around him, he explained his plan of action.

"This will be a land raid; we leave our longships here, with skeleton crews to guard them."

As he had expected, there was a murmur of discontent. A *Vikingr* surprise raid spread terror from the sea, not from the land. Sigrvard raised his hand and ordered silence.

* *The north-west coast of Spain.*

"Our objective is Gijon, the largest city of Asturias, on the headland. As it is their major trading port, there will be ample plunder for every man—gold, silver, trade goods and *thralls* aplenty. Our ships will be safe enough, once I have explained to the good citizens of Gijon that, should they harm our crews or ships, upon our return we will slaughter every man, woman and child in the city and leave it in ashes. Never underestimate the power of fear, my friends," he smiled.

As he had foreseen, the murmur of discontent became a chorus of approval.

"Once we have taken the city, we march south to their capital, Oviedo, and the seat of their king, Ordono. He has no time to raise an army to repulse us; he will have only his garrison and palace guard to field against us. As a *drengr* is worth three of his men in battle, I do not consider them a problem."

The laughter that ensued was the only approval of his battle plan he needed.

"Oviedo holds far more riches for us than Gijon. In addition to the plunder from the Cathedral, the Basilica and their existing church, sixteen winters past, they built two more churches—one a former palace—to add to our riches. My only concern for our men is, how will they carry all of this treasure?"

Now there was open laughter.

"My lord," came the expected question, "how do you know all this?"

Einar stepped in to answer on his behalf, "You have all forgotten? My lord is not only a leader in war but a Seer to the Jarl."

They nodded their understanding.

"Now, I suggest we prepare for battle."

As the council ended, Einar approached him with a bemused look on his face.

"Sigrvard, so you know all these facts, on which you base your battle tactics, from reading the Runes?"

Sigrvard deliberated on if he should let Einar continue to believe in the magic of the Runes or take him into his confidence. He decided on the latter.

"Yes, the Runes play a part, Einar, but the majority of my knowledge is a result of my trading interest with Vidar the *kauptmadr*. Our ships bring us not only trade cargoes but information. News of trade cargoes, rulers, politics, economy, strengths and weaknesses—particularly of their defences—from every country and port they visit, from all of *Midgard*."

Einar nodded his head slowly in understanding and admiration.

"And now, my lord, I had best prepare to bear your standard into battle."

* * *

The taking of Gijon was short, brutal and bloody. Their defences and garrison were quickly overwhelmed, with Sigrvard, Einar and the red dragon standard seemingly flying through the air for all to see.

The men knew only too well that if the standard went down, so had their leader—despite being protected by his thirty personal *huskarls*. It was not Sigrvard's way to direct the battle from afar, from behind a shield-wall, even though it was his first battle. His men knew he led from the front, taking the same risks as they; that he would always be in the fore, not following in their wake. For this reason, he had his men's respect, and he knew he could rely on them to enter the very gates of hell, if he so ordered. As none knew whom the *Valkyrie* had chosen to die that day, fear was pointless.

His men swept through the city, an unstoppable wave of death and destruction, killing, burning and looting everything in their path. As Sigrvard had predicted, the city presumed any attack would come from the sea and their defences were organised thus.

His men had been able to overcome the landside defences easily, then advanced through the city to the port, where they burned the ships in the harbour, effectively sealing the city.

As 'First Blood' came down on the Asturian guard's helmet and skull, Sigrvard caught sight of Einar to his right, banner held high, cleaving the air with his war axe. Many were destined to fall beneath the standard bearer's axe that day.

The battle was over as suddenly as it had begun. The surviving population of the city were gathered in the main square, kneeling in front of their captors. Einar had already ordered any survivors of the garrison be immediately put to death.

There had been great slaughter, pillage, rape and torching of houses in the city and the warriors' blood ran high. Sigrvard raised his sword to the sky. Their chant of 'Sigrvard! Sigrvard!' was heard all over the city.

He would not be surprised if the pall of black smoke now rising over the city could be seen by their king in his capital of Oviedo, some eighteen miles to the south.

Requisitioning the largest, palatial building in the square, Sigrvard ordered food and drink to be found and brought to him, then summoned his war council. Once assembled, he issued new orders.

"Make sure all our men are fed and given drink. What are our losses?"

"Slight, my lord," came the answer. "As far as the count of dead and wounded, less than a hundred."

Sigrvard added that tenth of his force to those he needed to guard their ships and calculated he would be marching against Oviedo with only five hundred men. He knew, although there was insufficient time for the enemy to reinforce the city, they would be facing some one thousand men and offered a silent prayer to Odinn that the strategy he was playing out would succeed.

"Send orders to bring our ships into the port and tie-up prows to the sea, and take what provisions they need aboard.

"Have each ship take their share of the men, women and children of the city to be sold as *thralls*, and to load the spoils they have taken."

"As you say, my lord."

"I will have no slaves on my ship. Load them onto the Raven and our three other ships. I shall forgo my share of their sale, which I shall distribute between our warriors."

"As you say, my lord. Your decision will be well-taken by your *drengr*, I can predict without the aid of a Seer," he smiled.

"First," Sigrvard continued, "bring ashore my fifty horses and riders, and have their leader report to me directly."

"My lord," Einar looked around at those assembled and spoke for them. "So, we are to fight yet another land battle though we are not equipped to besiege a city? Do not misunderstand me—the men are baying for the next victory."

Sigrvard allayed their fears, smiling at Einar, whom the men had nicknamed 'Odinn's axeman'.

"If my battle plan succeeds, there will be no need for us to lay siege to the city. You must trust me in this as your leader. As a Seer, I have read the outcome of our raid, and it is successful—and the Runes never lie."

There was a collective low growl of assent. He looked out at the darkening sky, lit only by the flames of the city's burning buildings.

"Tell your men to get what rest they can. I intend to be looking down over the city of Oviedo by noon tomorrow."

Once the meeting had departed, Sigrvard searched for, and found, a bed. He told his *huskarl* bodyguards to rouse him before dawn.

He breathed a sigh of relief as he was finally given the chance to take off his blood-stained shirt of chain mail and his protective layer of leather undershirt, and lie on the ornate bed, his sword close by his right hand.

* * *

The *herlid* marched one hour before dawn; Sigrvard and Einar were mounted, Sigrvard on his white stallion, Victory, his horsemen at the rear. He did not want them to be easily seen at the vanguard by the enemy; they were a crucial part of his battle tactics. He turned in the saddle to Einar, who still detested riding above all things.

"Einar, ride back and choose three of my mounted warriors as outriders. One is to ride south, in front of our force, the others to our east and west. Their orders are to ride back to the column with all speed, should they sight the enemy before we reach Oviedo."

"*Ja*, my lord."

In less than one hour, the riders returned at full gallop.

"Well?" Sigrvard questioned. The point outrider spoke out.

"Their army has marched out from Oviedo, my lord," he reported, "and has formed up in our path."

"Numbers?"

"More than ours, my lord, perhaps twice our number."

It was as Sigrvard had hoped—they had chosen to fight outside the city, so there would be no siege. He turned to the other two riders.

"Is there any high ground before we reach them?"

"None, my lord—only a small area of *skogland*, a mile or so ahead."

"Can we reach there before their army?"

"At their present speed, yes, my lord."

"Good." Trees would provide the cover needed. "Einar, prepare the men for battle and ask their leaders to attend me."

Some five minutes later, when they were assembled, Sigrvard gave his orders.

"We shall use the battle plan that has served us well in the past—the *svinfylking* formation."

Given to them by Odinn, the 'boar snout' had a devastating effect on the enemy. Its wedge-shaped formation began with warriors in single file at the point, then doubling their numbers with each rank back to its base.

This triangular wedge was designed to penetrate the enemy's centre; once this was achieved, and the enemy in disarray, the hand-to-hand slaughter could begin as the warriors dispersed either side of the incursion, behind the enemy and attacked on two fronts.

"Einar, you will carry my standard into battle and make full use of my shield-wall. My battle plan depends on the enemy being unaware that I am not leading our warriors. Understood?"

"Yes, my lord, but may I ask where you will be?"

"Watching you swing your blood-axe from a safe distance." Sigrvard laughed. They both did, for both recalled the moment in war-training when Einar had inflicted the only injury his friend had ever sustained. A careless blow as Einar, carelessly, practised his new-found fascination for the war-axe, slicing a sliver of skin from Sigrvard's right earlobe.

"To be serious," he stopped smiling, "the one weakness of the *svinflking* is if it is attacked by a flanking movement—and remember, the enemy have us outnumbered. I shall be ensuring that does not happen."

He turned to the assembly.

"May Odinn grant us victory!"

"Odinn!" As the cry rang out, the men took up the invocation for victory or death.

"To your men and your posts. I shall see you after the battle at our celebrations."

As his army moved forward, Sigrvard rode back to the rear and his horsemen whom he had left at the rear of the column as long as possible. From the dust raised by the horses, the enemy would think the number of warriors was greater than it was.

He reined Victory in and turned in the saddle to address his men, each of whom was now armed with an *atgeirr*—a thrusting spear—in addition to their swords.

"It is time," he made his voice heard. "Forget not, we have surprise on our side. They shall be devastated by the power of Odinn—we ride to victory!" A great roar of 'Odinn!' rose up from the fifty *riddari.*

Sigrvard led them west of the main column, then parallel towards the village of Posada, until they reached the small forest spotted by his outrider. He ordered his men to seek cover amongst the trees, but not to dismount. He looked up at the sun, now at its zenith. He would have preferred it behind him but the sun being directly overhead, gave neither side an advantage. Taking out the seeing-glass bequeathed him by Froda, he was startled by how close the armies seemed to be.

From his saddle, he watched the battle unfold.

As with every battle, it began with taunting insults, both ways.

'Your king is a *huglausi oskilgetinn* and you his *daufi bacraut!'*

'Cowardly bastard' and 'stupid asshole' were just the opening insults. There followed 'stinkfart', 'bow-legged carrion eater' and many more. That roused the blood but a battle could not be won by insults.

Einar ordered forward the triangle of archers and upon his cry of 'Odinn!' they loosed off a *skot-hrid*, one after the other.

The showers of arrows were made more deadly dropping from the midday sun and disrupting the reaction of many an enemy warrior choosing to look skywards at the wrong moment.

Almost immediately, there was a thinning of the enemy front ranks.

Sigrvard heard the war-cry of '*Ja*!' as they formed the boar's head and charged towards the enemy ranks as a scythe, cutting down all before it.

As Sigrvard looked through his eye-glass, he could see his worst fear was happening. The enemy had outflanked the boar's head formation, giving them no room to manoeuvre themselves into a position for single combat.

They were *vanfarinn*—in danger of losing the battle, his first.

"We ride!" he ordered his fifty horsemen. "Follow me; sweep around to charge them from the rear!" He gave a spur to his horse as his men followed. Almost upon them, he ordered his horsemen into a single line.

"Spears ready! *Ja! Ja!* Charge!"

As their rear ranks were decimated by the spears, the remaining enemy warriors turned in shock and fear to face the thundering hooves breaking through their centre. The flashing swords from the saddle were cutting a swathe of corpses through their ranks. As they did, Sigrvard's men were heartened and with a lust for blood and revenge, could at last turn and move freely in close combat. The slaughter that followed, many of his seasoned warriors told him later, was the greatest they had seen.

Sigrvard rode through the gap appearing in the shield wall and stopped by Einar's side as it closed. It was then he saw the enemy's standard bearer endeavouring to leave the field.

"A spear! Give me a spear, quickly!"

He leaned back in the saddle to gain maximum forward momentum, throwing the spear with unerring accuracy. He watched as the horse was brought down, throwing the standard bearer over its head. Sigrvard despatched three warriors from the shield wall.

"If he's alive, bring him to me."

He was alive. He was brought and forced to kneel before Sigrvard. One of the warriors held out the enemy banner and Sigrvard took it. The large flag was a simple design: a gold cross on a blue background. He handed it to Einar.

"Here, now you have two."

"And many more to come, I trust," Einar smiled.

Their prisoner was not smiling, but in fear for his life, trapped inside the shield wall. The battle was almost over, apart from small pockets still fighting. Those of the enemy who had not been slaughtered were in retreat to the city. Sigrvard ordered they were not to be pursued. His warriors contented themselves with looting the bodies and finishing off those who lay wounded. Sigrvard turned to the standard bearer.

"Do you understand our language?" he asked. The man had a regal bearing and his now discarded armour and sword were expensive. There was no reply.

"Have we anyone who speaks their language in our ranks?"

Einar thought carefully, scratching his beard.

"My lord," one of the *huskarls* spoke up. "I was taken by the Moors as a *thrall* and spent three years in one of their," he nodded in the direction of their prisoner, "galleys."

"Good, come forward and ask him his name and position."

The warrior did as he was bade. It took several minutes before Sigrvard had an answer.

"His name is Xured and he is not the standard bearer. He took the banner when its bearer was slain, hoping to take it back to the city. He is an advisor to the king and leader of his personal guard."

"Ask if his king was on the field."

The answer to that particular question came more swiftly, as their hostage laughed.

"He says no, the king is safe in his palace, in the city."

"How much do you think he is worth in ransom?" asked Einar.

"Nothing, my friend. I am returning him to his king as my *sendimadra*—my messenger."

Sigrvard turned to the warrior-interpreter.

"Tell him his god has smiled on him. Today, he lives. Come with me and bring him under escort. I have a message for his king."

CHAPTER TEN

"REPEAT what I say to the Asturian, word for word, understand?"

"*Ja*, my lord."

"Waiting for my signal, over the horizon, is a war-fleet of three hundred and fifty ships, with five thousand battle-hardened warriors eager for the kill."

He waited for his warrior to translate, carefully watching his captive's eyes for a reaction to his words. There was none. He continued.

"Tell your King Ordono that this is not a raiding party—more ships will follow. Our intention is to subjugate your country into a *Vikingr* kingdom for all time. There will be great slaughter."

Now there came a reaction into the prisoner's eyes, one of stark realisation.

"Your king can either surrender his throne or offer terms to save it, in which case we may leave him as a puppet ruler. Do you understand?"

"He does, my lord."

"Good. Now translate what I am about to say, very carefully."

"My lord."

"In the event your king contemplates taking further arms against us, he is a short-wit. Should he indeed take that path, we will lay waste to his land and raze every city, town and village to the ground. His people will become slaves and he will become known as 'The King of Ashes', over a barren country once known as Asturias."

The silence was palpable.

Sigrvard addressed his warrior-translator directly.

"Give him food, drink and a fresh horse, and pick out six of my *karls* to be his escort. I expect them to return here with him when he brings me his master's answer. Tell him."

"My lord, he says his king will honour the safety of your men, on that you have his word."

"Methinks I would as well take your word as his, Asturian," he smiled.

"He asks your name, my lord."

"Tell him, Sigrvard the Dene, and that, when he returns, we shall be found in Gijon. Now, begone."

At the meeting of leaders, there was a tension in the air as well as the feeling of anti-climax after the battle. Sigrvard decided his first action must be to quell any unrest amongst the men.

"What ails thee?" he asked.

The war leader who had obviously been delegated as spokesman stepped forward.

"My lord, the men's blood is still hot for the slaughter and cannot understand why we bide here, with Oviedo only a few *rost* to our south."

Sigrvard stood, feet firmly planted, arms folded and made eye contact with them, one by one.

"Listen carefully," his voice commanded. "I will not send any more of our warriors to Valhalla if I can take the city without an arrow loosed or a spear thrown. Earlier, I sent a message to their king, demanding his surrender."

The assembly laughed scornfully, as he had anticipated.

"By Odinn's *skagg!* Why would they seek terms with a small raiding party of some five hundred men?"

"They would not," Sigrvard agreed, "but they will with our war-fleet of five thousand men just over the horizon."

The silence was that of consternation. Then everyone began to shout at once. Sigrvard held up his hands and the shouting voices subsided.

"I am expecting the king's messenger with an answer within the next two hours. That answer will dictate our strategy."

"So, what do we do now?" one asked for all.

"We wait. We withdraw to Gijon and we wait. The men can transfer the gains from their pillaging onto our ships. I also need them battle-ready. At this moment, they need to be kept busy. I am ordering you now that I need all our slain buried side by side, with their weapons and personal possessions, in one large trench grave.

"Once done, have my horsemen trample the ground above so it cannot be found." He pre-empted their next question.

"No, we do not have time to build each of them a funeral pyre, or it could be ours. By tomorrow forenoon, we shall be either very rich or very dead."

Some four hours later, aboard the Red Dragon in Gijon harbour, his Asturian messenger and escort returned.

"I am glad to see you safe, Asturian, what news do you bear?"

"King Ordono and his counsellors deliberated at length on the payment to persuade you to leave this country and never return. They were of a mind to offer one thousand pounds in weight of silver, but I took it upon myself to tell them that would buy only enough of our land for his tomb, my lord."

Sigrvard smiled. *I am beginning to like this Asturian,* he thought to himself.

"I persuaded him that less than one pound in weight of silver, based on the size of your army over the horizon and awaiting your orders, would be the very least he must pay to save his throne."

"His decision?" asked Sigrvard.

"Five thousand pounds of silver bullion, my lord."

Einar's jaw hung open, *as well it might,* thought Sigrvard.

"And delivery to my ships?"

"Tomorrow, my lord, for it will take some time to assemble a wheeled convoy necessary for such a haul and to load it."

"Tell your king he has till noon tomorrow for its arrival. Later, and I call in the war fleet and take his country."

"The king has one concern, my lord. What guarantee can you offer that you will sail away from Asturias, never to return?"

"None," Sigrvard answered simply, "but I am sure your spies will report to you that we have sailed beyond the horizon to re-join our war fleet. The truth be known, Asturian, we head north. I have another battle to fight."

"I pity your new enemy, my lord."

They laughed as one and Sigrvard called for wine, before the Asturian's ride back to Oviedo.

"And what of you? Will your king reward your courage or lay upon you the blame for the loss of the silver?"

"Probably, the latter; at least I am not inclined to be here to find out," he laughed.

Sigrvard was not laughing.

"Would that I could take you with us but that is not possible as we venture onwards north. In the forenoon, bring with you only warriors you trust, who owe you fealty. You may, with my thanks, take for yourself and your men, one thousand pounds of silver, which I presume will be enough for you to start a new life away from Asturias?"

"My lord, I don't—"

"Then don't say anything, my friend. Einar, are there any ships in the harbour that are still seaworthy?"

"Yes, I think there are two small cargo ships, in case we needed them."

"Good. Have one provisioned and ready to sail on the morning tide."

"And now you had best ride back to your king with the 'good news'. I shall see you tomorrow forenoon."

"My lord."

As the Asturian rode off, Einar stepped forward.

"Sigrvard the Merciful, are you sure you have made the right decision?"

"Einar, he is a man of his word and has acted in our best interests, expecting no praise or reward. I would do the same if it were you in his place. Now, gather all our men together, except those on watch. I will speak with their leaders in the house in the Square."

The council meeting was short.

"I need you to explain to your men that we will be leaving Gijon on the late-day. We will not be sacking Oviedo."

Their response was predictable.

"But the men are expecting plunder, as is their right. What do we tell them without facing revolt?"

"You tell them they already have their plunder. They are leaving Asturias with their share of five thousand pounds of silver."

Sigrvard watched the reaction of the council with some amusement.

"So now, my lord, we sail home?"

"We sail, but not for Eirikrsby. There is more plunder to come.

"We sail to raid the Land of the Franks. Now, I suggest you tell your men all that I have told you."

As he sat by the window, thinking on the next stage of his voyage, he could hear the men on their ships and on the shore roar as one.

"Sigrvard! Sigrvard! Sigrvard!"

It was too warm that night for seal-skin sleeping bags and the men slept on the wooden deck, sitting upright in their rower's *sess* or ashore. Sigrvard reclaimed the ornate bed, leaned back and thought of Assi as he drifted to sleep.

* * *

"My lord, ten wagons approach with an escort of twenty armed men."

Sigrvard knew the Asturian warriors were no threat but he wasn't so sure about the king's men who were also part of the escort, led by Xured.

"How long?" asked.

"A half *stund*—half hour—my lord."

"Good. Tell the drivers of the wagons they may leave and return to Oviedo. Make sure they understand that is not a request."

Ten wagons would mean five hundred pounds of silver on each cart. He would divide the silver into two hundred and fifty pounds on each of his ships. Should he lose a ship, the loss of silver would be sustainable.

Sigrvard greeted Xured as he dismounted.

"My men will transfer the silver so come aboard my flagship, where we can make our farewells over a beaker of wine."

The two enemies, now friends, sat at the stern of the Red Dragon, watching the silver being loaded onto the ships as they toasted success.

"Your cargo ship is already provisioned, including feed for your men's horses. Have they ever undertaken what lies ahead?" Sigrvard asked.

"Only three who know how to catch the wind. As to oarsmen, none."

"Then I do not need to be a Seer to predict there will be many a blister before your voyage has ended," Sigrvard smiled, refilling their beakers.

"They will endure," Xured laughed. "I have promised them a share of the silver."

"And from here?"

"South from the Cantabric Sea and through the eastern straits to the isles of the Tyrrhenian Sea and warmer climes."

The fleet being ready to sail, Sigrvard stood and clasped Xured's forearm in farewell.

"Fair sailing, my friend, and may the gods be with you."

"Yours or mine?" queried the Asturian.

"Both," Sigrvard smiled. "Now is not the time to make enemies of the gods—any of them."

Sigrvard stood and watched Xured's ship clear the harbour and raise the sail once in open sea before it turned south.

He turned and gave the order for the Red Dragon to lead out his fleet.

As Xured crossed the horizon, he scanned the Cantabric Sea. There was no war fleet waiting for the attack order, nor had there ever been.

Xured's companions could not understand why their leader, stood on the prow, was shaking with laughter.

"Farewell, Sigrvard the Fox." He raised his sword in salute.

Sigrvard strode aft to consult Tryggr, his *styrismadr*.

"Your calculations, Tryggr?"

"I sail north, three miles out from the Carolingian coast—West Francia—until we reach our destination, the *oss* of the Gironda and the River Garonne. Unless the winds grow stronger, we should enter the estuary in two days, my lord."

"Good, *thakka*, Tryggr. We will talk later."

The leaders of each ship had received their orders, with a reminder it would be dangerous to underestimate the Franks.

Sixteen winters past, a *Vikingr* force had attacked Burdigala—Bordeaux—where the citizens thought they had driven them off. Stealth and the unexpected were well used in *Vikingr* strategy. They returned during the night and launched a surprise attack on the besieged city. This time, the tables were turned upon them. King Charles the Bald, of West Francia, broke the siege, forcing the *Vikingr* to retreat. Sigrvard had no intention of becoming entrenched in a siege.

The element of surprise being paramount, he deliberately targeted the city as it was celebrating a *Heilagrdag*—a Holy Day. Their defences, particularly the gates, would be depleted.

The city's noble families and those of rank, with their retainers, would be preoccupied in Christian services and their giving of rich gifts to the church to enhance their social status.

Sigrvard had ordered they land on the left bank of the river and regroup. The four-hundred-year-old Basilica of Saint Seurin, with the century-old Benedictine Abbey, was to be surrounded and looted, the occupants slaughtered before they could mount any defence.

He had ordered two ships from the fleet, on entering the Garonne, to forage and pillage the two villages of Pauillac and Blaye on its banks and leave no one alive who could warn the city.

Sigrvard further ordered that, as they re-joined their ships, one hundred of his men pillage and torch the warehouses and mansions of the rich city merchants by the river. If his strategy was adhered to, the raid on the city should be over almost before its citizens realised it had begun. They would be at sea before an effective counter-force could be raised. Einar asked how the strategy would affect his role.

"As my standard bearer, I wish you to hand over the flag to one of your *huskarls*, but only for this one battle.

"I have an important mission for you, but outside the city. I shall be with my horsemen. If the good citizens attempt to form any organised resistance, my horsemen will trample them into the ground. Their pure terror should ensure they break and run."

"And the mission?"

"This region has been producing wine for over a hundred years. I want you to take fifty warriors and sack the vineyard immediately to the east. Sack to your contentment but return to me with fifty barrels of their red wine—half to my flagship and half to the Raven."

"And this is important?" Einar asked incredulously.

"Would I say it, my brother, if it was not? Trust me. I promise you will know the reason once we reach home."

"I shall muster the men," Einar said grudgingly. "Odinn be with you."

Sigrvard's strategy played out well. The screams of terror and the sounds of slaughter from inside the Basilica could be clearly heard by himself and his horsemen. Behind them, Sigrvard could see flames and smoke beginning to rise into the air from the torched merchant mansions and warehouses. It had been his decision to hold his mounted warriors back and to use them as a 'shock force', where they were most needed. Within minutes, it was proven to be a wise decision.

From both left and right flanks came a mob, armed with swords and makeshift weapons. The citizens were intent on driving the attackers from their city. His men, now withdrawing from the cathedral, found themselves facing the mob. Sigrvard gave the order. Those at the rear of the mob were first to hear the sound of galloping hooves and turned, a look of pure horror on their faces. They had no time to prepare to defend themselves. The spears of the horsemen decimated the mob's rear ranks and the riders, swords and axes drawn, hacked their way towards the centre. The warrior, leading the men trapped by the mob, realised what was unfolding and formed a wedge with himself at the point, and they fought their way to the centre.

As they met Sigrvard's horse warriors, the two forces turned as one to face the broken ranks and cut down the mob as a scythe through an *akrlengd* of corn. As they broke before the onslaught, the survivors were ridden down as they fled. The square and streets around the Basilica ran with rivulets of blood. There was great slaughter that day.

* * *

As the warriors began sacking the Frankish monastery, a group of six or seven broke away from the main force and headed in the direction of the north end of the collection of low, stone buildings that formed the back wall of the monastery. Such activity would not normally warrant a second glance from Sigrvard but this time, something inside told him to follow his men.

As they hacked down the heavy oak door that hung beneath the ornate cross carved above the archway, the screams of the monks inside cut through the cold night air as they awaited their fate.

Before a unified supplication to their god was complete, as the first Denisc blade was about to dispatch one of the occupants to his maker, "STOOVA!" barked Sigrvard as he considered where he stood—it was the Scriptorium.

The flailing warriors froze as if caught in the icy blast of a Norse winter, as their leader's directive seared through the swirling haze of the candle smoke that swept around the room with a pungency that swamped the nostrils. The aroma caused Sigrvard's mind to leave his body in that moment, as it had many times before in his 17 winters. No longer was he the warrior-seer who had waded through muddied blood yet again in his young life. He was Osgar once more, but even younger than the nine winters he had been when wrenched from his Angle home.

The Osgar of barely six winters writhed as his young body sank deeper into the mudflats on the River Esk. A rich and bounteous source of the mussels much prized in nearby Streonshalh, but a bounty that was about to cost the youngster his life.

The pot containing half a dozen crustaceans was already lost to the treacherous muddy waste; soon Osgar would join them.

SPLAT! Osgar's gaze quickly shifted to his right where the end of a worn but substantial rope lay, beckoningly close. "Grab the rope," was the next thing the boy heard.

He knew not from whence the rope had come. He neither knew nor cared from whom it had come. What Osgar did know immediately was that if he could not make his right arm extend by two more inches, he was a dead Osgar.

An image flashed through his mind of a salmon struggling upstream as it leapt out of the water, spinning through the air to propel itself onwards and upwards. Instinctively, Osgar did the same and the extra impetus gained by his salmon-like manoeuvre meant—SPLAT—his right hand fell on the rope, followed quickly by his left.

As both hands grasped the hemp rescuer with heartfelt gratitude, the rope began to move. So too did Osgar. Face down in the mud, scooping mouthful after mouthful as he got closer to the sandy beach, he was helped to his feet.

The outline of the face he saw through his muddy mask was a tonsured face not much older than his. It was the face of a monk that sat atop a smiling countenance and lips that whispered, "There are safer ways to gather mussels."

Dicing with death may have been what preceded that moment but Osgar was still able to smile at his rescuer and thank him.

"By what name shall I thank my saviour?" said Osgar.

"Brother Benedict, but you can call me Ben."

But the young monk's demeanour soon changed when he noticed that the mud had slipped from his new friend's face to reveal a gash just below the hairline, which was issuing forth with blood.

"Come, I will tend thy wound." Benedict led Osgar down a long, dimly lit corridor towards the *enfermineria*, but they first passed through a room the like of which Osgar had never seen before, not that he had seen many rooms.

It was a moment that was to stay with him forever. Large candles held in stone sconces adorned the walls, one every two feet, and running down the middle of the room were two rows of raised dais sloping away from a central point, with a row of candlestands in between. There was one large candle for each dais but placed a foot from each of the *desca*, a safe distance from what lay on top of each, a sheet of vellum. Seated at each *desca* was a Scriptor whose life was devoted to God and the writing of documents to his everlasting glory.

"Hurry," said Benedict as he snapped Osgar out of mesmeric appreciation of the scriptorium. "Time to take in the sights after I have cleansed thy wound."

Benedict bade Osgar set his wringing wet arse on a simple but sturdy three-legged milking stool. He wiped the remaining mud from Osgar's face and reached for a small clay urn with a wooden stopper. To the patient it looked like a smaller version of the vessel from which his father drank mead.

But when the stopper was removed, a sweet essence wafted its way into Osgar's nostrils and a much-welcomed improvement on the stench of the muddy river wastes that had so nearly taken his life.

As Benedict inserted then withdrew a small goose feather—what else would a Scriptor have to hand—droplets of honey, which refused to stick to the aforementioned feather, fell to the floor but Benedict's hands were as swift as they had been in throwing Osgar the life-saving rope only moments before.

The safely secured droplets were smoothed into Osgar's forehead before Benedict drew the honey-soaked feather, which was actually a used calamus, across the gash to further stem the seeping blood.

Benedict beckoned Osgar to lie on the straw-filled mattress after he had applied a rough woollen poultice to the wound, held in place by Osgar's own hand.

"That should keep you out of mischief," said Benedict. "Though I doubt much could," added the young monk.

"What now?" said Osgar, worried that his family would be worried also if it was much longer before he returned home.

"You lie still for an hour while the honey stems then curtails the bleeding. Then you can go."

Benedict turned to leave.

"Wait," implored Osgar. "Will you leave me alone?"

"My friend. You are in God's care. Where on earth could you be safer?"

"But you will come back before the hour passes, won't you?"

It was a convincing enough plea, at which Benedict nodded, revealing the full extent of the tonsure that marked him as a novice monk. Osgar drifted away to a deep and instant slumber, a consequence of his battle with the mud that had almost claimed his immortal soul. Roused from his sleep that seemed to last hours but had been in fact just a quarter of one hour, he saw Benedict seated next to the cot on yet another milking-stool, and Osgar hadn't even seen as much as a single cow!

Before Benedict could speak, Osgar dived in with the question he had wanted answering from the instant he had set foot in the scriptorium.

"Tell me about that place, with all the candles and all the raised tables," for he had never before seen a *deisc*.

"And that smell," he added as Benedict opened his mouth to answer.

"Ah, yes," Benedict answered. "I'm afraid the Scriptors used up all the beeswax candles so had to revert to a more pungent alternative, pig's wax candles."

"My lord!" screamed one of his *huskarls*.

Instantly, Sigrvard spun around, narrowly avoiding an enemy sword. It was the last move that particular individual made as 'First Blood' shattered his helmet and skull within.

His mind meandering behind him for the moment, Sigrvard surveyed all before him. He thought of his horsemen, his *riddari*. His theory was now fact. For a second time, his mounted warriors had proven they could dictate the outcome of a battle.*

Sigrvard ordered Einar's chosen standard bearer to signal a withdrawal. They met with their men in the merchant's quarter on their way to the river, struggling under the weight of their spoils. Thanks to the total surprise of their raid, losses were minimal.

Their spoils were not. Gold and silver bullion, plate, crucifixes and coins; Christian books with solid silver clasps and set with precious stones; jewellery, furs and many *hundred silfrs* of ells of silks.

* *A month later, Charles the Bald formed a force on horseback, known as the Carolingian Cavalry. They were the forerunners of the French knights of the Middle Ages.*

The number of Franks taken for the slave market for sale as *thralls* was limited by the cargo space left on the longships.

Sigrvard looked back at the pall of smoke rising over the city.

As he did so, Einar came aboard the Raven.

"My brother, how went your *vin* mission?"

"Well, my lord. Your barrels of wine are boarded. I made the raid profitable by the spoils from the property of the owners—they were taken by surprise, with no time to arm their workforce."

Sigrvard turned and ordered, "Oars out!" He could not take the risk that the smoke over the town would be seen and result in the arrival of a Franken relief force. They rowed their longships hard, northwest up the Garonne, keeping an equal distance from each bank for safety. As they neared the mouth of the Garonne, they were joined by the two ships he had ordered to sack the villages on the banks of the estuary—their raids had also gained profit.

They reached the mouth of the estuary and the open sea. Sigrvard hove to and the fleet converged on the Red Dragon. He cupped his hands to his mouth and raised his voice to its loudest.

"Give thanks to Odinn—we return with the riches of our raids and battles won. Up sails! We sail north—and home!"

The warriors throughout the fleet raised their axes and swords in salute to the gods—and their leader.

"Sigrvard! Sigrvard! Sigrvard!"

It would have surprised him not had Charles the Bald himself heard their roar.

As he stood on the prow of the Red Dragon with the warmth of the setting sun moving slowly down his left cheek, Sigrvard's thoughts of plunder, like his first raids, were behind him. Ahead lay the prize that now had his attention—Assi.

CHAPTER ELEVEN

SAILS down, the fleet rowed up the inlet, approaching their home harbour. As they drew nearer, they could see the entire population gathered around the jetties, cheering their heroes' return. There seemed to be more villagers than Sigrvard remembered. He could see Eirikr mounted on his white stallion at the front of the crowd.

As the Red Dragon berthed, Sigrvard leapt from the ship as Eirikr dismounted and strode to meet him. He hugged his son in an embrace that almost cracked several of his ribs.

"*Vilkominn, min son!*" The Jarl held him by the shoulders, beaming with pride.

"*Thakka, min fadir!*"

"Come, let us go to the *langhus*, you can tell me of your voyage—I have many questions."

"As do I," replied Sigrvard.

Sigrvard explained he must oversee the unloading of their acquired riches—it would take over forty wagons—and allocate the shares. He must also thank the war leaders from Esbjerg, Skagen and Hantsholm and bid them farewell. He did not mention the fifty barrels of Frankish wine, which he would have taken to Vidar's warehouse by the harbour. Neither did he mention that from his larger share—as was his right—he would make payments to the wives and children or parents of the warriors who would not return.

Once his duties were completed, he ordered Victory saddled and rode to the *langhus* where his Jarl and father waited for him. First, he changed from his steel helm, chain mail and leather armour into a light tunic.

"*Hwae drincst du, min son?*" Eirikr motioned him to be seated.

"Wine please, my lord."

It was brought and they settled down for what Sigrvard knew was going to be a long meeting. He was right. As he told of their voyage, his father insisted on knowing every last detail of the battles and his strategies. When he reached the part played by his horsemen in the raids, Eirikr smiled and interrupted the telling.

"So, I knew you had an interest in horsemen when you were being trained to become a warrior and I taught you the use of strategy. Actually using them as a part of a battle is entirely your own planning for things to come. You were right to do so. Perhaps your calling as a Seer enabled you to do this?"

"Maybe, in part," Sigrvard answered, "but I would put this new strategy down to you teaching me the use of logic in battle planning."

Eirikr beamed with satisfaction. From this time, he would take credit for the strategy as his own, at every opportunity.

As Sigrvard ended his saga of the voyage, Eirikr asked the question he had deliberately left until last.

"The silver paid by the Asturians, what is its worth?"

"Five thousand pounds in weight, my lord."

The Jarl's goblet froze on its way to his lips. He repeated the question, Sigrvard repeated the answer.

Eirikr almost fell from his chair as he laughed.

"By Odinn's beard," he swore as his laughter subsided, "and I thought the *Vikingr* raid three winters past the ultimate in success. They took the King of Pamplona as a *gisl* and sold him back to them for a ransom of fifty thousand gold pieces."

"Do not forget the rest of our spoils," Sigrvard pointed out. "Gold and silver artefacts to be melted or shaved, precious stones to be set, *Kristinn* books to be sold back to them, jewellery, ells of silk, slaves to be kept or sold."

"Enough! Enough!" Eirikr held up his hands in submission. "*Lofkvadi*—the skalds will tell the Saga of Sigrvard for years to come—you will be immortal. The feasts to welcome your return will go on for a year," he laughed.

"Talking of feasts." Sigrvard was tired of the wallowing in his success. "I have a suggestion. As the wedding feast is only a matter of days away, why not hold them together? After all, the guests invited to one would also be at the other—and it would halve the cost..."

"I shall talk to Svein on it," he smiled.

"And on the subject of feasts, and my wedding *veisla* in particular, where is my betrothed? Why was Assi not at the jetty to meet me, my lord?"

Eirikr ceased laughing.

"She has been ordered by her father not to see you before the wedding, as is his right, or your wedding will not take place."

"Svein, *Oskillgetinn!*" His hand went to the grip of his sword. "One day I will kill him!"

"No, you will not," Eirikr said, frowning. "He is a proven warrior and a good man, but part of him dwells in the past with Assi's mother. Do not judge him too harshly. Remember, you are marrying the daughter, not the father.

"We both agreed the marriage would take place on the *Friggasdagr*, two weeks after your return," he went on, "so there are many preparations to make."

"*Ja*, my lord."

"And to other matters. Whilst you were away pillaging your way to becoming the richest man in *Jylland*, King Horik II decided it was time to join his ancestors in Valhalla.

"Our new ruler is King Bacsecg. I travelled to his court in Jelling just one *vikka* ago, to pledge my fealty."

"Do you think he will be a good leader, my father?"

"Take my advice, my son: *Man ma hyle med de ulve man er I blandt!*"

Eirikr had used that maxim before, when teaching him how to survive in politics: One must howl with the wolves one is among.

Sigrvard had followed that advice as he grew up. It would, he mused, be advantageous if he made himself known to this new king. The strategy for achieving this he had planned even before his return—albeit for a different *konungr*—king. He would put his plan into action very soon. 'Strike while the blade in your hand is still sharp.'

They drank more and the conversation continued.

"My lord, there seem so many more villagers on our return than when we left!"

"That is so. Even though we have insufficient buildings in which to accommodate them, still they come."

"But why so?" said Sigrvard curiously.

"Because of the growing reputation of Sigrvard, my son. A reputation that was growing before your triumphant and, may I say, bountiful, return. When news of the riches follows the news of your return, even more will flock here to be part of the new town that is Eirikrsborg!"

"What say you?" said Sigrvard in amazement.

"I knew one day the village would not be big enough. Not sufficient for its excellent location and potential wealth. I have thought long in your absence how, soon, you will take my place. I knew my confidence in you was not misplaced and from this time onwards, Eirikrsby is no more—Eirikrsborg lives."

A stunned, silent Seer sat, incredulous.

"As you will it, my Jarl, so be it."

"I do and it will. Now, more beer."

Soon, before Eirikr passed into drunken slumber, Sigrvard took his leave. His intention to visit Vidar waned the moment he stood and a short, aimless meander took him to home and his bed.

* * *

Thor was beating on his door with his hammer—or so it seemed to Sigrvard. He opened it to reveal an expensively dressed, corpulent merchant.

"VIDAR! *Velkominn! Hversu ferr?*"

"*Allt gott, thakka,* my friend. I am sorry I was not here to greet you on your return. News of your raids on Asturias and Frankenland have spread across Jylland and you are in danger of becoming a Skald's saga," he rocked with laughter.

"While you were busy amassing silver and other spoils I have been a little busy too, in the lands of the *Rus*. They are intending to settle in the lands between the Baltic and the Black Sea but are as yet fragmented. However, I predict that in several years' time, they will become valuable trading partners—by which time I shall probably be on my *daudadagr*."

"Ha!" Sigrvard snorted. "You are far from your deathday. As a Seer, I predict you will be a *langlifr!*" Sigrvard patted Vidar's ample stomach. "On the other hand..."

Vidar laughed and slapped him around the shoulders.

"So, now you return to our trading business?" he asked, as if needing Sigrvard's spoken confirmation.

"I never left," Sigrvard replied. "When I travelled to Jelling to swear my fealty to King Bacsecg, I took five barrels of Franken wine with me for our new king and his royal court. Where the king and his court goeth, his nobles and Jarls follow."

"And?"

"Here," Sigrvard handed him a scroll of leather scratched with the King's signature and royal seal. "What you hold, my friend, is a form of agreement that appoints us the sole suppliers of Frankish wine to the royal court."

"This is why you brought back the wine?"

"In the main but also for my wedding feast. Jarls from across Jylland will be there."

"And potential clients all," Vidar completed his sentence. "You are still a fox." His smile turned into a worried frown. "And just how are we supposed to supply the wine—a raid every week?"

This time it was Sigrvard who laughed.

"Not raids—trade, Vidar, which is where your experience and expertise is crucial. You are not associated as a *Vikingr* but as a respected merchant. What are your thoughts?"

"My thoughts," Vidar stroked his beard, "are that I shall be spending time in Frankenland," his smile returned.

"You will be at my wedding feast?"

"If I am invited—if not, I shall still be there."

One more of Vidar's friendly slaps and Sigrvard the Seer predicted he would have a broken shoulder.

"A drink to celebrate?" Sigrvard smiled and pointed to the barrel of Frankish wine in the corner of the room.

As the wine flowed, Sigrvard almost forgot that he wished to talk about Eirikrsby's name change.

"Vidar, a man of the world and no mistake," ventured Sigrvard.

As he was about to wallow in his friend's compliment, Vidar instead was required for a merchant's perspective.

"Eirikrsby has been growing beyond the village it once was. Some of that growth is due to your enhanced reputation, which is, in turn, growing the reputation of the place you call home, the home of Sigrvard, now Eirikrsborg.

"The population is increasing. We have itinerants from foreign lands, places some of our citizens have never even heard of. We have artisans and craftsmen, traders and merchants, even labourers who wish to be in no other place but here. Even I have a *thrall* who originates from far to the east. People create markets and people service markets and that in turn creates wealth, which in turn makes here a very nice place to be. And, thanks to Sigrvard, the great warrior-seer, a much safer place to be. It is also a place where the more people we have, the better it is for our business relationship."

Vidar fell off his stool, farted very loudly and rolled over, asleep.

* * *

Sigrvard's dreams were usually shrouded in mist, thereby allowing focus on the central element, but this was different. Brightness surrounded the magnificent sword, driven into rock-strewn ground by several inches. Perched on the hilt on either side of the jewelled pommel was a bird. A jet-black raven and a snow-white dove.

He could determine the dream was set as forenoon was coming to an end because the sun, being directly overhead, cast but a hand-sized shadow downwards. For a moment all was still, and central, but as the sun continued its path, the shadow began to stretch east slowly. Suddenly, the raven took off—the dove, unmoving—and flew north for a while before veering west and disappearing rapidly out of sight.

Sigrvard awoke, rose to his feet and made his way to where he kept his bag of Runestones. He was still mulling over the meaning of the dream as he brushed the sleep from his eyes and settled just outside the door on a wooden bench.

Normally, the stones would be emptied from their bag onto a wooden board for determination of their message. Not this time. Sigrvard tipped them into the flat of his hand then closed his fingers around the stones to form a fist. He then turned his hand over to deposit the Runestones on the board; just one showed its face, which had never happened before. He did it again, same result, and again, same result. Sigrvard did the same six times more and every time the same Runestone was the only one displaying its face—R, which he knew indicated riding.

He stared at the Runestone, understood what it indicated but had no idea what it meant. He mulled it over and over until he came to the same conclusion he came to each and every time—a journey, and a journey by horse, not longship. But where, when, why: all the usual questions, but this time questions he could not answer as a man or a Seer.

He had just decided that it would become clearer in the fullness of time when Einar entered the house.

"Groom-to-be, greetings. I have come for talks about your farewell to bachelorhood." Only Einar would take the opposite view of Sigrvard's impending union with Assi.

"Plenty of *Hnutukast*— bone-throwing— and *flytings*— insult contests—and most important of all, plenty of *bjorr*. Enough talking, time to start drinking."

Eirikr had given over his *langhus* to the throng that gathered for Sigrvard's celebration. As Einar had stipulated, there was *bjorr* aplenty, though most of the men had started their consumption in daylight.

The evening began with various drinking games, wrestling games and many a variation on weaponry skills, also known as 'showing off'. Proceedings continued in the same vein until but a few of those present were still vertical and even they had difficulty in avoiding farting, belching and, in some cases, urinating where they lay; bodies were strewn across the rush-covered floor of the Great Hall.

Einar then began to show off, though most of his audience were oblivious. He twirled his two-headed axe around his head and behind his back, then up over his head to catch it in mid-flight perfectly, before hurling it across the hall, splitting one of the large torches that hung on the wall into two.

Loud roars erupted from the now attentive throng and even louder banging of fists on tables followed approvingly.

"Odinn's axe-man!" roared Einar. "The axe is king," as he staggered back towards his seat alongside Sigrvard, axe regained.

"You see, my soon-to-be-married friend," slurred Einar, "the axe is without equal."

"Mmmm," murmured Sigrvard, "possibly, but the sword is too."

He kept his tone low, for he knew Einar would regard anything more specific as a taunt.

"Show us then, mighty Seer, why the sword should be feared more than the axe."

Einar turned, axe aloft, to the rhythmic banging echoing around the hall, all restraint wiped away in alcoholic stupor. Sigrvard hesitated but believing it might quiet his friend, who was just two beakers of *bjorr* from collapse, snapped to his feet. He drew 'First Blood' and in the same action, with a reverse flick of his trusty blade, flicked the flame from a nearby candle, leaving both candle and wick intact, before slapping Einar on the arse with the flat of the blade and returning the sword to its scabbard—all in the blink of an eye.

Incandescent with rage, which replaced impending drunken oblivion, Einar railed towards Sigrvard. All etiquette, rank and years of friendship went in that instant as his axe swung towards his best friend with only one thing on his warped mind—a death blow.

Einar got within a sword length of Sigrvard before two of his *huskarls*, Bjorn and Rolf, dived over the table and brought Einar to the ground, screaming and salivating like a *Berserker*.

He was still 'barking at the moon' when he was dragged, kicking and flailing, from the hall and thrown into a locked room for safety. By then, the evening and the celebration were over with just Sigrvard and his two 'rescuers' able to walk in a straight line. He hoped by morning two things: that he would have a clear enough mind to deal with the event that had just unfolded and that Einar's mind would be clear enough to realise potential consequences.

Just as daylight was piercing the gloomy eastern horizon, Sigrvard and his two *huskarls* made their way across the compound. As they creaked open the door, Einar was spotted curled up in one corner like a drowned rat. Still fuming, still drunk and barely awake, he scrambled slowly to his feet, using the wall for support to his none-too-stable legs. He stood there cowering before his Jarl, his friend, who had very nearly been his victim, although Bjorn and Rolf were slightly forward of their lord, still untrusting of Einar's demeanour.

Einar's thoughts, as his head started to clear, were spinning around, not knowing what to expect: he had considered everything from exile to execution, for had he not attacked his rightful lord? And, but for the swift actions of others, he could be standing there a murderer.

"What say you, Einar?" asked Sigrvard in a neutral tone that conveyed some optimism to his disgraced friend and standard bearer. A moment's silence before Einar answered, "I await my lord's decision as my actions have no reason."

"Only four witnessed what soured our blood feud, and the gods, of course."

Despite his alcoholic state, Einar knew a veiled threat when he heard one.

Sigrvard, with not so much as a single word, turned, walked between his *huskarls* out of the room, leaving Einar inside, still cowering, and the door wide open.

The next time Einar and Sigrvard met would be interesting. A thought that crossed both their minds.

* * *

Friggasdagr—the day of his marriage—was upon him. The day was mild with a hazy sun as the two seasons of the year met and summer began to take its leave. Soon, he would be *kvangadr* and a bachelor no longer.

His first duty as a bridegroom was to find a sword for the ceremony that had belonged to an ancestor. This posed a problem, until he talked to his father who told him a weapon from a living relative would be acceptable, giving Sigrvard his own sword.

"*Neiin*! Father, I cannot take your sword."

"Why not? Are you not my son? I shall not need it now in battle—Odinn has granted me a long life, but I am too old for raiding. I have more swords that will meet my needs—now take it!"

Sigrvard accepted it with due reverence and gratitude.

He made his way to the bath house with several of his *huskarls* in attendance. As he purified himself for the ceremony, his attendants' role was to instruct him on how to be a good husband and father.

At that point, normally, his best friend would be 'warning him' of the devious ways of a woman. But his 'best friend' was nowhere to be seen.

After bathing, Sigrvard finished dressing in his finest embroidered blue *kyrtill* and a fur-trimmed cloak fastened with a solid gold pin, in the design of the hammer of Thor, symbolising that he was the master of the marriage and to ensure a fruitful union.

He returned to the longhouse to find the pre-wedding transaction taking place—his *swaer* handing over to Eirikr, Sigrvard's family representative, his daughter's dowry. They now walked to the grove for the open-air ceremony to begin.

Assi was surrounded by her married attendants who undressed her. They removed her *kransen*, the circlet worn in her hair symbolising her maidenhood, to keep for the day she bore a daughter. Her hair was spread loose, a symbol of her virginity. She had preceded Sigrvard to the bath house, where she washed away her status as a maiden, while being instructed by her attendants as to the duties of a good wife.

The *brudr* was escorted to the ceremony by her young cousin, bearing the sword that was to be her gift to her *verr.*

As she entered the grove, Sigrvard suffered a sharp intake of breath, seeming unable to breathe out the air she took away.

He had never seen Assi look so breathtaking; her beauty shone like a beacon. Her long white *kyrtill* was embroidered with flowers and the Runes and on her head was her bridal crown, its silver points ending in a leaf design, with crystal stones set in the band, garlanded with red and green silk.

They watched as a goat was sacrificed to Thor, its throat slit and its blood caught in a bowl that was placed on the altar of stones and fir twigs soaked in it. The twigs—the *hlaut-teinn*—were then used to bless the marrying couple and their guests, by shaking the twigs to spray them with spots of blood.

Sigrvard presented his bride with his sword, to be held in trust for their son. She presented her sword to Sigrvard, symbolising the transfer of her father's responsibilities for her to her new husband. Svein would be pleased.

Assi's marriage ring, Sigrvard presented to her on the hilt of his new sword, then the bride offered him his ring on the hilt of her new sword. With their hands joined on the sword hilt, Sigrvard and Assi made their marriage vows. As they kissed, he knew his heart was lost forever, and was well-pleased.

After the ceremony came the *brud-hlaup*. This bride-running meant both parties must race to the *langhus*. The losers had to serve drinks to the winning party. Sigrvard had arranged for his horse, Victory, to be tethered nearby. Now, he sprinted to his horse and leapt into the saddle. Assi's party served the drinks that night.

When Assi reached the door of the longhouse, Sigrvard was blocking the doorway, his sword lying across the entrance. He took her by the hand and led her safely over the threshold. Crossing the threshold signified her transition from maiden to wife.

Now, the wedding feast could commence, beginning with the requirement by law, of the bridal ale. Assi performed the first of her duties as a wife and served the mead, mixed with a little of the sacrificial blood, in the two-handled bowl to her new husband.

Sigrvard lifted the cup in a toast to Odinn, took a sip and passed it to Assi, who made a toast to Freyja. By drinking together, they were now married in the eyes of the law.

Following tradition, Assi and Sigrvard were bound to drink mead together for the next four weeks, the 'honeymoon'.

The honey was believed to be a source of fertility.

Now the feasting began and would last for more than a week, but not all guests would, or could, remain for the entire duration. Sigrvard had been struck speechless when told how much food was there: horse, beef, pork, lamb, wild boar, venison, rabbit, chicken, goose—seemingly every meat known to man and every fish. Not to mention whole lakes of mead, beer and ale that would be needed for the week. It would have fed a small nation. Sigrvard predicted very few guests would remain sober.

It was a week to make merry with dancing, wrestling, strength and weapons contests, skald and *flytings*—insult contests, which could result in injuries, blood feuds and occasional deaths.

Wary though Sigrvard was after his bachelor night, nothing was going to mar this particular event. He could see no space among the hundreds packed into the hall, on *flets*, tables and standing.

Sigrvard and Assi were seated at the top table, Svein next to his daughter and Sigrvard next to his father.

"Serve the Franken wine now, but first to the tables of the Jarls and their retinues."

In the hall were Jarls from north to south—from Skagen to Hedeby—it seemed as if every Jarl in Jylland had attended. There were even Jarls from Sjaelland and Bornholm. It seemed Eirikr must personally know every Jarl in the kingdom.

He then saw his father beckon him from the floor, where he was in deep conversation with a red-bearded giant of a man.

"I am sorry, Assi. I'll be back in a moment."

"Take as long as you wish, Siggi. I am your wife now, it is my duty to wait," she said with a tipsy smile.

As yet, he could not swear whether she was being a dutiful wife or sarcastic.

"Ah, the groom himself," said the giant as he extended his arm.

Sigrvard took it. The man looked strong and healthy, despite his obvious age, and he must have been at least six foot two—unheard of for a Dene. Not someone he would like to meet in battle.

"My son, this is my long-time friend, Gautrek. We were young warriors together and fought many battles where the slaughter was great. I wished you two to meet as Gautrek is the King's *Hersir* and as such, controls all of his armies."

"The King has been following your exploits with interest, young Sigrvard, but not so young, I see," he corrected himself, "at seventeen winters. The Franken wine was an excellent strategy," he laughed, "but also your summer raids he found impressive, especially your strategy against the Franks." He paused to have his drink horn refilled.

"Of course, his battle tactics he learned from me," Eirikr boasted as he leaned over to enter the conversation.

"*Lodinkinni*—I know you of old," Gautrek laughed. "You would steal anyone's thunder—even the mighty Thor's!"

Eirikr joined in the laughter as he drank, though Sigrvard found his father's reaction to Gautrek's statement interesting. He was sure that anyone else calling Eirikr a liar to his face, even in jest, his sword would have answered for him. Gautrek must hold a very personal role in Eirikr's past. Gautrek turned to Sigrvard.

"Your father and I have known each other as brothers-in-arms for more than forty years. Should he give you advice, heed it.

"He was not known as 'The Fox' without reason, even back then," he smiled. "The raiding season is coming to an end and *vetra* is almost upon us, soon the time for wagons to be replaced by sleighs and to bring out the skates of bone. Before we know it, the feast of *Jol* will be upon us." He lowered his voice. "Once *Jol* is over, the King will be immersed in detailed planning with his war leaders. Do not ask about the plan—I am bound by oath and cannot tell you. After the feast of *Jol*, the King is sending you one hundred horses and one hundred riders, which he expects you to train and add to the fifty you already have under your control. I have given you time to plan for this but, Jarl-to-be, I must take my leave of you tonight."

"Can you not stay a little longer?" Sigrvard asked. "I would like to talk more with you."

"I cannot. As the King's *Hersir*, I have many tasks to fulfil before our army of warriors will be fully trained."

Sigrvard knew that to further questions, no answers would be forthcoming.

"And now, I must leave. I will pray to Odinn you have a long and happy marriage—with many children," he smiled; with a *handsal*, they said farewell.

"*Far vel Hersir*—I hope we meet again."

"Of that you may be certain, Scourge of the Franks."

He hugged Eirikr, turned and strode from the hall. Sigrvard looked at his father who shrugged. He knew nothing.

He returned to the top table as Eirikr circulated amongst his fellow Jarls. Sigrvard picked up his goblet of wine and toasted his new bride as he took her hand in his. The Jarls at the feast knew he was only a Jarl-in-waiting but were also aware of Sigrvard's reputation as a war leader and of his wealth, both from raids and as a merchant, trading from the Baltic to the Byzantine Empire.

There were rumours he had become the richest man in Jylland.

He did little to discourage them. At best, throughout the wedding feast, the Jarls treated him as an equal; at worst, with a grudging respect.

Assi had begun to yawn and was almost asleep on his shoulder when, thank Odinn, the time came to consummate the marriage. They rose to retire amidst cheering and much ribald laughter from their guests.

It was the law that they be accompanied by six witnesses who lit the way to Sigrvard's house. Assi was taken to the *hus* first by her female attendants and placed in the bed in her night clothing but wearing her bridal crown. Sigrvard arrived with his male attendants and removed the bridal crown before the witnesses, symbolising sexual union, and changed into his nightshirt before joining a nervous Assi in the bed.

The attendants and witnesses withdrew and the couple were left to consummate the marriage. The purpose of the law had been fulfilled: they could swear the bride and groom were in bed together and could confirm so if later called to testify to the validation of the marriage.

By the flickering light of the torches, Sigrvard gently removed Assi's nightdress and realised she was trembling.

"I have never lain with a man before," she explained. "I am sorry."

"You have nothing to be sorry for. It is I who should be sorry, I should have realised," he confessed as he climbed out of bed.

The window's shutter was closed, the only light coming from the oil lamps around the room. One by one, he put them out. The room was now in utter darkness as he attempted to find his way back to the bed. He heard Assi chuckle as he stumbled over a stool. As he returned to bed, Assi reached out for him.

"Assi, please believe me. As your *verr*, I swear by Odinn that I will never do anything to hurt you nor give you reason to regret our marriage."

He kissed her softly on the lips while putting her hand on his now erect manhood as they began to gently explore each other's bodies. They were still making passionate love as the sun rose.

They had little sleep and soon Sigrvard realised he must leave his house. He dressed hurriedly and even then he was just in time. As he opened the door, his wife's attendants passed him with knowing looks and giggles, and filed into his home.

Once he had gone, Assi's attendants dressed her. This would be the last hour she would wear her hair unbound and uncovered. Her hair was bound in the coiffure of the married woman and covered with the *hustrulinet*—the linen head-dress, which was the symbol of a wife.

Meanwhile, on his way to the *langhus*, Sigrvard was preoccupied with his deliberations on the necessity of a new, larger house to befit Assi's new status, and his own, and to accommodate the children to come, and the housemaids and servants they would need. If he became Jarl, he would cede their accommodation in the *langhus* to the families who had the most need. Inside the hall, he was greeted by the six witnesses assembled for the *morgen-gifu*—the morning gift—to be paid to the bride after consummation of the marriage.

The amount was calculated in relation to the dowry, one third, one half or, on Sigrvard's insistence, an amount equal to the whole sum of the dowry, also jewellery and new clothing.

Assi arrived with her attendants and the short ceremony began. The morning gift was intended to compensate the new wife for the loss of her virginity and to ensure her financial independence.

Sigrvard delivered unto Assi the keys to his house, symbolising authority as mistress of the household. The marriage had now met all the legal requirements. They held each other's hand as they left the longhouse, smiling. Once in the privacy of their bedroom, Sigrvard presented Assi with a small, light linen package, which once again brought a smile to her face. She slowly unwrapped it, much too slow for Sigrvard's liking but then he was a man. Her eyes lit up as she revealed a small, plain but elaborately edged amulet. It was no ordinary amulet for, as she slipped it onto her arm and slid it past her elbow, it glided smoothly across her skin, almost blending seamlessly as it sat comfortably twixt elbow and shoulder.

"Husband, it sits as if part of my arm but not where one would normally wear such an accessory, to be admired by wearer as well as folk."

"True, but this amulet is a bond between us that only we shall ever see. It will be hidden under your daily clothes and will only be visible when we lie together, to us."

CHAPTER TWELVE

THE twelve days of *Jol* was upon them, their first as husband and wife, and with it the three-day feast of the Winter Solstice, the shortest day, lasting only hours. The *Jul* itself would last over three weeks, until the *Julabot*—the Yule Sacrifice—when hopefully, there would come the brightening of days: celebrating the return of the sun, with the Skald reciting the *Solarjod*—The Song of the Sun—and the exchange of gifts.

By now, the goat, the symbol of Thor, protector of Midgard, the world of man, from the powers of Night and Death, would have been taken to the hall. The *Oskoreia*—the riders of Asgard, the souls of their dead ancestors, rode across the skies on the dark nights of winter. Before making their way to the *langhus*, Assi and Sigrvard decorated their evergreen tree with small, carved effigies of the gods, pieces of food, clothing and carved Runes, to encourage the tree spirits to return.*

Assi hung a sprig of mistletoe over the lintel of the door. The skalds told of Balder, the god of light and goodness, being slain by an arrow of mistletoe. His mother, the goddess Frigg, wept over his body. Her tears brought him back to life and also, falling onto the mistletoe, turned its berries from red to white.

Around the entrance to the longhouse, a crowd gathered to witness the giant Sunwheel.** At the signal from Eirikr, the wheel was set alight and rolled down the small hill to entice the sun to return to them. It was followed on its path by the children on their sleighs and

* *The origin of the Christmas tree.*

** *The origin of the Christmas wreath.*

bone-carved ice-skates on the frost-hardened covering of the frozen ice. It began to snow as they entered the great hall.

Eirikr and Svein took their places at the top table of the over-crowded longhouse. For whatever reason, Eirikr had placed Assi and himself at the centre of the table, he on Sigrvard's right, with Svein on her left.

Sigrvard realised that for the first time, he was leader of the feast, as the new Jarl. It was time to honour the gods to ensure the return of the sun. A wild boar was sacrificed to Freyja, the goddess of fertility, with their prayer for a good season in the coming year. The meat of the boar would then be served during the banquet.

The traditional oak *Jul* log had been decorated with sprigs of fir and holly; its carved Runes, provided by Sigrvard as Seer, asked the gods to protect them from ill-fortune. A small piece of the log was kept after the feast to protect the *langhus* and used to light next year's fire. As their glass beakers were charged and the traditional roast pork served, Assi drew Sigrvard's attention to the figure entering the hall: The Old Man of Winter.*

He was wearing a hooded fur coat against the snow and a long beard. Sometimes he would travel on foot or, as on this occasion, rode on a magnificent white horse. Some believed the eight-legged horse of legend was Sleipnir and the rider, Odinn.

This horse had four legs; Sigrvard should know, it was his stallion, Victory.

On the eve of the solstice, the children left their boots by their hearth, filled with hay and sugar for Sleipnir, Odinn's horse. In the morning, they would find small gifts from the god for their kindness to his steed.

"I wonder if," he leaned over to Assi to make himself heard, "we shall be visited by the *Jul* Goat?" He smiled.

"Why?" Assi answered mischievously. "Have you been a good boy?"

The legend told of Thor riding through the skies on a wagon pulled by two goats. The young of Eirikrsborg, dressed in their goatskins, went from house to house, singing and performing short plays, being rewarded with food and drink. The *Jul* Goat also brought gifts.

Eirikr struck the table several times with his hammer and called for silence, ordering all drinking horns and glasses to be filled for the

* *Upon conquering England, the Danes introduced Father Christmas to the Angles.*

minn—the Solstice toast. All stood; nearly all, as some were already not capable of standing at all.

"*Heilir Gags synir*!"

"Hail the Sons of Day!" The hall took up the cry.

Sigrvard held his glass goblet high in salute.

"*Tils Ars ok Fridr!* To the New Year and peace!" He knew there was little chance of that. No matter. Svein ended the toasts.

"*Glaedellig Jul!*"

The response almost raised the roof of the *langhus*.

"Husband," Assi laid her hand on his arm, "for our first *Jul* together."

She handed a linen-wrapped gift to him. Sigrvard unwrapped the cloth and picked up the newly-made *seax*. The blade was inscribed with runic characters, but it was the handle that caused him to draw his breath.

On its silver-chased handle was a dragon picked out in red—now the symbol of his clan. It was truly a work of pride and Sigrvard could recognise the work of his friend, the weapon-maker. He took Assi's hands and drew them to his lips. Pulling back, he reached inside his *kyrtill* and handed her his gift, watching carefully as she unwrapped it. She held the solid gold amulet in both hands as she examined the exceptionally fine workmanship. The design was that of two intertwined serpents, the symbol of her clan, their shining red eyes picked out in precious stones. As she turned it in her hands, she saw the runic letters inscribed on its inner side. She read:

'Sigrvard caused me to be made for Assi, his beloved.'

"It is the most beautiful thing I have ever seen," she spoke softly, her eyes misting. "I think we should be early to our home this night," she smiled. Sigrvard did not need persuading.

* * *

As law-sayer of the *Thing*, Sigrvard called the council to order. There were some thirty at the meeting, including plaintiffs, accused, witnesses, members of their families and clan and the simply curious, who looked upon it as entertainment. Seated at the head of the table, Sigrvard took the proffered beaker of ale and salted pike. Food and drink were provided for those present, as the proceeding could last for several days. He had been briefed on the first case—a divorce.

The accuser, Torstein, the wife's father, was seeking a divorce settlement on behalf of his daughter, Ranveig, against Borskar, her abusive husband—or so it was claimed. Sigrvard devoted all his attention to the witnesses' testimonies.

He was wary of divorce hearings, with good cause. Often, the member of the partnership with the most assets would seek a divorce to protect these assets from predatory in-laws.

Thankfully, this case was relatively straightforward, based on the use of violence and humiliation and where the wife had brought the larger part of the assets to the marriage. Torstein, the wife's father, claimed her husband had failed to afford his wife's relatives 'due consideration'—itself grounds for divorce under Denisc law.

Sigrvard called forward the wife to give her testimony. She claimed her husband, having taken drink as he did every day, had slapped her more than three times—the legal requirement for a divorce—and more by fist and foot.

"You have witnesses to this?" Sigrvard asked her.

"Yes, my lord. They are here at the *Thing*."

"Then I will hear them."

Following the testimony of the witnesses, the accused's defence of 'provocation' carried little weight, if any. Guided by Sigrvard as law-sayer, the jury of twelve men would decide on the verdict and the punishment.

Sigrvard advised them that if Boskar be found guilty, then a fine imposed was unlikely to be paid as he now had no assets. Equally, trial by hot stones would not satisfy his wife's clan. In Sigrvard's judgement, there was a very real danger of a blood-feud, given the thinly-veiled intentions of her family.

The spokesman of the jury stood. Sigrvard earnestly hoped they would temper the law with logic. Predictably, they found against Boskar Haraldsson. They took the only logical decision and pronounced him outlaw. The family of his now-divorced wife cried out in jubilation, their hands moving to the hilts of their swords and *seaxs*. Sigrvard nodded to the two housekarls by the doors, who moved forward to take position behind the clan to end any outbreak of violence that may begin.

He rose to his feet with arms outstretched and called for silence.

"The divorce and your punishment have been concluded. Boskar Haraldsson, as outlaw henceforth, you are banished to the great wilderness; any and all Dene is hereby forbidden to provide you with aid or assistance. Your enemies," Sigrvard studied Ranveig's family's reaction, "are free to hunt you down and kill you without penalty under law. Do you understand?"

Boskar Haraldsson hung his head and nodded.

Sigrvard was not displeased with the outcome. It had saved Boskar's life, if he but knew it. He would be escorted by two *huskarl* to the boundary of the village. Were he to remain in Eirikrsborg, he would, without a doubt, be slain in the inevitable blood-feud. Were he to take the path dictated by logic, he would leave Jylland and begin a new life elsewhere.

As he prepared for the next case, a messenger arrived and made his way up to Sigrvard, leaning over his shoulder to almost whisper his message.

Sigrvard could not move, an involuntary sob caught in his throat.

After what seemed to him an hour, he stood and addressed the assembly, "*Fyrirgef mik*—I must leave."

Once in the open, he took in several deep draughts of the cold air to clear his mind. The message had been short and to the point.

"My lord, your father, the Jarl, is dead."

* * *

Svein stood by the body of Eirikr, slumped in his ornately carved chair.

"My lord."

"What happened?"

"I do not know, my lord. He was well, calling for mead, when his arm seemed to stiffen and he dropped his goblet."

"Did he speak?"

"He tried, but the side of his face and mouth seemed to have fallen and his slurring was that of a drunken man. I put my ear to his lips and carried out his last order."

"Which was?"

"Sword. I drew it and placed it in his hand. He made a great effort and shouted 'Odinn!', and fell back into his chair."

"And that was his last word—to prepare a seat for him in Valhalla?"

"No, my lord. The last name on his lips at death was your own."

Sigrvard turned to face the Great Hall. Unlike the passing of Froda, he had been too late to take farewell of his father. To his surprise, he realised the longhouse was filling with the townspeople of Eirikrsborg, of all ranks and stations, with more arriving by the minute.

He had forgotten with what speed news—good or ill—was spread. He was aware of Svein passing him and taking up a position at the head of the silent crowd, joining Ulfr and Einar. As of one, all men, led by Svein, dropped to one knee. Sigrvard realised what was to take place—the swearing of the oath of fealty to their new Jarl, prior to the more formal ceremony to come. Svein drew his sword and spoke for all.

"Eirikr, our Jarl, is dead! All hail our Jarl Sigrvard! All hail Odinn!"

The people hailed their new Jarl as one.

"We give our oath of loyalty freely to our new Jarl," Svein continued, "in honour and truth. If any man here would gainsay Sigrvard, son of Eirikr, his absolute right, let them speak now and state their case." The silence in the longhouse was absolute.

"*Thakka*, Svein. Please give my people ale and bread before they leave the hall. I go alone to my *hus* to grieve."

"As you say, my lord."

Svein extended his hand to Sigrvard. In its palm lay the clan's Dragon Ring of his father. He took it and placed it on his finger. It was a perfect fit.

Eirikr's burial took place on the second day after his death, to give time for the arrangements to be made. Sigrvard was aware that his father must be buried adhering to the rules of the ritual. If the funeral rite deviated from tradition, or he was buried with too few grave goods, he would not find peace in the afterlife and return to haunt the living as a *draugr*—a shade of the dead.

Eirikr was to be buried, not cremated. He would, by entitlement of rank and wealth, be interred on a *langskip*. His status would justify the destruction of the longship.

Sigrvard had taken the decision, as son and Jarl, to have the interment on his own land, where his father would be with him for eternity.

Even as a Seer, Sigrvard could not have foreseen the future.

After discussion with Arne the shipwright, he had decided upon an elegant, ornately decorated, thirty-warrior Drekkar. He could hear his father's voice.

"Am I not a mighty warrior? Am I not a Jarl of great rank and renown? Have I not earned the right to the best of longships to carry me on my final journey to Valhalla?"

"One of the first things you taught me, my father, was that our greatest weapon was the *langskip*. Would you have me destroy our flagship and deny its warrior crew of their time of glory, their chance to join you in *Valholl*?"

Eirikr had snorted—his standard response to an argument lost.

It had taken Arne and 30 warriors to transport the burial ship on log rollers and sheer physical exertion to Sigrvard's chosen site. Next, a wooden structure was placed on the deck to receive the body and a tent-like large cloth placed around it. The time had come.

On Sigrvard's orders, a ditch the shape of the ship had been dug, into which half of the height of the ship had been lowered, its gunwales and dragon prow and stern remaining aboveground. Sigrvard took his place to carry the litter with his father's body onto the deck, accompanied by Svein, Ulfr and Einar as bearers.

The burial field seemed to contain all of Eirikrsborg: from housekarls and wealthy freemen and artisans to merchants and even *thralls*. He knew Vidar would not be there—he was on a trading expedition to the land of the Rus. There had been little time for other Jarls to attend, but he knew they would all be at Eirikr's *erfi*, the funeral feast to be held in seven days.

They placed the body, dressed in his leather armour under his full chain mail suit and wearing his highly decorated steel, silver and gold helm. With him, they placed his sword and scabbard, war axe, *seax* and finally, his shield placed over his face.

He also wore his personal jewellery of amulets, torque and finger rings, his silver cloak pin in the dragon sign of his clan and a silver hammer of Thor talisman. Symbols of his wealth were placed around him: glass, gold and silver drinking vessels, bone and ivory combs and lead weights for measuring out silver. Sigrvard had himself carved and placed the runic inscriptions at his feet. What came next, Sigrvard wished he did not have to witness.

Gunnhild, a member of Eirikr's household, had made the decision to accompany him to the afterlife. Sigrvard, for many years, had suspected she had been his father's mistress. He had been told, neither as Seer nor Jarl, that he could not interfere in the ritual.

As the body had been prepared for the longship, Gunnhild would fulfil the first part of the ritual by having sexual intercourse with six men, moving from one to the other. Once on the ship, they removed her bracelets and finger rings. She was forbidden from entering the 'tent' where Eirikr lay. She was given alcoholic drinks, sang and bade farewell to her friends.

For the final part of the ritual, she was dragged into the tent, whereupon the six entered and raped her in turn, the other warriors beating on their shields to cover the noise of her screams.

Then two held her wrists tightly and two her hands. An old woman, designated as the 'Angel of Death' for the ritual, placed a rope around her neck. As two of the men pulled the rope tight, the old woman took out a knife and stabbed her between the ribs, enabling her to join her Jarl.

Of that, Sigrvard had serious doubts but said nought.

At the given signal, some fifty men stepped forward with their tools and began to fill the ship with stones and soil; once covered, they continued to build the *haugr*—the grave mound—over the ship, creating a high tumulus.

As the rites had all been correctly observed, on top of the tumulus the outline of the longship was picked out in stone. As the crowd moved closer, from the top of the burial mound, his staff of power as the Seer, Sigrvard held up his hands for silence and delivered the death speech.

"We say farewell to a mighty warrior, leader and Jarl. He whom I was honoured to call father, and you assembled here your Jarl and protector of his people. 'The Fox' will now play board games with Thor and the mighty Odinn himself until Asgard is no more.

"Oh, mighty Odinn, prepare a place at your table for Eirikr the warrior at your side. Let his drinking horn be never empty. We shall join him soon."

Sigrvard the Seer lifted his rod to the heavens.

"Odinn! Odinn! Odinn!"

The assembly took up the chant.

"Eirikr! Eirikr! Eirikr! Eirikr!"

As Sigrvard turned his back to the crowd, they began to disperse.

CHAPTER THIRTEEN

AD 865

THE moon of *Morsugur* ended, heralding *Thorri*, the thirteen moons of the year, a winter that would change Jylland and England for all time. The two places of Sigrvard. A winter that would see Sigrvard come to terms with his own past and future, a winter beyond imagination or a Seer's omniscient powers.

Sigrvard now found himself trying to oversee and fulfil several responsibilities simultaneously. But such thoughts were a world away as he turned from the doorway and looked back towards a sleeping Assi. To where only moments earlier they had been locked as one, bonded by the love they felt for each other.

The flickering flames of the fire-pit produced an almost moving image of his beloved as it lit up her slumbering beauty. His thoughts, well beyond one of just 17 winters, were many. *The gods are smiling on me*, being chief among those thoughts.

Though a Seer, he could not foresee what lay beyond that winter.

Nor would he have wished to know what the gods had in mind for him and his own. Thoughts that were two edges of the same sword, a blessing and a curse, thought the warrior-seer, and often he had no control of the timing of either or both. In battle, it was all instinct and any pause to think could hasten the voyage to *Valhalla*. But in the comfort of his home and his wife were moments to be savoured, for he knew that as the weather improved, planning would soon begin for the raiding season.

Before the last flagons of *Jul* were downed, there were already rumours of a planned gathering of Norse warriors for what Sigrvard thought would be more than a raiding expedition. And while he had acquitted himself favourably on his first raids as a leader, his thoughts were now burdened with his new domesticity.

Will thoughts of home block instincts on the battlefield? he wondered.

As the breaking light of dawn glistened over the rooftops onto the fjord, Sigrvard heard Assi stir behind him.

"Come husband, come back and fill me with our love. The day ahead can wait a little longer," she said with a youthful wickedness. A smiling husband needed little persuading and the day indeed could and did wait a little longer.

* * *

Inactivity did not sit well with Sigrvard, although his Seer and Jarl duties did occupy time; but he yearned for battle. Nights with his beloved were a most welcome alternative to the day-to-day existence in Eirikrsborg, a distraction many would gladly give their place in Valhalla for. The slowly lengthening days as *Morsugur* became *Thorri* added a new life to the newly named town, as did the next stage in its development. Part of that development included the new home he was building for himself and Assi and any small ones who came along.

Thorri passed into the *manadr* of *Góa*, and he realised he had no choice but to delegate. The new home had progressed from the sinking of the first postholes to near completion with impressive speed, having brought in additional *Mastermyr* from Ribe to supplement his own carpenters. Major feasts and assemblies would still be held in the *langhus*. His current home he had allocated to the younger couple of a greatly overcrowded family house; he was sure Froda would have approved.

The new house was built on four *dagsslátta** of prime grassland, including one *akr* for Victory and a sizeable kitchen garden for Assi.

It had already become a major talking point, not only in Eirikrsborg, attracting the attention of the curious and the envious. Einar, his brother, who referred to the house as 'Sigrvard's Palace', had yet again proved his worth as overseer of the site.

Unlike the traditional *langhus* with its curved walls and accommodation for several families, their new home was smaller in length but

* *An area of land that could be ploughed in a day.*

larger in width—some 30 feet wide and 100 feet long—its walls straight and divided into separate rooms. The floors were lower than ground level to exclude draughts. The walls were wooden-clad and the wood-framed turfed roof wooden-clad, with supporting beams and reinforced dragon-carved gables.

As Jylland was not noted for its forests, Sigrvard had to have the Norvegr pine and soft woods, including expensive walnut, brought in by cargo ship; this had also proven necessary for their supply of wax and honey, the Sœnskr bees having to be imported. Shuttered windows to each external wall were also one of his innovations. The reinforced hardwood double entrance doors opened into a small entrance hall, giving access to the main hall of the *hus*.

At the far end of the hall stood two ornately carved tall-back chairs adorned with his dragon emblem and the Jylling-style S-shaped beasts with open jaws. On the wall behind the chairs hung the rod of the Seer, with runic inscriptions to each side, beneath them his dragon war-shield. Part of the hall had been partitioned as a weapons store and armoury. The Jarl's bedroom was the largest, with a freestanding box bed, its four short corner posts carved and painted with the dragon crest, breaking with the tradition of the master bed being fitted into an alcove.

The bed had linen sheets with a silk down-filled quilt and pillows; even the additional bedrooms had box beds, with wool quilts stuffed with down, and large sheepskins. The traditional wall-setts ran the length of both sides of the hall. Running central to the hall were stone heating-hearths, four in all, each with its own smoke outlet in the roof. The largest stone hearth was set into the spacious, south-facing kitchen, fully fitted with pots, pans, utensils and free-standing work tables.

A further door led into the herb garden and beyond, the smoke house and curing shed, house-servants' accommodation, a Saturday bath and sauna fed by a well and free-standing enclosed latrines; also, the one-acre field for Victory and the tack store.

As he left the new house, acknowledging his two *huskarl* guards at the door and striding back into the village, Sigrvard was not looking forward to his next meeting with Assi. As he crossed the threshold, she handed him a glass beaker of Frankish wine.

"My lord?" She could always tell when all was not well.

"Assi, I must be away for the next few days. I have ordered Einar to act as your steward in my absence. Tomorrow is *Mánadagr*. I shall return on *Ódinnsdagr*—I pledge you my word."

"But Siggi, must you go now?" Assi questioned him, the disappointment evident in her voice.

"I must, Assi. It is a command. I must travel to the Royal Court at Jelling.* As the new Jarl, I must swear my oath of fealty to the king. In this, I have no choice. I have trading goods for our new home stored in my warehouses by the quayside," he hastily changed the subject. "Take four of my housekarls as escort and select whatever you desire. I have already set several pieces aside to await your approval."

"The list I have in mind is as long as the road to Asgard," she smiled mischievously, steered in that direction by Sigrvard. "Tables, chairs, three-legged stools, linen, furs, storage chests, many lamps, decorations for the walls—"

"Enough!" Sigrvard held up his arms in surrender. "Remember we have only one house. I would ask only that your choices reflect our wealth—no, not the wealth of Sigrvard the Magnificent," he pre-empted her reply, "but rather, the visible evidence of our status and power.

"Also, I would ask that you select our house-servants, male and female, to meet our immediate needs, but as paid freemen," he insisted.

"Siggi, you are aware Einar will be far from happy with this. You know his views on your refusal to own *thralls*."

"Only too well; as you know, it is my legacy from Osgar the Angle. Brr! Odinn's father! Einar may be my blood brother, but he is a *miklimunnr*!** Tell him, as wife of the Jarl, he will follow his Jarl's orders and therefore, your own."

"When do you leave?"

"At first light, with my personal *huskarls*."

"Then we still have this night," she smiled. She took him by the hand and began kissing him tenderly.

* * *

* *The royal seat of Jelling, in the kingdom of Jylland, would become the royal capital of the unified kingdom of Denmark.*

** *Big mouth.*

Einar knocked gently on the door, which Assi soon answered.

"Greetings, mistress of the house. May the blessings of the gods be upon all here."

"Honoured friend of my husband, you are most welcome," she said. Assi smiled the smile of a friend. Einar, that of a snake about to strike. It was the closest he had been to Assi without Sigrvard nearby and he had great trouble controlling his ardour, which he hid with a sweep of his cloak.

She showed him to a seat and almost immediately the first of the potential servants arrived. Although it was dusk, Assi felt the hiring process would not take long, unless Einar was swayed by his feelings about the nature of *thralls* as slaves, rather than Sigrvard's servants. But then, Einar had never been abducted as a child.

Once the future servants had been decided—with little fuss from Einar, much to Assi's surprise—it was time for her to practise her hosting skills. She knew not of the near-death event that had taken place between Sigrvard and his best friend.

Nor did she have any idea how much and for how long Einar had lusted after her. Assi placed a drinking horn and a glass goblet on the small table next to the fire-pit.

They drank as friends, they talked as friends and they laughed as friends. Assi asked about his house in the forest. Einar was only interested in the forest between her legs where Sigrvard pleasured himself each night. She then rose to fetch more drink and as she turned away, Einar slipped a small pouch from under his *kyrtill* and emptied most of its contents into Assi's goblet, tipping the remaining small amount into his horn.

Amantia muscaria was the product of the red-capped, white-dotted mushroom. Crushed and dried, its powder was a powerful hallucinogenic that induced, among other side-effects, delirium and exhilaration, memory loss too. Some called it *Magic Mushroom.*

The outcome, as Einar intended, was carnal. Assi, unknowing and unwilling, succumbed. Her innocent involvement confirmed by her sighs of "Siggi, Siggi" as Einar penetrated her, again and again.

He cared not who she thought was inside her. He was, and that was all that mattered to him. Very quickly, Assi fell asleep and Einar placed her in her cot. He turned to leave and thought, *Again?* but again was never within his capability so he departed for the dark depths of his forest home. A setting that suited his own blackness for Einar rarely had company, save the occasional drunken wench he bedded; but they never stayed the night.

* * *

As Sigrvard approached Jelling, from a distance he marvelled at the defensive, manned wooden palisade, which must have been a mile long. As he approached the entrance to the King's stronghold, he was even more impressed by the biggest pair of gates he had ever seen. He wondered how many longships Arne could make out of the trees required in their construction. Bacsecg was not there to greet the entourage, kings didn't do that kind of thing, but Sigrvard, on dismounting, was escorted immediately to the Great Hall, which dominated Jelling from atop a man-made earthen mound.

He strode up elaborately carved steps and as if by magic, the hall doors opened to welcome him. Trestle tables and benches lined the walls, creating a pathway down the middle to the dais on which stood the longest, widest table Sigrvard had ever seen, fully eighty feet long yet still not touching the side walls. Walls that were regaled by more swords and axes than he thought existed in the whole of Scandinavia. But unlike the hall back home, Bacsecg's had fire-pits either side of the pathway, warming two very long lines of retainers, while serving the middle road to the high table.

The king awaited him, seated on an ornately carved throne.

"Sigrvard, Scourge of the Franks, I welcome you to Jelling."

He rose and stepped forward from his throne.

The king was not a tall man, several inches shorter than Sigrvard, but he was almost as wide as he was tall, and it was all muscle. Sigrvard learnt later that Bacsecg was renowned for his party trick, when too much beer had been quaffed. He would, from a crouching position, grip one end of the huge table and stand up, tipping the table at such an angle that all the plates, drinking horns and the odd drunken guest fell to the floor.

Bacsecg extended his arm and Sigrvard knelt on one knee to pay homage by kissing the king's raven ring, his clan crest. The king drew his sword, laying it horizontally across his knees.

Whilst touching the blade, Sigrvard swore the oath of loyalty to the king, whose courtiers acted as witnesses. Bacsecg motioned him to rise.

Following tradition, it was expected that the king would reward his Jarls well. Bacsecg signalled a courtier to step forward. As *beaga brytta*—the ring-giver—he presented Sigrvard with the gold arm ring, its design based on the sacred oath-ring of Thor. There was an instant bond between the wise King and the teen Seer.

"Come, walk with me," beckoned his host as they withdrew to the king's private chamber to continue what began as a formal exchange but soon became almost a full-blown council of war on a foundation of complete trust. As they talked, Bacsecg confirmed he was aware of his horse-warriors and their fame in battle.

"I have been following your progress with interest, Sigrvard. As you learned from my *Hersir*, Gautrek, I am furnishing you with additional horses to be used as bribes and peace payments, though there is a secondary reason as they will most certainly have other uses."

"A great expedition, my lord?"

"I cannot say more at this stage of the rumours that swirl around Jylland but I will tell you two things. One, there has been much talking at the highest levels and decisions are nigh. Two, I would ask you, on your return to your Jarldom, that you are ready to move towards a war footing with less than one moon's warning."

Sigrvard had learnt quickly that it was better to listen to Bacsecg than talk, so nodded assent.

"You will learn more at the *Althing*. I shall call for my southern Jarls at Hedeby at the appropriate time. By the time we sail, I expect your *herlid* to be fully armed, trained and battle-ready."

"You have my oath, my King, it shall be so."

A smile played about Bacsecg's lips.

"Unless, of course, you are more concerned with your new *langhus*?"

So, Sigrvard realised, the rumour that the king had spies throughout Jylland and beyond was no rumour, and evidently included Eirikrsborg.

"I am told," Bacsecg continued, "that your wealth may soon surpass my own."

"*Nei*, my lord. Mine is that of a *thrall* compared to yours."

Sigrvard had the impression he was treading on dangerous ground.

"A very wealthy *thrall*," the king smiled. It did not reach his eyes. "So, I have a Jarl, a Seer and an important merchant by my side; be aware, I may have use for all three."

"They all stand ready to carry out whatever orders they are given."

"An answer worthy of your adoptive father, 'The Fox.' But now, you must be tired after your journey, I shall have you shown to your quarters and assign you one of my house-servants."

House-servant or spy? Sigrvard wondered.

"Sit by me at our evening meal and we can discuss your thoughts on the best tactics to make full use of your horse-warriors."

* * *

The conversation went long into the night until Bacsecg slumped back in his chair and snored for the heavens. Sigrvard took his leave and was escorted to his quarters. But his journey abed was pleasantly interrupted by Gautrek.

"A word, my friend, if you so please."

"Of course, sire."

"It was with great sadness that I received the news of your father's death. He was a great warrior and my friend. At least I can take solace in the fact that he is feasting in Valhalla, waiting for me to join him."

"I am sure that will not happen for many years," Sigrvard smiled.

"And I never knew you were an optimist," Gautrek returned his smile. "But I am also here on the king's business. Are you prepared to receive your horse-warriors?"

"I shall be, in two weeks. I have allocated one hide of grassland, and the barracks and stables are almost completed."

"Good, then two weeks it is. I shall be accompanying them. I shall report so to the king. Although I have already informed him that you would be ready. Now, I must take my leave and wish you *God rejse.*"*

Again, a *handsel* and he was gone.

Sigrvard fell asleep as soon as his head hit the down-filled pillow that was the size of a small *knarr.***

Despite the enormous amount of beer he had drunk while with Sigrvard, Bacsecg was up with the dawn to bid his new ally farewell.

Sigrvard knew that with added speed, they could return home as night fell, which is what spurred them south to Eirikrsborg where they arrived just as the night-watch was lighting the braziers atop the northern gates.

* *Safe journey.*

** *Cargo ship.*

Sigrvard made straight for home. Assi leapt with joy as she turned at hearing the door open. He barely made three strides before she leapt into his arms. He carried her to bed where she welcomed him home properly.

Preparing food afterwards, Assi couldn't stop talking about all she had been doing for their new home, although she had another task to report to him.

"*Mein fader* has the fever and I have spent time with him also. Now you are returned, I shall replace his servant and tend him myself."

"Of course, my love." Sigrvard expressed concern for his father-in-law's welfare, before steering conversation elsewhere. He asked if her servant recruitment had been successful. She turned and smiled. "You will meet them tomorrow, forenoon. All were instructed on hearing of your return to present themselves here."

A most welcoming night followed the welcoming return, meaning a very happy Sigrvard rose and readied himself to meet his new staff. Assi insisted he take his Jarl's seat to meet his new house-servants from a position of power. He asked where she had found them.

"Your personal *karl madr* and my personal servant are freeborn Denisc, the others are Saxon *thralls*."

"Einar! He knew my orders."

"No! You do not understand. We bought the slaves, yes, but then gave them their freedom—they are now freemen and women and will receive payment for their work."

"Forgive me, I should have trusted you in all things."

"Yes, you should. And now I suggest you meet your new retainers."

First brought to him was his personal servant, Fynn the Dene, who would also be in charge of the other male servants. Sigrvard made it clear he demanded absolute loyalty.

"My lord, I shall earn your trust. My loyalty you already have ten times over." Nevertheless, Sigrvard had him kiss his crested Jarl ring and make his oath to Thor. The choice of Fynn was one he would probably have made himself and was comfortable with it. Next, Assi introduced her choice of Ulvild as her personal attendant, which Sigrvard also considered a good choice. The remaining servants were the Saxons: three male—Eadric, Cenric and Leofric—and six female, including the cook and kitchen maid—Cynburg and Eoforhild. The formality of meeting their master being over, Assi dismissed them.

"They are ready to move to our new house whenever you wish.

They have already cleaned it. In your absence, I chose additional furniture, wall hangings and lamps. Einar took responsibility for stocking the weapons store—enough for an army," she laughed. "I suggest, with your permission, Siggi, that you give me leave to organise the warming of our new home, to drive out any evil spirits."

"Of course," he smiled, "but family and close friends only—it is not a feast."

"*Thakka*, Siggi."

She leant over and kissed him on the tip of his nose, skipping away as he reached out for her.

Svein died the following *Thórrsdagr*, with Assi at his bedside. Sigrvard did his best to console her as she sobbed.

"Siggi, my father may have appeared uncaring and aloof, but that was his defence against emotion after the death of my mother. On my oath, he was a good man, and a good father."

"I do not doubt that, Assi. You know he had my respect."

"Oh, Siggi, what shall I do now?"

"Well, given that you inherit all of his estate, I suggest you purchase a small kingdom," he smiled.

Despite her grief, Assi laughed aloud through her tears.

Sigrvard prayed to Odinn that this would be the last funeral feast of the year.

Having checked the progress for the arrival of his horse-warriors, Sigrvard returned to find a listless and saddened, even confused, Assi, still mourning her father no doubt, but no… "Assi, please let me help. Tell me what ails you."

"Oh, Siggi," she held back a sob. "This was supposed to be a happy time, but now my father will never know his bloodline will live on. I am truly sorry for not telling you before."

"Telling me what?"

"I am with child."

Sigrvard sat motionless.

"Siggi, please forgive me."

"There is nothing to forgive—it is a gift from the gods. Do you know the birthing time?"

"I have spoken to the birthing women and they tell me I shall birth at the end of *Skerpla*."*

* *20 May-18 June.*

He took her in his arms and clasped her to him.

"I am sure your father knows now—he will be celebrating his grandchild in Valhalla. But now, we must plan for our new son.

"We must pray to Frigga and Freyja and sing the *galdr* to protect you and my son. I must see Vidar on his return. It had been agreed I would join a trading voyage to the east at the time of the birthing, from which I must now withdraw—I must be here for the birth and the naming."

Assi held him tighter, but said nothing.

"And we must have a silver key made for you to wear around your neck to ensure an easy birthing."

He left what they both knew unsaid: that his son's lifespan would be decided at birth by the Norn. Assi knew her new-born would not be safe until after the naming. Apart from the risk of death during the carrying time and birthing, if the baby was deformed or sickly, it stood the risk of exposure. It would be left to the elements to ensure its death. Should the child be healthy, Assi would signify her acceptance of the child by nursing it at the breast.

The naming would take place nine nights after the birth. Sigrvard would accept the child by placing it on his knee. Once named and admitted into the family, it could no longer be killed by exposure without it being considered murder. After naming the child, Sigrvard would perform the *vatni ausinn*—sprinkling the baby with water—which gave his son or daughter the right of inheritance.

Assi prayed to Frigga and Freyja it would be a son.

As the guests for the warming of the house arrived, they were greeted by Assi as the mistress of the household, signified by the keys to the house hung on her belt, and she accepted the guests' gifts. All invited brought firewood for the fire-hearths to banish evil spirits from their new home.

The gifts included bread and salt so the home would never know hunger, honey to celebrate the sweetness of life, lamps for lasting light and happiness and ale, beer and mead for prosperity and good cheer. Einar, true to his personality, presented Assi with a new broom.

"May your home be ever free of evil spirits, and as it is a woman's place to work," he smiled at his own wit.

"I thought work was a country to which you have never sailed," Sigrvard joined them. "But worry not—the horse-warriors will be with us in two days, when you will have little time for aught else. Please brother, have food and drink."

"Where's the drink?" was Einar's only reply.

Amongst the guests, Sigrvard had invited Balder, Magnus and Arne. Balder was his usual happy self, complaining about his workload for the *herlid*. Sigrvard, smiling with effort, asked him if he would rather be at the head of a full-frontal assault, which could, he assured him, be arranged. He declined. Sigrvard was relieved he had delegated Balder due to Einar's lack of sympathy with complaints.

Unlike Balder, Magnus, the weapons-maker, had become a friend. Although his workload had increased tenfold, his only comment was that he had brought in additional skilled men to ensure the desired quota was met.

Arne, the shipwright, also ranking as a friend, had also brought in skilled artisans to build and cover the ships that would be needed for this venture. When asked if he knew their destination, Sigrvard had answered truthfully that he did not and would not before the next *Althing*.

It was then he saw Vidar, guarding a plate of food in the corner of the hall, and walked over to him.

"So, my friend and trading partner, still a *skutilsveinn*, I see."

"I was never a trencherman," he protested, his mouth full of food. "I simply have a healthy appetite."

"When you meet your deathday and on your funeral pyre, I shall collect your blubber and burn it in my lamps," Sigrvard patted his friend's more than ample stomach.

"Then your house will smell of fine wine and exotic spices," he laughed heartily. "And I understand congratulations are in order, oh father-to-be."

"*Thakka*, but what of your trading trip to the land of the Rus?"*

"By Odinn's *skagg*, if I never hear the word Rus again, it will be too soon for me," he grimaced.

"Problems?"

"Not with our trading investment, we shall be rich twice over, but it was the voyage to Helheim."

"Come, my friend," Sigrvard took him by the arm, "let us talk where there are no ears—my private rooms."

* *Present-day Russia, Ruthenia and Belarus.*

Sigrvard poured Vidar a large glass beaker of red wine and beckoned him to be seated. “The voyage?”

“The voyage to hell. With their freezing winter, it is impossible to leave until the rivers begin to thaw. The route took us through the Gulf of the Finnr, up the river they call the Niva and into Lake Lagoda—the size of a small kingdom—at the mouth of the Volkhov; even our sails were frozen stiff as a corpse. Were it not for their silver mines and trading network in the east, including the Caliphate of Baghdad and Særkland—the Silk Land—I would have turned for home. The Rus, ruled by their King Rurik from Novgorod, are nothing more than *Sœnskr Vikingr.*

“Miklågard, which they call Byzantium—the great city—is the major trading centre of the East. Many of the Rus have found employment there as the Varangarian Guard—little better than mercenaries.”

“And we brought back?” Sigrvard interrupted him.

“An exotic cargo: silk and embroidered cloth, also glass, ceramics, salt, wine, fruit and spices; copper and lead for our jewellery-makers, quartz, and of course, silver from their mines.”

“Your estimate?”

“Enough for us to retire twice over,” Vidar smiled. “Remember, you are joining me on the next trading voyage.”

“That is what I needed to tell you, Vidar. I shall not be able to join you. I have horse-warriors and a *herlid* to organise and train, the birth of my son and can be called at any time to an important *Althing* by the king.

“Where are we raiding now?”

“I do not know—and that is the truth—but I think this will be bigger than any raid.”

CHAPTER FOURTEEN

IGGI, have you seen Ulfr?"

"Not of late, why do you ask?"

"I feel he is troubled."

"Is he ill, what ails him?"

"Not in the body," Assi frowned.

"Then what?" Sigrvard asked, perplexed.

"Since your father died, Ulfr feels he has no role to play. He spends his time sat with the other old men, telling tall tales and reminiscing on battles past."

"But what can I do?" Sigrvard was genuinely concerned.

"Return to him the spark of life. Were you to offer him a role, he would feel useful once more. When your horse-warriors arrive, surely his experience on the training fields could fulfil that role."

"Could? Of that there would be no doubt. He *would* be useful. He could instil discipline into the men—he put the fear of Odinn into me when I was training—and almost all the new warriors will be young in winters. I shall ensure he and Einar have equal rank—Einar still detests horses, so will no doubt welcome sole responsibility for weapons training."

Assi kissed him on the forehead. "You are a wise leader and a good man, my husband."

"No, Odinn has given me a wife far wiser than I," he smiled.

* * *

As Sigrvard sat for his regular early morning contemplation atop the rocky outcrop high above Eirikrsborg, he pondered how rapidly his life had moved in recent times. In less than nine moons, he had become a husband and Jarl. He had lost a father and gained a reputation. He had lost a mentor and friend but he was thankful to the gods that before the next *Jul*, he would also be a father. As he moved down the steep pathway, known only to him, he walked through the thick pine forest that wrapped itself protectively around his Jarldom.

Just before a sharp left turn and the short distance to home, he looked down the long, narrow street that ran the length of the town, ending at the gates. Then he saw a cloud of dust a little way short of the gates that were already opening slowly.

The horse rapidly closing on the town entrance was riderless until suddenly, a shape swung upwards from beneath the steed into the saddle. Sigrvard smiled. He recognised the rider.

It was Gautrek.

The townsfolk were already there in numbers as Sigrvard noted the huge assembly of horse and riders on the open area in front of the main gates. The people of Eirikrsborg were well acquainted with horse-borne warriors and justifiably proud of the fame brought to their home town by their warrior-seer's exploits; but this was different. His immediate thought, when he spotted the dust-cloud, had been invasion but that was soon a distant concern as he recalled his wedding feast when Gautrek, the king's *Hersir*, had forewarned him that he was to take responsibility for training one hundred of the king's warriors in the horse warfare that had served him so well in Asturias and Francia.

Gautrek slowed his mount to a trot and made his way up the slope to Sigrvard's home. He jerked his legs rigid in the stirrups and ejected himself upwards, out of the saddle and with a flick of his ageing hips, landed in front of Sigrvard. He went down on one knee and in a wide, sweeping, exaggerated movement swept his right arm across his chest and greeted.

"I am your humble servant, Sigrvard, Scourge of the Franks."

"Come here, you stupid old bugger."

They threw their arms around each other and hugged as long-lost brothers.

"What brings you here, my friend? And why the show?"

"Your new charges," he replied, "and I needed to prove that even old dogs can acquire new tricks, especially if it helps keep them barking."

"But so soon. I did not expect such company until *Goi*."*

"The king thought sooner rather than later would be better for more *riddari*."

Just then a rider approached the embracing friends. Sigrvard stepped back in surprise. Gautrek smiled broadly.

"Let me introduce you to my son."

"My lord."

A tall, muscular warrior, some nineteen winters, Sigrvard judged, dismounted and approached him.

"Geir, my lord."

"Geir, your horse-warriors are likely to prove crucial to the forthcoming *fólcvig*. Will your horsemen be ready?"

"More than ready, my lord. I give you my oath. My men know of your fame through the saga. If you take them through the very gates of Helheim itself, they will follow."

"The saga?" Sigrvard asked, amused.

"The saga of your raids on Asturias and the Land of the Franks, and your leadership in battle."

Sigrvard laughed aloud. Gautrek did too.

"You should not believe everything that is told by a Skald, Geir. But, to more pressing matters. Obviously, you have the trust of King Bacsecg and that of this wretch who sired you. You will now hold mine. From this moment on, I appoint you chief of the horse-warriors, answerable only to me, and I expect my every order to be obeyed, instantly. Do you understand?"

"Completely, my lord. By Odinn, I swear you will have the best horse-warriors in the known world."

"The best in the battle will suffice," Sigrvard smiled.

Their barracks had been completed on time: four self-sufficient buildings holding twenty-five men, the remaining half of each *hus* for their horses when indoors. The horses had been brought from Ísland, having first being taken there from Norvegr as part of their colonisation. They were noted for their stamina, being sturdy, strong and sure-footed. At an average pace of four miles in one hour, they were far faster in a charge over a short distance. Almost all the horses stood at fourteen and a half hands. They would be trained to walk, trot, canter, *tolt* and pace. Each rider would be responsible for his own mount's

* *Goi, the fifth winter month.*

health and fitness, as were Sigrvard's fifty existing horse-warriors, their horses being billeted with them.

After arranging for his hundred new guests and their mounts to be quartered and fed, he returned to his home where Assi was already busy preparing breakfast. Gautrek was invited but declined.

"I must away back to Jelling. There is much to be done."

And as swiftly as he had arrived, Gautrek was gone. Sigrvard sent word for Einar to attend him. No words were spoken about before, just a commander instructing his lieutenant.

Einar, avoiding eye contact, listened while Sigrvard explained the training he had planned for the *riddari*. He then took his leave, fuming at the change of leadership ranking.

The first day of training began before dawn, as Sigrvard intended every day would start. The day would not end until the darkness came and even then, there was advantage to be gained from practising without light. It would be intensive.

The training would come from Sigrvard, the tactics from the king or whomsoever should command.

There was nothing intricate to begin with, just several basic rules and manoeuvres, less to remember and easier to train as reflex. Thought and action as one, that was Sigrvard's mantra, drilled into one hundred minds that accompanied one hundred steeds.

But he could only work with what he had to work with and the varying degrees of competence. Some looked born to the saddle, others less so. By the time he finished with them, horse and rider would be as a single unit, in thought and action—like a chattering of starlings in the winter sky. The dawn was still some way ahead as Sigrvard addressed his new charges on the weapons field.

Each man stood alongside his horse and looked surprised as a number of *thralls* walked along the line, handing each rider a small sack. It was empty, which made it harder for them to fathom.

"Before we start what will be a significant stage in all our lives, I order you to place the bag given over your head."

Bemused looks rode along the line of warrior faces that had not a clue as to what was going on or about to happen. But they did as instructed.

"On my word, mount!" ordered Sigrvard.

Before that word had time to sink in, "Mount" came the order.

What followed became the domain of skalds for years to come.

What onlookers witnessed defied description. Some riders fell before mounting, some fell after, on the other side of their horse, some fell backwards and were kicked by their steeds, with many variations besides.

After a few minutes, Sigrvard called a halt and ordered the removal of the hoods that had so encumbered the drill.

"Look around, my brave *riddari.*"

They did so. Some of their company were astride their steeds, beaming with broad smiles, but not many. Most were unmounted and frustratingly so.

"By the time we are finished," said Sigrvard, "you will all be able to mount and dismount with your eyes closed."

Once those words had sunk in, frowns turned into understanding looks. It would not be the last time in the weeks that followed that the newest additions to Viking legend were to be surprised by the actions of the warrior-seer.

The training was intense but Sigrvard noted that as the intensity grew, so too did the rate of learning.

After the hooded start, the riders' next task was far more familiar or so they thought. The *riddari* collected their long bows and mounted for the morning session, which consisted of a shower of arrows at targets a hundred yards distance, followed by a charge at the canter, where arrows were loosed on the run. Surprisingly, despite the unwieldy *ybogi* long bows being a little too long to accommodate from the saddle, a high number of arrows on the run hit their 'straw-men' targets.

"*Gutt,*" shouted Sigrvard as the horsemen completed the forenoon session and settled down for food and drink.

Although there was much respect for the warrior-seer and what he was teaching, there were murmurings at the unwieldy nature of the long bows they had used since childhood.

Sigrvard had anticipated this and while his *riddari* were refreshing, two wagons pulled up to the weapons field and *thralls* began distributing bows that were fully twelve inches shorter than the long bows. They had not seen the like before; "They look like the bows of children" was the majority view.

Sigrvard spoke, "Take heed—I have much knowledge of such weapons from traders of my acquaintance, weapons that proved advantageous when foreign armies, such as the Magyars, attacked Francia.

"So, as soon as Gautrek informed me of my assignment to train you all, I have had my bowmakers working on providing these weapons for you."

But Sigrvard also had an innovation even more surprising than a shorter bow.

By utilising shorter shafts, the *riddari* rendered their arrows useless to the enemy who could not fire them back as they would have conventional bows.

Not unnaturally, there was a new-found appetite for the afternoon session and the new weaponry proved more accurate or rather allowed the *riddari* to improve their accuracy and firing rate. The shorter bow stave also provided the facility to fight in all directions, rotating in the saddle. However, Sigrvard was still unsatisfied. He called Geir, the lead *riddari*, to him.

"I wish you to take several runs and loose arrows, as you have been doing, but I want the rest of your men to observe. Then you shall return to me and I will instruct you further."

Geir did as bid and the *riddari* watched with curious though confused eyes until he returned to Sigrvard, who then addressed them all.

"You will have noted that the new bow is an improvement. But I wish to improve that even more. I noted that every few arrows loosed were released as all four hooves of Geir's horse were off the ground. And on each occasion, the accuracy was greater as, at a certain point, the horse being off the ground provides a brief, but steady, platform for release. You will now repeat what you have just seen."

The *riddari* went back to their task and were amazed at the accuracy of both Sigrvard's observation and their arrows.

The better bowmen began to develop the ability to fire backwards, into the enemy rear, as they rode past. An advantageous position from which to release as the enemy would never anticipate being attacked from behind, thereby rendering them more vulnerable.

They then moved on to spears that required a different set of skills and a completely different style of riding when compared to using spears as foot soldiers. They began with the longer spears, which enabled contact with the target, the enemy, without being close enough for contact by sword. They then switched to the shorter, stabbing spear, and the best of the *riddari* could get two or three short, sharp blows in before their steed took them past the target.

One of the advantages of spears was that several could be carried on horseback, meaning that after throwing some, the rider would have the option, when he only had one or two remaining, to cut and run or continue the fight. The very best could throw two spears at once.

The training continued apace. The days grew longer and so did the training and, pleasingly, so did the fluidity of the *riddari* and their level of competence. Indeed, the group made better progress than Sigrvard could ever have anticipated; he even thought, perhaps, the gods had a hand in the speed with which his new force learned.

And putting aside what Gautrek had said at the wedding about the king's plan, about which he was sworn to secrecy—Seer he might be but even he could not delve the depths of the king's mind.

But curiosity, now that was another matter, and the speed at which the *riddari* had progressed brought the prospect of meeting with the king, and furthering his knowledge of what he had planned, much closer.

After just four weeks, the *riddari* were ready. Sigrvard was amazed. He had been planning for at least three moons and it was not that he had intentionally made the training speedier to reach a quicker conclusion. It was just how quickly the king's men had adapted to the new way of fighting.

As the final session drew to a close, the final day of *riddari* training ended with the horsemen paired up with one steed per pair. The warrior on foot carried a tray bearing several beakers of beer, which he handed to his mounted companion.

The rider then set off to complete a circuit comprising the four sides of the training field; the first side of the square route was at walking pace, the next a trot at smooth pace, then a canter before the fourth and final stage—full gallop. The aim being to spill no wine, at best, but lose no beakers. Lundstrom, the best rider, ironically dropped tray and beakers on the last leg and suffered the forfeit of having to ride the circuit once again, naked, and facing the horse's tail. He took it in good jest while the rest of the group fell about laughing.

Laughter is good, thought Sigrvard. *Better than what they would face on the battlefield.*

Once fed and watered, the 150 *riddari* assembled for the last time on the training field. Sigrvard, on Victory, addressed them.

As he did, a line of *thralls* gifted each of the *riddari* a short bow each, of the type they had trained with.

"I had intended to award the best of you a prize"—murmurs broke out before he continued, "but"—low moans followed—"each of you IS the best. That is prize enough."

Roars of "Sigrvard! Sigrvard!" rang across the weapons field and through the streets and alleys of Eirikrsborg. Assi smiled when her husband's name reached their home. Sigrvard invited Geir to his home that evening.

He asked him to assemble the men the following morning for the journey home. Geir's smile went even wider when Sigrvard informed him that already, several large kegs of beer would be at the Great Hall for their consumption alone, for a job well done.

As morning broke, the *riddari* assembled in line abreast before Sigrvard's home. "You are special," he shouted at the top of his voice, seated on Victory. "Now go and do special things. Follow me home."

He called Einar to his side. "I charge you with protecting Assi in my absence. No greater trust can I have."

"And I, no greater gratitude."

The king's men were shocked at Sigrvard's announcement. They had not known his plan was to lead them home but when they were told, they were joyous.

He had explained to Assi and she understood.

"I will be but four days, maybe five, but I shall miss you every heartbeat of those days."

Einar also felt something: opportunity!

The Seer may have forgotten their dispute, he had not.

The journey back to Jelling went quickly. Sigrvard expected as much because he knew how well his *riddari* had been trained. The crowds of cheering Jelling folk who gathered to greet their returning warriors were impressed at what they saw.

As the *riddari* made their way along the long approach to the magnificent town gates, they went through an impressive routine of formation riding; columns of twos became a wedge, graduating back to a line, twenty horses across, before returning to pairs as they passed through the gates. King Bacsecg, who had witnessed the *riddari* approach, returned to his Great Hall where he sat awaiting his 'new' warriors and their tutor.

Sigrvard dismounted but before he could begin to ascend the steps, Bacsecg stepped down to greet him. Kings didn't do that, but he did.

"Warmest greetings, my dearest friend."

The pressure of his bear-hug indicated to Sigrvard just how well-meaning was the greeting.

They adjourned to Bacsecg's private chamber and discussed everything from warfare on horseback to paternal advice before Sigrvard took his leave for what he intended to be the fastest return journey ever.

Persuasive though Bacsecg could be, he knew it was a forlorn task to persuade his warrior-seer from his flight back to his beloved. Time enough for the Runes.

Bacsecg saluted as his guest began the ride back to Eirikrsborg.

Sigrvard turned as he passed through the magnificent gates, saluted back and turned south, digging his heels into Victory's loins but gently so, in persuasion rather than demand.

He knew his homeward journey should make an overnight camp unnecessary but he did not foresee events that would delay his return.

Several hours after his dawn departure, Sigrvard entered a small but thickly wooded valley with deep sides. *A perfect place for an ambush,* he thought, and instantly he heard a noise all too familiar—battle.

He spurred Victory up the side of the valley and was greeted by a scene of carnage that shocked him momentarily.

There were at least twenty raggedly dressed attackers clawing and slashing away at an even more raggedly dressed victim. What made the scene so shocking was the presence of at least forty blood-stained and limbless bodies strewn in all directions. When he noted more closely, the flailing arms of the figure central to the event, one wielding an axe, the other a huge sword, he realised—BERSERKER.

A legendary, fanatical warrior he may be, thought Sigrvard, *but he is doomed by sheer weight of numbers, unless…*

He spurred Victory forward and smashed into the assailing bunch without mercy. Very soon, twenty became ten and when ten became five, they fled a blood-stained place and two blood-stained warriors—Sigrvard and…

The two stood there, surrounded by bodies and body parts, neither spoke. Though there was just a sword length between them, neither regarded such as any threat.

The Berserker's eyes, very close together, almost as one, stared deep into Sigrvard's eyes. *What's to do?* thought the rescuer. The rescued lowered his weapons but still held them tight.

Then almost as a child, the Berserker burst in the loudest laughter Sigrvard ever believed possible from any human. He lowered 'First Blood' and also began to laugh, more moderately, of course.

"You are?" said the rogue standing before Sigrvard.

"I am Sigrvard of the Denisc, and you?"

"Helhest is what they call me," said the Berserker, in words Sigrvard could understand.

"What have I just interrupted here?" said the Seer.

"Nothing but a minor divert from my homeward journey."

And with those few words, the Berserker turned, stepped over several dismembered bodies, walked between several others and once clear of the killing ground, headed north.

Sigrvard was just about to place his hands on his hips in exasperation when Helhest turned, walked back between the bodies and plunged his sword into the body lying at Sigrvard's feet.

"For you."

He turned once more and in the blink of an eye was a distant thought as he strode, at near running speed, north. Sigrvard did not cease shaking his head until Victory had borne him several miles from the strangest event he had ever encountered.

His lack of concentration, as he made his way through a rock-strewn landscape, nearly proved costly as Victory, usually the most sure-footed of mounts, caught his front right hoof on an outcrop of stone that seemed to be growing out of the ground.

With lightning speed and agility, Sigrvard leapt from his steed and instantly checked his horse's hoof. Thankfully, Victory was none the worse, neither was he, then he noticed what had caught the hoof in the first place. It was not a rocky outcrop but a huge, carved obelisk, fully ten feet in length and half that in width and depth.

Closer examination of such a curious object was required. And what Sigrvard determined from his examination was to turn his head, in more ways than one.

He uncovered the stone block after scraping away what seemed years of moss and brush that had obscured it. But nature had been assisted because Sigrvard noted that the sides of the trench in which the obelisk lay, for it was no random block of stone, had been carefully dug out. And had it not been for natural movement of the terrain, it would have remained hidden from sight, which he determined was the very intent of those who had carried out its internment. Luckily, the sun was setting, for weathering had eroded the previously sharp runic inscriptions and shadows enabled pin-sharp definition, allowing what he who had carved the inscriptions had intended. As the Seer sank on bended knee, his blood ran cold at what he read:

Dawn broke such a colour as had never been—a portent heralded by a shaking of the air ten thousand times ten thousand more than thunder.

The earth did issue forth with the darkness of Helheim that stole the sun from the sky. All living creatures fled. Some hid, many died.

Eventual calm begat a new world, ash-covered as far as the eye could see.

Crops failed, beasts perished, people panicked.

Seventy winters passed—order restored but people watched each dawn, more fearful thereafter.

Sigrvard then understood the presence of the human skeleton he found buried under the obelisk. Not a sacrifice to the gods but a deed to hide for all time the message contained thereon.

He understood that the local Jarl must not have wanted such ominous Runes to become common knowledge. Knowledge that would undermine central control, knowledge that had to be killed, like the poor soul who carved such portentous inscriptions.

As a Seer, nay, as a Dene, he was more than familiar with Ragnarok, the End of the World Day. The day when the ground would shake and three uninterrupted, long, cold winters that would last three years—with no summer in between. In the aftermath, the world would be plagued by wars and brother would kill brother.

He was even more troubled as he slid his fingers in the grooves of the Runes. A vivid scene flashed into his conscious mind. He closed his eyes and the scene was even more real—dark, volcanic ash spewed skyward; two, three—no, more—seven, eight cone-shaped summits thrust from the earth's innards till streams met and the sky was black.

Even though it was a subliminal occurrence, Sigrvard could feel the dry, burning ash on his lips. He could do nothing. It would run through his conscious mind, which tried to clear the apocalypse, until he could decide what to do with the unearthed portent of doom and beyond.

Leave it be. That was his decision and it did not take him long to cover what had lain hidden for so long. Not only did he carefully replace the sods of earth but he took some nearby saplings of varying growth and replanted them around and on the slightly raised mound he had created. A few stamps of Victory's hooves in between the saplings and rapid growth in an otherwise remote area and once more, the hidden message would be hidden, erased—but not from his mind.

Sigrvard didn't even look back as he rode away, but he knew it was there, and he knew he would carry it for life.

As he climbed the last brow and Eirikrsborg sprawled before him, his only longing was for Assi.

CHAPTER FIFTEEN

AS *Goi* passed into *Einmánudur*, the feast of *Eostre** would be held to Ostara, the goddess of spring, and Freyja, for renewal and fertility. Gifts of coloured eggs would be exchanged. Sigrvard was now seventeen winters and stood five feet eleven inches, muscular with a well-trimmed blonde beard, gathered at its tip into a gold dragon beard ring, and taller than the average Dene, with only dim memories of his *fadelsdagen*, but knew it had been around this feast time. He had decided *Eostre* was as good a time as any to celebrate his birthday. He told Assi of his decision on the way to the *langhus* for the celebration.

"*Til hammómed amo*," Assi congratulated him.

"*Thakka*, but I would prefer we kept this to ourselves."

"As you wish, my lord."

The next day, Gautrek arrived with six *huskarls* as escort. It was a surprise, a point made by Sigrvard.

"My king asked me to travel to express how well-pleased he is with the progress of the mounted warriors." He mused at such a gesture to convey that which had already been conveyed. He wasn't wrong.

Over a beaker of wine at Sigrvard's house, Gautrek, sat facing him, leaned forwards.

"It is not for me to give you details of the forthcoming war, but I must impress upon you the importance of bringing your *herlid* up to battle-readiness. How many can you raise?"

"With my horse-warriors, *huskarls* and trained warriors, adding to the freemen farmers, artisans and field workers—with sickles and such for weapons—I would estimate around six hundred."

* *20 April-21 March.*

Gautrek scratched his beard thoughtfully.

"Their training is well in hand. So, this is a war, not a raid?" Sigrvard asked the obvious.

"This is why it is being called 'The Great Army', and that is all I can tell you. You must wait until the *Althing*, and now, if I can impose on your hospitality further, I need to rest."

"Of course, a room has been prepared for you, and setts in the hall for your men."

"Thank you, Jarl Sigrvard, then I will bid you goodnight."

Sigrvard was restless that night. Frisia? Frankenland? Where? Finally, he drifted into a fitful sleep.

* * *

At the beginning of *Harpa*, Vidar sailed for Serkland—the lands of the Arab. Before he left, Sigrvard asked him to bring back examples of their Islamic silver dirham coinage, usually melted down by the Denisc or used in jewellery.

"Silver coins?" Vidar's response was predictable. "Why? We have no use for them. Those we bring back, we waste time melting them down for use as 'hack-silver' for shaving down using our scales and weights. They are superfluous to our Denisc economy."

"It may not be so in the future. As a Seer, I have an idea this may change in times to come."

"In your role as Seer, I cannot but believe your predictions—as a merchant, you have made me wealthy in the extreme. Is there more?"

"Yes, my friend. Sometime after the birthing, I shall require half of our trading fleet to be converted to readiness for war."

"War? The one word that means loss of trade. I am loath to tie up half of my ships."

"*Our* ships, my business partner," Sigrvard reminded him. "I need them for my own cargo."

"Ah! Loot, the spoils of war," he laughed in relief.

"No, I need them adapted to carry horses."

Vidar stopped laughing.

"I am afraid this is not a request. It is an order from your Jarl."

"As you command—my lord," he added as an afterthought. "In that case, please return with the ships intact," he grimaced. "On a happier note, please pass on to Assi my prayers and hopes for a successful birthing—I feel as an expectant grandfather!" he smiled, as Sigrvard poured him a large drink.

"In a way, you are, my friend," Sigrvard returned his smile. "We both gain an heir to further build on that which we have achieved."

"And now, I must say *far vel*, my friend, I sail on the tide."

They hugged each other, more as father and son than friends.

The month of *Skerpla* passed quickly in battle training, local *Thing* meetings, hunting with Einar and his dogs and concern over Assi's birthing. He must admit, he did not entirely enjoy the bear hunting with Einar, whose hounds should have been guarding the gates of Helheim. Einar had three dogs bred from the *torvmosehund*, the ancient Dene 'swamp dog', bred for hunting large game, including bear.

One, he had named Raven after one of Odinn's wolves, the others Gifr—savage, and Vigi—the killer. He had chosen their names well. Sigrvard had also forbidden Einar to bring them across his threshold, near Assi.

At the beginning of the month of *Sólmánudor*, Assi's birthing began. The 'helper woman' midwife and the others to be there were called, and Sigrvard was barred from the birthing room. It was also the day before the feast of the summer solstice,* when the power of *Sól* was at its height. His son would be born as a 'Child of the Light'.

At last, the helper-woman summoned him.

"My lord, your prayers have been answered—you have a beautiful daughter."

Sigrvard wrestled with his hopes for a son.

"The child is free of deformity or blemish. Both the mother and child are healthy and well, praise be to Frigga and Freyja."

He realised the uppermost thought in his mind was relief and gratitude to the gods, if this was their wish. Once she approached twelve winters, the gods willing, he would ensure he arranged her a good marriage. After all, he and Assi would have ample time to breed a male heir to carry on the bloodline. He felt a sense of contentment as he went to greet his new daughter.

Nine days later, at the naming ceremony, surrounded by friends as witnesses, he held his new-born on his knee and sprinkled her with water, accepting her as his daughter. With Assi's agreement, he named her Astrid—divine beauty.

* *20 and 21 June.*

"Assi, the king has already held an *Althing* with our allies, the northern Jarls and their war chiefs, no doubt this will be the same. He will be looking to appoint additional war leaders whom he can trust to care for his interests on the forthcoming campaign."

"You?" asked Assi apprehensively.

"I know not. I cannot control fate, nor can I tell you when I shall return; the gathering could last several days. I shall give my brother Einar his orders before I leave.

"You will take your personal *huskarls*?"

"The king has limited retinues to twelve men. That is what I shall take, including six of my horse-warriors."

Sigrvard held her in his arms and kissed her long and tenderly.

"And now, I must prepare."

* * *

As he entered the gate through the palisade once more with his retinue, he could not help but be impressed by the largest trading centre in Jylland. He remembered even a church had been built, some fifteen winters past, as an expression of their intentions and the importance they set on visiting Christian traders. It was now mid-*Tvimánudur** and the height of the trading season. It would feature more prominently in the future, of that Sigrvard was certain.

*Heidabyr***—heath settlement—was comprised of over a thousand citizens, the majority living in small houses crammed together on east-west streets leading to the harbour and its many jetties; living in overcrowded, disease-ridden squalor, hidden beneath the town's prosperity. Lying as it did, forming part of Jylland's southern border, its defensive ramparts were semi-circular and faced inland, built of soil and rock, topped with turf and wood. The rampart was connected to the Danevirke, a defensive border running a distance of almost fifty miles, from the Schlei Fjord to the River Treene, thus enabling the Denisc to control all traffic on the Ox Road, the main north-south route, which itself ran through the Danevirke at Heidabyr.

To the south, a straight rampart ran between Selk Nor and the

* *22 August to 20 September.*

** *Hedeby.*

marshes of the River Rheide for ten miles, with only one gate and built as an earthen and timber wall with a V-shaped ditch.

King Bacsecg had evidently summoned every southern kingdom to this meeting: Jylland, Fynn, Lolland, Sjœland and Skåne. As they entered the turf courtyard of the king's fortification, Sigrvard noted in particular the flag of Norwvegy flying alongside the king's. As they dismounted, the now familiar figure of Gautrek, the King's *Hersir*, pushed his way through the throng of retinues and Sigrvard accepted his outstretched hand.

"Welcome Sigrvard, I am glad you are here. I regret, no armed warriors in the retinues are allowed into the main hall, the only exception being the Jarls and their war-chiefs.

"We have quartered your men nearby, and pottage and ale await them after their ride."

"It is not a problem, Gautrek," Sigrvard gestured to Geir to join them.

"Geir, greet Gautrek, the king's marshal. Your *fadir* has forgotten more battles than you will see in your lifetime."

"Indeed, my lord, something he has told me of, often."

"Gautrek, I am proud to present Geir, the commander of my horse-warriors, who, of course, you know."

"I am pleased with this. I have an idea your horse-warriors will be of great advantage to us in this venture."

"We stand ready, my lord. *Thakka*."

Geir returned to the care of his mount.

"Odinn's *skagg*! I could swear you grow taller with every passing winter, Sigrvard," Gautrek laughed. "Come, I will escort you to your quarters. The council will meet tomorrow forenoon, but tonight, you will feast and drink as the king's guests."

The Royal Feast had been much as Sigrvard had expected, from mussels and oysters to spit-roasted venison and beef and, it seemed, almost everything else in Midgard that was edible.

As with every meal, the *seax* and fingers were used, the silver finger bowls being changed constantly as they became greasy. There was one aid to eating the lobster, which Sigrvard had not seen before, a small silver replica of the hammer of Thor used to crack the shell before pulling it apart with fingers. Sigrvard found it ironic that the more Frankish wine the feast drank, the more it added to his trading profits.

What he had not expected was to be seated at the top table next to

Gautrek—the king's table, usually reserved for the king's most senior Jarls and advisors. It was now the forenoon and the great hall was filled with the Jarls from the south.

It was also filled with the stench of latrines, stale cooked food, candle wax and the smell of human sweat. It would not be *laugard-agr*—bath day—for another five days, not a tradition Sigrvard adhered to or that Assi would allow. The meeting was called to order by Gautrek, the king rising from his ornately carved, high-back chair to address the assembly. Following his thanks to all in attendance, he wasted no further time on pleasantries.

"It must be accepted by all present that we are outgrowing our kingdom. There is no longer land for all or soon, enough farmland to feed our people and the Denisc increase in number with every moon."

There was a murmur of assent. Sigrvard was also politically aware that the precarious, centralised power of the king was beginning to be challenged by Jarls constantly striving for more independence and the acquisition of more land. The lands they held in fealty to the king, they treated as their own autonomous kingdoms.

"We must recognise we have no choice but to expand our lands, and have formed an agreement to achieve this end.'

The reaction of the Jarls rippled through the hall as a wave of consternation.

"And whose lands do we invade, my lord?" asked the Jarl of Heidabyr, one of the most powerful.

"Angleland, my lords," the king stated simply, "but more than invade," he added but that was lost in a sea of noise.

Once more, the rumbling ripple of movement through the hall, as restless as cattle at the market.

"Which kingdom, my lord?" questioned Heidabyr, who seemed to be their self-appointed spokesman.

The king paused before answering, "All of them." For he knew there would be less threat to his autonomy with vast tracts of Anglo-Saxon kingdoms to distribute rather than the limited amount of land at home.

Sigrvard knew this would mean the Englar kingdoms they called Anglia, Mercia, Wessex and the kingdom of his birth, Nordumbraland. He also knew Jylland did not have a *herlid* large enough to achieve this alone.

Bacsecg raised his arms to restore silence.

"We do not go to England as *Vikingr* to raid but to conquer and rule a new land of the Deniscan. This new kingdom will provide estates, farmland, *thralls* and wealth for all my Jarls."

The assembly's rumble turned to one of approval. Bacsecg understood the power of greed.

"We shall not be returning to Jylland—except on our shields," the king continued. "As we speak, there is assembling a great fleet—more than the Englar would ever imagine. This invasion will be Deniscan-led, with our new allies, Norwegr, and will field the largest army. There will also be a smaller number joining us from Sœnskr and Irskr."*

A stunned silence fell across the Great Hall.

* *Sweden and Ireland.*

CHAPTER SIXTEEN

IT has been agreed by all members of this coalition that its overall leaders will be the sons of Ragnar Lodbrok, Hingewar—Ivar the Boneless—Halfdan and Ubbe. Under their leadership, each Jarl will be responsible for their own part of this Great Winter Army."

Sigrvard could immediately see Bacsecg's astute and devious reasoning in the choice of leaders. Their father, Ragnar, known as 'hairy breeches' due to his animal-skin clothes made by his wife, had been killed at the hands of Ællla, King of Nordumbraland. To his sons, this was a blood feud—revenge—fighting under their *Vikingr* raven banner.

Ivar, being King of the Dublin *Vikingr*, would explain their presence in the Great Army. Of all the possible leaders of the invasion, the brothers would die in battle rather than accept defeat. Bacsecg had made a wise choice.

Ivar was also reputed to be the wisest of the three brothers. Sigrvard had also heard that he was known as 'Boneless' due to him having no bones in his legs and must be carried around on a shield, but this Sigrvard would believe it when proven to his own satisfaction. He became aware the king had not yet ended his address.

"My command as your king is that your warriors and ships are on a war-footing by the beginning of *Gormánudur*,* and assemble at Vestervig, where the Lim Fjord meets the North Sea. The Great Army's camp will be nearby at Aggersborg. You have much to put in place and not least, to counsel your war-chiefs on what is expected of them. I will

* *21 October to 19 November.*

detain you no longer." As the assembly broke up, Gautrek pushed his way through to Sigrvard.

"Sigrvard, the king wishes you to remain until tomorrow forenoon."

"Do you know why, old friend?"

"*Ja.* For once, I do. As the most renowned Seer in Jylland, he wishes you to read the Runes."

"And what does he expect the Runes to tell him?"

"Simply, the outcome of the invasion."

"Oh, is that all? Gautrek, I am a Seer, not Odinn!"

Gautrek laughed. "I shall send for you in the forenoon, when the king requires your presence."

Sigrvard knew his reading would have to be dictated by logic rather than magic. He asked himself what Froda would have done in this situation. He received no reply.

Gautrek led Sigrvard into the king's private chambers.

"Ah, Jarl Sigrvard, the Seer. You have done the reading?"

"I have, my lord."

"And what do the Runes tell us?" There was a nervous edge to the expectancy in the king's voice.

"That the invasion will succeed, my lord, and England will become home to the Denisc."

"Thanks be to Odinn!" The king sounded relieved, then studied Sigrvard's reaction and the barely discernible pause. "But, Seer?"

"But, there will be great slaughter and kings on both sides will die. This conflict will take longer than anyone has anticipated."

"How long?"

"The Runes predict years rather than months, my lord."

"*Thakka,* Seer. But now, to Sigrvard the Jarl. Your prediction bears out my own opinion on planning for the invasion.

"Your reading has determined my course of action. I shall remain in Jylland to ensure its continuity and defence, should our enemies decide to try and take advantage of the situation. Once the Great Winter Army have consolidated their gains, I shall lead a Great Summer Army to reinforce you and ensure a successful outcome—victory."

He ordered wine to be brought and Sigrvard sat with the king as commanded.

"Sigrvard, I have talked at length with Gautrek and we are of the same mind. You will be my representative on the inner war-council of the Great Army, and speak for me in all things."

Sigrvard was not exactly over-pleased at the king's confidence in his abilities. "My lord, I thank you. I shall endeavour to speak on your behalf to the best of my abilities."

"Good. I am also entrusting to you an additional 1,000 warriors to be under your direct command and in the summer, I shall bring with me 100 additional horse-warriors."

"Again, I thank you, my lord."

Bacsecg stood, indicating the audience was at an end.

As Gautrek walked with him into the daylight, Sigrvard turned to him.

"Gautrek, you will be leading the Denisc *herlid*?"

"No, my friend. That is why the king asked you to speak in his stead. I remain to bring what will be the Great Summer Army up to battle-readiness. I cannot read the Runes as you, Sigrvard, but I think the conquest of England will take far longer than its leaders allow, even if our army stays together as one force. It is dangerous to presume every battle fought will end in victory, or that the Englar kingdoms will throw down their arms and submit. I have never known an army that did not suffer a defeat in battle, even if they win the war."

"I wish you would be with me, my friend, I value your experience and advice."

"Who will you take as your war-chief?"

"Einar, my standard bearer, to lead the warriors on foot, and Geir, who you met, as commander of my horse warriors."

"A good choice. And now?"

"Now? A battle I cannot win."

Gautrek raised his eyebrows in question.

"Assi," Sigrvard explained. "I must find a way to tell her I must be away for a winter or more."

"That is a battle even I could not win," Gautrek laughed. "I wish you well, my friend." He held out his hand. "*Far vel*, Sigrvard, and as a personal favour, do your best to stay alive."

"I intend to, my friend," Sigrvard clasped his hand and smiled. "I intend to."

On the ride back to Eirikrsborg, Sigrvard explained to Geir what had taken place. He listened in silence. Finally, he asked a question, but not one Sigrvard had anticipated.

"I have heard Ivar the Boneless is also a Berserker, is that true?"

"I have also heard so. If true, I thank Odinn he and his Berserkers are not at the head of my warriors." Sigrvard was unsmiling.

"But why?" Geir asked in surprise. "They are our fiercest warriors, with superhuman strength and are impervious to weapons."

Sigrvard sighed and tried to be logical. The Berserkers—'bear coats'—wore wolf and bear coats without armour. They fought in a seemingly uncontrollable trance, which Sigrvard was convinced was achieved by ingesting bog myrtle, fuelled by alcohol. He turned in his saddle.

"Geir, have you ever gone into battle with Berserkers?"

"No, but—" He had no opportunity to mention Helhest.

"I thought not. I have. They had the gall to inform me that, when in their howling rage, they did not differentiate between friend or foe, indiscriminately killing and maiming anything in their path—including our own warriors. They are unstable and uncontrollable. I would rather my warriors died at the hands of our enemies, not our own Berserkers."

Geir nodded in understanding and fell silent. As he dismounted, Sigrvard knew this was not to be an easy homecoming. He was right.

"Angleland?"

"England," he confirmed to Assi.

"Do you want our daughter to lose her birthright?" It was a rhetorical question.

"Assi, please listen to me. In years to come, the Denisc could face a breakdown of their way of life by too many hungry mouths to feed—even war between Jarls to gain enough land to ensure their survival. If order crumbles, our enemies will seize the opportunity to attack. The *only* solution is to expand the land of the Dene."

"But I know there will be women and children sailing with the fleet," she protested.

"Certainly, but not the wife and children of a Jarl. The only place I can guarantee your safety is here, in Eirikrsborg. I will not have my family—my bloodline—put at risk. I shall ensure you have adequate warriors to protect you. The king himself would not ask me to leave my family and estates vulnerable.

"When we settle in England, it will be as a family, with increased lands and power. As your husband and Jarl, I forbid you to join the fleet, because I love you. You are more precious to me than anything else in this world—even my own life."

Assi knew she had lost the argument but in her heart, she also knew Sigrvard was right.

"How long?" she asked in a subdued voice.

"I know not, even as a Seer. As soon as we have secured the kingdom, I shall send for you, or come for you myself. You have my oath."

"And if you are in Valhalla?" She held back a sob.

"If I am slain, then we have suffered defeat and you and Astrid are more secure here. The warriors I leave you, you will use to enforce your power as my wife to rule my—your—estates, do you understand?"

"Yes, Siggi."

"Assi, I love you." It was a simple statement of fact.

That night, Assi slept with a heavy heart.

* * *

Sigrvard had been wondering for some time, ever since he had returned to Eirikrsborg, when the king's plan would have more substance. Substance that was ever more solid when he informed the new Jarl he was to return with him in the forenoon. Einar was to accompany his Jarl on the journey north, along with the fifty *riddari* who were to join up with their northern counterparts under Einar, while Sigrvard would return to Eirikrsborg to finalise preparations for the bulk of his warriors, once he had attended the war council for final orders.

They made camp for their one night, just half a day's journey from the king's stronghold, before the war council, where the armies of Ubba, Ivar and Halfdan had assembled, along with the warriors of Bacsecg, Ivar's brother.

There was little desire or inclination for conversation so they took to their sleeping bags and they settled to their slumber.

Sigrvard struggled to sleep as he awaited the morning and the start of what he knew was more than a raid. The camp awoke as the early morning mist still hung heavy on the air but as it slowly lifted, the Viking army was shocked at what slowly revealed itself.

Stretched some sixty feet across between two huge oak trees was a long, plain and tall fabric screen. Hidden from the front, where Denisc warriors were rubbing their eyes at what they beheld, was the full extent of this mysterious manifestation. It stretched back at least a hundred strides with two walls closing up into the sharp end of a huge triangular encampment.

Denisc hands, immediately twitchy, grasped sword handles, spear or shield. But forward progress to inspect the newly arrived phenomenon, which most certainly had not been there as a drink-soaked warrior band had gone to its bed, was halted by Sigrvard. Their leader, clearly unsurprised, stood before his men and quietly ordered.

"No one is to approach. Our guests will not be disturbed. I shall engage when it is right."

Sigrvard wheeled away back to his tent, his men did as they were ordered.

Einar was close behind his Jarl as he threw himself onto his sleep place.

"They are here, then."

"They are," said Sigrvard who was ready for what came next from his trusty aide.

"You still think it is a good idea?"

"Yes," replied Sigrvard, who was never the most talkative first thing in the morning. 'It is a heavy burden to be both Jarl and Seer,' he used to whisper under his breath.

Einar was already on his way out of the tent flap as his old friend rolled over and wrapped himself in several woollen fleeces to grab what sleep remained to seek.

The newcomers were Berserkers. The warrior-seer had a secret weapon. When unleashed, even the battle-hardened Vikings regarded them with a combination of fear and awe.

Back in his cot, Sigrvard lay restless. He knew what to expect next and it had little to do with his sixth sense as a Seer.

The tent shook like the west wind as the flap burst open to reveal a familiar figure to Sigrvard.

"Ho!" it bellowed.

Helhest was back.

Before Sigrvard could react, his visitor was across the floor in an instant, wrapping his bear-like embrace around the man who had saved his life, lifting him off his feet.

"Greetings, my, mmm, old friend," for he could think of nothing else to say to a wild man he had known for all of the three minutes it had taken to butcher two dozen enemies.

Sigrvard offered his guest a drinking horn. Helhest chose, instead, the keg, which he raised and quaffed with extreme haste. Noting his host's quizzical look, he roared.

"Needs quick, never know when next drink."

Sigrvard asked, "What brings you and your men here?"

"We hear that big fight is ahead for you. You help me. I help you!"

Sigrvard thought about detailing the outline plan for what lay ahead, all that he knew anyway, ahead of the war council. It was a thought that he quickly dismissed. It would, in his judgement, be sufficient to tell his new 'friend', "Two days hence. Meet me at Ribe, dawn."

Helhest grunted, rose and rushed out of the tent as quickly as he had entered.

Sigrvard's mind and face were of similar blankness as he began to contemplate the war council, the Great Army, its assault on England, horses carried over the sea and his 'secret weapon'.

A secret weapon that had decamped and departed before he had changed his clothes and emerged to inspect his own men.

An 'ally' that went back to wherever it came from, and one that Sigrvard hoped was as ferocious as its reputation.

The meeting of the warrior chiefs was not until noon so after breakfast, Sigrvard offered Einar the chance to pit his wits against him, once more, on the gaming board.

"*Hnefatafl* and maybe a chance to learn from the master?"

Sigrvard was jesting. Einar was not amused but hid it very well.

As one game followed another, it was a familiar pattern to all those games they had played since their youth. Sigrvard trouncing his friend and Einar failing to learn as one should from reverses and setbacks.

Suddenly, it was after five or six humiliating defeats, for Einar, that their game was interrupted by one of Ivar's *huskarls*.

None of Sigrvard's retinue would dare but the messenger had ignorance to thank, though he little knew it, for being able to walk away unscathed after disturbing that which should not.

"My lord, King Ivar commands your presence at his pavilion for a council of war."

Sigrvard nodded with the slightest deference that even Einar failed to detect.

After the messenger's exit, Sigrvard whispered to his close friend, "So, obviously Ivar has taken the title of King of Dublin."

Ivar's tent was the largest in camp, with a pavilion of cloth sheets, hides and skins, the most luxurious of which, from a Minke whale, covered the entrance to the inner sanctum of the Great Army leader.

As Sigrvard strode closer to the pavilion, the two *huskarls* standing guard knew of the impending visitor and crossed spears were rapidly reversed while he was still seven strides from the entrance.

One of the guards pulled back the Minke skin and, being those four inches taller than the average Dane, Sigrvard arched his frame to step inside.

"Come," was the first word Sigrvard ever heard, directly addressed to him by Ivar whose right leg was hooked over the arm of a gilded throne. A keepsake he had taken a shine to on one particularly lucrative raid on a monastery outside Dyflin—Dublin.

There was the slightest of movement from the left arm, the index finger in fact, beckoning Sigrvard closer.

"Your reputation precedes you, Seer. I will need you to cast the Runes on this invasion."

Sigrvard immediately picked up on the word 'need' rather than 'want', or indeed any other word of command rather than request.

"Of course, my lord. I am at your command."

Sigrvard pulled the small velvet bag from behind his back, strung from the waist as always. He placed a white cloth on the table, carefully moving Ivar's wine-horn, taking care not to soil the divination with spilt wine.

Twenty-four Elder Futhark Runes and one blank fell on the cloth and in unison, as if so ordained by some ethereal force, lay there in neat precision, five times five. Some of the Runes fell face up, they were the ones to foresee the answer to Ivar's unspoken question. Those that fell inscription down were ignored. Sigrvard could feel Ivar's searing gaze burning into his mind but he would not give the crippled leader the satisfaction of hastening his determination from the Runes.

The Seer pinched the bridge of his nose, knowing the added delay would anger and intrigue Ivar in equal measure, and turned toward him.

"The Runes do not see a battle in this kingdom, although it will come. They see our army fighting in the north. They see also the conquest of England taking seven winters."

It must be catching, thought Sigrvard as he noted Ivar scratching his head before speaking.

"I can't see whether you are of more value as a Seer or a warrior," and smiled. At least Sigrvard thought it was a smile. He was about to respond when Ivar spoke further, "Although the application of logic and intelligence would suggest both."

Sigrvard felt uncomfortable under Ivar's gaze but the double-handed compliment countered the unease he felt at the suggestion that his usefulness as both warrior and Seer to the Boneless one meant twice the chance of not incurring his wrath.

"Tell me one more thing, and I seek your view as a warrior, not a Seer."

"Ask."

"Bacsecg has placed your *riddari* with ours, under the command of your standard bearer, answering to me. That I understand, but what of the plan for all *riddari* sailing to England separate from our main war fleet?"

A not unreasonable question from a cripple whose only interaction with horses was when his war-chariot carried him into battle. And even then, his perspective, of the horse's arse, hardly qualified Ivar to appreciate tactical analysis.

"Your brother decided, after careful consideration, that because there were an unusually high number of horses being taken across the *Anglis Kanal*, reducing the amount of time they spent on the uncertain open sea would minimise the chances of panic among the steeds. Once the two groups of *riddari* meet up on the coast, they will board the transport ships for the coast-hugging three-mile horizon journey down the coast of Francia.

"The ships would then turn north and sail towards the coast of East Anglia where they would connect with the main war fleet and its several thousand warriors."

Those details, conveyed to Ivar, were imparted to Sigrvard out of necessity by Gautrek from the king, ahead of the council that would accept the plan after a certain amount of posturing.

Posturing that Bacsecg had factored into the plan knowing his brothers, also sons of Ragnar Lodbrok, of old. Persuading them it was their joint idea, with equal influence attributed to each, ensured Bacsecg's intention was adopted.

But Sigrvard hadn't provisioned for Ivar's input, which was instant and, in fairness, perceptive.

"I am no Seer but a practical man. This plan has merit but I am thinking: would it not mean fewer supplies would have to be carried if the entire fleet met at Ribe then voyaged across to the coast of East Anglia, arriving together?"

"As the council wills it."

As Sigrvard and Einar entered the Great Hall, Einar for the first time, once again its magnificence was overwhelming.

"Come," roared Bacsecg from his place at the centre of the huge trestle table, with Ubba, Ivar and Halfdan, "let us feast before we talk."

Sigrvard noticed something different about the top table from his previous visit. The table had been cut in two and the equal parts had been pushed out to create a gap, occupied by a slightly higher table at which the sons of the legendary Ragnar sat. *Ingenious,* he thought to himself. *Bacsecg is prominent but no more so than the other three, except in reality.*

After much merry-making, Bacsecg and the top table of brothers and warrior leaders adjourned to his private chamber for the council of war.

From north and south, east and west, the Viking leaders sat at the round table that dominated the king's chamber. It was the largest gathering of Scandinavian warlords ever and the most significant, as the specially invited new Jarl of Eirikrsborg was about to find out. Before rowdiness broke out, Bacsecg rose to his feet. He glanced around the table, left to right, then right to left. Satisfied, he had their attention, he began with a quiet authority.

"For nearly one hundred summers, we have been a Viking over the sea to a divided land that offered much reward. Raids aplenty that enriched our coffers and our people but raids, nevertheless. A few longships here, several longships there; sometimes a few days, sometimes a few weeks.

"Foraging to survive when our supplies were gone then seeking enough to carry us back home. Some of our longships returned home with bounty, some very little and as we all have lost comrades, some did not return."

Sigrvard only had two raids to his credit while many of the heads nodding assent around him had been raiding since long before his birth. The king continued.

"No more small raids. No more hit and retire. BUT MORE!

"We have a new objective. Francia, for so long bountiful and vulnerable, is no longer either. They have become wise to our tactics and their towns are increasingly fortified. Their religious communities, previously rich pickings, now move inland and away from the threat of our raids.

"Times are changing. We must change also.

"We are *Vikingr* but we are also farmers. We will target the kingdoms of Angleland. We invade Angleland. We CONQUER Angleland."

The table-banging that followed was endorsement enough for Bacsecg, not that he needed it but universal approval from the war leaders ensured his brothers were kept in check.

"Now go to your beds but first, tell your warriors I will speak to them once assembled on the coast before we sail TO CONQUER ANGLELAND!"

CHAPTER SEVENTEEN

THE journey home for Sigrvard was uninterrupted. He decided that because future meant a lengthy spell away with the Great Army, one less day at home was not desired. Einar and his *riddari* would return to Eirikrsborg after a week's training with their counterparts of the Great Army.

Assi was her usual loving self to her Siggi once she had him to herself that evening, after he had dealt with the tasks being the new Jarl entailed.

While Sigrvard awaited the return of Einar, he had plenty to occupy his time. As the days were getting longer, fewer folk required his services as the Seer, meaning he could implement his plan to train extra *riddari*, for he knew not what awaited the Great Army in England now that the intent was conquest and not plunder. Always looking to innovate, Sigrvard introduced variations that to the neutral looked strange but they were all carefully considered and when possible, tested first.

The *riddari* training took place after forenoon of personal training each day when Sigrvard had already practised his weapon skills, particularly the sword. He had long been the most proficient of the Denisc with a blade but he had noted something in combat in Asturias that he wished to implement if it proved useful. But for that to be achieved, he had to alter the generations of swordplay every Viking mastered as a boy: hack and slash.

The Viking sword was simply a metal bar with two sharpened edges and a rounded point. There was very little stabbing, hence a concentration on sweeping, slashing blows intended to slice an opponent or simply knock him off his feet to finish him off. In Asturias, Sigrvard had noticed the enemy's use of a curved blade with increased cutting power but with less of an arc than a *Vikingr* warrior would be used to. He reasoned, as did the Asturians, that shorter arcs meant more blows could be unleashed in the same time a *Vikingr* could, thus increasing the chances of a death blow.

Sigrvard made his way deep into the forest behind his home and into a secret glade known only to him. Usually, it was where he went for the peace and solace of contemplation as a Seer, but this time, and for as long as it took, he went there as a warrior and Jarl.

At the end of the glade stood a lone pine tree, some six feet in girth; on either side was a straw target, the same kind of straw man he and Einar had practised on when they had begun warrior training. The men of straw were bound to the trunk as if they were to attack as a pair.

Sigrvard did not have 'First Blood' for his personal training; instead, he carried a heavier blade, by some five or six pounds.

He began with traditional wide arcs, which of course hit the target every time. And he counted to himself, one, two, three, etc., between each blow landing and how many he could count to before the next blow on the next target took a huge chunk of straw. He then changed tactic, after noting that he got to three almost every time between blows, sometimes four.

Using three as his mental marker, Sigrvard then tried to get more blows in for the three seconds his sword was on that flank.

He was able to match, and several times better that number until he decided it was time for the crucial test. He put the heavy blade down and took up 'First Blood'.

He was amazed at the outcome.

As he had anticipated, the lighter sword, after training with the heavier blade, enabled four and five blows on target in the same time because he reduced the distance through the air the blade travelled. A distinct advantage if he could train his men likewise.

Sigrvard returned to his home after welcoming Einar and the *riddari* on their return to Eirikrsborg. A good report from his second-in-command lifted his optimism even higher for the campaign ahead. And life that seemed good was to be even better, very soon.

The new Jarl was restless as the lengthening days moved inexorably towards the assembly of the Great Army, as *Goi*—March—moved into *Einmanuour*—April. He sat on a stool before his house, sliding his whetstone down from point to hilt and up the other edge of 'First Blood'.

He then flipped the sword across his lap to repeat the process, then flipped it once again to maintain the sharpening in an even manner. He mused at how many warriors he had sent to Valhalla with his trusty blade, a weapon that had served him well yet bore the indentations of every blow that struck either head or helm: indents that to remove by whetstone shaved off enough particles of iron for a grip as sensitive as Sigrvard's to notice. *Still many a skull to cleave or enemy to dispatch, methinks.*

"Ho," interrupted his musing and he lifted his head from his task towards the meandering figure of Vidar making his way up the wide steps to his front door.

"Ho, too, my friend. Welcome. What brings you to my hearth, for you know well that the Franken wine is long gone?"

Vidar grasped his chest with both hands and cried out, "That you should wound me so grievously hurts me, my friend."

They burst into laughter, hugged and sat down as Assi, almost as telepathic as her husband, emerged from the house with a tray on which was set a matching pair of glass goblets and a jug of red, FRANKEN wine.

"Hurt compounded by downright untruths. What manner of household is this?" cried the merchant in despair, until the broad smile induced by Assi's soft whisper, "My husband knows not that I have a cask for special guests."

Sigrvard's smile, though not as wide as Vidar's or his wife's, nevertheless sufficed to lay a hospitable air down for what was to follow.

"My friend, my partner and my heir, I have two reasons for wishing your company on this fine day, three if you count the wine. First, let me congratulate you and Assi that you are parents. I was never fortunate that way, too busy making money.

"Secondly, I come bearing a gift to celebrate you becoming Jarl and, I must confess a double-edged meaning behind my gift, appropriately, the second about which we will talk further, once you fill my glass again."

"Marek!" ordered Vidar and quick as a desert wind, Vidar's Arab *thrall* appeared with a long, linen-wrapped package that he offered his master with both arms extended.

Still seated, for moving such a frame as Vidar had developed in recent months was problematic, the merchant pivoted and proffered the package towards his host.

Sigrvard laid the package across his thighs and slowly unfolded the linen layers until his eyes were dazzled at what was revealed.

A sword. But this was no ordinary sword.

As a wordless Sigrvard slid his hands slowly over the impeccably finished blade, his eyes lit upon a single word embedded on the blade, just below the hilt.

'ULFBERHT'—Sigrvard had heard of the name but by legend only for what he held was nothing less than a sword for the gods. Viking swords were renowned but in the main for those who wielded them. They also had imperfections because, in Europe, the steel-making process did not produce enough heat to burn off those imperfections. But the Ulfberht sword was made in the Middle East from a process that produced crucible steel, also known as Damascus steel.

The lack of impurities in the Ulfberht's steel gave it a huge advantage because it made the blade more flexible and that enabled it to bend and thereby reduce the chance of it wedging in an enemy shield. Such a disadvantage in Viking blades had sent many a warrior to Valhalla early. The Ulfberht also kept its edge, literally, longer.

All such qualities meant that a sword like the one on his lap was rare outside the Mediterranean.

"But how, and why—?"

Vidar interrupted his friend, "I have many contacts west of Eirikrsborg and south of Eirikrsborg but, more pertinently, east of our town. And it is through one of my, shall we say, acquaintances from the direction that gives us the sun each day, I procured this as my gift to you.

"And before you say further, the second reasoning behind this gift is a thank you from the bottom of my heart, and treasure drawer, of course, for your investment in our business, which has enabled us to increase our wealth twenty times over."

Sigrvard, almost teary-eyed, rose slowly to his feet, hardly noticing the weight of his new sword. He waved it to and fro along his right side before gently swinging it across his front, from left to right and back again. 'Effortless' was the only word he could think of.

"Turn!" bellowed Vidar and as Sigrvard did so, a bright-red apple was aimed at his face.

In an instant, Sigrvard whipped the Ulfberht upwards and sidewards, slicing the apple into four equal quarters with no more than two flicks of the wrist.

"Words cannot—"

"Then none shall be spoken of the sword of Sigrvard, Scourge of the Franks."

The finest of Persian leatherwork that was the scabbard welcomed the sword of Sigrvard back to its resting place.

He would name it later but for now, it leaned against the wall, no more than a sword length from his right hand, which was where it would remain for the rest of his life.

They were dangerously close to the finish of the Frankish wine but with the briefest of interventions, Assi quickly replaced the near-empty jug with another that was abundantly endowed.

"Now, to business, my friend," said Vidar who was still two jugs away from the senseless jabbering of a drunkard.

Sigrvard, on the other hand, was not so distant. Something the merchant recognised but, with regard to his host's hospitality, said nought.

"I now talk to you as my business partner. Safe to say, your reputation has not only added to that of Eirikrsborg but in so doing has added considerably to our coffers. Not only are we attracting craftsmen from all over but also the materials in which they work; gold and silver from nearby lands as well as *dirhams*—coins—from the Arab world, which we melt down into bars. Copper and lead come from the Pennines and tin from Cornwall, trade that will only increase after the coming year."

Vidar winked at Sigrvard, not knowing what the Jarl knew that the merchant did not, but thought he did.

"Amber is coming from the land of the Rus and jet from Asturias. I have expanded our network of traders as far east as the Black Sea and the Caspian Sea, as far west as Iceland, Greenland and beyond. We are at a crossroads, my dear friend.

"And a crossroads that will see more riches than we can count in a thousand lifetimes."

But it was the current lifetime that was blurring Sigrvard's vision, so much so that he would be inclined to ask his friend to take his leave. A necessary course of action because it was part of Eirikrsborg folklore that Vidar the merchant once spoke, non-stop, for three consecutive days to an assembly of traders, the last of which—days not traders—

was to an audience that had been asleep, drunk, for the previous twenty-four hours.

Sigrvard slumped into his cot, kissed Assi gently on the back of her neck and fell asleep before he had rolled over onto his side.

CHAPTER EIGHTEEN

SIGRVARD had already said his farewells to Assi before he rode Victory down to the quayside, where he was joined by the entire populace, to wave the Eirikrsborg fleet off.

He could see the pride in Einar's face as he stood on the prow of the Raven, leading their vessels towards the mouth of the inlet. That made Sigrvard feel good.

He pulled Victory's bridle to turn, long before the longships were out of sight, and made his way past their home where Assi stood, one hand waving and blowing him kisses.

As Sigrvard and his fifty *riddari* made their way northwest towards Ribe, the Eirikrsborg battlefleet was sailing north through the Baltic and around the headland before dropping south towards the rendezvous point where it would meet up with the Great Army fleet just off the coast.

The route to Ribe was short enough for only one night's camping to be required so haste was not needed. Once the horses were bedded down for the night and guards set, the rest of the group retired.

An early start meant arriving at the Great Army camp mid-afternoon. As the Eirikrsborg contingent reached the top of the last escarpment before the coast, Sigrvard had a sharp intake of breath at the array of tents and pavilions that lay before him.

He tried to estimate what the various structures meant in terms of numbers of warriors but quickly thought better of it. Beyond the camp and across a wide sandy beach was an even more impressive sight, a host of longships at anchor. They were beached to enable not only swifter embarkation of the warriors but also to ease boarding for the horses. And so vast seemed their number that the longships almost formed another beach beyond the sand, which stretched towards to horizon, and beyond, to Angleland. Pondering for an instant a return to his homeland for the first time, Sigrvard realised that Ivar must have persuaded the war council it would indeed be better for the fleet to cross together.

Many thousands of men would benefit, on landfall, from a surplus of provisions with less reliance on foraging than a much longer voyage down the coast before turning North.

It would not be the last time the warrior-seer would be impressed with Ivar's logic. As Sigrvard and his men wended their way slowly through the camp, they arrived at the centre where four, equal-sized structures with a pavilion at the front of each stood. *Very politically correct*, he thought.

The *riddari* were stopped short of the four pavilions by several large *huskarls*. Their commander welcomed Sigrvard and asked him to follow him to an area just to the side where a slightly smaller pavilion stood, surrounded by ten even smaller structures for his men.

"King Ivar bids you rest and as the sun begins to set, he invites you to join him and the council at his pavilion." It was then that Sigrvard noticed the only difference between the four large pavilions—Ivar's raven banner fluttered furiously in the wind, a full two feet higher than the pennants of the other sons of Ragnar Lodbrok. As the sun was casting long shadows across the camp, Sigrvard strode towards Ivar's pavilion.

Clutched inside his long cloak in one of the many pockets he had Assi sew was a very large bottle of Franken wine. Not the biggest bottle from his hoard but sufficiently large enough for Ivar to note it was not an ordinary gift. And there were four bottles, all the same size, one for each of the brothers.

'One learns that when one is amongst wolves, one learns how to howl like one'.

Young I may be, he thought to himself, *but old enough to understand diplomacy*.

As the evening wore on, Sigrvard noted with interest how each of the brothers dealt with the bottle of wine they had been gifted.

Bacsecg set his bottle in front of him on the table. Ubba filled his drinking horn from his bottle and drank sparingly for some time.

Halfdan sliced off the top of the bottle with his sword and downed the contents in one.

Ivar was the only one to ask Sigrvard to join him in a toast, with Frankish wine, to their "success in the weeks ahead".

Before they retired to bed, the council was invited by Bacsecg to join him in his pavilion for a short council.

"I mean not to keep you from your slumber but I want you to tell your men that we leave on the tide, two days hence. They can do as they wish, short of killing each other, as long as camp is struck before that dawn and they assemble, ready to embark, when I will speak to them. But here and now, in the privacy of the war council, I say to you, we shall not return to Jylland until Angleland is our home.

"After decades of raiding and lengthy absences from our family and farms, we are turning raids into conquest and conquest into settlement."

The brothers and Sigrvard shouted with loud approvals. Ivar had words to add, but they could wait. But the warrior-seer knew in his water that what lay ahead was the stuff of sagas for many years to come. Before they led their men to their longships, the commanders addressed those loyal to them, with the same words Ivar imparted passionately to his followers, that conquest was a bonus to the 'real' purpose of the Great Army—REVENGE.

Ragnar Lodbrok, the most famous of all *Vikingr*, had been put to death in a most vile manner by King Ælla of Northumbria. It was alleged that Ragnar was tossed into a pit of poisonous snakes and as he lay amongst the coiling mass of loathsome adders, he sang his death song to the end before issuing a most portent threat:

"The little pigs would grunt now if they knew how it fares with the old boar."

And ever since, the skalds entertained the length and breadth of Scandinavia how 'the little pigs' greeted news of his death.

Now, it was coming to pass, that the leaders of the Great Army were set to unleash their wrath on the man, and people, responsible for their father's death.

It was part of Scandinavian folklore how each of Ragnar's sons had reacted when they first heard news of his demise and its manner.

Bjorn 'Ironside' was said to have gripped his spear shaft so tight that the print of his fingers remained stamped on it.

Hvitserk was playing chess and clenched his fingers upon a pawn so tightly the blood spurted from under his nails.

Sigurd 'Snake Eye' was trimming his nails with a knife and kept on paring until he cut to the bone.

But it was Ivar's reaction that seemed to be most telling. It was said, according to legend, that he demanded precise details of his father's execution and when that detail was forthcoming, his face became red, blue and pale by turns and his skin swelled with anger.

* * *

As the fleet was to make an early start the next day, Sigrvard decided on a rare early night to bed. He was halfway through his evening meal when Geir, now joint second-in-command with Einar, returned from his scouting mission around the perimeter of the Great Army's camp.

"How does it seem to you?" Sigrvard inquired.

"My lord, all is well but there is one matter that troubles me some."

"How so?"

"You did say that you counted 86 vessels in total for our fleet."

"Yes."

"But my tally from this very evening is ninety."

"Mmmmmm," mused Sigrvard, with a little understanding of what Geir said. "And do any of the longships at anchor appear menacing or different in any way, however small?"

"Curious that you should use the word small, my lord. Furthest away from the beach and almost hidden behind a rocky outcrop—some one hundred feet from the main fleet—are four *Skeid*, with very tall masts but each carrying two small, black sails and they all have a long, black shroud running around each vessel."

Sigrvard's "Mmmmmmm" grew louder with greater understanding—Berserkers!

Geir forced a facial expression somewhere twixt a smile and a frown, not knowing if the presence of such enigmatic warriors was help or hindrance.

The Jarl thanked him for his report and returned to his inner tent, smiling at the subtle way Helhest and his warriors had sneaked into the heart of the Great Army fleet and no one had noticed, until now.

Help methinks, thought Sigrvard, answering Geir's unasked question as he returned to his meal. He would tell the other commanders the next day.

Bacsecg walked through the throng of the Great Army, which had massed long before daylight. It was an impressive sight, thousands of *Vikingr* packed together but parting then closing behind the king as he made his way to the specially constructed platform to address them ahead of the greatest adventure in Scandinavian history.

Loud murmuring greeted his arrival—deathly silence fell as the assembly awaited his words.

"Saxon England is ripe for conquest. It is a land of many tribes waging war amongst themselves, to no end. We are Danes, we are Norwegian and we are Swede, but above all, we are *VIKINGR*!" *The roar must have been heard in Valhalla*, thought Sigrvard.

"We are many but we are as one," added the king.

Much shield-banging followed but Sigrvard's mind was clear enough to know the truth of his king's words. He knew the Saxon reliance on the *fyrd* was a weakness.

They fought to live; Vikings lived to fight. The freemen of the *fyrd* gave 40 days a year to their liege and provided their own weapons. Sigrvard could also, just, remember, although many winters had passed, that his father Deorwine had, like the rest of the village men, moaned about time spent away from tending their livelihood, relishing even less if they had to fight.

The Seer also knew that it was almost certainly the best time to strike, after decades of raiding that also provided much information about the lie of the land, quite literally.

The forts of the Saxon Shore lay idle. There were no imperious Roman legions to safeguard or rescue a threatened populace—a populace that was no match for the men from the North. Norsemen who had been turned from a marauding, ill-disciplined, though effective, fighting machine into a clever, organised and well-led, ruthlessly efficient killing machine.

The strands of loyalty that ran through every element of this Nordic alliance of convenience were as steel sinews binding each *drengr* to the man in front of him, to his side and to his rear—pulled tight, they were as one.

Once the approving roar of the assembly subsided, Bacsecg added but two more words.

"TO SHIP!"

And like lines of soldier ants, each man made his way flawlessly and efficiently to embark a ship, like Norwegian lemmings.

The three *Karvi* from Eirikrsborg and their complement of 50 *riddari* joined the six other seventy-five-foot long transport vessels of the Great Army, making a total of 150 mounted *riddari* who would be led by the warrior-seer, Jarl of Eirikrsborg. The remaining vessels, 29 *Skeid*, each nearly a hundred feet long, carrying 80 *drengr*, and 48 *Snekkja*, each with its fifty-six feet length crammed with eighty warriors and provisions comprised the greatest sea-borne invasion ever seen in the Northern hemisphere. Nearly three thousand warriors on 90 longships that would make the short crossing of the North Sea. Bacsecg's flagship led the flotilla with the ships of his commanders astern and once the final vessel cleared the sheltered cove, the invasion fleet turned south, keeping a precise three miles offshore until it was time to strike west.

The crossing to East Anglia was uneventful. The gods provided fine weather and favourable winds so there was less rowing and more sailing, which was fine by the men on board.

Rolf bandied words with his brother Torden, telling him he wanted a piece of England with a river for him to fish. Hengist told Jesper he wanted a Saxon wench 'with wide hips', several in fact, he wasn't fussy. Torsten wanted a farm on a hill, Mikkelson wanted a tavern so that he would never ever have to pay for beer again. Similar conversations filled the voyage a hundredfold as the Great Army moved steadily towards the Anglo-Saxon coast.

Spirits were still high when, on the fifth day, land was spotted by the look-out on Bacsecg's flagship. Sigrvard could just about make out the low-lying outline of a small island.

"Heave-to," came the order.

Murmurings of uncertainty came from the longships as they dropped anchor miles short of where they would normally do so. Indeed, many miles short of beaching their longships, which was the *Vikingr* way.

But such unrest vanished quickly as the ship's captains revealed to each crew the king's thinking behind such a tactic.

"The Anglo-Saxons saw us coming but only our lead ships before they sent panic messages across their land. They would only have seen the first few ranks of our vessels and assuming it was yet another raid, would have instructed their messengers accordingly. Once the entire fleet was anchored, the locals would have a different appraisal the following forenoon, a reappraisal that will be to our advantage once we disembark for parley."

In the morning as the sea-mist lifted, the *Vikingr* of the Great Army could see the tactical advantage of the island, later discovered to be called Thanet, lying three furlongs off the mainland.

The commanders met onboard King Bacsecg's flagship, 'The Wolf', shortly after arriving off the island. It had already been decided that the anchorage, on the windward side of Thanet, would be preferable to mooring on the leeward side, where they could be trapped, although there was little chance of the Saxons mustering enough ships to threaten nearly a hundred longships.

It took less than a day to disembark the entire Great Army, which set up camp on the island itself with two strategically placed longships as lookouts towards the mainland, one in each channel.

Those ships carrying *riddari* were positioned nearest to the mainland so that they could be the first to land. Ivar had a plan that he outlined to the assembled commanders.

"We will stay here in camp for two days. But at the end of the first, I think our young warrior-seer should take a raiding party of *riddari* to scout the land, secure fresh supplies and spread a little, shall we say, terror. That will not only capitalise on the shock of seeing so many of our longships in one place but also spread the news near and far that we are here and resistance is futile. It will also give our 'secret weapon' a chance to flex its muscles for our campaign ahead. Not to mention gathering much information to help us plan our conquest."

The next day, all *riddari* were ferried to shore. Once they had negotiated the narrow, sandy path to the cliff top, the group was divided into three sections.

Einar would ride south towards Dover, Geir would lay waste to any dwellings near their mooring while Sigrvard allocated his group potentially the most dangerous task—a foray deep into East Anglia, towards Canterbury, an important centre of Christianity, just 60 leagues from London.

The speed and mobility of Sigrvard's *riddari* would give them the advantage of surprise. The locals expected Vikings on two feet and not four. By the time the locals realised what they were up to, the *riddari* were back in camp, loaded with provisions and information.

Sigrvard instructed Einar and Geir to move their men slightly faster than walking pace but not at the gallop, which they would save for later, if pursued. "A trot" is how the Seer put it. They dispersed and were soon following their allocated task.

Half a day, one night and the following forenoon, the *riddari* reassembled, laden with sacks, chickens, a couple of goats, several pigs and one or two young blonde females, as far as Sigrvard could ascertain. More importantly, as their leader, he was relieved that one hundred and fifty *riddari* had ridden out and the same number rode back.

It was too early in a long campaign of conquest to lose warriors.

He thanked the gods for their benevolence.

Leaving several guards on the cliff top, Sigrvard led his men down the sandy path to the beach where corrals had been assembled. The horses were now on dry land and on dry land they would stay. Sigrvard, Einar and Geir returned to the fleet where their commanders and the king awaited their report.

It didn't take Sigrvard and his seconds-in-command too long to make their reports, which were, all three, strikingly similar.

Halfdan spoke for the leaders.

"So you encountered little or no opposition?" he said in a kind of disbelieving manner.

"Exactly, my lord. I doubt we encountered more than ten or twenty Saxons between the three groups," replied Sigrvard.

"It is as I predicted," interrupted Ivar, "they see we are here in number, the word has spread. Now, we wait for them to come to us."

After such a successful and fruitful reconnaissance, the king and his commanders decided to extend their camp, wait for the locals and then decide on their next course of action. That would be a case of when, not if. The island was secure, defendable and the Great Army had all it required with them or nearby. "What need is there for haste?" sneered Ivar.

As predicted, it did not take long for the locals to show themselves, though Sigrvard was the only leader who wasn't surprised that the entourage of locals that made its way along the cliff top was led by a fully-robed bishop, alongside a monk carrying a white flag. The delegation was not large enough to be threatening but not small enough to be derisory; the Saxons were used to the requirements of compromise.

After being searched for weapons, the delegation was led to a newly erected pavilion where they were seated at a lower level to the podium on which sat Bacsecg and Ivar. Sigrvard stood to the king's right and would act as translator, although the Viking leaders all spoke and understood English.

The bishop began to speak but was hastily halted by Ivar, who spoke with Sigrvard, "This is not a matter of religion. Who speaks for your leader?"

The bishop attempted to speak once again but was again prevented from doing so. At that point, the tall, clean-shaven warrior-like emissary who accompanied the bishop stood and addressed the podium.

"I am Aeldred, Thegn to King Edmund. I come in peace and ask you what it is you wish from your presence here."

It struck Sigrvard, and also Bacsecg and Ivar, how noble the way this young man, for he was little older than Sigrvard, conducted himself. He showed no fear, made no twitchy or involuntary movements but had a steely look deep in his eyes that forewarned anyone not to cross him.

"We wish to remain here before we continue our journey south to warmer climes to explore. We require to be left alone save obtaining from hereabouts sustenance for the duration of our camp."

Sigrvard knew, as the words from Ivar came out of his mouth, that no one present believed a word of what the translator imparted to the delegation. But for the present, that was a start.

Aeldred begged permission to engage with the bishop, which Bacsecg granted with a gentle nod and after a few moments, the Saxon warrior spoke to the commanders but directly at Ivar. Fixing him with a steely stare that would have shaken most men, he declared, "You may remain as our guests for one moon. Food and provisions will be brought to you every two days and left where the path reaches the cliff top. Should you require anything we do not provide, send an envoy and we will consider any such request, without guarantee it will be granted. Our offer is conditional that you and your men remain here and go no further inland than one league. Any action beyond what I have outlined here will be regarded as an act of war."

What a Vikingr this man would make, thought Sigrvard as he translated what Bacsecg and Ivar had already understood.

"Good, then you may go in peace," said Ivar in English to Aeldred and the bishop. "As you Christians would say, NOW."

The stern final word from Ivar caused Aeldred's eyes to betray his thoughts.

A red mist replaced the white retina. Sigrvard saw it. Ivar saw it and Aeldred knew it. But no further words were spoken as the delegation departed, not turning their backs on the podium party until they had moved a safe distance and closer to the cliff path.

Bacsecg called a council to his pavilion later that day and all commanders attended. The king, as usual, led the discussion but Ivar, as usual, dominated the talks that actually were not talks, merely him speaking, although the others did contribute.

"So, to sum up what has happened here. We wait our time until we choose when to leave but we scout extensively after calculating how long it will take them to raise an army and make our move one day before?"

Considering the intentions of the Great Army, the only barrier was the one-moon limit that had been imposed but, as usual, Ivar had a plan.

"We will cross that bridge when it is necessary."

The four weeks that followed were eerily quiet. Apart from the regular and subtle scouting missions of the *riddari*, there was no need to break the one-league boundary as the locals provided ample supplies, even for several thousand *Vikingr.*

Weapons training continued as usual and long, beer-quenching nights were the norm. Sigrvard ensured the *riddari* practised every day, but as there were more *riddari* than horses, he had to be mindful of overburdening the beasts; he rested them regularly.

Busy though he made himself, Sigrvard could not come to terms with retiring to his tent at night with no Assi to hold. As the month wore on, supplies began to fall rapidly, despite wagonloads of provisions every two days.

Bacsecg, prodded by Ivar, instructed the *riddari* patrols to carry out a limited amount of foraging, with no violence. News of the imposed restriction being broken would reach Edmund quickly enough without adding to it piles of Saxon bodies.

Camp supplies were duly supplemented but it only took a couple of days for Aeldred to return to the Great Army, with armed escorts this time, no monks or candles, although the mandatory white flag ensured the *Vikingr* knew how close to the edge they were pushing the locals.

"My lords, my king has asked me to inquire as to the reason you found it necessary to break our agreement."

Ivar dragged himself to his feet from his chair. The council had already met the night previous and agreed on the way forward, which Ivar took great delight in imparting to their Saxon delegate.

"You see, my friend," Aeldred squirmed but kept his demeanour in check, "we did not actually agree to your, er, suggestion. I think the word used was 'good', no more, no less."

A silence followed that could be cut by a battle-axe.

As Aeldred opened his mouth to respond, he was cut short by Ivar moving closer to his young enemy.

"Let me say this," he whispered into Aeldred's ear, beyond the range of anyone else present, before stepping back, "we require horses from your king, one thousand of them."

The entire delegation went ashen. Ivar smiled, sneered actually.

"Of course, that will take some time. You have two days to comply. Anything less than a thousand and any longer than two days, and we will regard *that* as an act of war. This is not an agreement or a request, this is a demand. You may go."

Sigrvard stood as motionless as he had since Aeldred had approached the podium, his translation not being required by Ivar. He doubted the young Saxon had ever been spoken to in that manner before.

Aeldred withdrew, not turning his back this time, expecting to be attacked at any moment, joined his escort and left.

Two days later, a herd of one thousand Anglo-Saxon horses was driven to the beach and into the corrals that had been hastily extended to accommodate them. Ivar knew he was on even more solid ground and moving ever closer to capitulation by his enemy.

Now that Sigrvard had the mounts to increase his *riddari* from just one hundred and fifty to a sizeable mobile force, he could start to allocate riders to steeds, riders who had been trained by himself in Eirikrsborg.

He wasted no time and at dawn the next day, the riders and their horses were put through their paces by Sigrvard and his commander, Geir. Einar stood on the side-lines, well away from the four-legged beasts he could never come to terms with.

Camp life was untroubled for the Great Army. Their base was well organised, well provisioned and well-disciplined and that was well noted by the regular spies who looked in on their 'visitors' from poorly disguised cliff-top observation points.

But camp life was not ideal for a roving *Vikingr* army that was used, outside winter months, to being on the move, and on the move they were soon to be.

As *Hastmanudur** approached, the war council met in Bacsecg's tent where the sons of Ragnar Lodbrok were eager to decide on the timing of their departure into the English hinterland.

"Soon," said the king, "but not that soon."

But before moans became dissent—Sigrvard kept a politically expedient silence—Bacsecg continued.

"We have the largest *Vikingr* army ever to set foot on these shores but it isn't enough. Yes, it is more than sufficient for raiding but we are not here to raid.

"We have to give Gautrek time to fashion the Summer Army that will join us after the *Jul* and when they are on their way, we will already be better placed to take what we came for."

Silence being assent, the council members went their way. Winter camp it was to be then, but probably the last one, or so they wishfully thought.

The commanders may well have had wives, children and mistresses to forget but Sigrvard did not want to forget Assi and his new daughter. He consoled himself that before Astrid got too much older, they would all be together in their new life in his old country. It was Sigrvard the father, husband and family man, not the Seer. Had he but delved further into that facet of his life, he would have been less optimistic.

The period before winter set in, when the Great Army would be battered by the storms coming off the *Mar Frisia,*** was spent reinforcing the tented encampment with a more rigid wooden framework. The entire site ranged over one and a half hectares and its V-shaped enclosure enclosed many structures, each thirteen feet square. Sigrvard and the war council did, of course, fare much better as their rank and privilege would dictate. Their place of abode was a much firmer wooden-framed building with an equal-sized pavilion at the entrance to protect the door.

Many a night was spent in Sigrvard's tent playing *Hnefatafl* and many a night, Einar suffered defeat. What disturbed Sigrvard was his

* *15 September to 13 October.*

** *Early name for North Sea.*

friend never learning and improving his tactical awareness. What disturbed Einar was being a loser.

Each night before he slept, Sigrvard pondered his situation, back in the land of his birth but not where he wanted to be—with Assi.

The war council met once again but this time it was more than camp reports about the number of broken heads after the regular drunken brawls.

"Sigrvard, how goes the *riddari* training?" inquired Bacsecg.

"If my lord will allow humour, they are chomping at the bit."

"And soon they shall. Ivar?"

"As we expected, our winter foraging drew no response from our unwilling hosts. The intelligence gathered during that foraging has allowed us to plan our departure. Sigrvard, you will continue to train the *riddari* as usual, we must ensure the Saxon spies have something to report back to their king."

Sigrvard did as instructed by Ivar, boosted by the knowledge that soon they would be about their task.

As *Eostre* drew near, all weapons training eased as the Great Army prepared for the festival. The reduction in activity was duly reported back to King Edmund's court and as the war council had anticipated, resulted in a similar easing of Saxon vigilance. From a distance, the spies saw activity within the camp but had no idea of its purpose.

Wagons were readied to carry a week's supplies for the *riddari* while provisions were being amassed for another purpose.

The morning before *Eostre*, the Saxon spies woke to the sight of empty waters around the Isle of Thanet. After several moons of the spectacle of hundreds of longships at anchor, the Great Army had gone, sailed away during the night. The Saxon spies rode like the wind back to the court of King Edmund and excitedly informed him that their enemy had vanished.

"God is with us!" exclaimed Edmund. But was he?

Aeldred was quickly despatched to Thanet with a detachment of two hundred *fyrd* as well as fifty warriors. They paused at the cliff top and viewed what had for several weeks been a hive of *Vikingr* activity. Now all was silent, still.

Once they had negotiated the cliff path to the beach, they proceeded cautiously into the camp, *fyrd* first, followed by Aeldred and his warriors. He allowed himself a brief smile for, brave warrior he might be, a pitched battle with Vikings was not to be relished. The Saxons made their way through the camp, meandering between hundreds of wooden structures, with flapping pavilion entrances the only noise. They reached the centre of the compound with its huge circular arena to be greeted by a most unexpected sight. Three *Vikingr* warriors on horseback, in full armour, standing before the largest of the camp pavilions.

Sigrvard, Einar and Halfdan.

This is a trick, thought Aeldred to himself.

It was.

Sigrvard beat his shield with his sword three times and roared, "*VIKINGR*!"

And suddenly, from within the seemingly empty huts and tents, burst forward eleven hundred and fifty *riddari*.

The massacre that followed was as brutal and effective as it was possible for such to be. The Saxons were scythed down in a matter of moments until Aeldred stood alone, defiant, surrounded by a mound of *fyrd* dead. Freemen who were more at home tilling and tending fields than trying to match seasoned ferocious Vikings on horseback.

The *riddari*, their bloody task almost complete, held off as Aeldred stood tall, shield and sword still at the ready, accepting his fate as it lay before him. The circle of riders slowly closed in on the Saxon leader as he considered one last option, killing one of the *riddari* and taking his horse and then seeing if he could outrun more than a thousand horsemen.

Just as he was about to convince himself of the prudence of his action, running away to fight another day, the *riddari* parted and through the gap rode Sigrvard on Victory, leading a jet-black Arab steed. He dismounted and walked towards Aeldred, bridle in hand.

The Saxon readied himself to make what would almost certainly be his last move in this life, a swing of the sword at Sigrvard.

But the Viking Seer extended his hand and offered the bridle and what it offered to a valiant enemy. No words were spoken.

None were necessary.

A small deferential nod, from each to the other, and Aeldred was mounted and away to safety, at a walk not a gallop.

I would expect nothing less, thought Sigrvard to himself.

Einar approached his Jarl and as if Sigrvard would expect anything more from his old friend, said, "Another Saxon to kill in the future when we could have done so now; what were you thinking?"

"You would never understand, Einar," mused Sigrvard to himself.

"Clean these bodies up and lay them out with dignity. They died well and deserve respect."

Einar knew to argue would be pointless and did as ordered.

As the last of the slain Saxons was laid out, Sigrvard mounted his steed and led the *riddari* out of the camp, followed by the provision wagons.

Up the cliff path for the last time, the mounted party turned east in the direction of Londinium before turning north on the old Roman road, Ermine Street, to York.

The Great Army stripped every hamlet and village of the recent harvest stored conveniently for quick transfer to the many empty wagons, also stolen. The benefit to the invaders would mean desperate months ahead for the Saxons. Bacsecg's plan was to clear Londinium and head for Verulanium before striking north. He wished to distance his mounted band from any potential strike from the old Roman town on the river.

Once clear, the *riddari* would forage and live off the land as they progressed towards their eventual target. Meanwhile, the fleet would make its way up the east coast, raiding town by town until it would anchor off the Humber Estuary and rendezvous with the *riddari* before the assault on York. That way, if the mounted army needed an escape route, it would be just offshore and if the *riddari* needed it, they could call on more than two thousand reinforcements at short notice.

The route north was eerily straightforward, so much so that Halfdan called for Sigrvard to cast the Runes. They were clear by portent that the journey to York would indeed be trouble-free.

Beyond that, the Seer was unclear. "I shall cast the stones closer to our destination," he told Halfdan.

The *riddari* continued their progress, foraging for just enough to last until the next settlement, no more. Why carry stores when they could eat off the land? The *Vikingr* did encounter occasional armed opposition but they served merely as practice for the ever-improving element of the conquering army that Sigrvard regarded as the future of their conquering force.

CHAPTER NINETEEN

IT was easy for Sigrvard to understand why Eofric was the intended target for the Great Army. Even as a boy of nine winters, he had been aware of the town's importance; he had even gone there once with his father, as it was just two days' travel from his Streonshalh home.

Founded by the Romans, it was the biggest settlement north of the Humber. Not only was it an important centre of learning but it was the epicentre of Christianity and a key player in Anglo-Saxon commerce, regionally and internationally. Merchants based themselves at its heart and traders from all the known world frequented Eofric for its prosperity and potential. It was that factor alone, learned from many a flagon-infused night with Vidar, that gave Sigrvard an insight into its value as a trading centre and why the Denisc had made it their prime objective. The commercial infrastructure was so important that even coins were minted there, the true mark of a vibrant economy.

There was also a double irony, not lost on Sigrvard. Saxon-born, he was returning to the land of his birth as a leader of the conquering Denisc who were following in the footsteps of their Frisian forefathers who had made the same journey four hundred years earlier. But unlike those ancestors who had settled alongside the indigenous population, peacefully sharing the bounteous land, the *Vikingr* would take that position by force.

The Great Army rested near Retford. The leaders decided to rest. Sigrvard decided it was time for contemplation.

He set off west with provisions for several days in the direction of the stone ring at Arbor.

Sigrvard made good progress, admiring the countryside of fertile soil and miles of forest and rivers. That the land of his birth was so bounteous was of no surprise but, as a child of eight, he had not appreciated as much as now, a man of eighteen summers. The irony was not lost that he was indeed coming home. He arrived at the stone circle just before dusk and had time to set up his tent before investigating the monument of fifty limestone slabs, set with a central, horse-shaped cove.

He imagined the mindset of its creators who must have had the majesty of the peaks in mind when they had created it. There was one narrow entrance and one wide one. Sigrvard entered through the smaller of the two, from a fairly nondescript landscape. Then he walked across the monument to the wider entrance, where he wondered at the spectacular view of the Peak District, which seemed to reflect the majesty of the gods or whichever deity they were dedicated to.

As the sun set, casting shadows across the plateau, Sigrvard sat down to eat. But no sooner had he sunk his teeth into a large slab of cheese than his victuals were disturbed by noise of commotion at the foot of the plateau where the path to the circle began. Sigrvard grabbed his *Ulfberht* and raced towards the rim of the plateau where he saw five ragged bandits surrounding an old man in monk's habit.

The bandits were obviously seeking easy pickings and were grabbing and pulling the man by his clothes and hood, stopping just short of using the weapons they carried. The assailed managed to squirm loose from his attackers and grab his staff to fend them off, or so thought Sigrvard.

What he witnessed then was beyond his wildest imagination.

The monk, with long white hair and full-length beard, must have been of holy orders; he flailed with his staff, sweeping in a wide circle and with each swipe catching one of his attackers about the head. Suddenly realising that they would actually need to fight for any ill-gotten gains, the men grabbed their weapons and suddenly, it was a different fight—to the death.

Sigrvard raced harder for he knew that arriving late on the scene, he would be unable to assist the old man. Then, attacked became attacker. Jabbing each of the robbers with the end of his staff with a rapid succession of pinpoint prods, he kept them at bay. One of them outflanked him but quick as a flash of lightning the monk pivoted on his staff and with both feet caught him in the chest and sent him tumbling.

Pivoting back on his staff to face the remaining four assailants, he smashed the skull of one of them, who dropped to the ground, dead.

Undaunted, those remaining attacked from the front and both sides. Sigrvard was still some way distant but closing fast as the triple attack began that surely would end in the old man's death. But the monk ran at his attackers and rammed his staff into the ground just before them as they poised to strike.

Pivoting over the advancing bandits, he quickly attacked them from the rear before they even realised what had happened.

Another skull was cracked but by then the first attacker was back on his feet, three against one. Sigrvard tripped. *I will be too late,* he thought. But when the monk dispatched a third robber by stabbing him through the eye and killing him instantly, the two left turned tail and ran away.

A breathless Sigrvard finally arrived but a threatening raise of the old man's deadly staff wasn't the greeting he expected.

"*Nai, nai,*" Sigrvard shouted in his native tongue.

The old man lowered his deadly piece of tree, glared at Sigrvard and whispered quietly, not out of breath as he should have been.

"Nice of you to turn up."

A stony, silent moment was followed by both bursting into laughter that echoed around the valley and seemed to follow the two surviving bandits as they fled.

"I am Sigrvard."

"A Viking, methinks," was the old man's less than endearing response. Sigrvard responded by grasping the handle of his sword still in its scabbard. The two stood there ready for combat but then laughter broke out again.

"Would you break bread with me?" asked Sigrvard.

"Indeed," came the reply from an individual who was obviously a man of few words.

They made their way to Sigrvard's fire and enjoyed what was left of the day's breakfast.

The Seer was the first to break the silence.

"I have never seen such fighting," he said with an element of surprise that was as much to do with the age of his guest as it was with the extraordinary combat display he had just witnessed.

Silence followed.

"I know not your name."

"William of Whitby."

The name spun around inside Sigrvard's head, sending him to another place. The name continued to resonate until he was no longer atop an Anglo-Saxon plateau but looking through the eyes of a boy of six or seven winters, among a crowd of onlookers standing before a stone cross where they listened to a shabbily dressed monk preaching to them. It was William of Whitby. He knew the face.

"…and Jesus expelled the money changers from the temple."

Sigrvard offered his guest a drink but said nothing of his previous encounter with a much younger William of Whitby.

"Frankish wine?" he said, not knowing that William preferred a good wine to beer; the offer was accepted.

Several infusions of wine smoothed any atmosphere that existed and Sigrvard pursued his interest in how William had routed the bandits.

"I wish to learn to fight in that manner."

"From me you will not." A steadfast reply convinced Sigrvard to leave it there, almost.

"Then, pray tell, where you learnt such skills, for skills they are."

"From a misspent youth along the Silk Road, before I found God."

"What call you this strange combat?"

"It is Bojutsu, which means staff technique using what is known as a Bo. It is an art employing a weapon as an extension of limbs."

Sigrvard let out a huge sigh. "Of course."

"Of course, what?" said William quizzically.

"My merchant friend, Vidar, told me tales from his travels of a European warrior-monk who protected traders and pilgrims on the road beyond Constantinople."

"That would be me," conceded William before sinking his teeth into a small loaf he had been given.

"But what are you doing here?" said Sigrvard who was growing ever more curious with each passing moment.

"I wander. I preach. I seek God and his goodness and I thank you for your, er, assistance and your victuals and bid you farewell."

* * *

As the *riddari* went past the Humber Estuary, Halfdan sent a scouting party to see if the fleet was at anchor; if not, the scouts were to remain until the fleet arrived then send word to him. It was just twenty miles from the Estuary to Eofric so the horse soldiers would make camp and wait. Unbeknown to the rest of the leadership, Ivar sent a spy into Eofric. In fact, he sent four.

Each was to check out one quarter of the town, from the river bank to the outer walls. Disguised as traders with appropriate goods from many countries, they would not arouse suspicion.

Meanwhile, after setting up camp deep inside a forest just a swift gallop from the town walls, the war council met to discuss their plan of attack.

As it was mid-*Gormanudur,** ironically 'Slaughter Month', there was very little daylight, being the first month of winter. Once the fleet was in position, it would sail up the Ouse into the heart of Eofric and coordinate with the *riddari* who would assault the town through its weakest point.

The date of the assault was set for All Saints' Day, 866. Although there was a code that war wasn't usually waged during winter, it wasn't part of *Vikingr* code.

"Why that day?" inquired Halfdan, echoing the thoughts of the rest of the council.

A cocky Ivar smirked as he delivered his answer, "I learned much in Hibernia about their religion. And because it is such an important feast day in the Christian Church, all the leaders, civic and military, will be at service that morning, in one place and ready for worship, not war."

Ivar learnt, once his spies had returned, that the worshipful gathering would take place in a location that played even more into his plans at annihilating the Eofric leadership in one fell swoop.

"It would also be symbolic—NOTHING can save them from the *Vikingr*, not even their God."

The Christian cathedral, St Peter's, sat within its own walled precinct and being self-contained, it herded its congregation into what would turn out to be a 'killing-field'.

"One way in, no way out," was how Ivar and the leaders saw it.

In one of his rare 'Saxon' moments, Sigrvard hoped their God would be with them that day.

* *14 October-13 November.*

The cathedral was a short distance from a bridge over the Ouse, which was where the warriors from the fleet would join up with the *riddari* for what was planned as a full-scale assault that would end the battle very quickly.

It was forenoon, two days before All Saints' Day, when the scouts arrived with the news that the battlefleet had arrived in the Humber Estuary. They gave the war council news that Bacsecg would time the fleet's arrival, just short of Eofric's walls, to allow time for the rendezvous at the bridge and the full assault on the cathedral.

Riding the incoming tidal swell meant the battlefleet needed just two oars per ship to make its way along the Ouse to the rendezvous point but even those two oars were muffled to allow silent progress. Meanwhile, Ivar sent his foot soldiers to just outside the town walls at the gate identified as the weakest point in York's defences.

Sigrvard's *riddari*, horse hooves suitably wrapped so that not even a single disturbed stone would be an alarm to the sentries who had been on guard all night, waited.

Just before the first glimpses of daylight emerged from the morning darkness, a line of six hundred horsemen silently walked across the open space leading to the West Gate.

The order, unspoken but understood, was simple: approach the gate and only raise a gallop if the alarm was raised.

Suddenly, movement on the wall. A sentry raised his warning horn but a well-placed Viking shaft pierced his throat and the horn never reached his lips. Sigrvard dug his heels into Victory's flanks and the *riddari* raced towards the gate, which opened slowly, the scouts had scaled the walls and York was open for business—*Vikingr* business.

The mounted force swept through the streets like whirlwind, cutting down any locals foolish enough to be caught in their path.

Sigrvard led his men directly to the cathedral precinct where they surrounded a packed St Peter's. The remaining *riddari* arrived, dismounted and were joined by the foot soldiers who raced between the horse curtain that surrounded the precinct. They battered down the ornate oak doors that the congregation had barred, insufficiently and optimistically.

The ensuing massacre within the consecrated walls was swift and brutal. Riders forced fleeing Saxons onto the swords of the *Vikingr* and foot soldiers drove worshippers under flailing hooves. It was later said that so blood-stained was the granite floor that it could not be cleaned and was replaced and the besmirched stone thrown into the Humber Estuary.

By the time the sun reached its zenith, Ivar, Halfdan and Bacsecg joined Sigrvard outside the cathedral.

"The Christian God must have been resting today," said Ivar mockingly. His brothers laughed, Sigrvard pretended to do likewise, outwardly.

Leaving a skeleton garrison, the *Vikingr* adjourned to their camp outside the walls that the *thralls* had erected while their overlords went about their blood business.

As the leaders ate and drank to their success, intelligence was being gathered. Information that confirmed that while the majority of York leadership, secular and clerical, had been butchered, the kings of Deira and Bernicia had escaped.

The brothers were not bothered about Osbert, King of Bernicia, but Ælla, their father's killer, was different.

"No matter," mumbled Halfdan. "All in good time."

In the four months that followed, the Great Army was comfortably ensconced in York, by which time the invaders were already calling it Jorvik. There was much drinking and gaming but Ælla and Osbert were not idle. They set about raising an army to retake the most important settlement in the North. Even the underlying matter of civil war between them was put aside as the two kings agreed to deal with the Great Army first and attend to their own petty squabbles after.

Sigrvard missed Assi every day and night. He longed to hold her and Astrid; was she walking, was she saying *Modir* and was *Fadir* yet part of her vocabulary? With each passing day and with every war council meeting, he was more determined than ever his family would join him when even the slightest possibility allowed, his earlier words be damned—"I am a Jarl; when I want my family, I have my family."

The Great Army scouts did their job as ever, so when the Northumbrian army advanced on York, it was of no surprise to Ivar and his commanders.

Sigrvard readied his warriors and *riddari* outside the walls of the city some distance from the battlements around the West Gate but well within arrow range. A makeshift, spiked, wooden wall was erected behind which Sigrvard readied his men, half his full complement of twelve hundred plus *drengr* on foot.

The remaining *riddari* were well hidden in the woodland nearby.

The spiked barrier was deliberately weakened, apparently incomplete, halfway along its length that, intentionally and on Ivar's orders, was directly in front of a section of Jorvik wall that was shrouded in scaffolding and makeshift screens.

Sigrvard was the first to hear the sound of branches and bushes rustling as the Northumbrians advanced towards them. He smiled as he wondered how the attackers would feel if they knew they were but a short distance, on either flank, of the mounted contingent of the Great Army that would be their downfall.

The Northumbrians broke cover and raced towards the spiked defensive wall, and despite a cloud of arrows, managed to reach the forward section of Sigrvard's position, relatively intact.

The *Vikingr* engaged with long spears while the *riddari* stood firm. At a given signal from Sigrvard, his *riddari* retreated towards the walls and were followed by the *drengr*.

The Northumbrians raced after them, determined to close the short gap between the two forces and enter the city to complete their mission. The defenders re-entered the city via the gate and were followed by a number of attackers though the bulk of the Northumbrians went for the gap in the wall nearby where the scaffolding was swept aside with ease.

The attackers were astonished at what lay before them.

A large curved area on which was arranged a large force of *riddari* and *drengr* forming a continuous line below a tall, inner curtain wall. The only break in that line was where the incursion entered.

They soon realised it was a trap.

The men from the North were swamped by the defenders' advance, which drove them back outside the walls and into the area that was surrounded by the spiked wooden barriers they had swept through just moments earlier.

Only this time, the deliberately frail barriers had been replaced by heavier versions, reversed, onto which they were driven.

Those Northumbrians who managed to get through the wooden stakes ran straight into the *riddari* who had emerged from their hiding place and were trapped between the two *Vikingr* forces—in a killing field.

The trapped were slaughtered on the spot and those who tried to escape into the city ran into Ivar's men who dispatched them with chilling efficiency.

The stench of death still hung heavy in the afternoon air over Jorvik, still a Viking city. A stench made worse by the huge pyre of fallen invaders that was burning away, well outside the walls.

Two *huskarls* dragged a pitiful, bloodied figure into the main hall where Ivar and the rest of his commanders sat on a raised platform.

The trail of blood left across the floor was wide and dark.

Ælla.

"It seems," began Ivar, "we shall not be joined by King Osbert. He has gone to his God, minus crown, and his head, I believe."

The hall filled with raucous laughter. Ælla wasn't laughing.

In fact, barely conscious, he seemed oblivious to his surroundings.

"But we welcome King, for now, Ælla. The man who murdered Ragnar Lodbrok, the greatest Viking of all, our father," as he swept his arm towards where his brothers sat, scowling at the man on whom they would soon exact their rightful revenge.

There were no triumphant speeches, exaggerated ceremony as Ælla, just hours earlier a proud king, was dragged to his place of execution.

'The Blood Eagle' was the right of the sons of Ragnar Lodbrok to exact rightful revenge for his death at the hands of Ælla. Halfdan was chosen as executioner and duly set about his appointed task.

The assembled throng of *Vikingr* warriors, still fuelled by battle frenzy, watched as Ælla was stripped and laid face down on the scaffold. The execution had been known to last hours but such was the savour with which Halfdan went about his assigned task, it took just moments.

He sliced open Ælla's back with his sword and pulling slowly towards the waist, severed the ribs from the spine and pulled his lungs out and flipped them over Ælla's shoulders, creating a pair of 'wings'.

Blood spewed on Halfdan and those *drengr* who stood closest to the platform. A cruel end for a cruel enemy who had thrown Ragnar into a pit of adders but Sigrvard, and he was not alone, admired the courageous way Ælla met his end. A Viking who met death through 'The Blood Eagle' was welcomed to Valhalla if he did not cry out at any point of the execution. Ælla was Saxon. Sigrvard felt he would have entered Valhalla or Heaven, either way. Even when salt was applied to the gaping hole where his back once had been.

Death was silent but not quick. Ælla did not die until the night passed. In the forenoon, Ivar was asked what was to be done with the body.

"Feed him to the dogs and what is left, feed to the pigs. The right ending for a dog who was a pig."

CHAPTER TWENTY

JORVIK was the Viking capital and dominated Deira.

What was left of the Northumbrian court sought shelter and refuge on the other side of the Humber, in Bernicia. The invaders set about rebuilding Jorvik and reinforcing their capital. A period of calm ensued and with it came an opportunity for Sigrvard, which he seized, in more ways than one.

He knew his newly acquired status within the Great Army would change his life and that of his family, but now that peace reigned across the land, his homeland, there was a pilgrimage he knew he had to make.

Three hours' ride northwest of Jorvik was the place of his birth. The place where his life had begun and where his family's had ended, ten winters before—Streonshalh.

It seemed to take forever but as he approached the top of the hill and bend in the river, which gave its name to the town—the strong bend in the river—*Streonshalh*, he was shocked.

He wasn't naïve enough to expect anything like the place he had been wrenched from as a boy of nine winters but the wind, the sea and the sand had buried what was left after the *Vikingr* raid under mounds of sand that blended into the river banks as if they had always existed. Sigrvard had seen enough but before he turned back to Jorvik, he had to see the monastery at Hild, whose land had been farmed by generations of his family. Soil from which had taken ages to scrub from beneath his fingernails all those years past. The place he had been baptised into the Christian faith.

As Victory took him up the steep road to the monastery, Sigrvard saw, well before reaching the site, the state of disrepair of a once glorious place of worship.

Maybe it was being back home and the memories that conjured up from the depths of his subconscious where they had been buried for years but he couldn't help but blame the *Vikingr*. Blaming them as he had back then. But no, it was the constant civil war between Deira and Bernicia that had caused such devastation as he beheld.

He swore on his life and the life of his family that he would see the restoration to former glory of a once magnificent construction. He had enough wealth for several lifetimes. He would spend some here.

On the return journey to Jorvik, despite the devastation and memories he had endured that day, Sigrvard felt the warmth of elation at his decision to restore Hild. He expected Assi would feel the same.

The day after his return from his roots, Bacsecg summoned the young Jarl to his private quarters.

"My trusted warrior-seer, I would that you play a game of *Hnefatafl* with me. I have heard your legendary prowess on the board is matched only by your excellence on the field of battle."

"My lord pays me a great honour for I too have heard that Bacsecg is as invincible on the board as he is in combat."

"Right answer, and the correct answer; shall we?"

The game went on well into the night; indeed, dawn's early light was imminent and yet the two protagonists were still locked in thoughtful strategy.

Drawn games of *Hnefatafl* were rare and even then only when the gamers were of the very highest level. Games that could not be settled did not necessarily indicate a settlement could not be achieved. While both kings remained on the board, the prize of victory was still on the table.

Now, thought Sigrvard. His determination had nothing to do with what might be considered a politically inexpedient victory over his king. Assi was his intent and of course, Astrid.

"My lord, may I be so bold as to seek a boon?"

"Ask away," replied Bacsecg without hesitation.

"I would that I send for my wife and daughter, who I have not seen since before she began suckling."

The warmth of the look that gripped the king's countenance was something Sigrvard had never seen there before, nor heard of. Bacsecg had a reputation, rightfully acquired, of stern forthrightness and an unforgiving attitude towards emotion.

"You have more than acquitted yourself as a worthy Jarl and warrior. Yes, send for your family. In fact, my flagship, which will not be required as yet, will comply with your wish with greater haste than our normal supply ship."

Sigrvard knew words could not express his true feelings at the success of his request so no words were spoken.

"Meanwhile, my young adversary, I think it prudent we put this intriguing contest aside for future recommencement, what say you?"

"As my lord wishes."

The walk back to his tent was more like a flight on clouds of ecstasy as he contemplated reunion with his family.

* * *

Ivar had enough of wallowing in the success at thwarting Northumbrian aspirations for Jorvik. So he turned his intent to Mercia, which for a hundred years had represented the strength of Angleland.

Leaving a garrison to control their new domain, the Great Army, led by Ivar, with Einar in command of the *riddari*, invaded Mercia and headed for Nottingham, which was taken in time to set up winter quarters; the Great Fleet, meanwhile, headed for the Tyne where they would anchor for winter.

Ivar set about fortifying his newly acquired town on the Trent, part of his scheme to establish a string of fortified centres across the land he was intent on conquering.

It was the success of fortifying Nottingham that led Ivar and the war council to decide they would winter there. Meanwhile, Mercia called for assistance from the only source available, Wessex. King Ethelred and his younger brother, Prince Alfred, quietly set about raising an army and provisioning their help for Mercia. Both sides readying for the confrontation that would determine the future.

Ivar called Sigrvard to his presence.

"I desire a reading of the Runestones. I have been most pleased with Sigrvard the Jarl and warrior, now would that I have the same feeling towards Sigrvard the Seer."

The stones were cast and it was all Sigrvard could do to rein in what he saw. *Prudence*, he mused, *was the order of the day* and it was that intent that guided him in the determination he imparted to the volatile and unpredictable leader who sat before him.

"My lord. A journey lies ahead for you but water is involved. Setbacks there will be but ultimate victory is your destiny, though from a different throne."

Sigrvard could see he had given Ivar much to ponder and that he was struggling to make sense of what he had heard. *Goodness knows,* thought Sigrvard, *what he would have made had I but given him a little more detail.*

AD 868

The scouts hurried back to Nottingham at the gallop and went straight to Ivar where they reported the combined Wessex and Saxon army was "two days from the Trent".

The bulk of the combined Mercian and Wessex force camped a mile from Nottingham while a delegation, under a white flag, approached the town from the West.

Ivar himself led the *Vikingr* representation out of the main gate.

Sigrvard accompanied him and as they left the fortified town, he wondered what precursor to full-scale battle would be forthcoming.

Little did Ivar know that Mercian King Burgred, against the wishes of his Wessex allies, was set to sue for peace. Vastly outnumbered, every move Ivar had at his disposal was a gamble so he refused to be drawn outside the walls to fight an open battle. And because the odds were stacked against him, when Burgred decided to buy off the invaders, Ivar accepted.

But the Anglo-Saxons were not without their own difficulties.

Despite being in the heart of home territory, they had supply problems because more men meant more provisions were needed. There was also the added difficulty presented by the *fyrd*, which comprised the bulk of their army. The impending harvest meant the men would soon have to return to their farms or lose their crops.

Ivar, ever the pragmatic optimist, reasoned that his Vikings could handle rationing better than the Anglo-Saxons, a situation made even better when Burgred delivered food to Nottingham.

A peace treaty was then concluded, which left Ivar his defensive centre of operation in Mercia a springboard to attack East Anglia. So confident was he in how he had fortified Nottingham that he decided to lead the Great Army back to Jorvik where he would spend the winter fortifying the *Vikingr* capital, leaving behind a formidable outpost on the Trent with access to the sea.

There was much joy as the Great Army returned to its power-base. The populace's delight that they were now safe from Anglo-Saxons to the west and Northumbrians from the north and the warriors who knew they would be in one place for a time before continuing their conquest, which was making good progress.

Sigrvard made his way back to his house in the city and slid off Victory, exhausted from his recent tribulations. His mind was filled with thoughts of 'sleeping for a week' but those thoughts vanished when he turned to see what was there before his home to greet him—Assi and Astrid.

It was a moment frozen in time that shook all he was—warrior, Seer, Jarl and man—into a husband and a father.

He raced towards his family; Astrid, a two-year-old replica of Assi, hid behind her mother's *kyrtill* at the sight of a man she knew not. Assi's smile lit up the dark afternoon as she hugged her man for the first time in many moons.

Inside the house, as Assi prepared food, Sigrvard sat on one side of the room staring across at his Astrid, she stared back. Less frightened than she was at first, she slowly edged towards this now much cleaner man who her mother had said to call *Fadir*.

Then, as only a child can do, Astrid darted forward and threw herself at Sigrvard and wrapped her tiny arms around his neck.

A tear fell from his face onto hers, Assi cried too. It was a moment Sigrvard would carry with him forever.

Assi and Astrid were not the only loved ones who came back into Sigrvard's life that winter. Vidar had accompanied them to Jorvik.

"Who else could be trusted to deliver this precious cargo to its destination?" was how Vidar described his motivation to his friend and heir. But Vidar had left it a day before turning up unannounced at Sigrvard's door, which turned out to be a very tight squeeze for the merchant.

"I see life continues to be good for you, my fat friend," joked Sigrvard as he hugged Vidar.

"*Ja*, I couldn't pass up the opportunity to visit the growing trade centre of the Viking world that Jorvik has become. Besides, you understand, I have to sample wines and foods from many lands that may add to our coffers via new trade deals, *ja!*"

Sigrvard could not counter his partner's logic nor would it have served him to do so. It would be one of the many meetings they would enjoy throughout the festive season just starting.

As winter took its grip on Jorvik, the population began preparations for Yule and *Jol*, for Christian and Dane co-existed as one, each allowing the other to worship and celebrate as was seen fit.

The Seer's household was full of laughter and love. Astrid seemed to grow older and taller with each passing day and never stopped talking. With each passing night, Sigrvard and Assi made up for lost time, with each of them thinking surely there would be an addition to the family as a consequence.

It proved a peaceful and joyful *Ylir** and once it passed into *Morusugr*, the promise of more daylight increased happiness throughout Jorvik. Ivar was happy that each passing day meant he was closer to implementing the next phase of the *Vikingr* conquest—East Anglia. Though he would not be there.

Ivar had addressed the war council and told them that Olaf the White, the Norwegian joint king of Dublin, had requested his help in capturing Dumbarton Rock, north of Northumbria, which had been occupied by the Picts.

"If we take those lands," Ivar reasoned, "we would not have to voyage around the tip of Caledonia to reach the Western Isles and Hibernia. Being able to cross westerly by land before taking our fleet to the Isle of Man and Iceland then Vinland and Greenland would be more preferable."

A year in one place that was not home, even though it was Jorvik, was a long time for any *Vikingr* but, as Sigrvard said to Assi, "All things come to an end, my love," as he leaned down to kiss her goodbye. It was a little harder for him to bid farewell to Astrid but he had a year of memories to cherish. He went down on one knee and lifted her chin gently up towards his face with his finger.

"Look after your *modir* until my return, Astrid."

As tears ran down her button-nose, Astrid nodded with just two words, "*Ja Fadir.*"

He took his *Ulfberht* and scabbard from the wall and left to join the

* *Ylir, the second winter month.*

rest of the Great Army, which the war council, persuaded by Ivar, had decided would march on East Anglia.

* * *

The Great Army cut a bloody swathe south towards East Anglia as it headed for Thetford. Not only did they live off the land but every town that was burned, every farm that was razed to the ground and every church and monastery that was pillaged sent a clear message ahead to East Anglia King Edmund that the *Vikingr* were coming.

And, in a change of tactics, all plunder went back to Jorvik on the longships that shadowed the Great Army on its march towards Thetford. It didn't take long for the Great Army to make camp at Thetford. They had done it so many times they could do so in their sleep, and sometimes did.

Ivar was not with the Great Army. After his success in defeating the Picts at Dumbarton Rock, he returned to Hibernia along with King Olaf, with much gold and silver. He told the other commanders, which now included Sigrvard, that there should be no more incursions that far north as, in his words:

"It is just not worth the effort. When we succeed in our conquest of Mercia and Wessex, we shall secure a land route to the Manx Sea and Hibernia beyond. The *Vikingr* world will stretch from the Baltic to Vinland."

Those were the last words Sigrvard ever heard from Ivar's lips.

The East Anglian army, such that it was, was vanquished but leaving the little matter of the throne occupied by King Edmund. He was spared briefly while he considered the Viking offer to "renounce his Christian faith, a religion they regarded as one of weakness, or die."

Edmund chose the latter and met his end tied to a tree as target practice for Denisc archers; his head was then severed from his body and tossed into a bramble bush.

With three out of four main Anglo-Saxon kingdoms now under Denisc control, only Wessex stood in the way of total control of Angleland.

The next part of the conquest plan was not, in Sigrvard's mind, the best of tactical moves. As one of the leaders of the Great Army, he addressed the assembled war council, after Halfdan had announced: "I will take part of our army to attack Cambridge while Ubba will take the rest of our warriors to subdue Northumbria, which will see us control the entire east coast."

"But, my lord, would not divide to conquer play into the hands of Wessex and give them time to strengthen their army?"

"I take note of your observations as a Jarl, not a Seer," responded Halfdan, "but that is what we shall do. This is not a board game."

Sigrvard could see the strategic importance of Cambridge as it stood above the boggy ground of the Fens and provided a practical crossing of the River Cam. It would also gain important port access to the North Sea. The Great Army took Cambridge while Ubba's men captured Peterborough before heading north.

Sigrvard did not sleep well that first night occupying Cambridge. He dreamed of nine ravens flying aimlessly in circles and the occasional thought of his two girls.

As the Great Army continued their westward march, deep into Wessex territory, Sigrvard, the warrior Jarl, mulled over in his mind, which most of the time was like a huge *Hnefatafl* board, the strategy by which the commanders planned their conquest of the last remaining Saxon kingdom.

The *Vikingr* invaders had already been in England for five years and after countless battles had lost many warriors and many leaders. And still there was unrest among the men who had come to fight then settle, not go on to fight again and again.

Sigrvard even heard rumblings of discontent from some of the warriors that if it was to be raiding only, as it seemed, they may just as well raid Gaul, which was closer to home. Ivar disappearing with a large portion of their force did not help either.

AD 871

As the Great Army pushed deeper into Wessex, it found progress slower than ever. The opposition was more determined than ever before and the *Vikingr* commanders knew not why, until it was learnt that commanding the Saxon force was the 21-year-old brother of King Aethelred, Prince Alfred. His 'hit and run' tactics hindered the *Vikingr* at every crossroads and river crossing, be it bridge or ford. Alfred seemed to be avoiding an open pitch battle, probably due to the proficiency of the *riddari,* thought Sigrvard.

Nevertheless, the Great Army arrived at Reading where they set up camp.

As 870 moved into 871, a large foraging party sent out by Halfdan and Bacsecg was intercepted by local levies under the command of Aethelwulf, Ealdorman of Berkshire, and defeated at Englefield. Four days later, Aethelred and Alfred brought the main West Saxon army to join Aethelwulf for an attack on the Denisc.

All invaders found outside the walls were slaughtered by the West Saxons but the *Vikingr,* led by Sigrvard's *riddari* swept out of the town and in the ensuing rout, Aethelwulf was killed.

Four days later, both armies had regrouped and a blood slaughter happened at Ashdown. Thousands lay in a bloody heap at the end of the day that proved a first major setback for the Great Army and a first success for the English under Alfred, although they failed to retake Reading.

The battle also claimed the lives of King Bacsecg and a number of his Jarls—yet more loss of leadership, thought Sigrvard, who had been lucky to escape with his life.

Over a one-year period, there were nine major battles between Saxon and Dane—the nine ravens of Sigrvard's dream.

Exhausted and depleted, Alfred and the Great Army, now commanded by Halfdan, sought peace. Halfdan took his force to winter in London. Alfred did likewise in Wessex.

Before the Great Army could move on Wessex, they had to return to Jorvik where a rebellion had ousted the puppet King Egbert and Archbishop Wulhere. Duly quelled, following the rebellion, the *Vikingr* returned south for its planned rendezvous with the Summer Army, under King Guthrum, that was soon to arrive and sail up the Thames. The Danes would then have a formidable force with which to crush Wessex, the only remaining obstacle to total domination of England.

Faced with such overwhelming opposition, King Alfred paid an enormous amount of gold and silver to buy peace, as well as the time to recover, reorganise and rethink their hit and run strategy, which still was not enough the repel the invaders.

Guthrum, who had played no part in the *Vikingr* conquest to date, used the peace bought by Saxon coin for a stop off in Francia where a period of instability promised rich pickings.

The Great Army made winter camp at Torksey, just seventy leagues from Jorvik, close enough for a cross-country 'scouting' mission, thought Sigrvard.

As always, the site had been well chosen and well scouted. It was easily accessible from the Trent and boats could be dragged out of the water for repair with ease, while the higher ground would offer protection from winter floods and any wandering Anglo-Saxon forces. It was also strategically located at a junction of several land and river communication routes.

The winter camp was uneventful but once the summer came, the Great Army moved closer to Wessex, sweeping through Mercia; underlining their domination of the kingdom, they made for the royal centre that was Repton.

Not only was Repton the winter camp of choice but, as a symbol of Mercian royalty, it was also strategic. Then there were the not inconsiderable royal and archepiscopal food rents held in myriad barns that dotted its fertile landscape. The Great Army would divide once more and while Halfdan took his force to Northumbria, Guthrum would head for Wessex by sea.

Sigrvard relished a return to Jorvik but his hopes were dashed under instruction from Halfdan.

"I have a task for you, my friend. I need to have eyes on our new ally when he confronts Wessex. Eyes that have been 'invited', shall we say. Guthrum sent word to me that he wishes to have your *riddari* lead his Summer Army against the Saxons so two can be accomplished in one, yes?"

It was a rhetorical question and both knew it, though Halfdan added, "I know you would wish for a homecoming but in due course, a most bountiful welcome awaits you as I have in mind you to become Marshal of Jorvik with, of course, an appropriate stipend of land and tribute as befits such status."

Intrigued as he was by the promise of such wealth and status, a reunion with Assi and Astrid would have been more welcome.

Sigrvard bit his tongue as he responded, "As my king wishes it, so it will be."

AD 875

Guthrum had set up camp in East Anglia and waited for even more dragon ships to arrive with fresh troops, then he sailed south to raid the Wessex shore. The Summer Army then disembarked and rendezvoused with fifteen hundred *riddari* under Sigrvard. The new force brought added pressure to an already beleaguered Alfred, forcing him ever more onto the defensive. The Danes won their initial confrontation with the Anglo-Saxons in Dorset, capturing Wareham, but it proved too close an encounter for Guthrum who was most impressed with the way in which Sigrvard's horse soldiers turned the battle by dividing their complement and outflanking the enemy. The fleeing Saxons were either trampled underfoot or cut down as they ran.

As Guthrum sat in his tent that night, Sigrvard sat with him.

"Seer, warrior, Jarl, wealthy trader, oh and yes, master tactician. Is there anything beyond the prowess of the son of Eirikr the Fox?"

"My lord honours my father, truly merited, as for myself. I try and use to my best that which the gods have gifted me. But as yet, I have failed to master weaving."

Guthrum, with a blank look, stared at Sigrvard. He stared back, then both roared with laughter as they clinked flagons.

"I too failed in that endeavour. A good thing we can both fight, then."

More flagons into the conversation, Guthrum turned to Sigrvard.

"I tell you truly, Sigrvard, *riddari* are the future of land war."

"I cannot argue against that, my lord, for it has been that aim that has driven me on in that particular art of war."

* * *

Once again Alfred had to sue for peace, which was soon broken by the Viking leader, but only after Guthrum had rested his host. He killed his Saxon hostages before leaving. The Anglo-Saxon king could not face the Danes in open battle but was able to hinder and annoy them with regular skirmishes that bought him time though he could not defeat them.

The campaign of ten winters bled both sides. Halfdan and the Great Army commanders recognised that repeated slaughter of their warriors could not speedily be replaced. Yes, more migrants were arriving from their homeland but, as had been, the original aim of the invasion, conquest and settlement, was as far away as ever it was. The newcomers wanted to farm.

The Saxons recognised too that the decimation of their forces could not be sustained but Alfred strived to indicate that reinforcing their army was easier than for their enemy. They were standing, and falling, on the soil they were defending, soil that was soaked with Saxon blood. Land that the *Vikingr* aspired to but land that WAS Saxon, land that they were invading.

A time of peace, reflection and planning followed. Guthrum took the Summer Army to Cambridge while Halfdan headed for Northumbria and Jorvik with the Great Army.

Progress north was speedy and the *Vikingr* column made camp overnight at Selby before a triumphant return into Jorvik the following day.

There was much feasting among the *drengr*, many of whom had fought fully ten winters. They toasted their fellow warriors who were feasting in Valhalla. They toasted to reunions with their wives on the forenoon, they toasted Halfdan and Sigrvard, by Odin, they even toasted the grass that grew in the meadow and the stars that shone down from the heavens above. It was a good time to be a Viking.

Halfdan summoned Sigrvard to his tent, inviting him to sit and dine with him. It was not a king and his subject, it wasn't even a commander and his trusted second-in-command. It was two friends, fellow warriors, exchanging stories of valour and sacrifice on the battlefield, and there had been a few.

"I want you to lead the Great Army into Jorvik on the forenoon," was a shock for Sigrvard to consider. He pondered what to say.

Decline? No!

Disagree? No!

"My lord, no greater honour can a *Vikingr* have."

"You have earned it, my Seer, my friend and I also confirm Sigrvard, son of Eirikr, as Marshal of Jorvik. You will be entitled to much land, rent and tribute for your service. Details will be drawn up in good time but for now, more *bjorr*."

Sigrvard made it to his bed just two hours before rising to greet the day he would lead the Great Army home. But before he retired, he sat under the stars in silent reflection. Moments later, he went to his tent and with quill and parchment, scribed a short note:

Please be so good as to attend the new Marshal of Jorvik at Hild Monastery on the forenoon, two days hence from this note.

He addressed it to William of Whitby and handed it to one of his *riddari* who was charged with it reaching the correct hands.

The fourteen miles to Jorvik passed in a heartbeat, or so it seemed. It wasn't that long past dawn when the advance guard of the Great Army, riding just half a mile before Sigrvard and his standard, got first sight of the walls of Jorvik, now fully restored.

Walls that had hundreds of citizens standing with banners and flags, arms waving for their returning heroes. The warriors gradually broke away and made their way to their homes, those who lived within the walls did anyway. Those who had farms beyond the city walls soon departed for their beloved ones while Sigrvard made his way to where Assi and Astrid awaited.

As he rode up the gentle slope to home, he saw two blonde figures on the terrace in front, Assi and Astrid, yet there was little difference in height. They might have been sisters; indeed, there were but sixteen winters between them so sisters they appeared.

"My, how you have grown, daughter," Sigrvard whispered as he held her to his chest while her mother watched on, tears gently moving down each cheek.

"I have missed you so much, *Fadir*. Did you miss me?"

Assi saw a tear drop onto Sigrvard's beard, answering the question but nine-year-olds need words.

"As to that, I can only liken it to being without air or water. A man needs both to live, I need you, and of course, you," not wishing to exclude Assi.

That family evening passed quickly as they shut out the entire world because their world was in that house. Astrid played with her toys, entertaining Assi and Sigrvard; Assi captivated Sigrvard, as always. And he felt the warmth of anticipation as Astrid's bedtime arrived with his bedtime to follow shortly thereafter.

Few words were spoken as Assi and Sigrvard enjoyed each other, over and over. None were necessary. Before they slept, he told her of his plan to go to Hild on the forenoon. She understood, she always did.

The three-hour ride to Hild was the best ride of his life. There were no enemy troops to fear as Northumbria was under the total control of

Halfdan's army, although Sigrvard knew of the occasional rebel forays south and was appropriately wary.

There was no death or glory charge into a bloody melee of hacking and slashing deathly intent at the end of his journey, simply the warm air and wistful aroma of heather upon the breeze. He knew his route would take him near the site of his old village but chose to leave that particular part of his past where it lay.

He spotted the ruins of St Hild monastery from some distance.

The white limestone towers pierced the deep blue sky with a broken outline of walls in between making it look as a sleeping dragon. As he rode closer, Sigrvard noted the campfire in front of the main entrance to the monastery's church, with a white-robed monk sitting beside it. He looked skyward and murmured to himself, "He's early. That pleases me."

"William of Whitby, I am pleased you could attend."

"A summons from the new Marshal of York, I beg your pardon, Jorvik, would not be one to decline, methinks."

"More an invitation," replied Sigrvard who was not sure how he should react to such semantics.

"Ironic, is it not, the cause of Hild's deterioration was not the handiwork of your warriors but your own kinfolk?"

"How so?"

"The infighting between Deira and Bernicia caused the abandonment of this place of worship and learning."

"So may that be but blame is not why we are here."

"So, why are we here? What is your intent for my being here, in the company of a Viking warlord?"

"I wish you to rebuild the monastery, at my expense, and oversee all that it was, all that it should have become and all that it will be."

Speechless was not a state William was familiar with nor the giving of gratitude but the gentle nod of his balding pate, which hid his smile, almost, was enough for Sigrvard.

Once that moment passed, William of Whitby turned to his surprising benefactor.

"What are you, a Saxon-born Viking Jarl, to get from this charitable venture?"

"Exactly that which is contained in your words, my aged friend."

Sigrvard paused for William's reaction. If there was such a facial expression for a frown/smile, then it was engraved on the scholar's venerable countenance.

"Explain, for you are no illiterate plougher of the soil."

"You are a scholar, a scribe and a maker of books, are you not?"

William nodded.

"My wish," continued the Seer, "is for you to chronicle how an Anglo-Saxon boy of a mere nine winters became a Viking Jarl, Seer and Marshal of Jorvik."

"But, my Denisc conqueror," said William, quite naturally retaining his sense of humour, "as you rightly indicated—I think 'my aged friend' were your exact words—such an undertaking is perchance beyond my lifespan, which is already on borrowed time from God."

"As part of my rebuilding of St Hild, you will create the most splendid of libraries and scriptorium outside Rome. You will enlist scriptors who will assist you. They will deal with general matters and knowledge while you will devote one day in seven to be privy to the innermost workings of that journey from Streonshalh and back again, which you will then assemble and present as the Jorvik Chronicle."

"And if God, who knows how such a book ends, should decide my allotted lifespan precludes the completion of such an undertaking?"

"Then it will be completed by another who still has many years to make up on your aged tally.

"You will appoint an abbot, at such time it is appropriate, and although he will oversee the day-to-day workings of the Abbey, it is you he shall answer to."

"And who do I answer to, Marshal?"

"To your God, and me, of course." Sigrvard was also possessed of a sense of humour. Both men, Saxon and Denisc Saxon, anticipated many hours of word games in the times to come.

It was decided that Sigrvard would travel to William's quarters at the Abbey, once they were constructed, for his chronicler to write the necessary details. William would visit Jorvik once a month to add to them.

On his return to home, Assi asked Sigrvard for his reasoning behind such a project—she knew about the monastery but not the chronicle.

"My love, the present peace will not last. There will be much unrest before there is lasting ease between *Vikingr* and Saxon but when we are as one, it is my belief that it will be the Christian God who will transcend all."

CHAPTER TWENTY-ONE

THE period of peace and prosperity had been hard-won.

The fertile soil of the Kingdom of Jorvik had drowned in the blood of Saxon and Denisc alike. But it was Saxon and Dane who lived alongside each other as neighbours. Pagan and Christian who worshipped in harmony. Two cultures, one city and how that city did prosper.

But, as Marshal and Jarl, Sigrvard remained ever vigilant.

Vikingr longships and trading vessels may have enjoyed the freedom of rivers and sea but landward always offered temptation to Mercia, Wessex and the ever-dissident Northumbrians. Deira and Bernicia had an uneasy truce but the lurking threat that came from Norway offered each, and both, of those kingdoms an ally, should they be so desirous of such a coalition.

Patrols from Jorvik, as well as a network of labourers and itinerant traders, were a vital source of intelligence to the Marshal of Jorvik, though he still managed to grow his wealth through his business. A business that flourished after the death of his partner and friend Vidar due to the inheritance the avuncular merchant left to him. He still maintained his warehouses and wharves in Eirikrsborg but Sigrvard centralised his power-base to Jorvik, which was rapidly becoming the crossroads of a Scandinavian trading network. A network that stretched from Newfoundland in the west to Constantinople in the east, and from the Baltic to the Mediterranean.

There were properly surfaced streets, a throwback to Roman occupation. Micklegate was the main thoroughfare through its centre to a new wooden bridge across the Ouse. The city was so important that even coinage was produced, yet another sign of its cosmopolitan image that attracted merchants and traders of many language and dialect.

Tradesmen and craftsmen descended on Coppergate, Micklegate and Sheldergate in droves but it wasn't only artisans who made Jorvik their home. Migrants erected wooden buildings with backyard wells and cesspits and trampled earth floors. Wattle-work panels formed narrow pathways and while congested, squalid conditions existed, they went unnoticed, if it wasn't too warm a day. A putrid mass of backyard waste, including animal and human excrement and rotting vegetation was mixed in with urine but still they came: spinners, weavers, blacksmiths and toolmakers; leather workers, bone and antler carvers, gold and silversmiths, jewellers, glass bead makers, bakers and butchers, the latter adding blood to the gutters that ran red from forenoon to dusk. Then there were the shield-makers and the fish and oyster sellers who plied their trade, like hundreds of others, to the accompaniment of the skald, the saga teller and the music from boxwood pipes and bone flutes.

Jorvik had an atmosphere and an air of nowhere else and despite his flourishing trade and commerce empire, Sigrvard relished the time spent away at their thorp north of the city. A home he cherished with Assi and Astrid whenever he could take them away from the city.

Sigrvard found the transition from the cut and slash of battle to the cut and thrust of commerce easier than he would have thought possible. It was far more lucrative and far less a threat to life and limb to barter rather than batter. The Jorvik Marshal could not have been busier nor could his domain, yet he still made it an important part of his daily regime to check out the marketplaces, especially Coppergate.

Coppergate was especially interesting for Sigrvard as he recalled the days of his boyhood when watching craftsmen take raw materials and turn them into practical items as well as works of art had captivated him: from huge oak trees that became longships to Arab *dirhams* converted into bullion or expensive jewellery.

Raw materials travelled many miles to reach Jorvik and travelled many hundreds more after transformation by every craftsman from goldsmith and silversmith to blacksmith. Leatherwork was also highly regarded and the Jorvik tannery's reputation was as widespread as the network of trading posts and merchants it serviced.

One of the first tasks undertaken by Sigrvard when he decided to relocate his business empire to Jorvik was to stock his thorps, dotted around the kingdom, with Jylland oxen, beasts renowned for their high-quality meat. Before half their number were butchered to provide meat for export, at near four years in age, they had already produced enough calves for both milk and meat, and leather, of course. Local materials were also much in demand. As commerce prospered in the city, greater was the demand for iron ore from local mines to craft weapons; although there was greater demand for ploughshares, sickles and pitchforks than axes and swords, another sign of the changing world of the *Vikingr*.

Antlers from the deer and elk of nearby forests were sought-after accessories for knife and sword handles, and hunting those animals also served to provide fresh meat as well as practising archery, which was a legal obligation. Jorvik attracted walrus ivory for decoration, silk for headscarves, amber for jewellery and Rhineland wine. Imports from the land of the Rus, China and the lands of the New World as far as Newfoundland, Greenland and the lands of the Caspian Sea and the Black Sea.

Seal blubber was a less celebrated though equally invaluable import into the Jorvik capital. Seal flesh was used to fry food and to feed the *thralls*. It was perfectly suited for that purpose as it did not sit favourably on the Denisc palate.

Sigrvard had one particular favourite destination in Coppergate. Jorg was the toymaker and the Seer was probably his best customer, certainly his most generous. Patronage of the toymaker by the city's leading citizen was also good for business. Jorg, one of the new wave of settlers from Jylland, was renowned for the intricacy of his carving. If it was wood, he could carve it. He was also without equal for ivory creations.

It was nearly the time of Astrid's birthday and Sigrvard had in mind a chess set that Jorg had been working on for several months. "Just the two queens left," he had promised the Marshal on his visit the week prior.

"Two queens," he had smiled.

The smile on Sigrvard's face disappeared temporarily as he left Coppergate and waded through the pools of piss and human excrement on his way home. He sometimes wondered what the Roman founding fathers would have made of their paved streets now swimming in shit.

Astrid was jumping up and down as her father returned home, eager to see what he had hiding behind his cloak.

"Show me, show me," she repeated over and over.

"Show you what?" responded her father, over and over.

Astrid feigned sadness. Sigrvard did likewise, although his long, thick blonde beard made it difficult for Astrid to tell.

Assi's maternal admonishment required no words. He knew he was teasing his daughter but he knew she loved it.

The morning of Astrid's birthday began for Sigrvard with his private contemplation. That day, as all days before, he spoke to Eirikr. He answered his own questions but then he and his father had been so close, it was as if he was there with Sigrvard. He mulled over the current period of peace. As Marshal and Jarl, it pleased him but as Seer, he thought ahead. It mattered little that he was Saxon-born and Denisc-bred when it came to knowing, with absolute certainty, the Anglo-Saxons would not rest while a single Viking held sway on their soil. They would not think twice about allying with others, notably Picts and Norwegians, to drive the Denisc back from whence they had come.

Sigrvard foresaw a different outcome but, as yet, it was still clouded in the mists of his mind.

He returned home to find that an excited Astrid had been playing with her gifts but they lay upon her cot. His daughter, not hearing her father enter, was moving around the room, light-footed as a wisp of a fairy dancing in the early morning mist—with the small sword he had gifted Assi on their wedding day. He was transfixed as his near-teen daughter showed swordsmanship he had not seen in war-hardened warriors.

The hand-eye coordination was impressive by itself but the speed and agility whilst executing elaborately effective hand movements made the hairs on his neck and arms stand erect.

His first emotion was pride, followed immediately by terror and the words that entered his mind thereafter—Shield Maiden.

Fear and pride are strange bedfellows and although he knew he would have to broach the subject at some point with Assi, that day was not this.

* * *

There hadn't been too much Northumbrian activity for many moons but attention was diverted to the other side of England when a messenger from King Halfdan arrived in Jorvik.

He was taken directly to Sigrvard who was presented with a leather message tube, from which he extracted a single sheet of parchment once he had broken the royal seal.

Greetings Sigrvard, I have a task for you and your excellent riddari. *Word has come to me from King Guthrum, a personal request. He seeks assistance in the next phase of the matter in hand, which you will understand cannot be committed to writing here.*

Sigrvard knew at once that Wessex was the 'next phase' referred to. With minimum fuss, Sigrvard messaged his commanders they would march two days hence. *Just enough time to tell Assi,* he thought.

He sent for Einar.

"You are herewith Deputy Marshal of Jorvik," he said in greeting as Einar presented himself to his Jarl.

"How so, my lord?"

"I am away on the king's business and I charge you to defend the Kingdom of Jorvik and my family. I can think of no better man to entrust that which is of the greatest value to me."

"And no greater honour can I have."

Einar left, leaving Sigrvard with the task of explaining, once more, that he was off to war. Once more Assi understood; once more, Sigrvard wished she need not.

"That is the way of our world, my love."

Whatever her reservations, Assi still marvelled at the impressive sight of her husband leading his column out of the city.

One day, she thought to herself, *he will go through those gates and it will be the last time I wave him goodbye.*

Sigrvard's force made good progress and met up with Guthrum and his army at Cambridge. The two leaders met in Guthrum's tent where he outlined their plan of attack.

"We will sweep south then west, where we shall take Wareham after dealing with Alfred and his force. Before we engage with the Saxons, we shall be reinforced by a fleet of our ships who will carry reinforcements into Portland."

It was to prove advantageous that Guthrum was able to sneak his landforce past Alfred and avoid confrontation until Wareham was secured. The Saxon leader had learned lessons from the *Vikingr* invaders and built a number of ships that set sail to head off the reinforcing longships. Alfred built the Saxon ships twice as long and twice as big as their Viking opponents but with one key design improvement that was to prove crucial.

The Saxon warships sat taller in the water and so towered over the longships, giving them the advantage when aiming down with sword, spear or arrow. And when boarding the longships, the Saxon warriors were able to leap down into their enemy vessels and the ensuing land battle was fought at sea. Assisted by a terrible storm that day, the Saxons recorded a significant victory.

Not only did that triumph prevent reinforcements making landfall but it also succeeded in sending previously unbeatable longships packing. However, the Saxons were unable to wrest Wareham back and so yet another peace was brokered. And yet again, the peace did not last. Once he had rested his forces, Guthrum broke out and pushed further into Wessex as far as Exeter, with Alfred in pursuit. Exeter fell to Guthrum but because he had lost so many men when his fleet was wrecked, he was in no position to defeat Alfred so once more peace was brokered and Guthrum took his forces to winter in Chippenham.

As ever, it did not take long for the *Vikingr* to set up camp and Guthrum called Sigrvard to break bread with him that first evening in Gloucestershire.

"We have not only taken stock of the land, my friend, from east to west but also of the Anglo-Saxon force. I feel the current stalemate has some time to run and so I am sending you back to Jorvik where your presence will ensure the troublesome Northumbrians and their wretched Norwegian allies are kept in check. My plans for Wessex and Alfred require me to avoid a war on two fronts, and that is where you come in.

"And, I am thinking, your wife will be grateful to me that I send you packing?"

Both men smiled, clasped one another and Sigrvard retired, sent word to his men they were home on the morrow and threw himself onto his cot for sleep.

Once they were well clear of Wessex and in the Denisc south of the Kingdom of Jorvik, Sigrvard thought to visit some of the southernmost parts of his domain. Something he had been unable to do since his reward from Halfdan.

"It will only add two days to our journey to Jorvik. What harm can that do?"

* * *

Sigrvard was most pleased how his lands were thriving. Barns were full, animals fat and his villeins were most diligent in their work, notably in collecting the appropriate taxes. Their application may have been sweetened with their Jarl being the only landowner in the entire kingdom who applied a bonus, should it be earned, come harvest. Indeed, his happy workers were productive workers.

By the time the *riddari* completed their incident-free homeward journey, the saddle-bags of the supply horses were laden with coin. Even allowing for the occasional donation to any church they passed on the way.

Sigrvard felt such un-*Vikingr*-like actions owed much to his mother's Christian influence, allied to him being back in the land of his birth. His men, on the other hand, thought not beyond the spoils they would share back in Jorvik.

As the column approached the south gate of the city, Sigrvard felt a sense of gratitude towards the gods for such bounteous land, his homeland, which was now his new home and his family's.

The reunion at home, for all from the humblest *thrall* to Sigrvard's itself, was that of any returning army, save for those who had fallen in battle. But, as since his first raids in Asturias and Francia, the Marshal ensured families of the fallen received the share their father, brother or son was entitled to. Once he settled back home, Sigrvard decided he would have some days with his family before returning to duties as Marshal, Seer and Jarl.

Einar reported to Sigrvard that there had been a number of small, isolated raids in his absence but mainly on outlying farms and hamlets; "nothing of great concern" was how it was worded. He did, however, add, "The strange thing is that all of those raids came from west and northwest of Jorvik, nothing from the north. There is some evidence of Norwegian presence in the raiding parties and from the Western Isles and Caledonia also."

"Double the scouting missions," said Sigrvard. "Tell our spies to make themselves be seen more often in their usual areas and instruct them, if necessary, more coin is available for more intelligence.

"Now, I desire some time with my family. Einar, you will continue as in my absence."

"My lord, I am grateful for your safe return and for the opportunity to safeguard your family and our city. But I must confess to a certain relief that I can now return to soldiering and scouting rather than sentry duty, you do understand?"

"I do, and my gratitude knows no bounds though the cart you will find waiting for you at your house, with certain things that used to be Saxon, will demonstrate that I did try to push those boundaries."

"My lord is as generous as ever."

Since the awarding of lands and thorps by Halfdan, Sigrvard had been a busy landlord and trader and had spent many a day visiting his various holdings spread over the vast area that was the Kingdom of Jorvik. He tried hard to please Assi by spending no more than one night away each time but knew his latest trek would take at least a week.

It would be a scouting mission that would also mean he could inspect his westernmost holdings because he was going close to the Wessex border in the west. He believed a show of force would warn off any hostile Wessex intentions. He weighed up several options before deciding he would send Einar to lead the scouting party that would comprise those who had garrisoned Jorvik while those who had campaigned with him and Guthrum would remain to garrison the city.

What would normally have been merely a scouting mission was made ever more necessary from the intelligence Einar had reported to him on his return. Avoiding a war on two fronts, as Guthrum put it, was uppermost in Sigrvard's mind as he made his way to the stables where he would give Einar final instructions.

Einar stumbled to the assembly point after his nightly flagon of ale and tried his best to take on board final instructions. That morning, Einar was just about the right side of a hangover to curtail the inner anger that just wanted to bawl at his Jarl: *Don't you think I can lead a scouting patrol without needing my arse wiped by a pompous Anglo-Saxon inbred!*

Thankfully, Einar curtailed his anger and it was fortunate he did as what Sigrvard imparted to him may save his life and keep his patrol safe.

"My trusted commander, I ask you extend your patrol beyond its normal parameters. I have word that the Norwegians, who do not see our coalition conquest of England in the same way as we, are courting the Northumbrian dissenters. I wish you to discover what presence there is of our Norse compatriots."

Einar pumped out his chest and struck his clenched right fist against his breastplate, something he thought impressed Sigrvard, but it didn't.

"*Ja*, my lord."

Einar didn't see the smile on Sigrvard's face as he turned to walk away. *He keeps trying*, mused the Jarl to himself.

The twenty-strong *riddari* swept out of the western gate and rode ten miles in that direction before swinging northwest.

Another day's ride further took them close to the Deira border where they came upon a group of Angles, numbering six or seven, with horses. Einar's eyes lit up. *Easy meat*, he thought, never for a moment wondering if what seemed too good to be true might be exactly that. And despite words to the wise from his subordinate, Einar smelled blood.

The *riddari* walked their steeds along a tall hedgerow that followed the ridge line that looked down into the dip where the Angles were resting. Einar gave the signal to mount and the *Vikingr* made twenty or thirty strides before the enemy was alerted.

The Angles did not, as Einar expected, rally towards them to engage; instead, choosing flight over fight, they mounted and sped north. Had Sigrvard been present to observe proceedings, he would have slowly shaken his head and thought, *Has Einar not learned a thing from years of defeat at Hnefatafl?* The answer, of course, was no. Led by Einar, the *riddari* raced after their quarry and seemed to close in on them as they climbed to the top of an escarpment before disappearing below the rim. As in the blind leading the blind, by the time his warriors realised they had been led into a trap—some three hundred Angles—it was too late. Nineteen of Einar's *riddari* were cut down in seconds; only Gilden survived because he was at the rear of the line. The inner leader inside Einar ordered him back to Jorvik to warn the city while he himself drove his horse into the centre of the Angle horde. Unlike his men who had died, Einar was dragged from his steed, bound and gagged and thrown back across his horse for the journey to the Angle camp. Of all the rides he had ever made atop a horse, this was the most uncomfortable. As he bounced up and down on the saddle, getting perverse satisfaction from his manhood being aroused, Einar was contriving a plan.

A scheme to turn an almost certain fatal situation to his advantage and exact long-awaited revenge on his best friend and blood-brother.

Einar's tortuous journey was soon over. The patrol entered their compound and as they removed his ropes and gag so that he could take water, Einar grasped his opportunity before he was dragged off to incarceration and almost certain death.

"Ho, I seek an audience with King Ricsige." Had it not been for the signs of wealth and rank displayed by his armour, it was doubtful if anyone would have paid attention; indeed, it was that which saved him from being cut down with the rest of his patrol as the patrol commander, who had noticed it and thought it worth taking him prisoner in the first place, listened.

"And pray, what would my king want with a miserable *Vikingr* scrote-sack such as you?"

"That is for men of rank to discuss, not a lackey," sneered Einar.

A well-aimed boot to the nose was the commander's response and Einar's reward for...well, being Einar.

Several moments later, a bloodied Einar was dragged, his feet still bound, into the hall where the king was dining. His retinue seemed more intrigued by their Danish 'guest' than he, gnawing away at a giant leg of lamb.

"And what is it our Norse kinsman requires from a humble Saxon that could be of the slightest interest?"

"Untie me and clear the room and I will tell you—my lord."

The king roared with laughter, his court did likewise.

"You have balls, I give you that, for now, for someone who is about to lose them, I am impressed. Surprised but impressed nonetheless."

The king had Einar's guards drag him to the other side of the crowded room and left him in a heap as King Ricsige threw his ample frame into a carved oak throne with huge cushions.

He reached for his *seax* and Einar swallowed nervously. Ricsige then reached for a nearby candleholder and scribed a mark, one thumb's thickness below the flame.

"You have until the flame reaches the mark to intrigue me. Then we dine, or you die and are fed to my dogs, they like raw meat this time of day."

Einar thought to ask if the king meant when the flame reached the mark or obliterated it but thought this wasn't the time for levity. He manoeuvred his body into a slightly more comfortable position, propped up against one of the hall's support beams.

"My lord, I am Einar, *Riddari* Commander of Sigrvard, Jarl of Eirikrsborg and Marshal of Jorvik."

That last title, which Einar used to impress, had quite the opposite effect. Flushed with anger, Ricsige reminded Einar that York was STILL the capital of the Kingdom of Northumbria.

"I am blood-brother and confidant to Sigrvard who has the ear of King Halfdan and I can offer you—Jorvik."

Einar now had the king's full attention.

Self-assurance bordering cockiness was Einar's demeanour as he put phase one of his plan into action.

"What is Jorvik, sorry, York, worth to you, my lord?"

Ricsige grew more attentive.

"Why would you betray your kin so readily?"

"I have my reasons."

Einar could have given vent to the bubbling envy that was boiling towards full-blown jealousy but he felt it would have undermined his scheme in the eyes of the king.

"After all those years of playing second fiddle to an Anglo-Saxon thrall—me of Viking blood—being snubbed and ridiculed, it is now time to turn the tables, turn being the word."

"If it pleases his majesty, I can give you your capital, and much gold, as York is both. The city is flourishing and trade from many lands is bringing in more wealth than can be counted.

"Make me King of York and I will hold fealty to you and pay you more in a year's tribute than you can imagine. Vikings have trade routes from Vinland to Constantinople and you need not raise a finger, save to count your gold."

"And your part in all this?"

"The throne of York, no more—for now."

"And how do you see this fantasy play out?"

"I steal your horse and escape."

The king jumped to his feet, knocking his throne backwards and alerting his nearby guards who raced to his side.

"Please, let me continue," pleaded Einar. "I take your horse, escape back to York and, in good time, when you have gathered sufficient forces and the city garrison is away, I will let you in through a secret tunnel known only to me and you will have your capital, your right."

"And my horse?" the king whispered ruefully.

"When you are ready, you will send me word; a messenger will have no trouble gaining entry disguised as a trader. I release your horse, which will return to you. His return is your signal."

"I have one condition," said the king. "You will ensure the wife of Sigrvard is taken hostage and safely delivered to me."

Released from his bonds, Einar and his new ally continued their conversation as aides readied the king's horse.

Einar turned towards the exit and freedom but as he reached the door, he turned to the king for one last demand.

"One more thing—your most trusted warrior will lead your incursion and he will be instructed that I must be dragged, kicking and screaming from the Jarl's bed chamber, after killing several of your soldiers, of course, and tied to a horse to be taken with your men as they leave York. Agreed?"

"Agreed."

While Einar was engaging in treachery, Gilden had reached Jorvik and informed his Jarl what had occurred.

"Einar is a wily fox, he will return. If not, they are sure to ask for a ransom."

Sure enough, it came to pass.

The king's horse was a fine mount and made short work of Einar's return to Jorvik where he immediately made for Sigrvard's quarters. Sigrvard was so delighted and welcoming at his friend's safe return, he bear-hugged him for the first time since his stag party. Einar felt a pang of remorse at the wheels of betrayal he had set in motion but it was too late.

"I was scouring my bedchamber for loose coin to pay your expected ransom, my friend, but the wily fox made good his own escape and on such a fine beast as well; tell me all."

"When my captors realised I was of rank and status, they threw me in, shall we say, less than secure accommodation.

"And when I was brought my evening meal, I, er, swapped clothes with the *thrall* who served me; he was dead and had no need of his rags. I took the serving tray and dish and simply walked free of my incarceration, made my way through the kitchens to the stables and picked the finest horse there, which, with the help of the gods, carried me back here."

"Praise be to Odinn that his axe-man returns."

"And he returns with news that will please the Marshal of Jorvik."

Einar went on to tell Sigrvard that he had overheard the Northumbrian leaders and the Norwegian commanders that they planned at the next full moon to sweep around the northern flank and attack Jorvik from the west.

"Then I shall be there to meet them and slaughter them to a man, every Saxon and Norwegian who stands with them."

"And I shall stand alongside you, my lord," said Einar.

"*Nei*, my friend. You have done your part. You will remain at garrison and safeguard my family and continue your impressive rebuilding of our capital."

A relieved Einar spent the rest of the evening drinking with Sigrvard before retiring.

Once more, Sigrvard bade farewell to his family as he prepared to lead half the Jorvik garrison out of the city.

"I will return soon," he smiled as he took Assi by one hand and daughter by the other.

"I am sure you will be well served maintaining my warehouses and their inventory," he added. "No one knows better than you, myself included, how my—sorry, *our*—business interests are conducted. Maybe one day, I will make you a partner, legally."

He smiled, she responded in mock chastisement, and they kissed once more before Sigrvard set off for what even he as Seer did not know was the most significant journey of his life.

Assi smiled as the *riddari* left Jorvik. She rubbed her hand over her stomach. *I will tell him on his return*, she said in her head.

CHAPTER TWENTY-TWO

DELIGHTED though Einar appeared to be, charged by Sigrvard to add the guardianship of his family whilst still overseeing the rebuilding of Jorvik, there wasn't much slaughter and glory to be had watching stonemasons and builders at their daily work so he was grateful that once Sigrvard returned, he would have scouting missions aplenty.

Nevertheless, he was impatient that there were workday endeavours to attend to first. But the side-line he had, having workmen restore one of the most desirable buildings in the city for his own use, more than compensated, especially as his supervision enabled him to pass costs onto his Jarl.

Then, one day, one of those moments changed destiny.

As part of his constructional supervision, Einar was required to attend restoration of a particularly ancient shit-house, *latrinae*, although that referred to a single occupancy depository.

The building Einar had earmarked as a present to himself was a communal toilet block, for which he had grand plans. His attendance was requested by the foreman in charge of a labour gang who informed him that a bricked-up door had been found that had been buried behind a mound of rubble.

Einar viewed the discovery out of curiosity simply because he thought there might be treasure hidden behind this unknown piece of Roman stonework. The labourers made light of the block-work so Einar and his foreman were able to light torches and enter a rectangular ante-chamber. The foreman failed to notice an *aureus** that lay near his sandal; he was more concerned at the fragile state of the roof that

* *Roman gold coin.*

looked ready to collapse any moment. Einar distracted the workman and swiftly recovered the coin, his mind spinning at the prospect of further treasure that might lie beyond the three tunnel entrances that ran off the ante-chamber.

"Sire, we need to support this roof before further exploration can take place."

"See to it," instructed Einar, "and report to me when it is done."

Two days later, Einar and the foreman returned to the ante-chamber but only one of the pair would leave, alive. Einar was not about to share 'his treasure' with anyone. As Alftan stooped under a piece of horizontal scaffolding, Einar gave a mighty shove to the vertical prop supporting it and several tons of heavy beams and stone blocks crushed the life out of the master mason.

Once the body was removed, Einar gave instructions that no one but he would be permitted to enter that room until he made it safe. The workforce, though wondering how a Viking *drengr* would do such work, made no further fuss nor question.

Einar returned later that day and with hammer and chisel, began to investigate the three tunnel entrances. He walked at least a mile along the first of them and emerged on the other side of the River Ouse. The second tunnel, also a good mile in length, emerged beyond the far bank of the Foss. *Clever people, those Romans*, he thought.

Einar set off along the third tunnel but stopped after a few yards when his hand rubbed along the wall and caught a recessed panel. He raised his torch for a closer look and saw that a cleverly disguised doorway, barely visible, was the reason for its concealment. Grateful he had brought hammer and chisel, Einar set to work cutting away enough stonework to crawl through.

It was a different kind of tunnel Einar found. Covered in cobwebs and rat droppings but no treasure. He followed the tunnel but this one was twice as long as the other two. He knew it was fully two miles as he had counted every step along its length until he reached a heavy brass and oak door barring his way. Luckily, it was not locked but secured by a huge iron bolt. It took quite a while for Einar, who was not muscularly endowed, to free the bolt and almost as long to heave the door open. The exit was set in a recessed part of a granite rock wall that led to a vista north of Jorvik, towards the hills and beyond. Wild brambles and brush added greatly to its secrecy.

What was the purpose of the secret tunnel, especially as there were two other perfectly functional tunnels for escape or clandestine arrivals?

The original Roman settlement of *Eboracum* had been sited, not on the nearby high ground, which would have been the norm for defensive purposes, but between the two rivers. That gave two sides of occupation, which needed no defensive construction.

Back in his quarters, Einar relaxed in his bedchamber, still pondering his tunnel discovery. The murder of the mason merited no thought at all. Always looking for a chance to exploit, he was sure there must be a way he could use the secret tunnel, once he had found the treasure, of course.

A flagon of wine was no way to prepare for his return to scouting the next forenoon but that didn't stop him. Alcohol took over and he was asleep in seconds. Once he sobered up, Einar knew there would be no better time to execute his treachery than at that point in time.

Sigrvard had only just left the city and would be two, maybe three, full days from reaching the area where Einar's false intelligence indicated Saxon incursion was taking place. So, plenty of time to send a message to Northumbria that Jorvik would soon be theirs, and their new king's, of course.

It was less than a day until the Northumbrian-Norwegian coalition assembled, under cover of darkness, at the rockface where Einar met them. The traitor was surprised that there were only around five hundred warriors, all on foot, of course, a point he made to their commander.

"Fear not, future King of Jorvik. The element of surprise afforded us by your cunning will mean we will have taken all we need from York before the population realises."

"And our exit plan?" inquired Einar.

"Ah, yes, you are to leave here bound, kicking and screaming, after killing several of my men and tied to a horse. How could I forget? After securing the Marshal's wife and daughter, yes?"

"Yes."

Led by Einar, carrying a single torch, the armed band made its way into the heart of the city, emerging into the main precinct in front of the cathedral before a soul stirred. They stormed through the narrow streets and headed for the main quarters of the garrison, cutting down all they met. They moved so swiftly that they reached the garrison quarters before they realised what was happening. The doors were barred and nailed secure while flaming torches were flung onto the shale-wood roof. The building was aflame in seconds and Jorvik was defenceless save for the few brave souls who battled valiantly to stem a tide that was not for stemming. Rape and pillage uppermost in most of their minds, the invaders swept erratically through the side streets. Einar had other ideas.

He knew where he wanted to go and that's where he headed with several heavily armoured aides. The two *huskarls* on duty outside Sigrvard's house were cut down in an instant, though they took several opponents with them as they died.

As crackling flames took hold on the thick oak beams of their bedchamber, Assi and Astrid praised the gods as they saw Einar enter the room through billowing smoke like some nether-world saviour. Their relief was short-lived.

As a blood-soaked Einar got closer, they realised he was neither saviour nor spirit. Flanking Sigrvard's trusted lieutenant, line astern behind each shoulder, were savage-looking Northumbrians. No true Norseman would follow Einar in what was about to happen. Einar's accomplices were also soaked in blood. No words were necessary. None were spoken. All present knew what was about to happen.

As one grotesquely scarred warrior advanced towards Assi, salivating as he loosened his trousers, he was halted in his tracks by Einar.

"Letta me first," he leered as his trousers fell to the floor, showing all present his manhood wasn't quite ready.

Any momentary hopes Assi may have harboured, that all the years of loyalty given to her husband by Einar would manifest in her greatest moment of need, vanished quickly.

"Allow me," whispered Assi, who decided to take the initiative in the moment she knew was to be her last in this world.

She sank slowly to her knees and lifted her ice-blue eyes upwards to engage Einar, face to face. Einar, never the brightest star in the firmament, couldn't resist the invitation to rest his now-erect member between the lips before him. Assi began slowly as Einar, distracted by the expected ecstasy, looked skyward.

Assi paused momentarily before snapping her snow-white teeth together, severing Einar's manhood at its base. As she spat the offending member across the floor, blood dripping from her lips, those same lips uttered, "No more like you," signalling the end of Einar's bloodline.

Assi leapt to her feet, grabbed the sword given to her by Sigrvard and swung it in the direction of the nearest Northumbrian, slicing off his helmet, and head, as one. Astrid grasped her sword and swung it at Einar, whose mind, not to mention his manhood, was elsewhere. The first arc missed but on its return trajectory, it caught Einar on the bridge of his nose.

The fool had thought no helmet was necessary.

What followed was swift as Assi and Astrid sold their lives, eventually, at a high cost to their rampant assailants. A cost that although its vengeance would be long in coming would be even more exacting than Einar could possibly ever countenance.

As pre-arranged, Einar emerged from Sigrvard's quarters, kicking and screaming, wielding his axe for effect, as several burly Saxons threw him across a horse, no saddle this time, and bound him tightly for his 'incarceration'.

The Northumbrian raiding party departed as quickly as they had arrived. Einar's 'kidnappers' made a very public exit through the bloody, smoke-filled streets of Jorvik while the bulk of their raiding group scurried away like rats through the secret tunnel, emerging well away from the burning city.

King Ricsige awaited the arrival of his turncoat Viking but his face dropped to the floor as only Einar entered his court when he had expected two accompanying females. Whatever currency may have been available to Northumbria, having possession of the family of the Jorvik Marshal as hostages was gone.

"Well?" exclaimed Ricsige.

"My lord, it is most unfortunate that Sigrvard's wife and daughter chose death rather than accept your invitation to court. We tried to take them but they fought like Berserkers and had to be killed."

"A Viking warrior who cannot take two females when leading a band of my personal guard is of no use to me—begone. We will speak further later."

Einar may have been slow on the uptake but he wasn't going to dally and risk decapitation when it fully sank in what Ricsige had lost with the death of Assi and Astrid. He quickly made for the stable and for the second time, used the king's horse to make good his escape.

He raced clear of the Saxon camp and put as many miles between him and Deira as possible. Then there was the not inconsiderable question of Sigrvard when he learnt of his family's fate.

Einar would have to go into hiding, but where? He couldn't go anywhere near the northern tribes after Jorvik. He couldn't go anywhere near Jorvik itself, maybe in the future but certainly not until some considerable time had passed.

He set off for the Isle of Man where anonymity may provide him with the best cloak for his evil actions. The timing had to be right. Too early a return to face Sigrvard would be suspicious, even if the man wasn't a Seer. Too late and any return may be just that, too late.

After more than a week of searching, Sigrvard reasoned Einar's intelligence was lacking. There was nary a sign of Northumbrian Saxon, let alone Norwegian Vikings, so it was back to Jorvik. But as they neared the city from the west, a rider approached the *riddari.* Never had Sigrvard nor any of his men seen a steed so whipped into a full gallop as the rider got near. He approached the Marshal, but at slower pace, as his previous speed might have earned him an arrow or spear through the head.

"My lord," said the rider as he gasped for breath while trying to speak.

"At ease, my good man, draw breath, take some water then say what you need."

"Jorvik, she burns."

Without hesitation, as his blood ran cold, Sigrvard dug his heels into Victory to follow the trail home, not knowing what he would find. As he drove harder and harder towards the city at breakneck speed, Victory was frothing with exertion. Nearing the outskirts, Sigrvard saw the smoke rising before he reached Micklegate, the southern entrance to Jorvik.

Heart racing, he galloped towards his townhouse where he could see the streets were strewn with numerous, mutilated bodies, freemen and *thralls,* women and warriors, Pagan and Christian alike. He jumped from his horse and raced towards the gate of his home, teeth gritted at what he might find.

Did they escape, did they hide, did Einar protect them as he swore he would? The answers to all three of his inner questions were the same. No.

He steeled himself for what he might find but it was still not enough.

Assi and Astrid lay beside each other, their naked, mutilated bodies in a death embrace. He could tell by the position of their bodies they had been raped, probably many times.

The flames inside the bedchamber were intense as the house filled with dense, acrid smoke, forcing Sigrvard to run from the burning shell. He doubled over until his stomach was retched empty of its contents. A handful of servants raced towards the room with pails of water but as he wiped away his tears with his forearm, he shouted, "Stop!"

His voice, a mix of grief and rage, rang out and they stood as statues.

"Let it burn! Let it be a funeral pyre for my wife and daughter. A beacon to light their way to the gods."

He turned and slowly walked back to his horse, mounted and made for Micklegate and, who knows, where to thence.

Victory wandered with an uncaring, unguiding Sigrvard, going where his steed took him.

A day, a night, another day, until he slipped from his saddle onto the moss-covered ground. Before he drifted into unconsciousness, he screamed to the gods, "Take me! I beseech your earth to swallow me whole and rid me of this burdensome world!"

If ever Sigrvard needed for his mind to take him to another place, it was now.

Osgar ran along the beach with waves swirling around his feet and between his toes. He looked towards the sand dunes where he saw three figures. He recognised the two females who were smiling at him.

He smiled back but did not recognise the young blonde boy who stood between Assi and Astrid. The sun shone on the ice-smooth surface of the sea. But then, a huge dragon emerged, belching flame that pierced the darkness between its jaws and swallowed all—Assi, Astrid, the sea, the sun, Osgar and the unknown boy.

Sigrvard's face was wet. Yes, it was raining but it was Victory's tongue trying to revive his master that woke him.

Sitting beside him was a face he did recognise, William of Whitby.

Why him, why now and why here?

He cared not for any question he had not asked but simply sat up.

No words were exchanged. Both men sat and waited.

Once they began, they did not stop. They spoke long past dark and long into the night.

"Perhaps you should be writing all this down," said Sigrvard, displaying a flicker of the man of a few days earlier.

"Perhaps I should—but then that would be a wasted exercise for this aged mind and these aged eyes forget nought. Mead?"

Sigrvard accepted the drink that had been warming by the campfire and they continued to speak. William told Sigrvard about the progress at Hild, he told William of the devastating raid on Jorvik.

As they rode back to the city, Sigrvard spoke more about his life than ever before to any other human. From before the moment he had been captured by the *Vikingr* to the devastation that had robbed him of his family.

In the week since the raid and Sigrvard's absence, the clearing up of a ravaged Jorvik was almost complete. His house had been left untouched, what was left of it, after his orders to let it burn as a funeral pyre for Assi and Astrid.

He called a council meeting of all eldermen and clerics.

"We are not Barbarian pirates. We *Vikingr* are farmers, fishermen, traders and merchants, and warriors, if required.

"We shall rebuild Jorvik, stronger and better than before. Dane or Saxon, Pagan or Christian, it is in everyone's interest for us to be successful. We can learn from each other.

"I am Jarl Sigrvard, Marshal of Jorvik but eighteen winters past I was born an Angle, near this very spot."

He pointed northeast and continued, "Streonshalh gave me life and I shall hold that life forfeit if what has been said here is not the truth. I pledge you my troth as an Angle and a Dane.

"My house will be razed to the ground, as will many other buildings. In its place, I will build a school for the young of Jorvik who will one day govern our city and our kingdom."

Next, it fell to the Marshal of Jorvik to investigate exactly how his city defences had been breached so easily as it seemingly had. Sigfried was the most senior warrior of the Jorvik garrison that had lost so many men and leaders when the raiders had burned down their headquarters. He presented himself to his commander with an understandable air of uncertainty.

"I am not seeking to apportion blame," said Sigrvard. "I seek only answers, assessment and information. First tell me of the attack, from the very moment you became aware."

"It was a normal morning and I was making my rounds of all sentry posts and guard posts. I checked the perimeter around your house and all *huskarls* were at their stations and alert. But as I approached the front gate of your residence, after coming from the rear, I heard screaming and saw a horde of…they must have been Saxons with some Norwegians and they fell upon us in a fury.

"I called to the *huskarls* inside your courtyard and ordered them to bar the gate and ensure the safety of your wife and daughter. Leif, my lieutenant, who was responsible for personal protection, carried out my instructions but then I was laid low."

"Yes, I noticed the limp—and your arm?" he asked, pointing to the half limb that hung from Sigfried's left shoulder.

Sigfried smiled. "At least it isn't my sword arm."

Sigrvard smiled back, then continued, "And what of events inside my house. Have you any knowledge?"

"I regained consciousness but by then the raiders had vanished. They came and went within the hour. I cannot fathom how so many came and went so quickly."

"You must investigate and pin down the first contact between the raiders and our warriors or population.

"Now, inside."

"Yes, my lord, of course. We found all *huskarls* dead outside the door to your bedchamber, save one."

Sigrvard's attention immediately sharpened. "Continue."

"Leif, though badly wounded, was still alive. I fetched him water and in between taking water, he gurgled but just a single word, over and over—Einar."

"Of course." Eyes bulging, Sigrvard's memory took him back to that bloody scene he had beheld when entering his bed-chamber that fateful day—in his traumatised state, he had not noticed Einar, and he should have. Einar, whom he had trusted with Jorvik and his family.

Why was there no body? Einar would have fought like a Berserker to defend his duty of protection.

"My lord," uttered Sigfried, bringing back his focus to the matter in hand.

"Yes, of course. Continue."

"We took Leif to the infirmary where he has remained ever since, unconscious, not a word since his ramblings of 'Einar'."

"And how does Leif fare now for I wish to speak with him myself."

"I fear that will be some time, my lord. I will keep you informed."

Weeks of intensive investigation failed to determine where the raiders had pierced Jorvik's defences. Sigrvard had let his men carry out their search while he scrutinised intelligence reports of Saxon and Norwegian movements as well as tending to the daily schedule of municipal matters.

Busy though his mind and body were, his thoughts would often drift and fill with the same two scenes, flashing intermittently from one to the other, settling on neither for more than a moment.

Assi and Astrid, smiling, laughing, happy. Assi and Astrid, mutilated, lifeless.

He snapped to his feet, mind focussed, and sped to where Sigfried was on duty.

"Exactly where have your investigations been carried out?" he asked.

"It would be easier to tell you where we have not looked, my lord."

"And where would that be?"

"The old Roman lavatorium. The stench would be bad enough ordinarily but the bodies of the slain that day were stored there until they could be buried. A task that has only just been completed, leaving me to complete my investigation with that building immediately."

"I shall require hammer, spade, crowbar and several torches; see to it."

Sigfried met Sigrvard at the lavatorium, Einar's intended domicile though the Jarl knew not. It had not been visited by Jorvik's Deputy Marshal since he had betrayed all he did in letting marauders in to do their worst.

The putrid smell was no hindrance to Sigrvard. After years of blood-sodden battlefields and decaying bodies, he was untroubled. *No worse than a hot day on the streets of Jorvik*, he mused.

Besides, several sprigs of jasmine and lavender sewn into his mask proved an effective deterrent to retching every few moments. It did not take long to discover the fake doorway to the secret tunnel, which he followed to its end. He had little difficulty prising open the door, which opened outward to reveal the escape route so easily utilised by the Saxon raiders to enter and leave the city.

Sigrvard's first thought was that he would ensure the last fifty yards or so of the tunnel was filled with stone blocks and mortar but then he decided instead on a more cunning, strategic plan.

Iron cross-beams, vertical then horizontal, hinged outwards would provide, should it ever be necessary, an emergency exit or a supply route for provisions or reinforcements for Jorvik.

The days passed and, despite the ever-present grief, Sigrvard felt the responsibilities of his position, and his several roles, and, without being self-centred, his importance to the continued growth of Jorvik. His commercial wealth continued to increase and he expanded into a number of market stalls in the city.

What he offered via those outlets was a microcosm of the city itself. He competed with others who sold local produce, fruit, vegetables and livestock but he also sold goods that were more difficult for his competitors to obtain, such as amber and walrus ivory from Rus and the east. He also employed superior craftsmen who turned antlers and precious material into jewellery, which was highly valued, near and far. But every night, he adjourned to his new house—it could never be a home without Assi and Astrid—a lonely man. Much beer was consumed, Rhineland wine too, though he had never been much of a drinker.

With Einar gone, there was no one to talk with, no one close enough to exchange battle stories and no one to beat at *Hnefatafl*. And no one to warm his bed.

Of course, there were servants and many females who would willingly share a bed with the most powerful man in the north, after the king. But not if that man were he. Night after night, he struggled for sleep in the vain hope that dreams of Assi and Astrid would come to him to ease his solitude and night after night, they did not come.

Each morning he rose and set about his daily regime. He even forgot about Leif, the one remaining witness to the Saxon raid on Jorvik, who lay unconscious in his sickbed. But came the day, several moons after he became a widower, when a messenger sent by Sigfried came to inform him that Leif was awake. Sigrvard raced to Leif's bedside and was warmed by the sight of his *huskarl* sitting up, eating broth.

Leif spotted the approaching Marshal and made to get up and stand to attention but he could not and fell back onto his bed in disappointment.

"*Nei, nei*, my brave warrior. It is I who should stand to salute you."

"My lord honours me. For shame I could not honour him in my duty to his wife and daughter."

"From what Sigfried tells me, you did all you could and were the last to fall," added Sigrvard who was close to tears as that day came flooding back.

"My lord, I thank you but I cannot take any credit for being the last man standing. That honour must fall to your deputy, Einar."

Sigrvard's ears pricked up. Eager to learn the truth but not wishing to push a wounded man not yet fully recovered, Sigrvard encouraged Leif to go slowly and in his own time tell his commander what had happened in the moments before he was felled by overwhelming numbers.

"Myself and the other *huskarls* stood our ground, waiting for the enemy to get close but it was made harder by the hindrance of so much smoke and flames. Einar rushed to us, covered in blood and his blood-covered axe in hand.

"He opened his visor to speak but before he could utter a word, he was felled from behind by a Saxon. He fell and was struggling across the floor to reach us but the Saxons stepped on him as they bore down on us."

Leif was obviously struggling to breathe due to his injuries but, so close to the truth, Sigrvard needed more.

"I was fighting for my life and was unsure what was happening each side of me. But I do know that your *huskarls* gave their lives doing their duty."

"Of that I have no doubt," the Marshal said. "And their families will be cared for, I promise."

"I was the last to fall but it was not a death blow and before I lost consciousness, I saw, through the black smoke, Einar despatch three enemies before he was overwhelmed. He fought like a Berserker but there were too many of them and he was carried, kicking and screaming, away. Then I remember no more."

Sigrvard looked up at the shaft of light streaming through the transom window above Leif's bed. Full of emotion and a combination of pride in the way his soldier and his best friend had executed their duty and the sadness of the outcome, he could not speak. Composing himself, Sigrvard stood. Turning to Leif, he spoke, "I cannot express the words to thank you, for more than you can know. But I can say that when you are ready to return to duty, it shall be as the new deputy-commander of my *huskarl*."

"Now it is my turn to not have the words to express. It will be my honour as well as my duty to serve you and Jorvik."

Sigrvard left with no small amount of joy in learning how Einar had served him but that joy was tempered by question after question. Why no body, what happened after and was Einar taken as hostage or for later execution?

But for now, Sigrvard planned to turn the full extent of his intelligence network to the task of finding Einar or news of his fate.

Unbeknown to Sigrvard, it would prove a thankless task, for his erstwhile second-in-command had been hiding, in full view, with a new identity on the Isle of Man, contemplating the timing of his return to Jorvik. Timing that could be life-changing or life-ending.

A week of increased scouting patrols and intensive intelligence gathering discovered nothing about the location of Einar, presuming that he was still alive. Nor would it. But with the absence of any ransom demand, what more could Sigrvard do.

If Einar were dead then surely the Saxons would have made use of that fact and heralded it across the land as a coup, the elimination of the Deputy Marshal of Jorvik, blood-brother to Sigrvard. It was that vain hope that kept the torch of optimism burning within. Sigfried supervised the installation of the iron grids that were placed at the end of the secret tunnel and reported that completion back to Sigrvard.

One thing that had irritated him since he had discovered how the Saxon force had breached the city walls was how or who.

As there were no signs of forced entry, it was evident that the door had to have been opened from inside, which then begged the question, by who?

Ironically, although Sigrvard could not connect the two, later that day, a battered and bloody Einar scurried back to the outskirts of Jorvik and so, commenced the pathway to the answers to those two questions, how and who.

Einar had to be convincing. His life depended on it.

A sentry at the west gate spotted the solitary rider from afar.

Normally, such a sight would not have aroused any suspicion but the erratic path taken by the approaching horse, and its rider slumped over the pommel, did.

Two riders were quickly despatched to investigate and with precision, when they got close enough, Einar slipped from his saddle and fell to the ground.

Rolf, one of the riders, immediately recognised Einar despite his battered and bloody face. Not wishing to make his injuries worse, the riders waited for a cart to take Einar to the infirmary, although Sigrvard, who had been informed immediately Einar had been recognised, commanded his friend be taken to his private quarters.

Einar slept for two days, or so it appeared to Sigrvard and the orderlies attending to his wounds, which were considerable.

The traitor was clever enough to feign slumber whenever anyone approached. He also ensured that Assi's parting gift remained his secret by rolling over whenever anyone attempted to inspect his wounds in the area of his nether regions.

He knew he could not feign his condition forever but just long enough to get his story straight for the inevitable conversation with Sigrvard.

The Marshal insisted on daily news of his friend. His safe return was just the lift needed to brighten his life as a widower.

CHAPTER TWENTY-THREE

The Ring of Death

AT long last, Einar was ready to speak with his blood-brother, who surprised him with a gift that made even hard-hearted Einar feel humble. A *thrall* entered the room, walking behind the Marshal, carrying a gold double-edged axe in one hand and a helmet in the other. The weapons were laid on the bed as Sigrvard sat in anticipation.

"You must have much to tell me, brother, but first, how feel you?"

"Like I have been trampled by a band of Berserkers."

Sigrvard laughed, Einar feigned laughter.

"If you feel well enough, please tell me what happened to my wife and daughter. I know it will pain you to relive those terrible moments but I must know if they suffered."

Einar had thought long and hard over the previous months how exact and how truthful he should be. After all, the wrong word or errant piece of information and Sigrvard would treat the rest of his body in the same way Assi had his manhood.

"By the way, I could not find any sheep so I have arranged for Saxon twins to provide you with a little reminder of our wenching days," said Sigrvard with a smile.

"Too kind, sire, but I feel it will be some time before my body is sufficiently recovered, though I thank you dearly."

"No mind, they will be ready when you are."

Einar quickly changed the subject to the Saxon raiders.

"They caught us all by surprise and even the wall sentries were unaware until it was too late and the garrison was ablaze and the incursion had reached your compound. They seemed to know exactly where they were going and it was obvious they were targeting your family."

"That suggests we have a traitor in our midst, would that I had him before me now. He will suffer unspeakable horrors before a long, lingering road to death ends with me sending him to Helheim."

Surprisingly, Sigrvard never heard the loud gulp that made its way down Einar's throat, mainly because he coughed to disguise it.

"I'm so sorry, brother, forgive me. It is too much too soon. I do not wish to be insensitive, I owe you so much already. We shall continue in the forenoon."

Excellent, thought Einar as he relished more time to make his recounting of the attack more convincing.

"The forenoon would be good, Sigrvard. Until then, I will gather my strength."

"Do so. I need you with me as soon as the gods will allow."

Einar wondered how long he could keep up the pretence; as long as he wanted to stay alive, he reasoned.

Sigrvard decided to give Einar some undisturbed time but he was also planning his return to normal. And what better occasion than to ease him back into weapons training, for had he not been imprisoned, beaten and restricted to a cell and an infirmary cot for many weeks? No way for a *Vikingr* warrior to live.

* * *

Einar watched from the side as the warriors went through their paces.

Single combat until one of each pair struck a death blow, or what would be a death blow on the battlefield for these *drengr* were so proficient at their art, pulling away at the last moment was safe enough. Only pride suffered with a tap on the arse.

Sigrvard approached Einar from the side and as he turned to face his friend, the Jarl tossed his gift, the new axe, in Einar's direction, which he caught with his usual dexterity.

"Ah, see one and all. You never lose it."

Einar smiled as he slid his bruised hand through the leather loop on the axe handle. Sigrvard knew his friend was back.

"Maybe I should have given you a boy's axe as you are still recovering?" teased the Marshal.

Einar sneered. *He is definitely back*, thought Sigrvard.

"*Fight, fight, fight,*" roared the watching warriors. None present knew of the night Einar had nearly slain the Jarl. If they had, they would not have been so eager to see blood-brother against blood-brother.

"*Nei,*" said Sigrvard. "Einar is not yet fit for a fight."

Suddenly, the axe flew from his hand and sliced the ground between Sigrvard's feet.

"Odinn's axe-man is ALWAYS ready!" answered Einar as he beat his arm on his shield. The watching warriors roared their approval as Sigrvard looked at his feet and the axe buried twixt them.

"Just like old times, eh, Einar?"

The pair circled each other, an even pace, not too slow and not too fast, as they sized one another up for the first move. Einar brought his axe towards Sigrvard's left and his shield, sufficient to send his friend stumbling backwards though he stayed on his feet. Einar followed up too quickly and was caught off balance as Sigrvard caught him on the top of his brand new helmet with the flat of the blade, but enough to make his head rattle.

They locked arms like a pair of rutting stags and struggled to throw the other off-balance. Being the taller man, Sigrvard had the advantage but Einar was agile and somehow managed to lock his leg behind his opponent's right knee to throw him to the ground.

Normally, that was the signal to end the contest but Einar threw himself on top of Sigrvard and pinned him down.

The crowd loved what they were seeing for no one had ever bested their Jarl. And the Jarl was none too pleased at being flat on his back for the first time since he was a child.

Wishing to be magnanimous whilst retaining some dignity, Sigrvard reached up and held Einar by the arms to push him clear and for a moment, hesitated. Einar was not wearing shoulder armour, merely a woollen tunic with loose sleeves under a leather vest.

Sigrvard's left hand wrapped around Einar's upper right arm and he felt an amulet, which was unusual for a warrior in training. Unusual though the presence of such an adornment was, it was the size of it that shocked Sigrvard. It was small, too small for a man, more a woman's decoration.

Einar could not move for Sigrvard grasped him with vice-like grip.

"What is this, my friend?" said Sigrvard as he slid the sleeve higher to reveal that which sent a cold shiver through every pore of his being.

ASSI'S AMULET!

Sigrvard, with a mighty surge from within, threw Einar from his body as a child might toss a ragdoll.

"What is this?" Sigrvard roared, so loud it stunned the crowd to silence as he held Einar's arm aloft, bearing the love token he had given Assi on their wedding night.

In his stupidity, not to mention the agony of losing his manhood, Einar had not realised that only Sigrvard and Assi knew of the amulet's existence.

Einar was shaking visibly and raised both arms in supplication.

"On our blood-oath, I swear Assi begged me to take it for safekeeping to prevent it from becoming Saxon plunder…"

For the briefest of brief moments, Einar recognised a flicker of belief in his friend's eyes.

"…and return it to you."

In the moment of silence that followed, when the entire world seemed to stand still, as soon as those last five words left his lips, Einar knew all was lost.

"Why did you not disclose that to me? Why wait until I discovered for myself? I am Sigrvard, Jarl of the Denisc!" roared Sigrvard. "I have slain many in battle with honour and now I claim the right of blood feud and vengeance for my murdered wife and child—a duel to the death.

"Traitor. Murderer."

Einar knew not where to look as he became the focus of a betrayed friend and his entire tribe.

"By all the gods, you must believe me," bleated Einar who was condemning himself with every word he uttered.

"Tomorrow as the first light breaks the darkness, the Ring of Death, on the weapons field."

Sigrvard turned to Sigfried and nodded. His commander turned to the traitor.

"Then so shall it be. What say you, accused?"

Einar could feel the eyes of the world upon him. He stepped back from Sigrvard and mouthed the words, "Believe me, you must believe me," but no sounds issued forth. It was as if the gods themselves had heard enough. His only hope was if the flicker of belief he had seen in his friend's eyes became a raging fire; but a Seer knows the hearts of men.

"On the morrow, forenoon," and with those words, Sigrvard walked away.

Huskarls and warriors formed the 'Ring of Death' with their shields. The eight feet square cloth on which a duel to the death normally took place was dispensed with.

No one gave the order. Sigfried took that decision.

Each combatant had three shields to call upon but that was all.

No one present could interfere under pain of instant death. This was between accuser and accused.

Einar entered from the west, facing into the rising sun. Sigrvard's choice, as it would send a blast of sunshine into Einar's eyes and start the day as uncomfortable as Freya could make it. He carried two axes, one double-bladed and one single blade, with extra-long shaft.

Sigrvard carried 'First Blood' and a shield, with the *seax* given him by Assi tucked inside his boot.

"No Ulfberht?" quipped Einar, trying to make light of the moment.

"Ulfberht is meant for warriors to kill or be killed by. You are not worthy. A traitor. As a Jarl, I choose 'First Blood'."

"I have always been the better warrior," hissed Einar with venom, "and I shall prove it as I send you to Valhalla."

"Valhalla is for honourable heroes. When I kill you, you will take your place in Helheim."

The blood-brothers circled each other very slowly, Einar making a point of touching the amulet when he saw Sigrvard's gaze attracted to it.

"That is mine," said Sigrvard in response, "and when I separate it from your arm and your arm from your body, it will go with me to the afterlife where I shall reunite it with Assi."

In true *Vikingr* fashion, the pair exchanged insults before a blow was struck.

Einar opened with, "*Saurigr Saxar Skitkarl*—you dirty Saxon bastard."

"*Hrafnarnir munu hafa þik*—the ravens will have you," was the reply.

"Dickless son of a whore" really hurt Einar who failed to understand just how a smiling Sigrvard knew.

"One day when your wounds were being dressed, I saw, well, nothing."

Thinking back to his many nights of passion with Assi, Sigrvard smiled again; knowing his Assi, he knew exactly what had happened to Einar's dick. Wiggling his smallest finger at Einar simply rubbed it in and had the desired effect, an angry lunge from the double-axe. Odin's axe-man he may have been but lunging with a swinging weapon was not the best tactic when fighting for your life. Sigrvard simply side-stepped and Einar stumbled past him, with a tap on the buttocks adding to his embarrassment.

Not carrying a shield, despite having the advantage in terms of weapons, Einar was vulnerable when either axe-bearing arm was wide of the body, leaving arms open to attack. That's where Sigrvard drew first blood when his sword caught Einar between his coat of mail and shoulder pad.

The traitor reeled away as much in shock as in pain but swung an axe to deflect 'First Blood'; but the damage was done.

The two battled on, blow and counterblow, with neither gaining the advantage. Both exhausted, they took steps backwards for recovery.

"*Þu berd eins ok litil pika ginnar*—you fight like a little bitch!" spurted Einar.

"*Gor mik eigi, heimskt troll*—don't disrespect me, stupid troll."

Einar had always been sensitive about his lack of height and reacted by leaping forward as Sigrvard hesitated. The move bowled the bigger man over and Einar hung on for dear life, both men keeping a tight grip on their weapons.

As they lay there in the mud, Sigrvard whispered, "Why?"

"You were always Eirikr's favourite. Saxon *thrall* while I am full-blood Viking and son of his best warrior."

Sigrvard said nothing as they rolled on the ground, neither giving way to afford any advantage to the other.

"Still no reason why you led the enemy to our hearth."

As they staggered to their feet, Einar spoke, "Why should I not lead them to your thorp? I lived in your shadow from boyhood. You, Eirikr's favourite, replacement for a dead son.

"Who was I? An expendable warrior who would never gain land except by conquest. This I was offered by the northern Angles of whom I am now one. You should know from me that your wife and daughter screamed like stuck pigs as they enjoyed the attention of my North Angle friends."

Sigrvard felt the blood boiling in his body as he sped forward at his best friend who had mirrored, in reverse, Osgar's transformation from

Saxon to Viking. He needed no further incentive to destroy the evil before him, but he got it, and confirmation that Einar was at the heart of his family's death.

"Come on, Scourge of the Franks—or should that be Siggi?"

Sigrvard was incandescent on hearing a word that had only ever come from Assi now issued forth from the bile he used to call friend. All the years of training and restraint, care and caution and trained reflexes went. He was simply a man bent on vengeance and nothing was going to stop him.

Einar swung his axe but instead of deflecting, Sigrvard slipped his blade inside and severed Einar's hand, still grasping the axe, at the elbow. It flew towards Sigrvard and caught him on the earlobe.

"It matches the wound I gave you in our youth," said Einar through the pain of gritted teeth.

"But this was a better blow. I see you recall our youth when we were blood-brothers."

Einar, still reeling from the severed arm, swung his second axe and although Sigrvard was quick enough to defend the blow, the axe deflected down and caught him just above his ankle armour. Blood issued forth.

"You don't have me yet, old friend," gloated Einar.

Sigrvard could take most things, even from a traitor, but he drew the line at sarcasm.

With Einar's axe momentarily embedded in the mud, Sigrvard spun around and with the shield he had just picked up, cracked his opponent on the side of his head, bowling him off his feet.

Back upright, both combatants stood catching breath for the next assault, though Einar was breathing the heavier. He was losing a lot of blood and getting weaker with each passing moment. His brain was spinning at triple speed, working out how he could survive long enough to finish off his friend before he himself was finished. And therein lay the difference between the two warriors.

Einar was all training and reaction, and reluctant training at that, while all those hours of blending practice with reflex had produced a warrior who did not need to think—Sigrvard was all reflex. He didn't even need to think how quickly he could finish Einar off, his only thought was vengeance and how he could extend Einar's suffering to avenge the suffering inflicted upon Assi and Astrid.

That momentary lapse of reason by Sigrvard gave Einar an opportunity and he took it. A mighty heave of the axe took Sigrvard's shield away from his grasp and left him unprotected, save for his sword.

Einar leapt through the air to press home his advantage but Sigrvard recovered his concentration and rolled back onto his back, catching Einar square on the chest and throwing him through the air until he smacked his body on the ground, taking all breath from his body. Winded and wounded, Einar could have been finished off there and then. A more merciful Sigrvard would have done just that for any warrior, let alone one who had fought at his side for more than ten winters and more, but mercy was not in Sigrvard's heart.

Einar had lost any right to mercy long before he had engineered the deaths of Assi and Astrid and long before he had opened the door for the Saxons to ravage and destroy. Einar lost everything the instant he let the accumulation of jealousy, lust and envy manifest into that moment he had decided on betrayal.

'First Blood' was raised high. And with hate and vengeance surging through his body, with more power than he had ever mustered in his life, Sigrvard brought his blade down on Einar's unprotected head—no helmet, he never learned.

The blade cleaved Einar from crown to cusp and the Ring of Death gasped.

"Two faces for a traitor, appropriate," quipped Sigrvard.

He swung his sword and severed one half of Einar's head, which flew several feet away. The grotesque sight of the remaining 'head' atop the body of Einar, which staggered from side to side, looking like it wished to speak, was unreal.

Sigrvard stepped to his left and with a reverse sweep of his blade completed the decapitation. And still the headless body staggered aimlessly, seemingly seeking a final resting place before Einar sank to his knees and rolling over onto his back.

Sigrvard was not finished.

Even battle-hardened *Vikingr* warriors retched at the rapid succession of Sigrvard's sword swipes that eviscerated the vanquished as he lay in a growing pool of blood.

"Enough!" shouted Sigfried.

"Enough," whispered Sigrvard as he dropped his sword and walked slowly through the Ring of Death.

He spoke not a single word as he locked himself away for days after. He had killed his best friend who had killed his family.

What else was there for one of the richest, most powerful men in England? He knew not what.

CHAPTER TWENTY-FOUR

TIME meant nothing to Sigrvard; save for the minster bells, he would not, other than daylight, have known how long since he rose and how soon to bed. His officers and clerics kept him aware of the workings of Jorvik, which seemed to be as smooth as necessary. What did, however, focus his attention were the daily intelligence reports that kept him informed of activity beyond the walls, which did not fit into the category of civil or commerce.

He had not, nor never would want to, forget the combined Anglo-Saxon assault on Jorvik that had shattered his existence and taken from him the three most important people in his life, including the one on whom he took vengeance for the deaths of the other two.

But soon his life of public service and accountability would change tack and his future would rely heavily on his previous proficiency and expertise on the battlefield.

Sporadic raids were still taking place but were on the periphery of the kingdom and inflicting little damage or loss on the Jorvik exchequer or Sigrvard's personal wealth, which was steadily growing to such a level he did not even bother any more to tally his fortune, though he reminded himself from time to time that more in his coffers meant a speedy advancement to the work rebuilding the monastery at Hild. His chronicle, on the other hand, was a different matter.

Since the death of William of Whitby, overseer of the rebuilding and his chronicler, whilst building continued apace, the stone chest containing the chronicle had remained secure under his bed. He had a plan in mind but, to use an expression he favoured, 'it is an idea which as yet has no shape'.

It had been some considerable time since Sigrvard partook of his morning contemplation. Indeed, the last time he had been alone with the thoughts such occasions gave him had been the day his contemplation was disturbed by bandits robbing a lone monk in the wild heathland southwest of Jorvik. That day was the day he had first met that lone monk, William of Whitby.

I must revisit the stone ring soon, was a thought that often crossed his troubled mind for he knew that until rebuilding of Hild was complete, there would be no alternative place for such mental easing.

His morning ablutions were disturbed by the gentle rapping of knuckles on the door to his bedchamber. Gentle enough to be the knuckles of Megan, his maidservant, but arresting enough to ensure that he answered.

"My lord, Leif waits without. Shall I bring him in?"

"Of course," and she was gone in an instant, returning almost as quickly with Leif, hero of the attack on Jorvik and now second only to Sigfried in the Marshal's command hierarchy.

"My lord, I have news just brought by an outrider that the king will be here soon."

Sigrvard was a little perplexed as he knew that Halfdan was away fighting Picts in Caledonia. Then Leif explained.

"King Guthrum expects to arrive within the day and his messenger awaits permission from the Marshal of Jorvik to take back to his lord."

"Of course; would it ever not be so?"

Leif departed, leaving Sigrvard scurrying for his clothes though Megan, in the meantime, had laid out his workday attire for hasty dressing. He knew also that the ever-efficient housekeeper would ensure that by the time he returned from initiating hasty plans for the royal arrival, his formal robes would be there too.

Instructions were sent for wood to be supplied to the royal suite, which needed fires lit immediately as there was no specific timespan for Guthrum's arrival. Food preparation had to begin even faster as the numbers arriving were not forthcoming in the message just delivered. For the rest of the day, Sigrvard pondered on the reason for such a visit though he felt sure it had something to do with Guthrum's recent declaration of himself as King of all Anglia.

There were venison, beef and lamb aplenty in salt-water barrels and enough beer and wine to sink an average-sized longship.

However, Sigrvard knew never to underestimate what a Viking

could eat or, more importantly, drink. Fresh fruit grew in vast amounts inside and outside the city walls and there were enough bakers in close proximity to supplement those employed in the Marshal's residence.

And Megan had already informed local weavers that fresh woollen blankets would be required by the afternoon to complement the imported silk sheets always kept clean and pressed for surprise guests. And surprise hosts, as Sigrvard was most certainly that day.

The approaching column could be seen from the city walls as the advanced riders came into view, and what an impressive sight too. It was mid-afternoon and thanks to an efficient household and an even more efficient housekeeper, the Marshal of Jorvik was ready to receive his royal guest and his retinue, which must have numbered at least one thousand.

The *courtage* was welcomed in the vast parade area that was twixt Sigrvard's quarters and the minster, in the dead centre of Jorvik.

As the king dismounted, Sigrvard, in his full Marshal regalia, moved forward to greet him. That was what you did when kings came to call. He knelt on one knee before Guthrum had time to tell him not to bother with ceremony. Probably fortuitous as both guest retinue and host population would have expected the full protocol.

Guthrum took Sigrvard's right hand and helped him up.

"Forgive me, my good friend and ally, for arriving unannounced but what I have to say needs to pass from my lips to your ears and your ears alone. Any and all subsequent discussions between us should be likewise restricted to us."

"I am most pleased to welcome the King of Anglia to the Kingdom of Jorvik. My home is your home as long as and for whatever reason you wish it, my lord."

While the king's brigade was taken to the newly rebuilt garrison quarters, Sigrvard escorted Guthrum to his private chambers.

"I will take my leave of you, my lord, and after you are rested and refreshed, I will be pleased to share my humble pantry with you, and I am sure you will welcome some of the newly imported Francia wine, which is now at home in my cellar."

"Indeed," replied Guthrum. "Your fame as a trader and merchant is exceeded only by your fame as a warrior-seer, which is considerable in itself. I look to share both with you shortly."

Sigrvard had not yet organised a sauna facility in his new home but had prepared the next best thing for Guthrum—a hot bath.

And not just any hot bath. Sigrvard had, fortuitously, already secured a supply of medicinal waters from nearby Goathland—Harrogate—by the cartload to bathe his battle-weary body. But the king would enjoy it first. There was always the possibility of export and a trade deal to be done if the king enjoyed his mineral ablutions. Megan ensured servants were on hand to assist the king. He certainly needed no encouragement when told of the benefits of Goathland water.

As the sun still hung low in the western sky, bringing with it a blood-red sunset, Sigrvard welcomed King Guthrum into his Great Hall.

"Just the two of us?" inquired Guthrum when he spied the vast array of food, bread and fruit that lay before him on platters of gold and silver. "I doubt you and I will consume all this," continued a smiling monarch.

"Fear not, my lord. That which is not eaten will keep and that which will not keep will be distributed to the city poor."

"Very magnanimous, Marshal. Another aspect of your reputation, which is known far and near.

"Now," clasping his hands together, "let us eat before we talk."

The two ate and talked as old friends for not only was Sigrvard a loyal supporter of Guthrum, he was a trusted confidant also.

"You will be most aware of the threat still posed by your northern neighbours and let me not forget to give you my sincerest condolences for the loss of your family and it is that which I need to discuss.

"We, that is you, are more than capable of keeping those dissident Saxons subdued but you will also be aware that allied to the snakes in the grass Norwegians present an all the more formidable challenge. My spies across the Kattegat inform me that the Norwegians have been gathering men and provisions for several moons now and are almost ready to cross over and join with the Northumbrians for a renewed assault on recovering Jorvik."

"I too have been aware of such issues," said Sigrvard, "and your arrival is most timely. I was about to suggest to King Halfdan that I might lead an expedition up to Deira and Bernicia to, shall we say, remind them of their place in the order of things here in the north."

Guthrum leaned over to Sigrvard.

"You have to know that Halfdan and Guthrum are of one accord when it comes to the ultimate aim of subduing all England. If you take an army and ravage the north, preferably before the Norwegians can get their giant feet under our Denisc table, that will send a message to Northumbria. A message that will pass even further north to Caledonia but also will resonate as far as Wessex and the ears of King Alfred.

"It is past time we removed this northern threat for all time. It must be impressed upon them that they can no longer attack the Danelaw without retaliation resulting in their total annihilation.

"But do not harm the royal family. If you kill their king, his place will simply be taken by another. Try to find a royal hostage to ensure that peace will be maintained. Their treasury is yours as is what spoils you may let your army share."

As that sank in, Guthrum continued, "The truth of the matter, and I can trust no other in these isles with what I am about to say.

"Should the next phase of our plans to conquer all of England and extend Danelaw from the North Sea to the Hibernian Sea and Anglia to the Western Isles be unsuccessful, then any united nation will be Saxon-ruled, not Denisc."

Sigrvard murmured under his beard and nodded in accord.

"Two minds as one sit at this table, my lord."

"And there is the not insignificant matter of vengeance, methinks. A path you already took steps along with your recent, er, Ring of Death?"

Sigrvard had not thought of vengeance since that day he had fought Einar. Maybe that was a good sign that the grieving process was starting to ease. Now he could give more time and thought to Sigrvard the warrior, not the widower.

"How many men can you muster, including your renowned *riddari*, without under-garrisoning Jorvik?"

"Comfortably two thousand, possibly five hundred more."

"As I estimated. Another two thousand would lean any confrontation in our favour, would you not agree?"

"Indeed," said a smiling Sigrvard, "but that would take time, my lord, time I fear we do not have."

"Splendid, then so shall it be. By the way, did I mention that two thousand of my men are awaiting orders to make their way to Jorvik to place themselves under your command? One thousand are camped out of sight two miles away and the other thousand are sitting comfortably aboard longships that sailed up the east coast from Anglia as I came overland."

"No, my lord made no mention of such wonderful news, unless my ears were lazy at the time."

"Maybe; pass that roast boar platter. Such tasty fare."

They retired early that night. Sigrvard to begin preparations for his expedition north, Guthrum for a second spell in his hot, mineral bath, though the latter was made more enticing by the presence of several young female *thralls* he had taken a shine to, and they him.

As Sigrvard watched Sigfried and Leif quietly and efficiently manage several thousand *drengr* and *riddari*, he thought back to the start of the Denisc invasion when such an exercise would have quickly deteriorated into mayhem and pandemonium.

It proved a seamless exercise by which the men under arms, preparing to leave Jorvik, reported to two distinct assembly points: Guthrum's contingent retiring south with him assembled outside the south gate while the section joining with Sigrvard and the Jorvik garrison assembled in front of the garrison quarters.

"May the gods be with you," whispered Guthrum as he bear-hugged Sigrvard.

"And may they keep a weather eye on your march south."

Guthrum wondered if they would meet again and under what circumstances. Sigrvard had no doubts about 'if' but had no shape of an idea of the circumstances. What he did know was how important it was for the Kingdom of Jorvik and the future of Danelaw that he succeed in the coming weeks.

Throughout history, when battles were fought, they were usually named after the nearest settlement or terrain feature, be it river or cairn, lake or mount.

But when Sigrvard and his *Vikingr* army faced the mass of Anglo-Saxon and Norwegian warriors for a battle to decide the future of Northumbria, they did so on a flat, anonymous field of brush, heather and thick brambles. Sodden with days of continued rain, Sigrvard had concerns about the disposition of his *riddari* and when they should be used. It was a portent of what was to come.

After the initial showers of arrows failed to disperse either side from engaging, the two hordes raced towards each other.

The *Vikingr* wedge initially forced the enemy back, and back again, towards a thick copse of willow trees but the coalition force rallied and their counter-attack forced the *Vikingr* to retreat, and then some more.

Sigrvard ordered the *riddari* into action but as soon as hundreds of hooves hit the swampy ground, that swamp did its best to swallow all, riders and steeds.

Spotting the difficulties their opponents were gripped by, Hakon, the Norwegian Jarl who was the coalition commander, swung his forces, reserves and *thralls* alike, into the fray.

It was a bold and opportune move that looked likely to win the day as the *riddari* struggled to control their mounts before they could even engage in combat. Slaughter was looking the likely outcome, until the gods intervened, in a way.

From the head-height combination of heather and brambles emerged what looked like a vision from Helheim. At first, it looked like a mass of dark, shapeless, fur-covered animals, upright but looking like they would be more at home bounding forward on all fours. None present on that nondescript battlefield had seen its like before, save Sigrvard.

Berserkers.

By the time that thought had entered his mind, Sigrvard saw them smash into the coalition as a tidal wave that didn't just sweep through the enemy, it swept them away. The carnage that followed was witnessed by the *riddari* and *drengr* who at once realised that their part in the battle was done.

Moments was all it took. The few Saxon and Norwegian warriors left ran for their lives. The Berserkers ran after them, save one.

Sigrvard had never seen a Berserker on a horse but he recognised the figure on board a steed that would not have looked out of place pulling a plough—it was Helhest.

"Once again, my friend, I am in your debt," as he hugged the Berserker leader, being better prepared this time than the last occasion when it had nearly cost him several ribs.

"But pray tell. I have not seen you since your ships slipped in to join the Great Army fleet, how many years since?"

"You not need me. When left Jylland, captured trader ship and got better offer."

"What better offer?"

"Him Emperor in Constantinople. Need guarding body so Helhest take warriors, become Varangian Guard. Plenty gold, plenty black women."

It was difficult for Sigrvard to see through the bushy, black beard that was almost bramble-like in its coverage of Helhest's face, but he was sure there was a smile in there somewhere.

"We go back. Done here."

Again learning from last time, this time Sigrvard was quick enough to grab his maniacal comrade to hug him farewell. Then he was gone.

Sigrvard's force made camp well away from the field of slaughter that won them the day, a swamp piled high with rotting corpses, providing carrion for both winged and four-footed predators.

As Sigrvard sat outside his tent pondering his next move, most likely to be a move on the Royal Court at Durham, seeking hostages, a group of soldiers advanced.

They were dragging a not very willing figure, female in shape but not manner. Leif threw the prisoner to the floor in front of Sigrvard, declaring, "This vile creature has put four of my men in the infirmary and two others in the ground, on top of what she did on the battlefield today."

Intrigued, Sigrvard approached, ensuring first that she was securely bound.

"Tell me more," said Sigrvard, "about today."

"Before the Berserkers intervened, this—I don't know if she is Saxon or Norwegian—she was fighting like a Berserker, if I am to be truthful, my lord."

Screams rent the air as the girl, for she was no more than seventeen or eighteen summers, reacted to Leif's words.

"I am no Saxon *thrall*. I am Norwegian royal blood. I am Erle, daughter of Jarl Hakon, and granddaughter to the king."

By the time she had realised her anger had played right into the hands of an enemy for whom such a prisoner was beyond gold, it was too late. And Sigrvard was relieved his battle-drained warriors would not have to march further and seek in Durham what had just fallen into their lap, by the grace of the gods.

"Secure her, and then again, chain her, hand and feet, to a cart-wheel and post men within stabbing-spear reach all night. We march home in the forenoon."

At first, Erle was in stunned silence. When she realised the night that lay ahead, she began screaming again.

"And after she is fed and watered, gag her. I wish to sleep tonight."

As he enjoyed his evening meal, Sigrvard began to ponder and after a moment or two of reflection, he sent orders for the hostage to be brought to him.

When she entered his tent, Sigrvard dismissed her escort and she stood there, alone. Gone was the fearsome 'Shield Maiden' who had fought so confidently on the battlefield, more than a match for any man she encountered; instead, before the man who had captured her stood a frightened young girl, not much older than his beloved Astrid and not very much younger than Assi.

As Sigrvard was about to address her, Erle recovered her previous bravura.

"Is this where you exact your tribute, Viking?"

"Say what?" responded Sigrvard, somewhat bemused.

"A virgin of but nineteen summers, is that not the stuff of *Vikingr* dreams?"

"Not this particular Viking," replied Sigrvard, hardly able to resist a smile.

"The reputation of your kind precedes you."

"And what of *my* reputation, pray tell? What do you know of Sigrvard?"

She looked him in the eye.

"I hear you have a foot in two camps. Saxon-born, now Viking-bred."

"Then you will know that I am one who may be considered the best of both worlds. That is why you are here now."

"I do not understand."

"I have never taken a woman against her will. I was raised to treat a woman with respect and have been able to so do despite, shall we say, for the tendency to do otherwise being uppermost in the Viking male mind. My position, which I have earned, allows me to maintain my stance and influence others who may wish to do otherwise."

"You still make little sense to me," she replied.

"You are my hostage. As we speak, a messenger is on his way to your father to arrange your safe return, which will be done in two days after we parley. If terms are not agreed, then you will remain our hostage as collateral for any peace terms agreed.

"You will be hostage in name only. As befits your noble rank, you will be treated as if one of our own ladies of noble birth, starting now."

Sigrvard picked up his saddle bags, clapped his hands to summon two maidservants, walked towards the tent flap and turned to address a stunned Norwegian princess.

"*Godda nott, sof þu vel*—good night, sleep well. My bed is your bed."

When the messenger returned early the next forenoon, he immediately reported to the camp commander who took him to Sigrvard. The message from Hakon, which was handed to the Marshal in a leather tube, was simple and to the point:

My lord Sigrvard, I implore you: do not harm my daughter.

I will meet you one hour before dusk on this day, exactly one mile north of your camp, and for your understanding of my honour, five miles in advance of our camp. I will be alone, save for a scribe and my loyal second-in-command.

I ask you are likewise accompanied so we may agree terms for my daughter's release.

As agreed, the two leaders met in a vast, open space where any, if there were to be, attempts at assault would be too obvious for any effect.

"My lord Hakon. In exchange for your daughter Erle, I demand you withdraw all current and future support for the Northumbrian Angles and Saxons and persuade your allies to withdraw north of the Tees and stay there. I realise the former is more within your power than the latter but in saying that, it is your withdrawal from these shores I seek most."

Hakon mused for a moment before giving his answer to Sigrvard's demands.

"I love Erle more than life itself. Life her mother gave up to bring her into this world. But I cannot accede. I have pledged my word and my honour to Northumbria to stand by them until the end, whichever way that particular wind blows. I know of Sigrvard, Scourge of the Franks, but I also know of Sigrvard the Seer. Both would understand that pledge cannot be broken."

Sigrvard nodded for what his enemy spoke was the truth.

"So, how say you we settle this? I have no use for a hostage save for my terms as explained but neither do I have need nor motive to kill her."

"I am a wealthy man. I have vast territories and farms back in Norway but I also have vast tracts of lands and a treasury full of coin and bullion and other luxuries that I know would be of interest to a famed trader such as yourself."

"Your point, my lord?"

"My point is this. I cannot give you what you request but what I can offer is a treaty whereby I remain in England and, as commander of the forces that oppose you, ensure we stay north of the Humber, expecting that you will wish to remain south of that estuary. In return for this proposal, my daughter will remain with you as guarantee of my adherence to what we agree. And I will, should you take her as your wife, name you as her husband, heir to my estate that will pass to her on my death and to you as her husband.

"What say you?"

It was more than Sigrvard might have expected, notwithstanding the suggestion of marriage to someone he had captured but two days earlier and who was his prisoner.

"Agreed," said Sigrvard.

"*Gutt*, let the scribes draw up the documents while we toast our new agreement."

Several hours and two documents later, the two parties went their separate ways, leaving Sigrvard to break the news to his hostage about their prospective nuptials.

You are to return with me to Jorvik and be my 'guest' for a spell, was how Sigrvard rehearsed it in his mind on the ride back to camp.

When he put it to Erle, adding that her father would write her in due course, she took it surprisingly well. It wasn't the way she saw her future exactly, but an arranged political union, in the guise of a marriage, was the way of the world for a maiden, whether she was Saxon or Norwegian.

The march back to Jorvik was via Whitby where Sigrvard wished to see how the rebuilding of the Hild Abbey was progressing.

While there was a schedule in place for construction, Sigrvard made it a priority that the ground on which the monastery stood and its immediate environs were consecrated to the Christian God, so he was able to lay William of Whitby to rest in holy ground.

Erle made her home quickly on their return to Jorvik. The letter from her father duly arrived. She read it first in private, then, as per instruction, to Sigrvard:

Beloved daughter,

It is with both a heavy and joyous heart I write this to you.

You are of an age to marry and were it better circumstances, I would prefer a union that was based on love more than politics, as with your dear mother. But that cannot be. You are a hostage in but name only, though you are a guarantee of my word to Lord Sigrvard.

He is a good man, for a Dane, and will treat you with the respect and courtesy your rank merits. In time, you may marry and in more time, you may feel in your heart that you are matched. That is for God and you to decide. I hope grandchildren may come along and I hope you have a long and happy life. Fadir

Erle quickly made a friend in Megan who was of a similar age so giggling as they went about the task of running Sigrvard's domestic affairs was usually the order of the day. It was something Sigrvard got used to and, truth be told, the return of laughter to his orbit was most therapeutic. He also got used to Erle serving his evening meal, something he found favour with each subsequent time it happened until it became the norm.

Very quickly, Erle's presence moved well clear of her being guarantor for her father's adherence to the peace agreement.

She took an interest in Sigrvard's accounts and soon thereafter took charge of them.

As time passed, the running of Sigrvard's thorps was never smoother and never before had his accounts been so ordered.

From being most useful, Erle became indispensable and was granted both a housekeeper—naturally, she chose Megan—and a generous personal allowance.

He found her presence calming at the end of a working day that swung to and fro between commerce and municipal meanderings.

"Please stay, join me."

The words just came out one evening as Erle laid a platter of chicken in front of him. There was no pre-thought or devilishly cunning plot of subterfuge, no carnal intent nor hidden agenda, simply a young man wishing the company of a young woman who was now part of his life.

A life from which such a presence had been missing for far too long.

In the years that followed that first meal together, Sigrvard looked back, many times, trying to recall what they had spoken about, but failed. All he could remember that one minute they were alone in a huge dark room lit only by a huge fire, and the next moment, shafts of sunlight were dancing through the sandstone mullion windows.

They spent many a night dining together. She tutored him in the etiquette of royal dining while he was fascinated by her acumen when it came to business.

On the day of his birth date, they shared several bottles of Frankish wine. It was not all they shared.

Erle slipped smoothly into the mineral water hot bath that had become part of Sigrvard's nightly routine. He was leaning, tipsy, against the side of the bath as she stepped out of her robe and the light from a nearby candle caught her maidenhood as she walked gently down the steps and across the warm, vitalising water to him.

His manhood needed a little coaxing but once her gentle touch took him in hand, she mounted him and for both of them the explosions they enjoyed inside each other were the first of many they would share.

As they lay together in front of the huge fire that warmed the tepidarium, Sigrvard asked Erle how she had become so adept at household affairs.

"My father is a great leader," she would say, "but he struggles to organise which breeches need washing and which need repairing and which are simply fit only for the hounds to sleep on. The running of his household was my Jarldom while he ran his."

The relationship between Sigrvard and Erle, after just a few moons, was no longer that of captor and captive, and then it suddenly struck him one night after dinner when they were discussing the felling of timber on his thorp lands, north of the city.

"So, when the trees are felled, the timber is brought into the city but what of the branches and the sawdust from axe and saw? Are they just left to return to the soil?"

"Yes," he replied.

"So why not do this? You have many a street urchin on the streets of Jorvik that would be better employed, and away from the distraction of petty thievery, gathering up twigs and branches. Twigs that could be sold as kindling to the good folk of the city and branches that could serve as roofing for sheds or outbuildings. Then you have the sawdust that could also be gathered and bagged and either sold as bedding for the many small animals kept for winter food. The produce that does not sell will simply be diverted into the Marshal's household, thus saving expense on the household purse.

"Such activities would serve as a basic income for those children to support themselves, if they are orphans or their families, which will, of course, welcome such additional income. We would also provide commission on top that would add incentive and productivity."

Sigrvard simply sat there, open-mouthed in amazement and admiration.

"Of course. Do it, tomorrow."

She smiled. He smiled. It was a new path leading to a very new road. Soon afterwards, Erle became household manager to the Marshal of Jorvik, officially. Unofficially, she was charged with running Sigrvard's business empire, which had been way beyond his control ever since his civic duties had increased with regional responsibilities following King Halfdan appointing him to the Regional Council.

When he told her of her new duties, she jumped up and down with joy, hugged him and then Megan, who she danced with a little with the biggest smile Sigrvard ever saw.

He told himself how often he forgot that she was just beyond her teens and not a mature woman of some years. He felt a spark deep inside that had not been felt for two years and more.

Assi and Astrid were still in his head but now he recognised that Erle was in his heart.

The new householder manager to the Marshal of Jorvik quickly instituted the process of kindling and sawdust that added a small, though consistent, income stream but also improved civic well-being.

As for Sigrvard's well-being, Erle was taking care of that. He woke beside her one morning and as she stirred, he turned to her.

"I wish you to arrange something."

"Of course, my lord, what is it?"

"Our wedding."

Once the surprise was past, the ceremony was shortly thereafter.

Sigrvard wanted not what he had experienced before and with deference to Erle, the only ones present were themselves and the Christian priest who pronounced them husband and wife.

On their wedding night, Erle told her husband, "I am with child."

CHAPTER TWENTY-FIVE

THE following two years were the happiest Sigrvard had been since he had wed Assi. He struggled at first to accept to be happy again—guilt, he thought—but once he realised Assi would want him to grasp any happiness he could, it became easier. He also knew that Assi and Erle would have been good friends.

While domestic and commercial harmony were the order of the day in the Kingdom of Jorvik, Sigrvard still kept abreast of the political climate across the border from Danelaw, where Wessex remained the only obstacle to a Viking England.

The paradox of Alfred's naval success was not lost on either side. The force that had long terrorised and exploited through their waterborne warfare to its fullest extent suffered its first reverse. Small in scale though it was, it planted a seed that was to grow.

Alfred also reorganised that which had once proved a weakness in the Saxon armoury, the time constraints of the *fyrd.*

Now a rota system was in place whereby half that obligation of fealty stood to arms while the other half went about their workday chores and when those parts of the *fyrd* swapped over, it meant that at any one time, the Saxons had a standing army ready to move. Alfred also organised a series of fortified *burghs*—or *boroughs*—from Cornwall to Canterbury, a curtain of steel that would be the first line of any defence to further Viking incursion and a staging point for any incursions into Danelaw the leader of the Anglo-Saxons deemed necessary. Those towns, as they grew, added to the commerce of Wessex as Alfred also recognised the need for a balance between military and economic affairs. Neither side was strong enough to sway the balance of power either way, both had a land bridge between the North Sea and Irish Sea, and from the English Channel to the North Sea.

But any advantage, however small it may be regarded, was with the Saxons. They only had one dangerous border, that with Danelaw, but the would-be conquerors had Wessex and Mercia to the west and Northumbria to the north.

That impasse led to yet another peace being brokered between the opposing forces. But more significantly, the Treaty of Wedmore that came into being formalised the sketchy agreement that had been in place for the previous eight years.

The alliance between Mercia and Wessex was further strengthened by the marriage of Alfred's sixteen-year-old daughter Aethelflaed to the Mercian ruler Aethelred II, as it provided a positive power-base from which the Saxon alliance was able to retake parts of the Danelaw, piecemeal.

That part of the Great Army that had decamped to the Continent returned in 885 AD and besieged Rochester until the town was relieved by a Saxon army led by Alfred. Some of the routed Vikings fled back to the Continent while others joined up with Guthrum in East Anglia. Alfred adjourned to London for the winter. The incessant toing and froing, when at first one side then the other seemed to gain pre-eminence, was getting tedious, not to mention expensive in terms of cost and loss of lives.

Guthrum recognised that what he had confided into Sigrvard several years earlier was coming to pass. The balance of power was swinging more often, and for longer periods of time, in favour of the Saxons and their God. So Guthrum agreed to peace.

The two kings, Alfred and Guthrum, agreed to meet at Wedmore, deep into Wessex territory and conveniently situated on raised ground in the Somerset Levels between the River Axe and the River Brue.

Alfred chose to limit his retinue in size so as to not belittle Guthrum who had to travel the span of Wessex to reach the village where history and his own life would change forever. A show of power not lost on Sigrvard or his king.

Sigrvard was one of the thirty most honourable men of the Denisc army who formed part of Guthrum's retinue that day and one of only four to attend the secret meeting between the two kings before the religious ceremony in which Guthrum would be baptised.

Alfred and Guthrum sat in close conclave with an occasional

involvement for the Saxon cleric with Alfred and more regular interaction from Sigrvard. Guthrum turned to Sigrvard.

"You are a Seer and were you not a Saxon?"

"Indeed, I am Saxon-born," he said.

"And how see you the current situation between Saxon and Dane?"

Sigrvard thought deeply about his answer. He had three options and three alone, any one of which could send the peace parley tumbling. Did he speak that which he felt Alfred would wish to hear or did he offer the words that his king would wish?

The only other alternative was to give his own opinion, which may upset both rulers.

"I am a Dane who was born a Saxon. If I can reconcile my life both as a Saxon and a Viking, then why cannot Alfred and Guthrum be reconciled to live peacefully together, one respecting the boundaries of the other?"

Then, breaking protocol, Alfred addressed the Seer directly, "You counsel wisely, my Saxon-Danish friend, and we will take your words unto us."

With a wave of the hand, both kings ushered their advisers out of hearing distance and continued their talks.

The baptism of King Guthrum took place in the River Parrett with Alfred as godfather and Guthrum's sole sponsor. The Saxon ruler saw the conversion as a great achievement while Guthrum privately regarded it as nothing more than politically expedient. Guthrum's conversion did nothing to loosen Danish grip on the land he had already acquired by conquest. It only served to garner Guthrum recognition among the Christian communities he ruled but it also legitimised his own authority and claims. By adopting the Christian name of Athelstan—also the name of Alfred's eldest brother—Guthrum's conversion reassured his newly acquired subjects that they would continue to be ruled by a Christian king rather than a heathen chieftain.

From a political and power perspective, the new codified treaty saw all the English not under Viking control—effectively, ALL England—submitting to Alfred, King of the Saxons.

Just one tantalising step from being King of England.

Once Guthrum had totally immersed himself into the River Parrett and emerged as Athelstan, the retinues of both kings, Saxon and Denisc alike, adjourned to the Great Hall in nearby Wedmore to begin twelve days of ceremony and celebration.

Sigrvard observed from the periphery as the grand and the noble of Denisc and Saxon royalty celebrated a new convert and another period of peace and trade.

As a child of nine winters, newly captured by Eirikr, he recalled Froda telling the Jarl, "This one is like an eagle." That night, in the Great Hall of Wedmore, those same eagle-eyes spotted a familiar face in the crowd when the only faces he should know were those in Guthrum's retinue.

Try as he might, he could not recall a name for the attractive face of a well-dressed Saxon woman, obviously of status and rank and no older than he, but much less battle-weary.

Eventually, after two more flagons of mead, he garnered sufficient courage to ask. He approached her from the rear and tapped on her right shoulder. She turned, slightly startled, and they each uttered a single word at the same time.

"Sigrvard."

"Cynfrith."

They embraced and the tears flowed, hers more than his. They tried to speak but cacophony ruled that historic day so Cynfrith took him by the hand, as she had all those years earlier. They went outside where the moon shone on the smooth surface of the river, casting a silver path from the moon to the riverbank where they sat.

He didn't know where to start. She saw that and spoke first, "Please forgive me. When Svein sold me, I didn't even have time to seek you out to bid farewell. Indeed, it was suggested that it was in the best interests of my health not to contact he who was betrothed to Assi, daughter of Svein."

"You have nothing to reproach yourself, Cynfrith. It is I who should be sorry.

"I wanted to find you. I would have bought you. But Eirikr advised me that to pursue the matter, in light of my impending nuptials, would be unwise. Please, continue."

"I was bought by a well-known Eirikrsby trader. A good man. Vidar, I think was his name."

Sigrvard smiled, knowing that his friend's motivation in purchasing Cynfrith was of the sincerest kind.

"He," continued Cynfrith, "ensured I was sold to another good man—Ralph of Tewksbury—a fellow trader of good reputation. And before I knew it, we were on a ship loaded with merchandise, and on our way to Wessex."

"And in the twenty winters since we, er, last saw each other?"

Both blushed, although she could not see beyond Sigrvard's hair-laden face.

"I married Ralph soon thereafter and he had no issue with taking on a *thrall* who was pregnant."

Sigrvard gasped. He had to ask but was unsure if he wished the answer.

"You were pregnant?"

"Yes, my son, Eric, was born exactly nine months after we, er, last saw each other. Your son Eric is now a man of twenty summers."

Trying to let the enormity of what he had just heard sink in, Sigrvard took a moment. "Does he know of me?"

"When he was of ten winters, I told him Ralph was not his father. When I was asked to be part of King Alfred's retinue—Eric is commander of his bodyguard—I told him there was a good chance the man who fathered him would also be here.

"Whether or not he would meet that man was his decision. I for one would not have sought you out. Fate decided you find me. The next step is for Eric to take, or not."

The following forenoon came a moment Sigrvard never thought he would experience—meeting his son.

Cynfrith walked along the riverbank to where the swans gathered in their favoured feeding spot and waited. Sigrvard followed soon thereafter and the three of them stood under the welcome shade of a weeping willow tree. Cynfrith took the lead from the two bashful men and was straight to the point.

"Eric, this is Lord Sigrvard, Marshal of Jorvik, Advisor to King Guthrum and Seer to King Halfdan.

"My lord, this is Eric Sigrvardsson, Commander of King Alfred's Royal Guard, my son...your son."

The two men stood and looked at each other. Eric, blond and muscular, stood a good four inches taller than his father. Each saluted the other with clenched fist across the chest.

"I will leave father and son to talk. I shall return and hopefully find that you have not killed each other and have instead learned more than you know at present."

Cynfrith walked away from them with elegance and poise. What followed was a process that both men found easier as the day wore on. Non-judgmental and with no hidden agenda, the more they got to know each other, the less the previous twenty years seemed to matter.

"I would like to invite you to join me in Jorvik. I am expanding the city and my military provision could be an ideal place for someone of your accomplishments, of which I have heard much since we have been here at Wedmore."

After a brief pause, while Eric mused on Sigrvard's offer, he added, "I have made a similar suggestion to your mother but she has declined."

"I too must decline, sire. I thank you. A place alongside a warrior of such repute is what any soldier of my age can only dream of.

"But my time and place is here with my mother and I have a duty to my lord, King Alfred. In time, the peace between our peoples may strengthen and in that case, I would wish to play my part.

"If war is required, so be it, then I would wish to play my part too."

Sigrvard's heart beat with the pride of a thousand drums. *That is the answer I would have given*, he thought to himself.

Before leaving for Jorvik, Sigrvard repeated his offer to Eric and Cynfrith. Again, they declined. Eric escorted Cynfrith back to her lodgings then made his way to Alfred's camp to ponder on a day he could never have imagined. Sigrvard went back to the Great Hall where celebrations continued. Although there were only a few hundred attending at Wedmore, Sigrvard felt they must have consumed most of the Wessex reserve of ale.

Whatever state of intoxication he would normally have endured had been tempered by meeting his son—his unknown son. But he had more important thoughts to muse upon rather than drink himself senseless to celebrate the baptism of a Pagan King who thought of it as mere political expedience.

He threw himself on his very comfortable wool and down bed that was almost the size of a longship and, not even trying to sleep, tried to make sense of it all; a four-year-old son in Jorvik waiting to hug him home, a twenty-year-old son who maybe would be glad to see him gone. Pleasured and troubled thoughts merged into one as he finally found sleep.

His dreams were usually short and to the point but this time it was different, more like a skald's rendition of a saga.

There was a familiarity about the scene with a sword as the centre-piece. Standing proud and upright, glistening in the bright sunlight, was Ulfberht. And that was where normal ended.

On one side of the grip, perched peacefully on the hilt, was a dove; on the other side, a squealing, squawking raven, wings flailing but seemingly unable to take flight as if glued to the hilt, and getting ever angrier as each fruitless flapping of its wings took it nowhere.

Then, in an instant, Cynfrith replaced the dove, Erle the raven.

Just as suddenly, Torbjorn replaced Erle and Eric became Cynfrith but the final apparition, before Sigrvard noticed the shadow of the sword, was Osgar standing next to Ulfberht, holding the hilt with his left hand. Towering above Osgar, right hand holding the other side of the hilt, was Sigrvard. The shadow cast by the sword was in the shape of the Christian cross, the top of which seemed to be pointing to nowhere in particular.

Sigrvard woke long before Guthrum's retinue was to depart. He lay there in his most perceptive Seer mindset, trying to translate the dream, when his servant announced the arrival of Cynfrith and Eric.

The goodbyes were kept simple, formal and polite. Sigrvard hugged Cynfrith. Father and son clasped arms, right arm to right arm, right hand into right elbow.

"I will make my offer no more. It is always there. Know this, my son. I am with you and for you. Always a place at my side for you, and whatever you wish, Cynfrith, if it is of this world then it shall be yours."

"*Takk Fadir*—you see, I have been practising," smiled Eric.

Sigrvard wept unashamedly and hugged Eric and his mother before making his way to join up with Guthrum's retinue to prepare for their journey, each back to their world. Both father and son knew they would meet again. Both felt concerned what the potential circumstances could be of such a reunion.

As the *Vikingr* column prepared to leave Wedmore, a large force of Saxon horsemen approached. Immediate reaction from Guthrum's retinue was 'attack' but once King Alfred was spotted at its head, expectation was different.

Alfred approached Guthrum.

"My lord Athelstan,"—It would take the Denisc leader some time to answer to his Christian name—"I offer you my personal bodyguard to escort you to the border with your lands."

Guthrum looked at Sigrvard and a simple nod of the head was assent for acceptance. Alfred continued, "My people may not be so well disposed to Vikings on their land and may well not be aware of our new peace. So I bid you well and anything you require while you are in Wessex shall be yours, save the crown." Alfred smiled at that; Guthrum could do nothing but match the Saxon's mirth.

"Eric is my most valued commander and he will be your escort. Safe journey."

As Guthrum's *courtage* made its way out of the village, Sigrvard did not look back. There was no point. He knew Cynfrith would be watching and, perhaps, silently weeping. That thought was uppermost in his mind, even though his son was escorting the group. But Sigrvard was taken by the conspiracy of ravens, away to the east, that took flight as the hooves of the column horses disturbed their peace and scattered them north. Even if he had not been a Seer, it would have been difficult not to read portent into that.

CHAPTER TWENTY-SIX

RIC informed Guthrum they would march northeast along the Severn Estuary to, as he advised, "avoid some rather troublesome local chiefs with whom even Alfred has problems."

They would then swing due east for Danelaw.

All went well until the first night camp was set. King Guthrum took ill and high fever all night had all praying for his newly baptised soul. The fever broke as dawn lit up the sky but Sigrvard sought out Eric for what to do next.

"We are not far from Tewkesbury Abbey where the monks are renowned in their application and knowledge of the medicinal arts. I propose we send outriders ahead to forewarn them of our arrival and the reason for us needing their help. Being a direct request from the king should ease any concerns, on both sides."

A sound plan, thought Sigrvard.

The entourage duly arrived at a magnificent Tewkesbury Abbey and, being Vikings, the vast majority of the entourage could be forgiven for thinking what fine plunder must be contained therein.

But the health of King Guthrum was the only thought on the minds of Sigrvard and Eric, who took his responsibility as Alfred's representative most seriously. Outriders sent ahead ensured that the Abbot at Tewksbury had his *enfermeria* fully prepared.

The king was rushed there on arrival.

"Now all we can do is pray," said Abbot Eolfric. "My finest physicians with the most advanced medicines and herbs available will, if God wills it, have your king well very soon."

Trying to act reassured, Sigrvard thanked his host and made his way to the quadrangle at the heart of the monastery, adjacent to the abbey itself.

He sat on the low wall around the central fountain that gurgled fresh, clear spring water into a large circular pond. In silent thought, he swept his hand slowly backwards and forwards as he contemplated the repercussions should Guthrum die.

"You will not find any mussels in there." Sigrvard wheeled around at the familiar voice.

"Benedict!" He immediately recognised a friend from what was an age passed.

"Osgar," said the now grown novice he once knew as he reached with arms open in greeting.

They hugged. They wept and as the tears flowed so too did the questions that followed rapidly.

"After the raid that took you away, I had nowhere to be safe so I decided to head for more welcoming climes and ended up at Tewkesbury Abbey where Eolfric took me in. I made good progress within the monastery and am now Prior with full responsibility for the Scriptorium, your favourite place if memory serves me well—your turn, Osgar?"

"Sigrvard is how I am called now, old friend. Where do I start?

"It was more a new world than a new life when I exchanged being a Saxon for being a Viking."

They talked for hours, oblivious to the reason Sigrvard was there at all. The deeper their conversation, the further and further away they became from what they were than to what they had been all those years ago.

Sigrvard got more excited as one of those rapid thoughts he encountered from time to time raced into his mind.

"You must come to Hild Abbey as my Abbot—there, I have said it."

Sigrvard explained all about William of Whitby, the Chronicle and the renovation of the Abbey, as well as Jorvik and its importance to the north, the north that was home to both Benedict and Osgar, now Sigrvard.

"This is so sudden. I have so many good years here but the pull of returning north is overwhelming. I shall seek the Abbot's counsel."

As if by fate, the Abbot was walking towards them.

"Good news. King Guthrum is well and will be able to resume his homeward journey on the morrow, should he so desire."

"If you would excuse us, my lord Sigrvard," and Benedict walked the Abbot to one side.

Moments later, Benedict returned to his old friend.

"What time do we leave?"

The pair hugged joyfully, each making subconscious plans for what lay ahead.

Eric escorted Guthrum's entourage as far as Repton then turned for home. His farewell with Sigrvard was dignified and correct in every respect. They saluted each other. There was no hug, they had done that the previous evening, with the wish that the next time they met would not be on the battlefield.

"Now that would be some contest," Sigrvard said to his son with a smile. Eric smiled back but said nought.

Guthrum headed for East Anglia while Sigrvard, and the new Abbot of Hild, advanced in the direction of the Kingdom of Jorvik.

* * *

"It has changed much since I was last here," said Benedict.

"I would hope so, considering you were but a child," answered Sigrvard.

They made their way to the Marshal's home where Sigrvard was overwhelmed by Torbjorn throwing his arms around him.

Erle did likewise but was blushing as she noticed the cleric behind Sigrvard. "Later," she whispered in Sigrvard's ear.

"Honoured wife, please meet my oldest friend and a reminder of my days as a child in these parts, Benedict, the new Abbot of Hild Monastery."

"Welcome indeed, my Lord Abbot."

After showing Benedict to his room, Erle excused herself to see about her household duties in preparing food for the evening meal. Then she absented herself to put Torbjorn to bed while Benedict and her husband sat before the fire to reminisce further.

"I am sure you have much to catch up on," she said politely. Sigrvard showed Benedict into the ante-room behind his dining quarters. The Abbot of Hild was astonished at the array of vellum, quills and numerous pots of varying sizes and content, mainly ink. There was a variety of mixing bowls, pestle and mortar in abundance as well as large amounts of leather binding and just about everything required by a scribe or illuminator in the best-equipped scriptorium Benedict had ever seen.

"Not what I would expect of a Viking Jarl, my friend."

"Maybe not but I was most inspired by King Alfred's path towards the written word he expressed when I spoke with him at Wedmore and that word was to be English, not Latin. A dead language of a dead people is not for a new country that lurks within the bowels of this land waiting to explode like some huge fart, though it will suffice for now."

He smiled, as did Benedict.

"I was also well pleased to learn of the king's plan to chronicle the years of Anglo-Saxon history previous to, and including, the commencement of his reign. Somewhat akin to my Jorvik Chronicle, though my story will be of a much humbler ranking.

"And," continued Sigrvard, "this is your domain for my Jorvik Chronicle."

Benedict, looking a little perplexed, turned to his friend as Sigrvard lifted what appeared to be a small stone sarcophagus onto the bench that dominated the room, with a *deisc* at either end.

"Contained herein is what William of Whitby, your predecessor, wrote before he went off to annoy his God, leaving peace to reign here on earth."

It was said with enough suggestion that love was at the heart of Sigrvard's comment about his old friend, wishing he had enjoyed his company more than the gods had allowed.

"I will make brief notes ahead of your regular visits to write and continue William's work. But those notes will be brief. I expect the full-flowing language used by William, of which you are more than capable, to be forthcoming. Thus, the record of my journey will be preserved."

Benedict inspected the vellum sheets and seemed most impressed with William's work.

"I see William was a true artist. It will be an honour to continue his work."

"This Chronicle is for the future and will not be seen by eyes other than yours and mine until we are long returned to the dust from whence we came."

"May I ask why, my friend, you undertake such an endeavour?"

"Skalds and sagas are the Denisc way to honour the past. The

Anglo-Saxon way is the written word but therein lies a danger of misrepresentation.

"As it is only your kind, clerics and monks, who are able to record, it stands to reason your observations, present company excepted, are likely to be less than complimentary."

Sigrvard paused slightly before continuing, "As a law-sayer, I have to see both sides of any dispute or argument. It is a perspective that has much to commend.

"I once heard the story of a figure in your Bible, Solomon, who was famed for his wisdom because he weighed up all views carefully before reaching a judgment. I wish the Jorvik Chronicle to provide such a balanced view."

"As you wish, Osgar—apologies, Sigrvard. It will take some time."

"I know I can trust your discretion, Benedict, but I ask of you to grant me one favour."

"My dear friend, if it is within my power, by God's grace, that request I will gladly grant."

"I am glad you mention your God, the same God to whom I was joined in baptism many years before I even knew what a Viking was. Before each time you bring your quill to bear on the finest vellum, I wish your sacrament of confession and the confidentiality therein to safeguard what passes between my lips and your ears."

"Of course, as you wish, so shall it be."

"Conveniently, you will take up the Chronicle from the point of the Treaty of Wedmore and our fortuitous reconnection at Tewkesbury. And one final stipulation!

"When you complete each additional page, you will bring it to me. I shall read then add to what is an already significant amount of vellum in this chest. A chest you will eventually bury in consecrated ground at Hild, on my passing. Understand?"

"Understood."

Their return to Jorvik began what for Sigrvard and the city was a period of sustained growth. Sigrvard's prosperity grew to legendary proportions—easily the wealthiest man in Danelaw or Wessex, he was rumoured to be wealthier than anyone in the Viking world. While he ruled his commercial empire, as well as the Kingdom of Jorvik, much of the success his empire enjoyed was due to the organisation, planning and execution, which was down to Erle and Marek.

Marek had been an invaluable assistant to Sigrvard in the years since Vidar died and had grown into a man of stature and wealth as Sigrvard's trading partner and manager as well as a friend.

"Life is good to me, my lord," he would often say to Sigrvard as he contemplated all he had achieved since he was brought to Eirikrsby from the Mid-East as a boy *thrall*. But always, in his jet-black eyes, Sigrvard noted a lack of spark. Little did the Marshal know that Marek was simply homesick, though he never showed it. Still but four winters younger than Sigrvard, he harboured hopes of returning home one day and maybe seeing his parents and siblings once more.

It was near mid-summer, as *Skerpla* moved towards *Solmanudur*,* when a strange sight was beheld just before the River Ouse bend that led into the heart of Jorvik. Three strange vessels sailed up the river—not enough in number to pose a threat, though they were escorted along each riverbank by mounted militia. The citizens of Jorvik had never seen their like before, but Marek had, as had Sigrvard—they were Arab dhows.

By long-established protocols, none of the three vessels attempted to dock, they anchored mid-stream and a group of five men, four in armour, one carrying a white flag, and a fifth, a distinguished-looking gentleman in flowing, elaborately decorated robes and wearing a *keffiyeh*—headscarf. Obviously, a man of means as his head-dress was topped by several peacock feathers and the biggest jewel anyone in Jorvik had ever seen, including Sigrvard who was at the quayside to greet the dark-skinned stranger.

Before either the Marshal or the newcomer had chance to utter a single word of greeting, Marek raced forward and threw his arms around the stranger, almost knocking his *keffiyeh* to the ground, ignoring all preliminary greeting protocol.

"ENGKEL!" he screamed.

"A thousand pardons, honoured Marshal—Salomon Abdul Rachid al Ahram Badi at your service, but I prefer 'Solly' as it leaves time before the sun sets for things of greater importance."

I like this stranger who is but not a stranger, Sigrvard thought to himself.

It was just about to register why there was such familiarity about this man when Solly whispered, "My cousin Vidar has spoken so highly of my lord Sigrvard, Scourge of the Franks, Seer and honoured Marshal

* *13 June to 12 July, month of the summer solstice.*

of Jorvik, not to mention business partner of the aforementioned scoundrel who I have not seen for many years since—how goes it with the ridiculously rich blood of my blood? Away in some far-off foreign place making more riches?"

Marek and Sigrvard looked at each other before the Marshal spoke, "It is with much sadness I have to report to you that Vidar died several winters past."

Solly paused for a moment. "Well, I suppose if there is any kind of deal to be made wherever he has gone, Vidar will be the one to accomplish that."

Ice well and truly broken, Sigrvard took his guest to his private quarters where a feast, speedily prepared by Erle, awaited, while first giving instructions that fresh fruit, food and water be taken immediately to the three dhows, for which gesture Solly thanked his host most graciously.

Erle and Torbjorn joined Sigrvard and Marek to eat as Solly answered the Marshal's burning question, "Why are you here?"

"The story began with Vidar taking control of Marek's welfare, at my request, and that of his parents as our region was being threatened by the Ottoman Turks."

"So Marek, you were not a *thrall* as I was led to believe all these years?"

"No Sire. But Vidar thought such subterfuge was necessary for the safety of all concerned."

Sigrvard smiled; he knew how clever his old friend could be.

"So my friend, any blood of Vidar is my friend. What is your purpose here in Jorvik?"

"I have come to return Marek to his rightful home."

Sigrvard looked at Marek, Marek looked back, then both turned their attention to Solly.

"I wish to buy my nephew's freedom with the contents of one of my ships, all three if necessary."

The Marshal stroked his beard with finger and thumb.

"No."

Those at the table sat up, stunned.

"No," continued Sigrvard, "that will not be necessary."

Sigrvard turned to Marek, who was as confused as all at the table, except the Marshal, and with sincerity in his voice that all could hear, said: "You may have been a slave, or so was thought, but over the years, first to Vidar, then to myself and Erle, you have proved yourself invaluable over and over more times than I can count on the beads of Vidar's abacus, which I treasure dearly.

"You have your freedom—do as you wish. I would that you remain but given this opportunity, I will understand if you choose to return home."

A tear appeared in Marek's eye, several more with his uncle.

"A toast!" snapped Solly and laughter broke out.

"In that case," Solly changed mode, "I suggest on the morrow we discuss the trade for the merchandise from East of Byzantium that threatens to burst the bulwarks of my ships, in exchange for"—a chuckle—"what trinkets you might have squirrelled away here in Jorvik."

Sigrvard thought back to his instant reaction to Solly, back on the quayside, *I do like this stranger.*

The rest of the evening and well into the dawn, except for Torbjorn, the group exchanged stories from battles to banter, travel to trauma, friends long gone and friends just made.

Sigrvard suggested early in the forenoon that a few hours' rest should be enjoyed before any business be transacted. All agreed. Sigrvard and Erle joined Torbjorn, who had been asleep for hours, while Marek showed Solly to his room.

On the morrow, Sigrvard was amazed at the display of fine goods Solomon showed him in the hold of his flagship: bolts of silks piled from keel to lower deck, amphorae of spices, figs and olives, as well as boxes of amethyst as well as the finest Persian carpets. And hanging from pegs on the walls of the hold were row upon row of knives and swords of the finest Damascus steel.

"And my other two ships are similarly endowed, my friend. Now, I have shown you mine, it is time for you to show me yours."

Back on the quayside, Sigrvard, along with Marek, escorted Solly to the Marshal's most precious warehouse.

Inside, stacked floor to ceiling were racks upon racks of walrus ivory, Cornish tin, Welsh gold in boxes, elk antlers, some much bigger than a man, fox pelts, bearskins and much more.

"I think this is a good day for both of us," said Solly with a smile.

"I tend to agree," responded Sigrvard.

The four-way meeting between Sigrvard, Erle, Marek and Solly lasted but a few minutes. "A good way to trade: brisk, with brevity and bounty," said Sigrvard.

The rest of the day was spent with Marek organising the transfer of goods, ship to shore and shore to ship, while Sigrvard escorted Solly around the City of Jorvik.

That evening, all four gathered for a farewell meal. A joyous occasion tinged with sadness, for Sigrvard and Marek especially. Solly and Marek took their leave to rest for their long voyage ahead.

Sigrvard sat for one last glass of wine, telling Erle he would join her in the bath soon.

A knock on the door was quite a surprise for Sigrvard, who shouted: "Enter."

"A guest seeks your permission to enter, my lord."

It was Solly.

"Forgive my late intrusion, my lord, but there is something left that can only be between us two."

Intrigued, Sigrvard invited him in and poured a glass of wine.

"First, I must remind you that our mutual acquaintance, he of my blood who is no longer with us, may have appeared the fool but no shrewder man ever walked this earth."

"I cannot disagree."

"Then you will have some understanding of the gift I bring you that Vidar obtained for you. A gift that is beyond unique. Nothing of its like has ever existed nor will ever exist again."

The Seer was beyond intrigued as Solly produced a small, highly polished box of teakwood from India and handed it to him.

Sigrvard opened the box and inside was a small glass phial, no more than two inches long, containing a clear liquid.

He didn't have to ask an answer to his question, which was already forthcoming.

"I am fully aware of the Viking philosophy to death and the willing acceptance of same by all *Vikingr*, from the day they are born. But Vidar said so much good for so many people, already and yet to be, is from Sigrvard that such goodness needs a full life term, and more. Obviously, dying in battle is preferable though the element of such uncertainty may render this gift ineffectual. However, should the cause of death be injury or illness or something similarly non-violent, the gift will come into its own."

"I do not understand," mumbled Sigrvard.

"Vidar travelled to many distant places, places we shall not know of for many, many years. North of India, he got lost on one trade trip and found a mysterious, mountainous region of pious, spiritual monks, it was called *Tufan.**

"Vidar told me, 'My life turned there.' He found many things that confounded him and astounded him in equal measure.

"One remarkable discovery was the large number of monks who were two hundred years old, or more, and not being old."

Such ages Sigrvard found beyond comprehension but the relevance of Solly's words in relation to the gift was soon to become clear.

"Vidar brought this gift of life back from *Tufan* for you. You must drink the liquid within the phial and replace it with several strands of your hair as well as a few drops of your blood. Reseal the phial with its wooden stopper and seal with wax to ensure its integrity."

"And all that will stop me dying?" said Sigrvard incredulously.

"No, but after you have passed from this world, your soul, contained within the phial in your blood and hair, will become as one, mix with the remaining droplets of the liquid that were there previously and infuse into a family member of your blood.

"That member will then have your soul, that person will be you, again.

"All that was you, all that is Sigrvard, will then assist in their evolving life as they face the trials and tribulations ahead."

* * *

Sigrvard did not sleep that night; how could he? He had always felt, growing older, that as he acquired more and more responsibility, there was more he had to do to manage that responsibility. Was the gift a blessing or a curse? He would never know, maybe.

Sigrvard, still deep in thought, stood on the quayside, waving goodbye to Solly and his oldest friend, Marek. But not before they had concluded a trade agreement, in perpetuity, that would ensure a continuity of commerce between the family of Sigrvard and the family of Marek, as long as there was a single member of each family drawing breath. A trade network that stretched from Vinland in the west to India and China in the east.

* *Ancient name for Tibet.*

CHAPTER TWENTY-SEVEN

AS Jorvik prospered, Alfred plotted. Sigrvard's spies kept him well informed with intelligence from the periphery of the Kingdom of Jorvik by 886 AD under the rule of Guthrith, some three years since, but beyond was a different matter. But as the 'White Fox' grew older, he grew more cunning.

Gathering intelligence may have increased in difficulty as Saxon and Dane, Pagan and Christian, lived side by side, but the growth of Jorvik's commercial empire meant their traders and merchants covered the land from Cornwall to Carlisle and from Bridgnorth to Benfleet. They were very observant traders with eyes as sharp for a new fortification as for a good bargain to be had, especially those in the pay of the Marshal of Jorvik, from whom they also got a premium rate in barter.

The special bond between Sigrvard and Guthrum also flourished in the years that followed Wedmore. And, being the younger man, the Marshal of Jorvik would visit East Anglia at least once a year, usually by longship. "Easier on ageing bones," he would say.

In his forty-first year, Sigrvard took his son Torbjorn, now seven winters, on his first sea voyage. Down the east coast of Danelaw to East Anglia where they were to be guests of Guthrum, or Athelstan as he was known to his Christian subjects. The boy was so excited, though that did not stop him throwing up in the early hours at sea.

"You'll get used to it, I did," said a heartily roaring Sigrvard. And he did. So much so that by the time they were reaching their destination, Torbjorn, with a little help from the steermaster, was guiding the longship through particularly benevolent waters with both arms straining to control the steerboard. Sigrvard was confident his longship would be safe enough on the short voyage due to her speed, despite the growth of Anglo-Saxon naval activity. Though the escort of six other longships, laden with produce for the southern market and the Continent, did help put Erle's mind at ease.

His mind drifted back to when longships had ruled, many winters since.

Guthrum had become a father-figure to Sigrvard in recent years and watched, as doting 'grandfather', while Torbjorn enjoyed the king's gift, a jet-black colt racing around the paddock adjacent to Guthrum's palace.

"He shows he has much of his father's skills on horseback," said Guthrum.

"Truth be told, my liege, he is much abler in the saddle than his father. I learned; he was born with such ability in-bred."

The two laughed and toasted their good fortune.

"But now we must talk Anglo-Saxons, Sigrvard. You know I trust you above all men and I know you have gathered much intelligence about our wily adversary, King Alfred. We must share our intelligence, for only unity will help us prevail or, at worse, survive in our new home we have fought so many years to secure."

"You have my agreement on that, Sire."

"So, how see you the present situation, from what you have learned?"

"From my years rebuilding Jorvik, I have become well-versed in reinforcing what the Romans left behind; very clever, those Romans. The stone walls are now even stronger than when they were raised so I am intrigued to see Alfred employing a similar strategy, if I may play upon that word. The Saxon King is building a series of strongholds based on old Roman towns and settlements by reinforcing existing structures as well as extending and building new ones."

"Apart from the obvious, to what purpose?" inquired Guthrum.

"Alfred is attempting to present a barrier to Denisc expansion while at the same time making large sections of Wessex impossible for us to cross."

"I have also had reports of this building programme but there seems to be more to it than simply building fortifications," mused the king.

"Indeed so. Not only are the Saxons building military strongholds, these 'burghs', as they call them, are replicating what I am doing in

Jorvik. A strong and secure military power-base provides protection, real and perceived. That in turn attracts people and commerce, and taxes.

"Trades flourish when a population feels safe. It has worked in Jorvik and my spies report it is working even better in Wessex."

"Can we not do likewise and improve on what you are doing in Jorvik?"

"I think not, Sire. Alfred has also reorganised what was once a weakness in Saxon military philosophy. He has reorganised the *fyrd* and established a system of rotation as well as passing a law that all *fyrd* members must live within a dozen miles of their burgh."

Guthrum nodded, fully aware that in former times the *Vikingr* knew that the forty-day obligation of fealty to serve in the *fyrd* was problematic. Such service generally interfered with the harvest—no men meant no harvest, no harvest meant no crops and that meant starvation.

"Alfred has recognised, as have I in Jorvik, the unbreakable and necessary bond between economic stability and military organisation—plus the one big advantage they have over us."

"Which is?" asked the king eagerly.

"The centralised leadership of Alfred. Think back to when we first came, in the 860s. The Saxons of the 890s are a far different proposition and are not the weak opposition they were then.

"And we, well, at our best, any coalition between the various Scandinavian factions was fickle but we had a common goal then. Now, and for recent years, we seem to have been spending our time chasing Saxons and Mercians the length and breadth of this land, or being chased by them. And that has taken its toll."

Guthrum nodded. "And at the slightest suggestion of difficulty, our so-called allies think nothing of darting off to Hibernia, Caledonia or even the Continent, leaving us that have settled here to spill our blood in their absence."

They mmmm'ed in unison and downed another neckful of mead.

All too soon it was time for Sigrvard and son to return home but not before another gift for Torbjorn. A sword.

"That will one day, hopefully, ensure the continuation of the influence of the Denisc on this land we now call home," said Guthrum as he handed the blade to a wide-eyed Torbjorn.

It wasn't long after his return to Jorvik that Sigrvard learnt of the death of Guthrum. His twelve-year reign as King of Anglia, of Saxon and Dane, Christian and Pagan ended, unusually for a Viking, peacefully. Sigrvard knew that with Guthrum, the dream of a coast-to-coast Danelaw also died. On hearing the news, despite his sadness, Sigrvard smiled. He knew Guthrum's battlefield exploits over more than forty winters as a warrior were more than enough to have earned him his rightful place in Valhalla. But losing such a wise and clever leader at a time when the Anglo-Saxons under Alfred were biding their time did not bode well and Sigrvard did not need to be a Seer to see that. To lose a pivotal leadership figure when the enemy's leadership was going from strength to strength was a signal for disaster.

And so it was to be.

After the death of Guthrum, his words were borne out when the Viking presence in England fragmented. Some went to Caledonia where they could control the sea routes to Shetland and the Orkneys as well as Iceland and Greenland and down to the Isle of Man.

A force of Vikings went back to the Continent while those who chose to remain sought the relative safety of the Kingdom of Jorvik. That dissolution should have given Alfred the incentive to press forward but his hesitation almost proved costly.

AD 892

After two years, there was one last, great attempt by the Northmen to establish Danelaw as the dominant power in England. A huge fleet of two hundred and fifty longships arrived in the estuary of the River Lympne in Kent and rowed four miles upriver into the Weald. Locating an old, half-built fortress, they set up camp at Appledore.

Reinforcements came later that year when the Viking chief Hasteinn brought a further eighty ships up the Thames estuary and built a fort at Milton, taking the new Viking presence up to the levels of the Great Army of 866. Guthred, who had succeeded Gulfrith as King of Jorvik, broke his truce with Alfred and with the Northumbrians prepared to support the newly arrived Vikings from the Continent.

And in 893, after the Vikings occupied their fortresses in Kent, Alfred's army cleverly set up a position between the two forces so that they could oppose in either direction if either king's forces left its encampment.

Sigrvard's *riddari* was part of Guthred's Jorvik contingent that, like the Saxons and very unlike the forces of the Great Army, had an increased equine presence. Most useful in the elongated game of cat-and-mouse that was the general theme of the latter years of the Saxon-Viking conflict.

Once again, stalemate was the order of the day and Alfred used some of the riches from his improving economy to buy peace.

Rich gifts of coin were given by the Saxon leader to Hasteinn who reciprocated with oaths and hostages. Hasteinn even went as far as having his two sons baptised and sponsored by Alfred and Ealdorman Aethelred.

But once again, the Vikings broke their truce with Hasteinn, ravaging the area around Benfleet and huge areas of Hampshire and Berkshire while the Appledore Vikings raided well inland, as far as Wessex itself.

While that group of *Vikingr* were attempting to take their plunder back to their ships, the force from Northumbria and East Anglia, led by Sigrvard, gathered a fleet and besieged Exeter.

As had been the format for some time, the combat was either chase and run or sieges.

Alfred had been making his way to help his son prevent the Vikings from loading their ships with plunder, but instead he diverted and took the bulk of his army to Exeter where he attacked the Vikings, successfully lifting the siege.

The king then sent part of his army to Benfleet where they captured Hasteinn's camp and captured or destroyed all the Viking longships.

Sigrvard returned to Jorvik to gather reinforcements but he confided in Sigfried, now his Supreme Commander, "I fear the climax to this conquest is at hand and I fear for the future."

Sigrvard only had two days at home with Erle and Torbjorn, not even enough time to inspect progress at Hild though he was pleased when Benedict reported the rebuilding was almost complete.

But he did see what progress was being made with the Jorvik Chronicle and was joyously pleased that, in Torbjorn, Benedict had a willing and very able pupil when it came to writing Latin text and illustrating manuscripts.

When Alfred was in Exeter, the Viking armies that were encamped at Shoebury went up the Thames and after being joined by the Sigrvard reinforcements, continued along the Severn to Buttington.

But they were confronted by a huge Saxon army that besieged them for many weeks until Sigrvard and his warriors were starved out and defeated by a Saxon force that had been strengthened by the Welsh who were as keen to end the Viking presence as the Saxons were. The surviving *Vikingr*, with Sigrvard amongst them, fled back to Essex. Once again they were reinforced by a fresh influx from Northumbria and East Anglia and drove across country for the gateway to North Wales and the Isle of Man that was Chester. However, and indicative of what Sigrvard had felt for some time, as at Buttington, the English besieged them in Chester and starved the *Vikingr* out of their fortification and forced them to flee.

The year of 894 saw the continued demise of the *Vikingr* forces and once again, they went backwards and forwards; from Wales to Northumbria, East Anglia and Wessex, until they ended up in London where they set up winter quarters.

It was all going wrong for Sigrvard and the *Vikingr* cause and the final insult occurred when they tried to ravage the area near Chichester and the locals not only vanquished them, killing hundreds, but also captured some of their longships.

The Vikings showed Alfred they were not quite finished when, in 895, an English army attacked their fortress by the Lea and were put to flight; however, it was but a small setback for the Saxons as Alfred built two fortresses lower down that same river so the Vikings were unable to get back to their ships and were effectively trapped.

The Vikings made for Bridgnorth on the Severn, near the Welsh border, where they built a fort, staying the winter. But the end was nigh; Alfred knew it and so too did Sigrvard, who had taken a Saxon arrow to his ankle, where his armoured legin had ridden up his calf just a moment before the shaft hit its target.

In the summer of 896, the Vikings who had arrived in 892 departed. Sigrvard led the remainder of the Great Army back to Jorvik, which was still the *Vikingr* capital despite constant marauding by Wessex.

Sigrvard sat before his roaring, oak-fuelled fire in his quarters at Jorvik, his left hand clutching his favourite walrus-ivory drinking horn while he leaned on his right. Erle sat across from him, wanting dearly to speak but understanding that much troubled her husband. He had been home for several months and had gotten gradually quieter with each passing day. Often he would disappear, for hour after hour, into the ante-room he so favoured when he really wanted to be alone.

But that night he turned to Erle who had been running his trade empire on her own for some years now while he led his *riddari* across hundreds of miles of what was rapidly becoming Anglo-Saxon England.

"I am weary, my love. I am nearing my fiftieth winter and have been slaying and butchering for more than thirty of those winters. I wish war no more. Does that make me a coward?"

She dashed across the polar bear-skin that decorated the space between their chairs, dropped to her knees and did something no one else would ever have the courage to do.

She grabbed Sigrvard by his bushy red beard and shook him vigorously.

"Don't you ever let me hear you talk like that. If you even think that again, I will take a sword to you myself and you know damned well I might well thrash you."

Sigrvard lifted his eyes towards her. He said nothing; but as he held her and their embrace became a love-embrace, which ended up in the mineral bath, he knew he had fought his last battle.

Sigrvard was making increased use of the mineral bath because his injured ankle had turned and festered as he had ignored it. Fortunately, Erle had forced him to have it treated by the medicinal monks at Jorvik Abbey; but despite improvement, he was left with a limp he managed to disguise when out in public.

The uneasy peace that existed between Danelaw and Wessex suited both sides, for different reasons. Less time dashing all over the land engaging with the *Vikingr* meant more time for planning and plotting for the Saxons while the Denisc simply took stock of their situation. It was a situation Sigrvard understood only too well, and it was not good.

Around the Kingdom of Jorvik, apart from the odd Northumbrian raid, it was quite peaceful. The treaty that Sigrvard had brokered with Erle's father was still intact and made even stronger by the bond of her marriage to Sigrvard and the fact that they had provided an heir to Hakon's estates, both in the north and Norway. But Viking settlements in the southeast were most vulnerable and as soon as the settlers in East Anglia were under threat from a joint Wessex and Mercian force trying to claw back territory, it became necessary to go to war again.

And despite his physical limitations, Sigrvard had to respond when the call came for help from the Danes of East Anglia.

Despite the ankle injury impairing his mobility, Sigrvard was still the best horseman in the *riddari*. He was also able to tolerate the pain because his son Torbjorn, now of fourteen winters, was able to accompany him when he assembled his force to help the East Anglian Danes.

However, despite their prowess in the field, the *riddari* were powerless to combat the network of fortified *burghs* King Alfred had established across the south. And the Saxons were becoming so adept with their new navy that the pre-eminence the *Vikingr* longships had enjoyed for decades no longer existed.

Valiantly though the Vikings fought, they could not match the Anglo-Saxon enemy, which continued to show as a force lessons they had learned from AD 866 onwards.

Sigrvard could see the Denisc were worn out. He told Torbjorn, "King Alfred has completely rebuilt domestic opposition to our presence. He has also supplemented his military capability with a support infrastructure of taxation that, supported by his *fyrd* rotation, means that the Saxons are almost on permanent war-footing, which we cannot match."

Sigrvard understood it was nearly the end of the dream of a Denisc England. By AD 896, a lack of progress against the Saxons sent the penniless Danes, notably those from the south of Danelaw, scurrying to the Continent.

As they prepared for their much depleted and much dispirited force to board ship for the voyage back to Jorvik, Sigrvard confided in his son as they sat by the campfire. Torbjorn had proved himself on the battlefield as a warrior and as adept, tactically, at fourteen as Sigrvard had been all those years before.

"Danelaw is still ours, just, but getting smaller. Wessex is Alfred's. But soon, my forecast," he continued, "of one God and one nation will come to pass and I fear that one nation shall be Angleland. I charge you, my son, that you will, with your mother's help—should I no longer be here—fight to the full extent of your heart and soul, which is Angle and Viking, to preserve Jorvik, kingdom and citizens."

"*Ja Fadir.*"

"We are done here. Tomorrow, we go home."

As much as it were possible, Sigrvard and the rapidly maturing Torbjorn ensured that Jorvik maintained its position as the most important centre of Danelaw. But it would soon be time for him to take a wife.

"But I am in no hurry, *Fadir,*" he would say. To which Sigrvard would reply, "But I am not getting younger and as you are my heir, so too do I need you to ensure the continuation of our bloodline."

The marriage was arranged soon thereafter. Torbjorn would marry the youngest daughter of Sigfried, Sigrvard's second-in-command.

Erle continued to be the power behind the trading empire. Hild was now the newest and grandest Abbey and monastery complex in the whole country, greater even than Canterbury, with the finest library and scriptorium in Christendom, as Sigrvard had wished. He was also well pleased at his own improved skill with a quill. Comparisons with Alfred would not go away.

Marek's trade deals kept the gold flowing into Jorvik from the east and goods flowing back in return and were it not for the uncertainty of the brittle peace that existed over the entire country, Sigrvard would have been tempted to say life was good.

He confided in Erle one night, in the still welcoming mineral waters of the newly rebuilt bathing room.

"I sometimes wonder what Alfred and I could have achieved if we had not spent years trying to kill each other."

"But, my love, you have together created and maintained Danelaw, which is on the brink of becoming one nation with Wessex, in which we all can live and worship in peace."

"But at what cost do two nations become one?"

"A cost worth paying, you as a trader must surely see that."

"I am the Seer, my love, but you are wise beyond your years."

Sigrvard smiled and disappeared into his ante-room.

* * *

Sigrvard rolled over in bed and as his flailing arm slapped the mattress, he awoke with a start—Erle was missing. But no sooner had that dread hit him than she entered with bread, wine and cheese. His favourite breaking of fast served by an astonishingly beautiful wife.

"The gods do indeed smile down upon me."

"As mine does on me," she replied.

How could he have forgotten that each Sunday, Erle attended mass in their private chapel just down the long corridor of their accommodation wing? That thought was always accompanied by his promise to himself that he would one day furnish them with a dwelling beyond the walls of Jorvik, a country home with fields and a kitchen garden, but with occasional flashbacks to what had happened to Assi and Astrid at his thorp still embedded in his mind, he never got around to it.

Erle had become Christian soon after the birth of Torbjorn but it was no sudden decision as she had been brought up in Norway before coming over with her father to Northumbria.

She had known of his childhood as a Saxon whose mother was Christian, but she also knew that he and his father had followed the old ways. And because she had been with Sigrvard for many years more than he had shared with Assi, she knew how much his mother Aebbe had influenced him with Christian ways.

Erle was happy in her religion and even happier that Sigrvard never interfered with either her participation or that of their son. True, she often wished she could discuss her husband following the same path as Guthrum, but she never pushed him either.

The subject did crop up on one of their nightly immersions in the mineral bath. Sigrvard's "Maybe" was the strongest indication, ever, that he would consider it.

He felt at his most comfortable spending hour after hour in the warm mineral waters that eased his battle-ravaged body. He felt even better when, more often than not, bathing turned into love-making. The only pain he felt then was that of ecstasy but it was more than worth it.

Usually, before they took to the water, Sigrvard would spend time in his ante-room.

Erle never entered that domain nor ever inquired what went on in there, though the fact that Abbot Benedict and occasionally, Torbjorn, were the only other visitors did give her a clue that it was due to the Jorvik Chronicle, of which she was aware. She often wondered about the ink-stained hands that Sigrvard would carefully wash before stepping into the bath, but she never asked.

The marriage of Torbjorn and Brynhild took place the day after Torbjorn's fifteenth birthday and there was much happiness and feasting in the entire city. Torbjorn was happy because his bride was young and pretty. Brynhild's family were very happy, and much richer, while Sigrvard was very happy that a second bloodline would follow him, knowing that Eric was also part of that bloodline.

FINAL CHAPTER

ERLE entered the bedchamber and was startled to see an empty bed. Sigrvard was nowhere to be seen, which, considering he could hardly walk when she had put him to bed, gave her good cause for concern. She was just about to raise the alarm and call the guards stationed outside the room when the door to Sigrvard's ante-room creaked open.

"There you are," she said with relief.

"Where else would you expect me to be?"

He made his way across the room, ably supported by his trusty *Ulfberht.* He mumbled, loud enough for Erle to hear that which she had heard a hundred times before, "Not the most appropriate use for the best blade in the world but it is part of me and I shall use it as I see fit."

She noted the ink-stained hands again so she knew what he had been about, but said nought. *He must be finished by now,* she thought.

As if he read her mind, Sigrvard spoke, "The chest is complete. You know what I wish for you to do."

"Yes, my lord, my love. I shall comply with your wishes."

Having discussed that the stone casket was to be buried nine feet below the surface, one foot for every year of his pre-*Vikingr* life, she would inter the Jorvik Chronicle at the site of Sigrvard's thorp, north of Jorvik, after he passed.

"And my servants, for they have never been *thralls* to me?"

"They shall not be sacrificed, as you wish it. They will be part of your house as long as it stands."

Erle had sent word to Cynfrith and Eric that Sigrvard was near death. Despite the best medicine and help, Benedict insisted on bringing from Hild, the old injury had seen a bloody bruise climb slowly up his leg to his torso. Whatever poison had taken hold of the seer-warrior, it was not about to relinquish that death-grip it had secured. Restricted though his movements were, Sigrvard refused to be incapacitated.

He called Torbjorn to his bedside and they discussed the disposition of his estate, as it affected him. Both did well to contain the emotion welling up inside.

Sigrvard then called Erle to him.

"My love, I fear it is not long now. We have spoken all words needed from the first day we met. Our hearts know each other.

"I am secure knowing my estate will be in the same caring hands since you first took charge. No better person is there."

Despite his suffering, mental strength and fortitude compensated for a deficiency in physical strength and Sigrvard was still able to walk to his mineral bath every evening before joining Erle in bed where his limitations in movement were no hindrance.

The bath-chamber was where Sigrvard finally agreed, at his suggestion, to be baptised. Only Torbjorn, who was his sponsor, Benedict, who performed the ceremony, and Erle were present.

"This is between me and my God," said Sigrvard.

"God or Wodin?" whispered Erle.

"Either, or both. It serves no purpose to alienate either in my position.

"Just one more thing," added Sigrvard.

He reached around his midriff for the velvet bag he had worn ever since he had become a Seer-to-be. All those years ago. "Where have the years gone?" he would muse.

"One last reading of the Runes," he smiled.

The stones tipped out onto the board and without hesitation, or request, Sigrvard revealed their determination.

"One God, two nations become one, for all time."

He gathered the stones up and put them away for the last time.

"I do not fear death, though it has come for me so often we are old friends. As Jarl of the Denisc, I will feast in Valhalla. As Osgar the Angle, heaven will suffice. Perhaps after many summers to come, someone will read my words and the reading of my life will be understood. And the times I have lived through will be clear also. I have lived in the reign of five kings, many gods and acted as counsellor to

Guthrum as we negotiated peace with Alfred of Wessex, giving advice that led to the birth of Danelaw. I think I am ready to join Eirikr and Froda.

"What tales we have to tell and what tales we shall be told."

Suddenly remembering that he was about to re-join the Christian Church via baptism, Sigrvard added, "God willing." He cleared his throat and assisted by Erle and *Ulfberht*, made for the bath steps and his conversion.

* * *

Sigrvard's bedchamber was kept in subdued light as his eyes were troubling him. Daylight streaming through the windows was bearable, just, but after dusk, wall-sconces and candles were the only brightness, save for the main fire. Erle ensured servants kept the fire well-fuelled with seasoned oak; the smell of woodsmoke reminded both Erle and Sigrvard of their early relationship. He raised his head towards those near and dear to him who had gathered around the foot of his bed, forming a half-moon that began at his left hand with Erle and ended at his right hand with SIGRVARD!

In between, from Erle onwards, stood: Torbjorn; Brynhild, his wife; his grandson, Torbjornsson; Benedict; Cynfrith; Eric; Eric's son and Sigrvard, making nine in all. But what the dying Seer saw, which his family and friends could not, was more than was. Directly behind those nine figures were nine others, no longer of this world. Assi stood at his left, just above Erle, and on his right stood Eirikr; in between, again forming a half-moon was Astrid, the boy-child he had seen in a previous dream at the beach, alongside his dead wife and daughter, his mother Aebbe, father Deorwine, sister Godkifu and brother Godwine and Froda.

Two half-moons, one full circle made of two half-circles. The room descended into darkness for Sigrvard's eyes, even the fire's brightness dulled. Sigrvard felt a warmth leave his body and a small globe of pulsing light hovered before him. He wanted to touch it—he could touch it—but he did not need to. It was as if, like a trained will-o'-the-wisp, waiting for permission.

Sigrvard felt himself nod his head in assent and the globe danced through the air, unseen by anyone but he.

It hovered above Erle, then Torbjorn, then each in turn, hovering momentarily before moving on to the next, ending with Sigrvard. The light then moved forward and began by hovering above Assi, before moving on. Sigrvard noted that the globe hovered longer over the boy figure between Astrid and Aebbe.

The light then moved along the line before moving, very rapidly, between the boy-child and Torbjornsson, his grandson, faster and faster until there was a brilliant white-light bridge from grandson to boy-child. The bridge then morphed into an aura that engulfed Torbjornsson and from grandson to grandfather, a light bridge was formed. All that was Sigrvard passed into his son's son. All that would have passed from Sigrvard to the boy-child also passed to Torbjornsson.

"He is at peace now."

Erle smiled as a single tear slowly trickled down her cheek onto Sigrvard's lips. She was sure she saw him smile.

She whispered to herself, "Osgar the Saxon and Sigrvard the Viking depart. In peace, I shall join you in Valhalla or heaven. As long as agreed, Jesus' birth, celebrate as has always been."

Lo there, do I see my father.
Lo there, do I see my mother, and sister and my brothers.
Lo there, do I see the line of my people back to the beginning.
Lo, they do call me.
They bid me take my place among them in the halls of Valhalla,
Where we shall live forever.

Osgarsigrvard

EPILOGUE

AS Simon reached the last few pages of the several hundred Chronicle vellum sheets he had read, there was an itch, metaphorical, he felt compelled to scratch. However, he resisted the temptation to skip to the last page for verification but he still could not shake off the feeling that there was something different about the latter pages of the manuscript.

He had read words that had begun from the hand of William of Whitby and those from Abbot Benedict but he was starting to notice a subtle difference in script from the death of Guthrum onwards, AD 890.

There was what he could only describe as a human 'soul' flourish in certain letters and certain words that were undetectable to all but the most expert eye.

He was determined to get to the bottom of his 'itch' and have a damned good scratch but he had become so immersed in the Jorvik Chronicle that it was more a case of the Chronicle itself reaching out and grabbing him by the throat and pulling him in, refusing to take no for an answer.

It was as if Simon, who had been born in Whitby, was destined to be part of the Chronicle itself. It had certainly been an all-consuming task, yet he had never tired of the beauty created by a combination of ink, quill and mind as letters on vellum that were magic, pure and simple.

The script had been gloriously consistent since the first page but towards the end, Simon felt that there was a slight difference in style that he felt compelled to utilise spectrographic analysis.

His intuition was correct. Though very cleverly disguised, the last few pages had been written in a different hand. Incredible though the Jorvik Chronicle was in its own right, there was something even more incredible. Simon's heart was pumping at a rate of knots when he realised he was now reading the final words of a dying man. A Viking Jarl who had been dead for nearly thirteen hundred years and Simon had read HIS diary, HIS words.

And as if reaching forward through all those centuries, Sigrvard was determined to have the final say.

As Simon lifted the last sheet of vellum, his attention was diverted to where the side wall of the casket met the base.

A barely perceptible crevice revealed a narrow roll of vellum, which he carefully extracted. Barely four inches by one inch, the note bore just thirteen words:

The hand of Osgar the Angle, Sigrvard the Denisc, caused me to be.

At the other end of the casket, in another barely visible crevice, was a small glass phial. It had a wooden stopper but was further sealed with wax. It had been so well secured that Simon could just make out a lock of matted red hair. *Something that will need extra-careful analysis*, he thought.

He had sat reading the Jorvik Chronicle for three days solid—travelling across twelve centuries had been invigorating; probably adrenalin, he thought. Now he was done.

He removed his spectacles, pinched the bridge of his nose between thumb and index finger then sat in silence, contemplating.

He sat for a very long time.

His journey from 9th-century England had begun with words written by William of Whitby, continued through Benedict, Abbot of Hild Abbey, and had ended in the hand of the man central to the Jorvik Chronicle, Angle-born Osgar who had died as Sigrvard, Denisc Jarl and Seer.

A fusion of two cultures, two peoples and two religions. The very embodiment of two nations that became one—England.

The warrior-seer, dead but not gone, would not have wanted it any other way.

Simon pinched the bridge of his nose, placed the last sheet of vellum on its predecessor, sealed the casket, switched off his laboratory light and headed home.

He would sleep tonight.

As silence enveloped the laboratory, the casket on a bench at the centre of the room began to glow. A small globe of light emerged. It danced around the room like a deranged will-o'-the-wisp, and raced towards the far wall, which was covered, end to end and floor to ceiling, with books. The globe swept rapidly along each and every book, on each and every shelf, and went back into the stone casket from whence it had come.

Bill Nesbitt

Bill was heading for a career in academia as befitted a man whose long list of talents included: being a published author, musician and singer, travel writer, one-time member of the American Screen Actors Guild, linguist, Master of Martial Arts. However, whilst at University, he was recruited by Her Majesty's Government and spent a career in intelligence, serving his country in a role not even his family knew about. It was a role to which he sacrificed body and soul, literally. Broken in body but not spirit in the service of his country, even when Colonel William Nesbitt retired he was not on the public Census and no medical records existed for him from 1948 to 2002.

Bill covered the full spectrum when it comes to creativity. A Whitby-born native Yorkshireman, he began writing poetry and fiction as a very talented schoolboy. He diversified into song writing and folk-singing before he became a widely respected author, penning such respected works as *Last of the Cold War Warriors*, *Last of the Cold War Warriors II*, *The Kyushu Contract* and *When Twilight Ends*, under his pen name Sean Collins. His expertise in the world of travel writing came to the fore, under his own name, with *Travails Abroad*, a brilliantly funny account of disasters abroad. He also found time to become a world-renowned artist with exhibitions all over the globe.

In fact, Bill could do pretty much anything when it came to creativity, except finish his lifetime passion, *The Jorvik Chronicle*. Sadly, Bill died in 2017.

In 2019 a friend, Brian Beard, suggested finishing what Bill had started. His widow Jenny agreed and the result is the collaborative work, *The Jorvik Chronicle*.

Brian Beard

The Jorvik Chronicle is Brian's first novel. A former history teacher, he is an experienced football writer, broadcaster and historian, with more than a dozen autobiographies under his belt. His bibliography includes: *The Breedon Book of Premiership Records, The Three Lions, On This Day, Aston Villa* and *Collins Gems Disaster Survival.* He has written football autobiographies for: Kenny Swain, Don Goodman and John Ward. Formerly a 'ghost writer' for George Best, Brian is a well-known broadcaster and football historian and is Associate Historian to the Football Association and member of the Association of Football Statisticians. He is the longest serving football reporter for Sky Sports with well over 1,200 games plus another 1,250 or so for many regional and national media outlets. This debut novel allowed Brian to indulge in his twin passions of history and writing as he picked up the baton that was so tragically dropped by Bill Nesbitt.

Due for publication in 2021:

Brian Beard

JORVIK CHRONICLE II
SEED OF SIGRVARD

Two grandsons of Sigrvard—one of Anglo-Saxon lineage and the other of Viking heritage—driven by the spirit of their warrior-seer forebear, venture east and west.

Bjorn establishes first European contact with native North Americans, nearly 600 years before Columbus—and creates a mystery that lasts more than a thousand years. Harold travels east—blazing a trail Marco Polo will travel, nearly four centuries later—in search of the secret of eternal life, in the mountains of Tibet. Instead, he discovers the invention that will change the world forever.